Prepare for
Ascension .. CHRYs

Enjoy

E. J. Clark
3/6/09

Brooks a. agnew

The Ark of Millions of Years Volume Three: 2012

Unlocking the Secret

by
E. J. Clark
&
B. Alexander Agnew

Front Cover
by
Roy Young

AuthorHouse™
1663 Liberty Drive, Suite 200
Bloomington, IN 47403
www.authorhouse.com
Phone: 1-800-839-8640

© *2008 E. J. Clark & B. Alexander Agnew, PhD All Rights Reserved*

No part of this book may be reproduced, stored in a retrieval system, or transmitted by any means without the written permission of the author.

First published by AuthorHouse 5/20/08

ISBN: 978-1-4343-8064-7 (hc)
ISBN: 978-1-4343-8063-0 (sc)

Library of Congress Control Number: 2008903057

Printed in the United States of America
Bloomington, Indiana

This book is printed on acid-free paper.

Table of Contents

THE DEDICATIONS — 5

THE FOREWORDS — 6

PART ONE — 15

The Coming Cataclysm of 2012 — 15

The Oldest City in the Americas — 175

The Tetrahedron — 185

The Other Worlds — 205

The Cataclysm Survival Plan — 240
- Location — 242
- Shelter — 244
- Food and Water — 254
- Water — 256
- Water purification — 257
- Survival Supplies — 260
- Clothing — 268
- Optional miscellaneous items — 270
- Important Documents and items — 272
- Money and assets — 273

The Grand Finale — 279

The Trees of Life — 363

Update — 377

PART TWO — 388

The Spirit Race — 388

Unlocking the Secret   **418**

Past Life Awareness   **430**

Manifestation of the Future   **457**
- Step One – Getting in the heart.   461
- The Breaths   462
- Step Two – Learning to intend with intention   470
- The Eighteenth Breath   470

Conclusion   **477**

Table of Illustrations   **479**

Index   **492**

The Dedications

I, E. J. Clark, first wish to dedicate this book once more to my wonderful cat Youshabel, who died during the writing of the first chapter from lymph node cancer. The loss of my writing companion took its toll as I found it very difficult to write without her lying by my side.

Second, I wish to dedicate this book to you, the reader for whom the book was written.

This book is dedicated to the Queen of the universe who poured light into my heart and love into my mind so that these wonderful words flowed from me like desert flowers after a gentle spring rain. The touch of the goddess raised me from the ashes of mortality like the phoenix. My joy pools peacefully in the palms of her hands like pure water, waiting to wash the life inside me.

Brooks A. Agnew

The Forewords

Each volume of *The Ark of Millions of Years* is the perfection of the previous volume, and each volume is the sequel of the previous book. Therefore, in order to fully understand our writings, they need to be read in proper order.

Both volumes 1 and 2 have recently undergone revisions to correct minor errors in edits and a few errors in text. Additional text was added to volume 2. All three books now have their front cover design on their spines. This will help to readily identify the books when shelved. Again, the reference chapter in volume 1, "The Beginning," will serve this book as well.

Volume 3 of the trilogy will be the last book of the series, mainly because having written three books on the birth and ultimate destiny of our earth, our knowledge on the subject is now exhausted.

Our main concern is 2012 as it looms on the not so distant horizon. It should become our main focus worldwide with terrorism and warfare taking a secondary position. Because time is of the essence, we are asking our readers to spread the message of these books to friends and to various organizations to which they may belong. If so desired, your authors will even come to groups to speak and present a PowerPoint program on our findings as presented in these books. Arrangements can be made through the information found on the back cover.

The first chapter is exceedingly long; however, we didn't want to break it down into smaller chapters and in the process break the train of thought. Therefore we recommend when tired to simply bookmark it and return later.

For the most part, the first two books of the trilogy have received a warm reception. It is too early to determine the impact volume 3 will have on its readers. However, if history repeats itself as they say it does, your authors will be likened to Noah who once preached a flood was coming upon deaf ears whereon only a few were saved; this time it is a global cataclysm.

We are living in "the best of times," in "the worst of times," and in the end times. Take warning from this book and "prepare" both spiritually and temporally while you can, for the prophesied end times are at hand. You alone will determine your destiny and perhaps the destiny of your family members.

E. J. Clark

Part Two of this book was written in the year 2015. The fact that it has been published in the year 2007, eight years in the past, should be no surprise to the reader. That is to say, once the reader completes this book, he or she will have an understanding of the Observation Effect and its relationship to time.

The Universe is the mathematical sum of the intentions of every sentient being in it. Regardless of whether sentient beings are awake and aware or not, the formula cannot be usurped by any force. Not even God, or a whole host of gods, can change that. The free intention of any being is the charge and right of that being to exercise it to his or her will. Should God change the intention of a single sentient being, the entire universe would cease to exist. The faith that holds energy together to form matter would be destroyed forever.

God must let us fail, love, die, and even kill for whatever reason we choose. The purpose of this book is to awaken the reader to the idea that everything past and future can be affected by the intention of a single sentient being. Of course, should millions or even billions of sentient beings, such as humans for instance, apply their intention in a focused and coordinated manner, there is absolutely no limit to what could be created, or, for that matter, destroyed.

One thing must be made absolutely clear. The beings of Earth have a choice. Don't think for another moment you have to march inexorably down the path of eschatology to Armageddon. When you are done with this book, you will all realize that we can all take a new path to a world far away from the woes of the prophets. There is no blasphemy in this, we can assure you.

There are thousands of "self-help" books on the market. They may each have their merits. But you want the tools you need to personally stop the cycle of failure in your life and move toward success. Don't you? We'll try to bring this to you as easily as we can, but there is not much time. There is a need for enlightened and awakened people producing positive energy and success. We need thousands of you. Millions would be better. In here, you will learn how to access your life energy.

You will also learn about the tool of *clearing*. When a person fails at something, they often say, "I will never do that again." Or they may declare, "I will never allow that to happen again." In fact, they have already sent out the energy to guarantee that they will in fact do it again and again. They may proceed in business, or love, or in any sort of pursuit of happiness to the same place and fail, over and over again. Most people will say something like, "Well the powers that be just don't want me to have that." Another favorite we hear is, "If it is meant to be, then I guess I'll be successful. If it is not meant to be, then I guess I won't." The notion that the universe has a destiny for each person, from which they are powerless to deviate, has been the ploy of governments and religions since the dawn of time. It is also false.

The first thing a person must remember is that they are eternal beings having a mortal experience. You are not the calcium and protein filled with water that warms your bicycle seat. You may have been born like most mammals, spewing amniotic fluid and gasping for air and reeling from the shock of evaporation against your skin. You may feel your world as a cold or hot thing of pleasure or pain through the billions of electrical sensors on your skin. You may experience your environment like a chaotic smoothie poured into your head through delicately designed tympanic stereo. But it isn't like that at all. The nano-world that fits into a mere three dimensions is only a comma in a twenty-four-volume set of instruction manuals for reality.

The being that makes up the person you *are,* is only temporarily occupying solid matter in the form of your physical body. The real *you* is older than you can imagine. In fact, the entire universe is folded up inside of each and every human soul in the universe. It is a total agreement between every sentient being in the universe. If one sentient being were to leave this universe, the entire composition would collapse back into the void and have to start all over again with a new total set of intelligences in agreement.

You must realize before you lay this book down that you are *Source*. You are a god. You have the seed of greatness and glory inside of you. Not to rule or lord over the masses, but to serve. Religions have been working since the dawn of civilization to build and control congregations by telling people that they cannot get to heaven unless they are members in good standing of their religion. They sing about love, but they preach one universal message: fear.

Fear is around forty times more powerful than love at manifesting the future. A young mother who had terminal cancer approached a dear friend of ours who is a Catholic priest. She was bewildered as to why she was going to die. It wasn't fair. She had prayed every day since she was a little girl, after her mother died of cancer, that she would not get cancer. With kindness of an absolute saint, he said, "My God, woman. I would be completely shocked if you had lived your life thus far without getting cancer. You manifested it with your own fear."

The universe does not discriminate. Whatever energy is sent out to the universe from a sentient being will vibrate everything that will sympathize with that energy. If you send fear out into the universe, then products of fear are what you may reap. If you send out products of love, then that is what you may reap.

One word of great advice here. It does not matter how you are loved by others. It only matters how you love them. Do not be surprised if you aren't loved by everyone. Even Jesus had enemies. In order for you to work the law of attraction to its fullest positive effect, you are strongly advised to master loving everyone.

Keep in mind that this is nigh impossible if you do not do one thing first. You must love yourself. This is the second of two great commandments Jesus gave the world. He said, "Thou shalt love thy neighbor as thyself." Notice the huge difference between this commandment and the other ten commandments. The Ten Commandments all begin with, "Thou shalt not..." This commandment begins with, "Thou shalt..."

Also notice that the book was recorded in Greek. With Greek logic, one needs only realize that the actual precursor to loving your neighbor, is to love yourself. That being the ultimate key to the universe, we will endeavor to lift you to the point where this is possible. If we can accomplish this one thing far and wide enough, wars will end forever.

You have eons of experience. And that means you have learned many things through those experiences over countless mortalities of one kind or another. Although all experiences are for a person's expansion and growth, they can also establish patterns or habits or *scripts* that form blockages in the flow of energy.

The construction of these blockages or mirrors is done by the individual. They form an echo wall that short-circuits the Life Force over and over again. The presence of these wall surfaces acts like a mirror, reflecting the life energy instead of letting it flow through to fulfill the person's dream.

When conducted by a clearing practitioner, *clearing* is effective at removing these blockages or mirrors. That means the obstacles to the flow of life energy can be skillfully identified and removed forever. Although people may profess to do *clearing* in one workshop or another for groups of people, *clearing* is a one-on-one process during which people are changed forever. There is no "workshop high" that wears off a week or two after the event is completed. *Clearing* is a permanent life-change.

When a person's life energy is allowed to flow freely, his or her intentions can be fully empowered. The intentions of a human being are the most powerful creative forces in the universe. In fact, they *are* the creative forces in the universe. That means if you ever wondered about the identity of the creator, take some serious time and look in the mirror. Look into your own soul.

Manifestation is the literal creation process of a human soul. Each soul has all the potential and tools of godhood built into it. All a person has to do is remember who they are, and that their potential is absolutely unlimited. Then, that person needs the toolbox to do the work of creation. That is what this book is about.

There was a book published back in the year 2006 called *The Secret*. It was part of a revolution in awareness and enjoyed the most amazing marketing and advertising efforts in the history of the self-help genre. It did a wonderful job of arousing the faculties of millions of people around the world. It attracted the most dynamic lecturers and showmen to help explain the benefits of the *Law of Attraction*. After reviewing history since *The Secret* was published, the authors were urged to publish the tools necessary to unlock that secret, and carry that back to the year 2007 to see if a new timeline could be realized.

Millions of people were convinced the law of attraction was functional throughout the universe and would apply to anything they wished to accomplish. What they lacked were the tools to meet the conditions of the law. They put their pictures up on their refrigerator doors. They dreamed and hope and wished, but not enough energy could be mustered to turn the planet. This is why we wrote this book and brought it back to the year 2007. The provision of these tools, along with the desire of millions of souls to reap the wealth of the universe, will be enough to redirect mankind away from where it is now in the year 2015. We can't give you all the details, but believe us when we tell you it is vital to the condition of Earth that the planet achieves a critical mass of *cleared* and functional souls at the *empowerment level* for Earth to survive.

With the momentum that swelled in the year 2007 with *The Secret* marketing effort, we strongly felt it was necessary to move our start date back to that year. If a message of awareness could be constructed in the past, utilizing the momentum of *The Secret*, we felt it was possible to empower enough human beings in time to avoid the events prior to the year 2015.

Read and grow, friends. We need you.

Brooks A. Agnew

Part One
The Coming Cataclysm of 2012

In volume Two of *The Ark of Millions of Years*, in the chapter "The End Times," we wrote of what has been predicted by the Tzolk'in calendar and prophetically foretold by the words of Christ in the Bible to occur at the End of the Age that the Greeks called the *Suntelia Aeon*. We wrote of the event rather than delving into the consequences thereof mainly because it is an unknown. It wasn't until your co-author, Brooks Agnew, was being interviewed on a radio talk show when the talk show host asked, "Do I need to fear the upcoming event?" that we realized much more is needed to be written of the event in order to "prepare" the world, lest everyone is caught off guard. Bear in mind we are predicting the unknown but it doesn't take a rocket scientist to understand the "great shaking" of the Earth will be a cataclysmic, global destruction of the world as we know it. The answer to the radio talk show host's question is, "Yes, if you are not prepared for the event, then you need to fear it," as we will bring out in this chapter.

Since the writing of volume 2, the "signs of the times" have been increasingly manifesting as natural disasters just as we predicted that it would. Approximately eight months after the Indian Ocean earthquake and tsunami, Hurricane Katrina struck the U. S. in August 2005, causing extensive damage to the costal regions of Louisiana, Mississippi, and Alabama. New Orleans was inundated by Lake Pontchartrain when the levees protecting the city failed. The subsequent flooding resulted in catastrophic flood damage and major loss of life. As of March 2006, the death toll had officially risen to 1,599 (1,800 by June), and was still rising with over 3,000 still missing or unaccounted for. A million people were displaced. It is an ongoing humanitarian crisis on a scale not seen in the U.S. since the Great Depression. Until Katrina, Hurricane Andrew was the costliest natural disaster in the history of the U.S. Estimates have now placed Katrina as the costliest natural disaster in the nation's history. Two weeks later, Hurricane Rita brushed the Florida Keys and struck the Texas coast. Although it didn't cause much damage, it did result in the loss of millions of dollars to the business economy in the Houston–Galveston area because most of the two cities were closed down and evacuated.

Less than two months later, on October 8, 2005, an earthquake measuring 7.6 on the Richter scale struck the northern Kashmir area of Pakistan. Parts of India and Afghanistan were also shaken. Kashmir lies in the area where the Eurasian and Indian tectonic plates are colliding. In ancient times, the collision of these plates resulted in the uplifting and birth of the Himalayas. The Pakistan city of Balakot was completely destroyed because it was located on a major geological fault line. There are plans to rebuild that city in a new location. The confirmed deaths in Pakistan are 79,000 and still rising, with 75,038 injured. Most of the wide-spread, affected areas are in mountainous regions. Millions were left homeless and hungry facing the approaching harsh Himalayan winter. Villages were reduced to rubble, and later rain-soaked rubble on unstable ground triggered landslides that blocked roads, hampering humanitarian efforts. All communication was lost. Airlifting of humanitarian aid was difficult due to inclement weather conditions.

A string of aftershock earthquakes, some measuring a magnitude greater than 5 on the Richter scale, continue to rock the area. At last count there have been 1,500 aftershocks that continue to occur daily. In addition the death toll in India has risen to 1,329 with 4,500 injured, and Afghanistan reported 4 killed. The earthquake is on a catastrophic scale never seen before in this region.

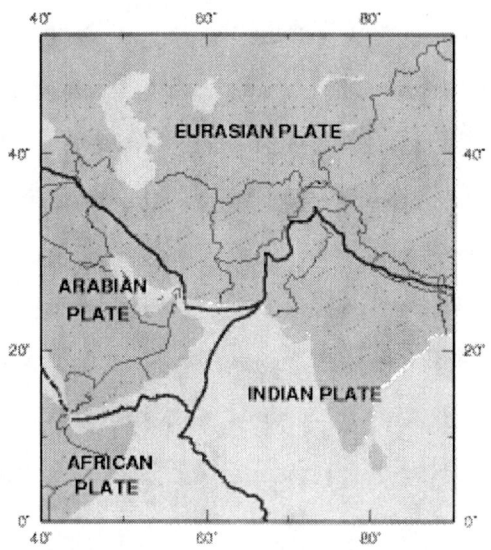

Figure 1 - Eurasian and Indian Tectonic Plates

During the first week of October 2005, Hurricane Stan cut a path of destruction through Central America, causing a week of torrential rain to pummel the region. Creeks that normally stream down from the highlands turned into raging rivers, causing flooding and landslides. In many parts, overflowing rivers carried away houses and people, washed out bridges and cut off communications. El Salvador had to evacuate more than sixty-two thousand people to safety, and Guatemala evacuated more than thirty thousand.

To make matters worse, a moderate earthquake rocked Central America even before Hurricane Stan had weakened into a tropical depression. The 5.8 magnitude quake caused the collapse of a rain-damaged highway bridge in Guatemala and sent thousands of frightened Salvadoran residents into the streets.

Tragically, the Mayan village of Panajachel, located in the shadow of a volcano on Lake Atitlan, Guatemala, was buried in a torrent of mud and earth following a weeks worth of driving rain. The estimated loss of life stands at fourteen hundred. Hard-hit Guatemala reported that four hundred landslides had occurred, causing damage to eleven bridges and twenty-five percent of its paved roads in addition to damaging thirty percent of its crops. Hurricane Stan claimed sixty-seven more lives in El Salvador, fifty-one in Mexico, ten in Nicaragua, and four in Honduras.

Meteorological experts say the upcoming season could be as violent as the record-breaking season of 2005, which recorded twenty-seven tropical storms, including fifteen that became hurricanes. These storms affected 3.6 million people in the nine countries of Mexico, Guatemala, Belize, Honduras, Nicaragua, El

Salvador, Costa Rica, Panama, and the Dominican Republic. The number of people impacted by the 2005 storms jumped dramatically from 2004, when only 14,400 persons suffered. Update October 10, 2006: Fortunately, the hurricane season was not as violent as predicted for the U.S. and the Caribbean; however the typhoons that hit Asia and the Philippines, were the largest and strongest on record.

In February 2006, another major landslide buried the entire mountainous village of Guinsaugon, located in the central Philippines, following heavy rains. Reports indicate that a minor earthquake in the area may have triggered the landslide. It appears that the mountain that rose just above the village simply collapsed onto it, killing an estimated one thousand souls.

The Indian Meteorological Department reported on December 14, 2005, that the four major earthquakes which occurred in the past one year, including the one that triggered the tsunami, were due to the seismic activity in the same tectonic plate boundary, but there was no link amongst them. The earthquakes were totally independent and appear to be just a coincidence. However, they further noted that earthquakes continue to happen.

Since December 26, 2005, more than two hundred wildfires have burned an estimated 3.7 million acres in Texas, destroying more than four hundred homes in addition to crops, animals and wildlife. On April 2, 2006, it was reported that sixty-three tornadoes swept through the eight states of Arkansas, Indiana, Illinois, Iowa,

Kentucky, Ohio, Mississippi, and Tennessee, killing twenty-eight people. The destruction caused by these tornadoes will be in the millions of dollars, not counting the misery inflicted on those involved. Less than a week later, on April 7, 2006, a line of severe thunderstorms and tornadoes swept across the Southeast, leaving devastation in their wake. Powerful winds, dangerous lightning, softball-size hail, and driving rain pulverized homes, ripped up trees, flipped cars and killed at least 11 people in middle Tennessee. And, the tornado season has only just begun as of this writing on April 8, 2006. According to the National Weather Services Storm Prediction Center, the number of tornadoes in the U.S. has jumped dramatically though the first part of 2006, compared with the past few years. At this same time last year only ninety-eight tornadoes were reported compared to four hundred already reported in the early spring of 2006.

On the west coast of the U.S., the coastal areas have been experiencing long periods of heavy rain for several months, resulting in much flooding and storm damage. All has been attributed to El Niño. Parts of Europe also experienced torrential rainfall that resulted in flooding and much damage to towns and homes.

Pestilences are categorized as natural disasters too. It seems as if cancer is more prevalent than it was forty years ago. When your authors were children, cancer was relatively unheard of. Now it is common among adults, fairly common in children, and occasionally seen in babies, with some being born with the disease.

AIDS is now a global epidemic. The human toll and suffering due to HIV and AIDS is enormous. In some countries it is out of control, particularly in Africa. Since the beginning of the epidemic, more than 15 million Africans have died. In parts of that continent, an entire generation has been lost, leaving Africa with 12 million AIDS orphans. It is estimated that worldwide eight thousand people die daily from this pestilence and more than six thousand become infected with HIV every day. More than 25 million people have died of AIDS since 1981 with 3.1 million having died globally in 2005.

Avian bird flu now looms menacingly on the horizon. If the bird flu virus succeeds in mutating enough to jump the species and infect humans as a contagious disease, this new scourge will be more deadly than the bubonic plague that nearly wiped out Europe. Deadly viruses are mutating to infect humans at a rate never seen before. At least one new disease is jumping the species barrier from animals to humans every year. AIDS, avian flu, SARS, and new variants originated as animal diseases. Don't forget the West Nile virus either. In recent years this virus has been spread all over the planet by birds that were initially infected by mosquitoes. Mosquitoes, who subsequently vampire blood from these infected birds, spread the virus by biting humans and animals.

Drought is also categorized as a natural disaster when large areas are affected, causing crop failures that in turn can lead to famine, especially in developing countries. Rain failure is not the only problem associated with harvest failures. Other problems include soil infertility, land degradation, erosion, climatic changes, and swarms of desert locusts that can destroy whole crops and cause livestock diseases. As of January 2006, at least 10 million people are affected by the current food crisis in Africa, with Niger being the worst-affected country. The UN directed an appeal for the U.S. to contribute $240 million toward food aid for West Africa. Practically every American has seen and been moved by the haunting images on television of starving, skeletal children with swollen stomachs in African aid camps. Is it even possible to know the mortality rate?

The Associated Press reported on May 19, 2005, in a follow-up on the Indian Ocean earthquake of December 2004, the following statement: "The trembler 'delivered a blow to our planet' that was felt for weeks. The quake shook the Earth's entire surface. Ground movement of as much as 0.4 inch occurred everywhere on Earth's surface, though it was too small to be felt in most areas." Scientists now believe the Asian earthquake may have accelerated the Earth's rotation, shortening days by a fraction of a second and that it has caused the planet to tilt an inch more on its axis!

Along with the Office of U.S. Foreign Disaster Assistance (OFDA), CRED (Centre for Research on the Epidemiology of Disasters) maintains an emergency disaster database called EM-DAT. An event is categorized as a natural disaster if it kills ten or more people or leaves at least one hundred people injured, homeless, displaced or evacuated. An event is also included in the database if a country declares it a natural disaster or if it requires the country to make a call for international assistance.

According to the EM-DAT, the total natural disasters reported each year has been steadily increasing in recent decades, from 78 in 1970 to 348 in 2004. Typically about twenty thousand lives are lost yearly to natural disasters. In recent years the death toll has far exceeded the normal figures.

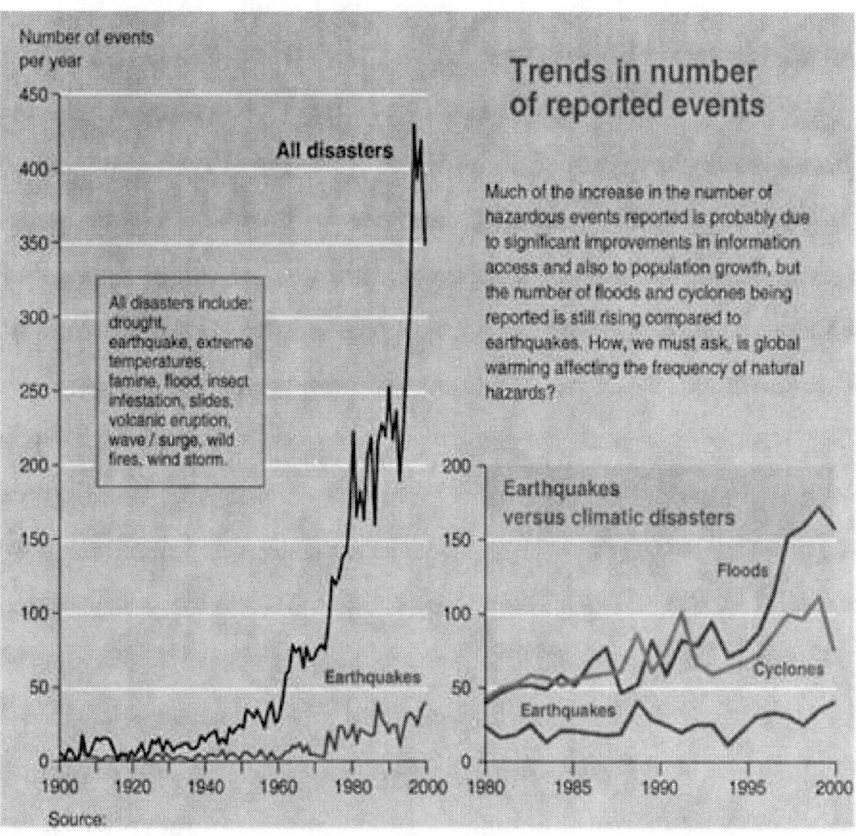

Figure 2 – Global deaths by natural disaster

So what is going on? Scientist believe global warning is increasing the temperatures of the Earth's oceans and atmosphere, leading to more intense storms of all types, including hurricanes and typhoons. Warm winters produce warmer ocean waters and warmer atmospheric conditions. When the warmer atmospheric air currents are drawn up from southern areas and collide with cold northern jet streams, the result triggers violent thunderstorms that spawn tornadoes.

While that certainly is a factor, your authors believe there are other factors involved, as written in volume 2 and briefly summarized as follows: The ancient "key" to understanding the creation was restored back to Earth in volume 1 of *The Ark of Millions of Years*. It revealed that our Earth was a binary planet composed of two parts, one spiritual and one temporal. When they united about 6,500 years ago, the two Earths were in harmony. Volume 2 of *The Ark of Millions of Years* disclosed that the two Earths are now out of harmony with each other. Each planet has a unique frequency or pitch to its vibration. When they were united their vibrations were in harmony, much like a harmonic cord in music. Over time, negative forces or vibrations have overpowered the positive forces exerted on the planet, creating a new sound of disharmony. The newly created sound is a wobbling sound, called a modulation, that forms when two vibrations are out of phase with one another. The new vibration is causing a degradation in the harmony between the spirit Earth and the physical Earth and can cause, we believe, destructive forces of great magnitude. The two planets no longer vibrate in the harmony that is described in the Bible as cosmic groanings that "travaileth in pain" found in Romans 8:22.

They are out of tune with each other, producing sour modulations that are resonating throughout the planet and being manifested as natural disasters. Consequently, the negative vibratory forces are causing the two planets to begin to separate. The separation process will be fully completed on December 21, 2012, when the "great shaking" of the heavens and Earth occurs. Until then, it will be calamity after calamity until the final End Time cataclysm.

From December 21st through the 23rd 2012, our sun will be crossing the middle band or galactic equator of the Milky Way for the first time in about 5,125 years. Of course, all the planets orbiting our sun are on the same path. Our planet Earth's position during December 21st through the 23rd will be located in the "dark rift" of the Milky Way, which contains the magnetic axis of the super-massive, spinning black hole located in the center of our galaxy. Our planet will once more be literally sailing the "cosmic sea" for three days as it did in ancient times, its spiritual counterpart that is. Egyptian legends say that Noah and his entourage arrived here by "sailing the cosmic sea" on his great ship, the Ark of Millions of Years. Of course, it was the spirit Earth that sailed across the "cosmic sea" with Noah's entourage on board the great ship. The spirit Earth then united with the physical Earth in this dimension, which resulted in the Earth becoming a binary planet as documented in volume 1. This union is called the Union of the Polarity and was anciently symbolized by a six-pointed star, as documented in volume 2. The ancients believed that a transdimensional portal or an Ouroborus, as they termed it, existed in the "cosmic sea." If indeed a spinning black hole does exist there, and scientists now say it does in fact exist there, then spinning black holes can be transdimensional portals as documented in volume 1.

In volume 2, page 157 and re-pictured below in Figure 4, is an illustration showing how the Milky Way will appear in 2012, as viewed from Sagittarius. The bottom half of the illustration shows the Milky Way, which was viewed in ancient times to be a great

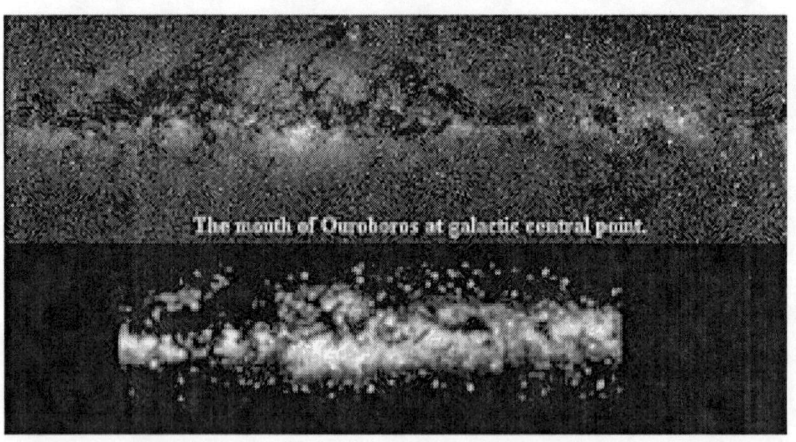

Figure 3 – The rift in the Milky Way

serpent of light that is actually swallowing its tail forming a circle. Look closely on the bottom half; do you see the serpent swallowing its tail? When the circle Ouroborus is formed in 2012, it marks the End of the Age when the transdimensional Ouroborus portal was believed to be opened. However, the "dark rift" or "cosmic sea" was viewed as part of the Ouroborus portal. Scientists today know that the "dark rift" contains a monstrous, super-massive, spinning black hole magnetic axis. The following illustration shows the position of Earth during its three-day transit of sailing the "cosmic sea" in 2012. Our sun's path of the ecliptic takes it right across the center point of our galaxy, the galactic equator, where it conjuncts or crosses the Mayan Sacred Tree that is the Milky Way. Some web sites call the conjunction point of the sun with the Milky Way the galactic center. This is incorrect. The sun crosses the exact center of the Milky Way at its galactic equator. The galactic center is where the black hole is located. If the sun crossed the galactic center, it would be "swallowed up" by forces feeding the black hole.

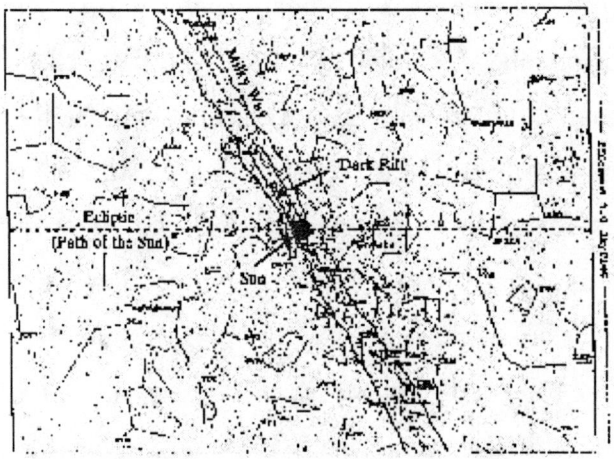

Figure 4 - The sky as it will appear in 2012

As the spinning black hole devours everything near it, in

return it gives off tremendous energy that radiates for millions of miles in all directions; however, most of its strongest energy flows along its magnetic axis. Over the next five and a half years, Earth will be steadily moving closer and closer to the spinning black hole magnetic axis that will be another factor affecting the weather conditions, some of which we are beginning to experience now. Your authors have noticed very windy conditions over the entire planet for the last six months. In the past, April was never windy, instead was traditionally known to be rather cool and rainy. Not so, this year (2006).

April has been extremely windy and hot in the U.S. There was no usual spring season because winter seemingly changed into summer almost overnight. Most of Europe, Canada and the U.S. fried in the highest temperatures ever recorded, starting in mid-June and lasting to late August. Your authors believe the closer we move toward the spinning black hole magnetic axis, the greater the energy radiating from it will affect our planet, probably in the form of three-hundred-mile-an-hour winds, heat, intense storms, and erratic weather patterns. Summer temperatures of one hundred degrees or more Fahrenheit may become the rule rather than the exception. Right now we are beginning to experience something best described as the "outer bands" of a hurricane. For six months of the year the Earth, in its orbit around the sun, will be on the far side of the sun that will shield it somewhat from the effects of the radiating energy of the spinning black hole. As it continues its orbit during the remaining six months, Earth will be closer to the magnetic axis of the massive, spinning black hole and will be unshielded by the sun. The effects will be pronounced, worsening each year till 2012. Even winter months will gradually get hotter and may reach the point where there will be no winter cold but rather an endless, hot summer.

If this occurs, the global impact will be disastrous because crops will wither in the fields, creating food shortages and famine, both for man and beast. Countless wildlife species will perish. With this type of heat, the polar ice sheets and glaciers will melt rapidly, in six years rather than the predicted two hundred years, raising the ocean's sea level twenty feet or more. In 2006, scientists reported that a record number of glaciers have already melted around the world, especially in the Arctic regions.

The Antarctic regions have experienced less polar ice melting. This is because the tilt of the planet exposes the northern hemisphere to more of the radiating heat of the magnetic axis of the black hole. Antarctica is shielded somewhat from this heat energy mainly because of its "down under" position. In December 2006, Canadian meteorologists reported that a three-thousand-year-old ice shelf, the size of eleven thousand football fields or forty-one square miles, snapped free from an island near the North Pole, probably from global warming. As sea levels rise, coastal areas and coastal cities will flood. London, England, will be under water as will the entire state of Florida. Los Angeles, New York, Seattle, Houston, Galveston, New Orleans, Mediterranean cities, Rio de Janeiro, etc., will all be under water. The impact will be staggering.

Global warming is being caused primarily by our planet approaching the magnetic axis of the spinning black hole. Another factor affecting global warming is that some of the "dark matter" of the universe is being converted into light and heat (*The Ark of Millions of Years* 2, 125–126), resulting in the entire universe experiencing a "warming period." Add to that the effect of fossil fuel burning and greenhouse gas emissions, then the complete picture of the causes of global warming emerges. As you can see, most of global warming cannot be prevented.

Since December 14, 1997, the massive, spinning black hole in the center of our galaxy began to pulse huge amounts of energy out to the universe. The pulsing energy has already destroyed a "beeper" satellite in June 1998. If the energy continues to rise and pulse, it will eventually destroy all our satellites around the Earth. If the energy in 1998 can destroy a satellite, think of what it will do in 2012 when we are directly in the path of destruction.

We also believe it is the combination of two factors, one of that is Earth moving closer to the massive, spinning black hole magnetic axis and the other the negative vibratory forces in process of separating the two Earths, which is causing disastrous effects on the planet and that will continue to do so until 2012. It is the destiny of our planet.

Figure 5 Our Spiral Milky Way Galaxy viewed from above with location of our sun

The above illustration is not completely accurate because on December 16, 2003, Australian astronomers discovered an extra cosmic arm in the Milky Way that they believe wraps around the outskirts of the vast galaxy, likened unto a thick gas border or halo as illustrated below.

Figure 6 - Extra cosmic arm halo surrounding the Milky Way Galaxy

Another new discovery is that the Milky Way is not in its middle age but it is still forming and growing by absorbing small satellite galaxies into its own disk. In 1994, it was discovered that the Sagittarius Dwarf Galaxy was in the process of merging with the Milky Way Galaxy, and then in November 2003 another previously unknown galaxy, called the Canis Major Dwarf Galaxy after the constellation in which it lies, was found to be colliding with the center of the Milky Way. These cannibalized galaxies add thousands of stars to the vast haloes around larger galaxies. Recently, the analysis of spectral satellite data has confirmed that our solar system is not originally from the Milky Way, but from the Sagittarius Galaxy—exactly as we predicted four years ago! This is clear and decisive evidence that Earth and possibly our Moon are not from this galaxy, exactly as we explained to you in 2004 with volume 1.

When we view the Milky Way at night from our back yards, remember we are looking at the central portion of our galaxy from an edge-on view from the outer arm where we are located, as pictured below.

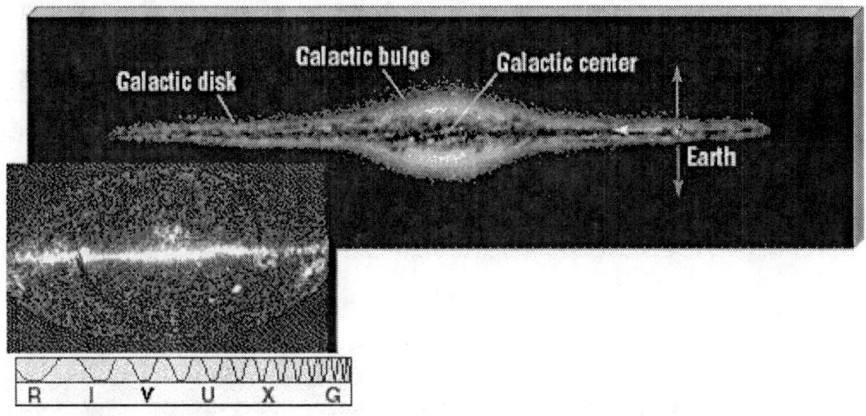

Figure 7 - Milky Way Galaxy "Atlas Image [or Atlas Image mosaic] courtesy of 2MASS/Umass/PAC-Caltech/NASA/NSF"

The Milky Way is a gravitationally-bound collection of an estimated two hundred billion stars. Our sun is just one of these stars in this typical barred spiral galaxy that is about ninety thousand light years in diameter. The sun is also located roughly twenty-four thousand light years from the center of our galaxy. The Milky Way is so named because from Earth's vantage viewing point, it looks like a band of white light or a river of "spilled milk."

Figure 8 - The Milky Way band of white light stretching across the night sky. Notice the rift or dark void across the center.

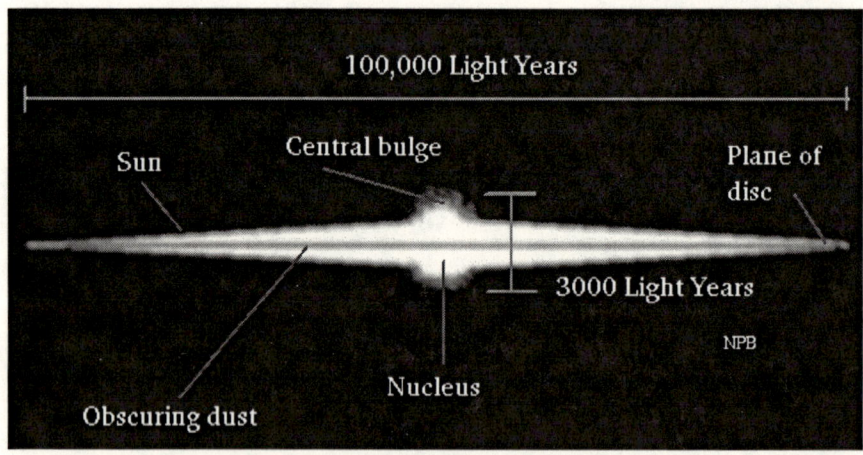

Figure 9 - Structure of the Milky Way Galaxy. Image credit *www.astro.keele.ac.uk/workx/milkyway/page.html*

Our Milky Way Galaxy, as are all spiral galaxies, is comprised of three main components, namely a disk, a bulge, and a halo. The disk contains gas, dust, and young stars in its spiral arms. The dense bulge in the center of the disk contains mostly old stars and no gas or dust. The halo is the home of a few, scattered stars and globular clusters and is also home of dark matter. It surrounds the Milky Way's spiral disk and bulge.

The view of the galactic center (bulge area) had always been obscured by immense, thick, dark, nonluminous dust clouds until x-ray telescopes came into use in 1998. NASA's Chandra X-ray Observatory finally lifted the fog, and we can see what is going on. It was confirmed in 2003 that indeed a monstrous, super-massive black hole exists in the center of our galaxy. If that wasn't enough, in 2005, UCLA astronomers presented the first evidence that tens of thousands of smaller black holes are orbiting the monstrous black hole at the center of the Milky Way. These smaller black holes and neutron stars are expected to gradually be swallowed by the super-massive black hole. This black hole has already swallowed many billions of stars' worth of material. The galactic center is turbulent. Hot fog plasma of multi-million-degree gas appears to be escaping from the center into the rest of the galaxy. Chandra revealed that hundreds of white dwarf stars, neutron stars, and black holes are bathed in this incandescent fog of multi-million degree gas.

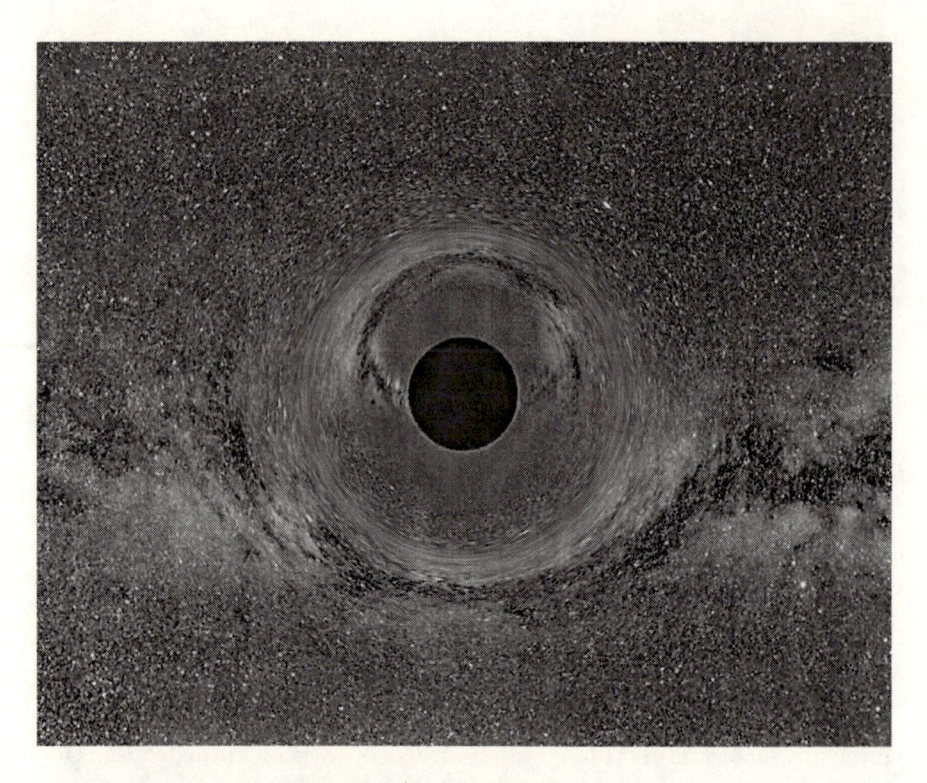

Figure 10 - A (simulated) black hole of ten solar masses as seen from a distance of 600 km with the Milky Way in the background. Image taken from Wikipedia, the free encyclopedia website (Redirected from Black holes).

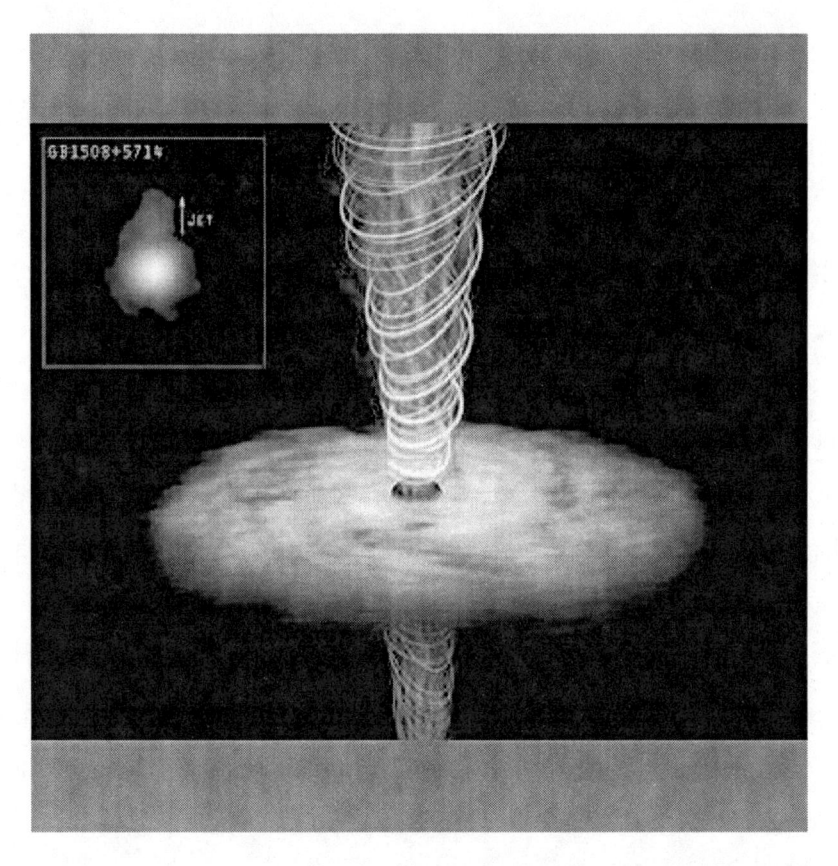

Figure 11 - A black hole spewing out violent jets of matter and energy that can be millions of light years in length. Image credit (NASA/Reuters)

Why the astronomy lesson? Because on the Mayan End Time date of December 21, and continuing through the 23rd, 2012, our planet Earth will make a three-day transit through the "dark rift" of the Milky Way, passing directly in front of and through the center of the magnetic axis of the monstrous, super-massive spinning black hole that lies at the center of our galaxy. Although Earth will still be about twenty-four thousand light years away from the massive black hole, it will, however, be in the direct path of the energy emitted, defined as the electromagnetic axis of the black hole. Stated simply, the black hole emits energy along its magnetic axis through which the Earth will travel in 2012. Because of its enormous size, the energy path or magnetic axis of the spinning black hole can quickly traverse twenty-four thousand light years' distance, emptying and filling the "dark rift" region. Around December 11, 2012, the electromagnetic axis energy of the black hole will be affecting the electromagnetic field surrounding the Earth, causing the oceans and seas to heave out of bounds. High winds, raging electrical storms, thunder, and torrential rainfall will commence globally as in the days of Noah, the result of the interaction of the two electromagnetic force fields. Airplanes and ships will be grounded. The intensity of the storms will cause a global power outage. Satellites will be destroyed. All things will be in commotion, causing men's hearts to fail from fear for fear shall come upon all people (Doctrine and Covenants 88:90–91 and Qur'an 6914).

Prophecy says that in the End Times the Earth will be darkened by a great cloud. These clouds are the dark, nonluminous dust clouds, called dark nebulae, located in the "dark rift" known to the Maya and the ancient world as the "cosmic sea." As Earth sails the "cosmic sea" it will be completely shrouded in inky, jet-black clouds of pitch-black darkness. The light of the sun, moon, or stars will not be able to penetrate the dark nebulae for three days and nights in fulfillment of Zechariah 14:6–7: "It shall be in that day that there shall not be light, the glorious ones will wane," or "the bright ones will fade." All the lights in the sky will appear to go out.

The Sixth Seal of Revelation, at the End of the Age, will be opened just prior to Earth's entry into the "dark rift." As our planet starts to make the transit, it will immediately start shaking and trembling from the energy blasts from the super-massive black hole and from the smaller black holes surrounding it. The "dark rift" is supercharged with destructive energy forces of unknown strength. Earth's to-and-fro reeling motion, described like that of a drunkard, is recorded in Isaiah 24:20. Shaking movements of the planet will cause the stars to appear to fall. Revelation 6:12–17 and Doctrine and Covenants 88:87 both describe the opening of the Sixth Seal with a great earthquake where the mountains and islands are moved. Then the Earth is enveloped into darkness, black as sackcloth as the heavenly luminaries fade.

The black, interstellar dust clouds, located in the "dark rift" will make the moon appear to turn red as blood in color before its light is completely obliterated by the dark nebulae. The planet will experience a rough ride for seventy-two hours in complete darkness. Perhaps this is why the "dark rift" is called the "cosmic sea," because all things in this area ride rough blasts of energy much like a ship rides rough waves in storms. Of course, another reason is because Noah's great ship literally sailed through the black hole transdimensional portal to arrive here, thereafter called a "cosmic sea." This transit through the "dark rift cosmic sea" was foretold to be cataclysmic as the world would be destroyed by earthquakes with few survivors.

The cataclysmic belief was held by the ancient world on both sides of the continents. In the Americas, most notable was the Mayan/Aztec belief that this World Sun would be destroyed by earthquakes. Plato, a Greek philosopher, referred to a cycle of catastrophe at the End of the Age. John recorded the cataclysmic event in Revelation, as did the prophet Joseph Smith in the Doctrine and Covenants, the Old Testament prophets Isaiah in Isaiah 24:20, and Haggai in 2:6. If mountains and islands are moved, it will be caused by tectonic plate movement from the "great shaking" of the planet. Your authors believe that just prior to our planet's entry into the "dark rift", or about ten days out, the oceans and seas will begin to heave themselves out of bounds, further flooding already flooded coastal areas and cities. High winds, raging electrical storms, and torrential rainfall will accompany the angry, heaving seas. New Orleans' levees may hold but tidal swells of 50–150 feet will surge over them and ruin the entire city. Coastal cities around the world will be further flooded, having been previously flooded by rising sea levels caused by polar ice cap melting. Panic will ensue as the unprepared citizens of this planet will realize the full, dire gravity of the situation and feel the helplessness of impending doom (Doctrine and Covenants 88:90–91).

Imagine three days of darkness with the Earth reeling to and fro. Imagine the thunderous noise of mountains rising, land masses sinking, and volcanoes erupting. Imagine the creaking, popping noise of buildings and homes disintegrating into a pile of rubble. Imagine the horror of piercing screams of dying people in the darkness…maybe your own family, if not yourself! Hurricane-force 300 mph winds fueled by intensely hot solar flares of plasma energy may sweep across the planet, the result of the sun's corona being affected by the electromagnetic axis of the black hole.

Imagine the intensely loud roaring of these destructive winds. What is not shaken down, or blown away, will be burned to a crisp by globs of solar plasma energy erratically striking the ground. In addition to all of the above, the magnetic axis of the spinning black hole may cause a planetary pole shift. The death toll will be staggering, in the millions, possibly even one third or more of the planet's population. Think about it. Possibly one third "raptured," one third killed, and one third left behind to face the tribulation years? Currently the world's population stands at 6.5 billion souls. Do the math. If 2.166 billion are killed, the rest are either "raptured" or survive. We doubt 2.166 billion are "raptured" from the living. The number is probably much smaller. Those left behind will have to face the tribulation years post-2012. Evidently, enough survive to satisfy the population requirements for the great tribulation years as defined in Revelation. We can only speculate and guesstimate the numbers as it is in the unknown zone.

Then suddenly the darkness will dispel when the light of the heavenly luminaries return after Earth has finished its three-day transit "sailing the cosmic sea." As with the approach of Earth toward the "dark rift" so will it be as it leaves the "dark rift," meaning the heaving seas, raging electrical storms, thunder, high winds, and torrential rainfall will continue for about two more weeks till Earth has cleared all energy paths of the electromagnetic axis by moving out of the area. Revelation 16:21 indicates there also will be a great hailstorm, every stone about the weight of a talent to add to men's misery. But, with the passing of each day, the storms will gradually become less intense.

Slowly, the survivors will emerge from hiding places to face a destroyed world, thrown back into the Stone Age, with no electricity, no Internet, no radio or television, no operational cell phones, no land telephone service, ruined cities, no heat, little food, scarce water, gasoline shortages, damaged highways, makeshift hospitals, and governments in chaos. With businesses and companies in ruins, former jobs will be gone, banks will be disabled because buildings and money records will be destroyed. There will be no computers. Money will be worthless. Stores will be looted. Satellite communication will be destroyed. With no communication, there will be no National Guard to keep law and order. Every man, woman, and child will have to fend for his or herself in order to survive. Those in northern climates will be experiencing winter without heat and maybe without shelter. It will be a time of great peril as a lawless, desperate people will be a dangerous people. Mind you, we are not trying to incite fear with these points of prediction. We are merely awakening you to the sense of reality that may be experienced by those who are asleep to the events around them. They will be reacting to their environment, rather than acting upon their environment. You are now informed, and can thus position yourself to not be fearful when these times occur.

Is this not the total destruction and collapse of the world's economic system spoken of in Revelation 18? Verses 8–24 tell us that this collapse will come quickly and will happen globally in one day. Those survivors who are left behind will mourn for the former world's economic system and for all the material things and modern comforts they used to have (Revelation 16:11–19).

Survivors will see a changed Earth. Land configurations will be different. Climate may change suddenly if Earth tilts more or even straightens up. If this should occur, the seasons will change as well as lengths of day and night. If a number of volcanoes are erupting, the volcanic ash clouds could block the sun's rays sufficiently to cause another "mini" ice age lasting many years. Of course, this is all speculation, but most environmentalists agree that major climate changes have occurred in the past suddenly. We cannot predict what we do not know, but a global cataclysm of this nature will certainly cause drastic, abrupt changes. Things will never be the same again.

Below are two future world maps showing how the world may appear after the 2012 cataclysm. The first map is based on visions Gordon Michael Scallion received, over a period of twenty-five years, of upcoming changes to occur by 2012. His maps cover changes for all continents, as well as new islands that will be created, rising from the oceans' floors. Giant-sized color copies of these maps may be purchased from his web site. He graciously gave us permission to use his map images in this chapter.

According to his *Future Map of the World*, most of Western Europe and the Mediterranean countries have disappeared. One thought to remember is that Rome and Israel must survive in order to fulfill the requirements of the Book of Revelation and the words of the prophets. Nevertheless, his maps are significant in that he foresees a global cataclysm occurring no later than 2012, causing drastic land changes. Keep in mind, however, that there is a "New Jerusalem," in the formation of the United States, and Rome could mean the empire of capitalism that rules the world like Rome once ruled the world. The Holy Roman Empire is nearly reestablished with the consolidation of the world banking system with three major unions: the European Union, the North American Union, and the Asian Union. The North American Union, consisting of Canada, the current United States, and Mexico, was signed into existence in the summer of 2006 by George W. Bush.

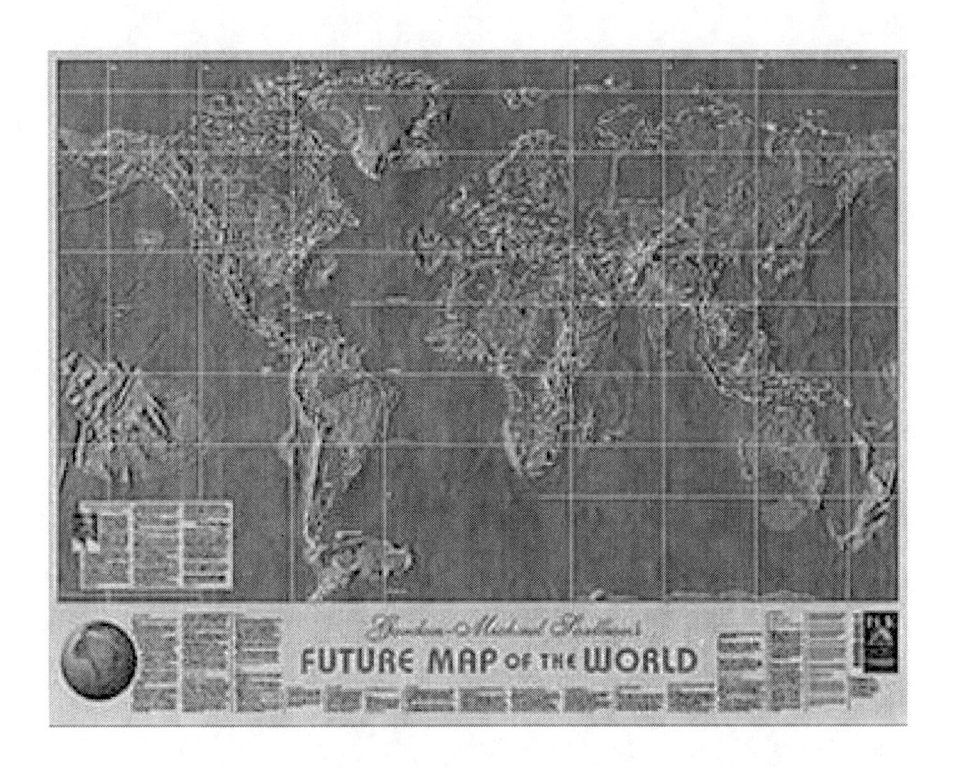

Figure 12 - Gordon Michael Scallion's *Future World Map*

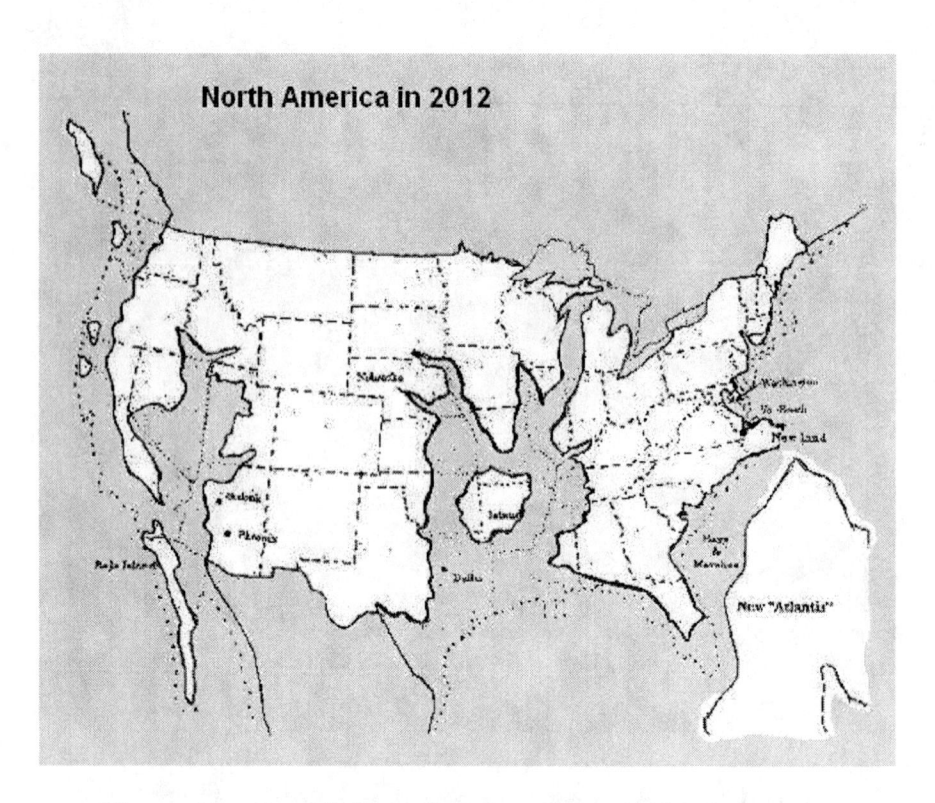

Figure 13 – An additional *Future Map of North America*

As written in volume 2, the "raptured" spirit Earth with its resurrected and translated righteous beings departed at the beginning of the transit into the fourth dimension through the Ouroborus for the commencement of the Golden Age and coming millennial reign of Christ. Will the spirit Earth actually pass through the spinning black hole? There again we do not know.

The black hole is about twenty-four thousand light years away from the "dark rift"; however, we envision the massive, spinning back hole creating a very long and large tornado-like tube vortex or wormhole along its magnetic axis, having an opening from the Ouroborus that leads to and through the black hole entrance into the fourth dimension. Another possibility is that the electromagnetic axis of the black hole, by its spinning, turbulent action, creates a negative energy field in the "dark rift" that literally opens a wormhole portal and will keep the wormhole open perpetually as long as the spinning black hole's magnetic axis continues to flow into the "dark rift" region. Either way, the spirit Earth is destined to enter the portal into another universe, a spiritual fourth dimension. Without the "key" knowledge of the Union of the Polarity, it would have been impossible to "crack" the Mayan calendar 2012 meaning. The survivors of the cataclysm will be those who are "left behind" to salvage destroyed civilizations. Some of the believing non-valiant survivors will know they are "left behind," but the vast majority will believe those who disappeared or are missing and unaccounted for simply died during the cataclysm. It will be the beginning of judgments predicted to come forth from God to bring about repentance.

The cataclysm will probably be the catalyst that brings about one-world government, one-world currency and attempted one-world religion; the old governments having collapsed. The survivors will eventually organize a New World Order. In a few years communications will be restored, some cities repaired, governments installed, and jobs created. The restoration process may happen even quicker because help, most likely, will come from outside sources. After the 9500 BC cataclysm, who came first to restore civilization? The Nephilim, of course, using the Emerald Tablets of Thoth as a pattern ("The Brave New World" in vol. 1).

Their system of enslavement of mankind is nearly in place as we speak with the formation of the economic one-world government. Who do you think will come to restore civilization after the 2012 cataclysm? Yep, you've got it, the Nephilim! They are still working as technically advanced aliens from another planet. They will claim to have witnessed or to have had knowledge of the cataclysmic event happening and to have come to help Earthlings restore civilization. They may come peacefully and offer their help, but only if mankind will accept their aid. Because the Nephilim are "fallen sons" of God, they will profess a strong *belief* in God and may even say they were sent here by him to offer their assistance. Having no other place to turn for help, in desperation, mankind will eagerly accept their offer of assistance.

In volume 2's "The End Times" chapter, we calculated the, "space of half an hour" in Revelation to be approximately twenty-one years. The twenty-one years following 2012 may be the time frame allowed to rebuild civilization. Crustal changes may also speed up the restoration process because continental drifting during the cataclysm might move the continents closer to each other. With the immense ocean barriers removed, or at least the distance made smaller, countries will be able to work together and share resources more easily. New, unheard of, superior technology will be introduced by the Nephilim in all fields. Miraculous medical cures will be brought forth. No disease will be incurable.

But, as always, there is a high price to pay for technology.

As the Nephilim restore civilization, countries will be armed "to the teeth" with new, advanced weaponry in order to keep peace. However, the Nephilim will secretly stir up and instigate problems in the Middle East in their plan to exterminate the remaining Jews, Muslims, and Christians. When the world's economic and political systems fully collapse, a new world leader will emerge to offer solutions after the newly installed governments run into difficult and seemingly unsolvable problems. All this has been carefully orchestrated by Lucifer with the help of his demonic forces and the fallen Watchers (Nephilim) to gain complete control of the world as written in volume 2. Payment for "dancing" with Lucifer and his Nephilim pied pipers will be allegiance. The rest of the story is told in the chapter "The End Times," in volume 2.

In "The End Times" chapter of volume 2, we made the statement "…**it is possible to predict the time of the *Rapture*,**" and "**it was meant to be predicted by this generation.**" This is because the ancients left "evidence" as a reminder of the upcoming 2012 event for the generations that immediately precede 2012. Barring any unforeseen incidents, most of us will probably live for five and a half more years to witness the coming 2012 events, so we are the generations meant to know and to be warned to "prepare."

What kind of "evidence" did the ancients leave as a reminder of the upcoming 2012 event to our generations? We use the plural of "generations" because more than one generation is living at a given time. Our grandparents, parents, children, grandchildren, and even great-grandchildren may all be living during the next five and a half years. Five or even six generations of families could all be present to live through 2012. The ancients left messages through symbolism and pictorial images preserved on substantial structures, meant to endure to our time, so that we would see their messages of warning "to prepare." Most of the evidence has been right under our nose but we have misread them because we lost most of their true meaning by 1850. May your eyes be opened, as ours were, with what we are about to present and as we now believe correctly interpreted as follows:

The Tree of Life motif appears in all cultures, in both the ancient and modern world. Its symbolism has different meaning to various cultures depending on the culture and time frame; however the common thread found in all societies is that the tree specifically connects the three regions of man known as Earth, heaven, and the underworld.

To the Mayan/Aztec cultures, the Tree of Life or Sacred Tree represented the Milky Way. Often the Bird of Paradise/Quetzal bird, a stylized representation of the Big Dipper representing God, the Father (Itzamna), is shown sitting on top of the Milky Way. As a representation of the Sacred Tree, the Maya chose the flowering Ceiba tree. Its branches represented heaven, the trunk represented Earth, and the roots of the tree represented the underworld. It was the path to the Ouroborus linking Earth to heaven and hell and the portal through which gods pass freely.

The most impressive depiction of the World Tree at Palenque may be seen on the carved sarcophagus lid of Lord Hanab-Pakal II. His tomb was built deep within the heart of the largest pyramid, called the Temple of Inscriptions. His massive tomb lid shows the dead king resurrecting to eternal life along the axis of the World Tree or the Milky Way. Encoded on the tomb lid is the 2012 date by the upside down U-shaped serpent bar. The serpent bar, representing the ecliptic path of the sun, forms the cross-piece of the Palenque "cross" or World Tree in the illustration below.

The message being conveyed to onlookers of his tomb lid is, "when the path of the sun (ecliptic) crosses the exact midpoint (galactic equator) of the Milky Way, I expect to be resurrected." It was understood by the Maya that when the sun conjoined the galactic equator at the center of the Milky Way, it was the End of the Age and the Day of Resurrection, which calculates to December 21, 2012, on the Gregorian calendar. This piece of knowledge was imparted to them by the Mayan calendar. The World Tree was an instructional depiction of the future 2012 End Time date.

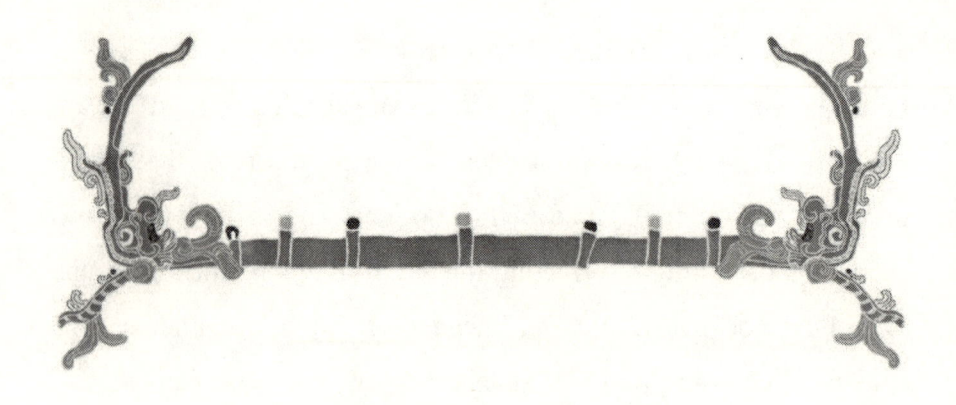

Figure 14 - Serpent bar

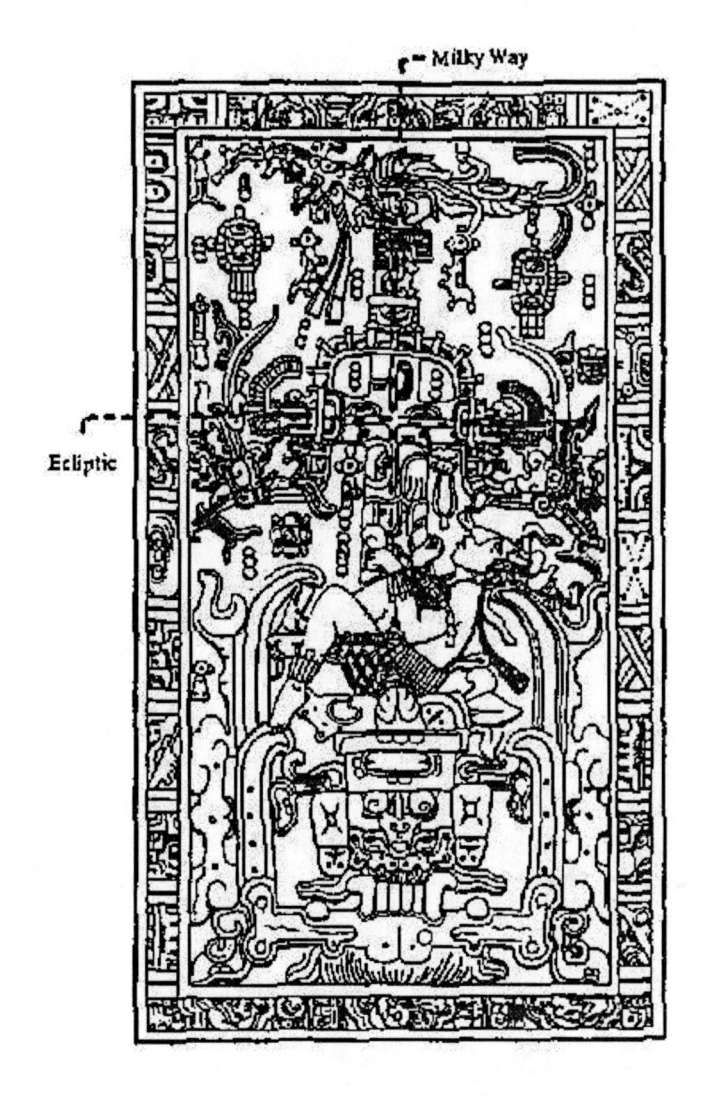

Figure 15 - Pakal's Tomb Lid. Image credit: www.Alignment2012.com

Figure 16 - The Mayan stylized World Tree. The Milky Way, its rift, heaven, the underworld, and the path of the sun are all depicted herein. The "+" marks the end of the aeon (age) (conjoining of sun) in the center of the cross. Earth is symbolized by the crocodile shown in the rift at base of the cross.

Figure 17 - Reproduction image of Panel from Temple of the Cross found in Palenque.

Images of the Mayan stylized World Tree are most notably found in Palenque. The above image is found there in the Temple of the Cross. Another variation of the World Tree is called the Foliated Cross and is found in the Palenque Temple of the Foliated Cross. After much study of the Mayan stylized crosses, your authors wish to present a new interpretation of their symbolism that will fly in the face of traditional thought, as follows:

These stylized crosses are depictions of the Milky Way cosmic event that will occur in 2012. The serpent bars are the path of the sun. When the path of the sun crosses the exact midpoint (the center of the cross), it will mark the End of the Age or the Great Year. If you look at the image above, the "dark rift" is depicted, located below the exact midpoint near the end of the cross where it attaches to the base. Earth is represented by the crocodile and is shown as being in the "dark rift" when the sun conjuncts the center point of the Milky Way. At the top of the cross is the Bird of Paradise (Quetzal Bird) representing Itzamna (God) in heaven.

These stylized World Trees were instructional guides to remind the populace what was going to happen at the End of the Age. The message was literally "carved in stone" in the sacred temples of Palenque. Pakal (Pacal) is also depicted as a dead spirit wearing his burial clothing, handing over his rulership to his eldest son. Remember, the son is noticeably smaller than the father for a very good reason! The scene takes the message even further as the dead king expresses his belief of a resurrection from the dead at the End of the Age through use of symbolism. Note: we prefer to use the old spelling of Pakal, the king of Palenque.

Your authors believe that these images have obviously been misinterpreted by others as we continue with our interpretations. Was Pakal a Christian? The answer is, probably a resounding YES! In volume 1, we wrote that Votan, a grandson of Noah, founded some cities as documented in Mayan writings burned by the Spanish that survive today as oral traditions. Palenque was thought to be one of those cities. It was Votan's mission, along with that of others who accompanied him, to restore civilization and bring the gospel to the ancient peoples of the Americas.

Votan probably founded the ancient settlement of Palenque, followed by Pakal I (died AD 612), later succeeded by Pakal II the Great (AD 603–683), who either started or continued building the famous "stone city" on the settlement site, followed by his eldest son, K'ihnich Kan B'ahlam (Chan-Bahlam), who added to the city complex after his father's death. Kan-Xul, the younger son of Pakal, succeeded his older brother in AD 702, at the age of thirty-eight. During his rule of twenty-three years, he completed the building of Palenque. It is estimated that only five percent of the city has been recovered from the jungle growth. Although Pakal was a giant King, being a descendant of one of the giants, he apparently was receptive to the Christian teachings of his mother and grandmother and accepted the gospel knowledge of the one true God of the universe.

A recent new find confirms that Pakal was a descendant of Nephilim because the south jamb of the Temple of the Foliated Cross and the north jamb of the Temple of the Sun shows the partial standing figure believed to be that of Pakal's son, Kan-B'ahlam, who had the genetic defect of polydactyly. Pakal passed this genetic trait onto his eldest son, Kan-B'ahlam, who had both six fingers and six toes as depicted in a scene found on Pier B and C of the Temple of Inscriptions. This is an extremely rare genetic trait. Carvings depicting the physical deformity were visual proof or mark of divinity as descendants of Nephilim Elder gods who had the genetic trait of polydactyly. In ancient times, the Hebrews viewed this as a corruption of bloodlines. The following pictures prove beyond any doubt that Pakal was of very close descendancy from either Nephilim or giant lineage, as he inherited his giant size from Nephilim directly or from descendancy of a giant.

Figure 18 - Pakal with Nephilim pocketbook, a true mark of authority

Figure 19 - Pakal's son, Kan-B'ahlam with six fingers from Pier-B

Figure 20 - Pakal's infant son, Kan-B'ahlam, with six toes from Pier C

Figure 21 - Pakal's son Kan-B'ahlam with six toes from Pier B

In the Andes, multiple digits were so frequent that the Quechua Indians of Peru had a single word for it—*ttapta*—meaning "the birth of a person with six fingers" (Lounsbury, personal communication). As written in volume 1, that particular region was a "Mecca" for the Nephilim Elder gods. In Europe, Raphael's *Sistine Madonna* shows the extended right hand of Pope Sixtus II having six fully formed fingers.

The names of Votan and Pakal have been wrongly associated as belonging to the same person. They were two separate individuals and several hundred years apart in time. It could be that Pakal I was confused with Votan; however, Pakal II is sometimes called Votan. Later research found Pakal II was preceded by Pakal I, creating the confusion. Few researchers know there was a Pakal I before Pakal II, and Pakal I may have been an uncle of Pakal II.

Pakal II was most likely a Christian who believed in Christian principles, given the amount of light and knowledge that he had. He probably believed in the one true God, had knowledge of a heaven and an underworld hell, was baptized, and believed in a savior (Quetzalcoatl) who would resurrect him from the dead in 2012. Reports from native and Catholic sources all agree that the concepts of Christianity and the practice of baptismal rites were possessed by the original Mesoamerican colonizers many centuries before the coming of the Spanish priests.

Therefore Pakal, a Mayan king, would have been baptized in the name of Itzamna (the father), Bacab (the son), and Echuac (the holy ghost). The Mayan term for the ceremony, *caput sihil*, means "to be born anew (again)." No Mayan person could marry or be priests unless they were baptized (Jakeman, M. Wells, *The Historical Recollections of Gaspar Antonio Chi: An Early Source Account of Ancient Yucatan*, Provo: Brigham Young University Publications in Archaeology and Early History, 1952, 103). Most likely, Pakal expected to enter the fourth-dimensional heaven with the Earth, a prophetic teaching of the Tzolk'in calendar used by the Maya. K'ihnich Kan B'ahlam carried on the teachings of his father. He built the Temple of the Cross, the Temple of the Foliated Cross, and the Temple of the Sun. He was dedicated to teaching his subjects the same principles as did his father before him.

Pakal's ancestry is believed to go back to the Olmec/Jaredite civilization. His maternal roots carried Christian beliefs either from the teachings of Votan or from their more ancient Olmec/Jaredite beginnings. Engravings on the Panel of the Cross trace the genealogy of K'ihnich Kan B'ahlam, the son of King Pakal, to the Olmec/Jaredite King Kish—U-Kish Kan, a royal ancestor of the Olmec/Jaredite culture whose name appears in the ancient Toltec/Nephite record now known as the Book of Mormon in Ether 1:18,19, and Ether 10:17,18.

The next image below is a picture of the Foliated Cross. This panel is found in the Temple of the Foliated Cross. Here Pakal is depicted as passing his throne on to his son, K'ihnich Kan B'ahlam. The Foliated Cross differs from the World Tree image above in that it symbolizes the Maize God, whom the Maya called Hun Nal Ye, who gave the gift of corn for sustenance to mankind, a belief found in the Popol Vuh creation accounts. The Foliated Cross teaches that the Maize God is one of the creators of heaven, Earth, and the underworlds as symbolized by the Milky Way. The Popol Vuh teaches that Hun Nal Ye (the Maize God) was the son of Hun Hunapu (the chief creator god).

Without getting into a long, detailed dissertation of Mayan beliefs, essentially the Popol Vuh's teachings parallel the Christian belief that Christ was the son of God. In Peruvian and Mayan/Aztec legends, Viracocha/Quetzalcoatl are names of the pre-mortal Christ, who was credited as being the giver of corn to man and was known to them as being one of the creator gods or a feathered serpent. In this light, it appears that Hun Nal Ye is another Mayan name variation for Christ. The Mayas speak many regional dialects. Each dialect gives different names to the same person; that has created some confusion in the understanding of their culture and religious beliefs.

At Palenque, inscriptions found on temple walls inform us that Hun Nal Ye, the Maize God, raised the sky in one phase of creation from the primordial sea. This happened when he positioned the World Tree at the center axis of the cosmos.

Your authors believe that the message of the Foliated Cross is a symbolic representation that the Maize God/Christ is the creator of the cosmos as represented by the World Tree. Itzamna (God), represented by the Bird of Paradise in heaven, stands at the head of the Maize God/Christ, indicating the father-son relationship. The Mayan World Tree is also a motif of resurrection and life as is the symbol of corn. Interestingly enough, the Maize God/Christ was associated with a resurrection as symbolized on the Milky Way World Tree. It seems quite evident the World Tree Foliated Cross associates Christ with a resurrection on the 2012 End Time date by its serpent bars crossing the exact midpoint of the cross, indicating the return of Christ. Many Maya today believe that the second coming of Christ will occur on that date.

Figure 22 - Reproduction image of panel in Temple of the Foliated Cross. Note the tremendous difference in height between the father (left) and the son (right).

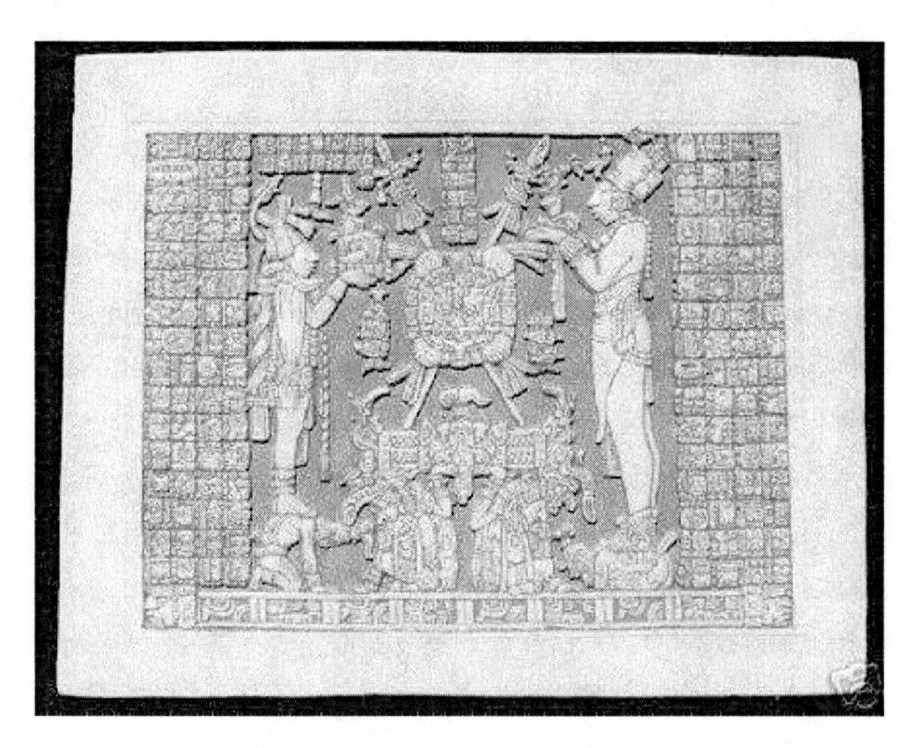

Figure 23 - Reproduction image of Temple of the Sun panel. Note the tremendous difference in height between the father (right) and the son (left).

This panel image comes from the Temple of the Sun that was built by Pakal's eldest son. It commemorates the passing of Pakal's kingship authority to K'ihnich Kan B'ahlam (Chan-B'ahlam), his ruling successor, after the death of Pakal. Your authors are going to "loosely" interpret the meaning as we view it. In the center of the panel, between Pakal and his eldest son, is a shield with crossed spears (a symbol of war). The shield has a picture of a sun jaguar head (symbol of deity) mounted over a serpent bar that rests over the two lords of death. Pakal and his son stand on the backs of two Alux dwarfs. The serpent bar is the path of the sun (the ecliptic) that meets the midpoint of the World Tree Milky Way (drawn in center of serpent bar) in 2012.

When this happens the lords of death will be defeated, or in other words the resurrection day happens on that date. When the dead are resurrected, death is defeated. The sun jaguar is a representation of God's war upon the lords of death, who are defeated on the 2012 End Time date. The panel confirms Pakal's belief that he will be resurrected on that date. At the same time, the scene recalls the beginning of time by the Hero Twins of the Popol Vuh (each twin is held in the palms of Pakal and his son), who became the source of life through a magical rebirth after becoming captive sacrificial victims. Embraced in the scene are themes from the Popol Vuh as well as Christian beliefs. This fact shows that there were others of the city who stuck to their old, ancient religious beliefs and were considered non-Christian even though the Popol Vuh did parallel some Christian beliefs. It appears that the Popol Vuh is an early mingling of mythology with Christian doctrine. Pakal's sons kept their political power and position by pleasing all religious people, a very clever ploy in tumultuous ancient Mexico. In addition, the symbolic cross evidence found at Palenque suggests Pakal and his sons may have been viewed as great prophets in their time.

Our interpretation of these temple panels are not in line with current thinking of archeologists, but by the same token archeologists do not have the correct understanding of the Mayan End Time date as we have come to understand the event. Once the

Mayan End Time date is clearly understood (the World Tree Milky Way, serpent bars, Tzolk'in calendar, path of the ecliptic, dark rift, sign of End of the Age, etc.) then it is rather easy to interpret the temple panels in Palenque.

K'ihnich Kan B'ahlam built the Temple of Inscriptions over his father's tomb. The temple was so named because of all the Mayan glyphs located on the temple walls. Simple readings of the glyphs indicate that they give the genealogy of Pakal, a seventh-century king. Further interpretation of the inscriptions located on temple panels appear to justify why Pakal should be king as well as significant events in his own life. The following is a loose interpretation to emphasize the phrase "and it came to pass."

> And Pakal was born March 6, AD 603 (9.8.9.13.0 8 Ahau 13 Pop) and descended from great kings throughout the centuries, whose names are here recorded. AND NOW IT CAME TO PASS that on the 29th of July, AD 615 (9.9.2.4.8 5 Lamat 1 Mol) Pakal was anointed to be king. AND IT CAME TO PASS that on the 25th of January, AD 633, he ascended to the throne. AND THEN IT CAME TO PASS that on the 30th of August, AD 684, Pakal, the king, died.

The phrase "and it came to pass" or one of its derivatives, occurs 526 times in the Old Testament and 87 times in the New Testament. This phase is not unique to the Bible as the ancient Toltec/Nephite/Book of Mormon record utilizes the same phase 1,381 times. The fact of the finding suggests the phase is Hebrew in origin and correlates with Nephi's statement in the Book of Mormon, "Yea, I make a record in the language of my father, that consists of the learning of the Jews and the language of the Egyptians."

Palenque was built in the Mayan Classic Period (AD 200–900), mostly after Book of Mormon times, but the language style on the Temple of Inscriptions closely parallels the style found in the Book of Mormon. If the Book of Mormon is an ancient Nephite/Toltec record as it claims to be, it should be no surprise to find descendants of Book of Mormon people using the same glyph writing style and terminology in Palenque. It could be that Palenque was the last great bastion of Christianity in Mesoamerica before the collapse of the Mayan/Aztec empires as it was considered the most important religious and political center in the Yucatan of its time.

The same elements and themes from Palenque are found in the Mayan ruins of Copan, Honduras, expressed as the Cosmic Tree, foliated god, and serpent bars. Elaborately detailed, larger-than-life statues of Copan's rulers, described by art historian Linda Schele as "a forest of kings," fill the Great Plaza. These sculptures represent the sovereigns as "sacred Cosmic World Trees," known to us as the Milky Way World Tree. Waxaklajun Ub'aah K'awiil (18 Rabbit) was the thirteenth ruler of Copan, reigning from AD 695 to his death on May 3, AD 738. Seven of the statues in the Great Plaza are those of 18 Rabbit, depicting himself as various gods. Perhaps the most famous of these statues is the one of him depicting himself as the Maize God/Christ World Tree, holding the double-headed serpent bar (ecliptic path of the sun) that is crossing the World Tree at its galactic equator. Symbolically, 18 Rabbit is teaching onlookers of the resurrection date of 2012 that occurs when the sun crosses the galactic equator at the End of the Age, and he is associated with the return of Christ for the harvested righteous. At the same time, the now dead 18 Rabbit is expressing his belief that the Maize God/Christ will resurrect him on that date.

Figure 24 - 18 Rabbit in Copan holding the serpent bar in his hands.

In the central area of the coast of the Gulf of Mexico, near

the city of Papantla, in the state of Veracruz, Mexico, are found the Mayan ruins of El Tajin (AD 600–1150). The name means thunder or hurricane in the Totonac language but its more ancient name of Michlan means the "abode of the dead." Below is pictured a panel from the Pyramid of the Niches.

Drawing by Daniela Epstein

Figure 25 – El Taijin's version of the Axis Mundi. Note the wormhole with many dimension fringes listed around it. On 2012 it opens…one more time.

This picture is the Taijin's version of the Axis Mundi. The bodies of two entwined serpents encircle the central hole. The serpents represent the serpent bar, the Life Force, and an Ouroborus that is formed from the entwined bodies of the two serpents. They entwine at the conjunction of the galactic equator on this particular Axis Mundi that represents the 2012 winter solstice sun; the knot itself is a symbol of "movement" in the heavens, as perhaps movement into the fourth dimension. The central hole is the dark rift

Ouroborus portal that is opened on that date. The fringes, inside the central hole, probably represent the many dimensions opening into heaven represented by the sky band. Above the sky band (representing heaven) are more fringes that probably represent the same multiple dimensions of heaven.

Earth is represented by the turtle at the base of the Axis Mundi or Milky Way. On the far right and left are figures that are standing in the waters of the underworld and encircled by the Life Force. They appear to be deceased and are awaiting the resurrection on that date. On the left, standing near the Axis Mundi, is a priest who appears to be teaching the king, who is holding his serpent bar scepter, the Maya symbol of power and authority. The priest appears to be teaching the king, who is standing on the right, about the cosmic event and time of the resurrection. Again, here is found the remnants of the Christian belief of a resurrection to occur on the 2012 End Time date. Other panels found around the ball court depict scenes from the Popol Vuh and Xibalba, the abode of the dead. Therefore these picture panels appear to be instructional aids or reminders about the coming End of the Age events.

According to Mark Pinkham's book, *The Return of the Serpents of Wisdom*, the ruins of Angor Wat in Cambodia reveal a temple with a version of the tree/cross motif similar to that of Palenque. We haven't been able to locate a picture of this particular cross; however, we do know that Angor Wat was first built as a Hindu shrine and later was changed to a Buddhist shrine. It would stand to reason that they knew about 2012, too, because they understood Precession. The events of 2012 would reflect their religious ideology.

New important finds by your authors do confirm the concept of the Union of the Polarity was known in Mesoamerica. Two-headed red jaguar thrones have been found in Tula, Uxmal, and Chichen Itza. Volume 1 documents the finding in Palenque.

Ix, one of the days on the Mayan calendar, was the day of the Jaguar and of Obsidian, "on that heaven and Earth embraced" (Nicholson, 1938, 76). The day that heaven and Earth embraced is the uniting of the spirit Earth with the temporal Earth. It was important enough to the Maya that a day glyph commemorating the event was placed on their calendar.

Figure 26 - Ix Mayan Day Glyph

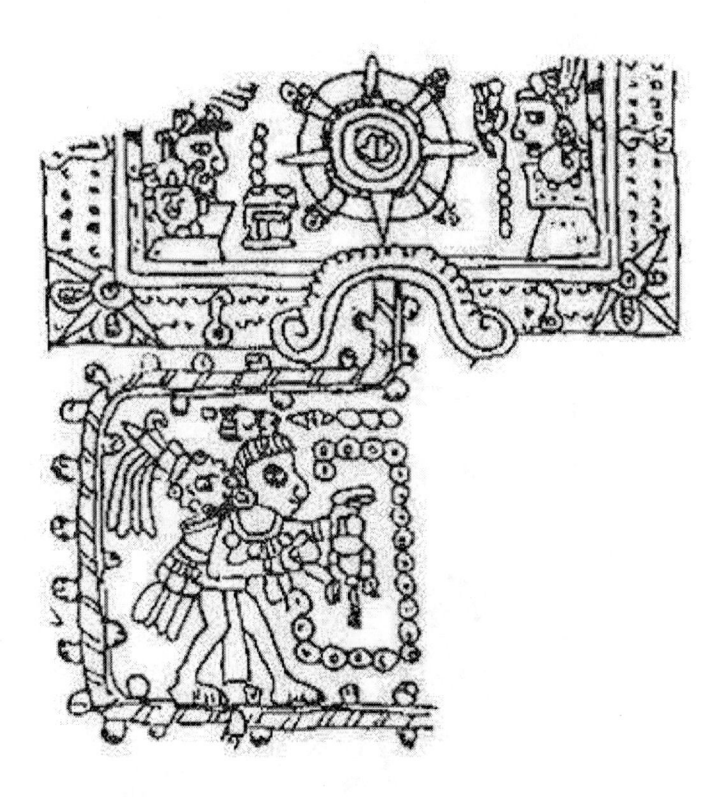

Figure 27 - Image redrawn from the Mayan Codex, Vindobonensis. Note the wormhole with serpent bar passing over it, denoting the End of the Age right in the center of the Milky Way.

The redrawn image above comes from the Mayan Codex Vindobonensis. Mayan prophecy says a ladder will emerge from the center of our Milky Way galaxy in 2012. Using the ladder, from out of the center of the Milky Way will emerge the serpent rope carrying the god Nine Wind (Quetzalcoatl/Christ). Some Mayan accounts describe him sailing down on a winged ship. Note the curved serpent bar midway of the Milky Way marking the End of the Age in 2012. The ladder appears to be a wormhole or stargate into another dimension.

Figure 28 - Close-up of serpent bar with emerging ladder

Figure 29 - Babylonian symbol for the sun.

Figure 30 - William St. Clair tomb logo for the Holy Grail.

The symbol for the source of the serpent rope matches the Babylonian symbol for the sun and the logo for the Holy Grail found on the tombstone of William St. Clair at Rosslyn Chapel, Scotland. The Mayan symbol for deity, pictured as the source of the serpent rope, is another evidence of their Chichimeca ancestors having Babylonian/Sumerian roots.

Figure 31 - Stela #11 from Izapa. Note the marks of crucifixion on his wrists.

Pictured above is a redrawn image of Stela 11 from Izapa. According to current thought of Mayan scholars, the drawing depicts Cosmic Father (the winter solstice sun) in the "mouth" of Cosmic Mother (the "dark rift" or "birth canal" in the Milky Way). The outstretched arms mean halfway or midpoint of the Milky Way where the solstice sun conjuncts in 2012, or a "measuring of time" event. When the celestial alignment happens in 2012, Cosmic Mother will give birth to a New World Age.

Figure 32 - Used with permission from John Major Jenkins, www.Alignment2012.com

On the north side of the ball court in Izapa, the above image is found. Here the same theme is repeated and interpreted by Mayan scholars as First or Cosmic Father (One Hunahpu) = the December solstice sun that is sitting in the middle of the Milky Way "canoe" sailing the "cosmic sea." The background is part of the Milky Way that rises over the solstice horizon marking the midpoint of the Milky Way where the sun conjuncts in 2012 (upside down u-shaped serpent bar). The outstretched arms indicate a period ending a "measuring of time" event. In the Popol Vuh creation myth, this astronomical convergence was encoded as the rebirth of One Hunahpu.

Your authors do not fully agree with either of the above interpretations because **both images clearly show a bearded white man or god**. Both images are of Quetzalcoatl/Christ, holding crucifixes, whose message being conveyed by the carvers in stone to viewers is, "At the End of the Age on December 21, 2012, I shall return to commence a New World Age." The first image even appears to have crucifixion marks on his wrists. The second image meaning is correct except for the figure in the canoe that has been misidentified as One Hunahpu instead of Quetzalcoatl, the Mayan name for Christ.

Other steles in Izapa clearly contain recognizable scenes from the Mayan creation account found in the Popol Vuh. This would indicate that perhaps there were two religious points of view from two or more different groups of people living in Izapa at the same time. Izapa is considered a Pre-classic Maya territory (600 BC–AD 200) and was an important religious and political center 300 BC–AD 50. It was during those years the Izapa area experienced a population increase indicating various different peoples made it their home, and it was during those same years that the many steles of Izapa were carved. It is entirely possible that a Christian community lived amid other tribal communities of different religious belief in and around the Izapa area as is substantiated in the Book of Mormon. A few of the stele or carved pictures contain mixed images from both the Popol Vuh and Christian beliefs, probably to satisfy both groups of believers or to demonstrate the similarity in their beliefs.

Figure 33 - Izapa Stele 5

Of course, we have to mention the famous Stele 5 monument found in Izapa. The image above is an accurately redrawn picture of the actual stele. Many interpretations have been applied to this engraving. We would like to offer ours. Obviously, in the center stands the Tree of Life representing the Milky Way or Axis Mundi. Its branches are reaching into heaven, and the roots lead into the underworld. The square in the main trunk represents the "dark rift" portal that is being guarded by two Watcher angels or cherubim. In heaven is the curved serpent bar directly over the tree branches—located in the exact center—with a bar going through it that represents the path of the ecliptic conjoining the December solstice sun.

This symbolizes the 2012 Precession End Time date. Hanging upside down (on the left) are two fish suspended from heaven, representing a resurrection to occur in 2012. Below the fish are two hummingbirds sipping nectar from a dragon Life Force symbol. Hummingbirds and fish symbolize eternal life. They are taking or receiving eternal life from the creator, symbolized by the dragon Life Force symbol. Around the tree are several seated individuals dressed in Babylonian-style clothing.

Mormons believe these seated figures, on the left, represent Lehi and his wife, Sariah. However, the style of dress suggests an earlier time, perhaps Jared's family (Jaredites)? The horned headdress is rare in Mesoamerica. The feathers between the horns are symbols of death and royalty associated with deity, such as a priestess. The fringed parasol or umbrella is both a Mayan as well as an Old-World symbol that represents royalty or a person of high rank. It is perhaps suggesting the seated figure under it is a high priest. An inverted question-mark symbol near the mouth of the high priest suggests that he is speaking or teaching. He holds a scribe's stylus in his left hand that indicates he is literate. On the forehead of the high priest is a small skull head with a piece of the fruit from the tree in its mouth, which suggests he is teaching or talking about the coming resurrection and eternal life. Above him are several figures standing under a death symbol that indicates they are dead and are awaiting the coming resurrection. All seated figures appear to be teaching or telling others about the resurrection set to occur at the End of the Age. Incense burners are offering prayers to heaven on their behalf. The figure with a hood over its head touching the tree may represent those people who are unbelievers and blind to the truth.

Izapa was first an Olmec (Jaredite) site and later was inhabited by the Maya, Aztecs, and a bearded white race (Nephites/Toltecs). One angel appears to be giving some of the fruit of the tree to a man with outstretched hands. Next to him and under the arm of the angel, on the left side, are two fish (fish can represent believers) that also appear to be ready to eat of the fruit. The fruit represents the plan of salvation unto eternal life, to be discussed in "The Grand Finale" chapter of this book. It is a symbolic message of a resurrection unto eternal life. Reaching down into the underworld are the roots of the tree that reach down to the watery abyss of the Netherworld.

In summary, the stone was probably used as a method of instruction to religious groups, as Izapa was a great religious and political center in its heyday. Because the characters in the picture seem to be of a period or age much older than when it was carved, it may portray a historical event in the past such as the first settlers or Jaredites (Olmecas) telling the story. It is important to note that

Izapa was an early Olmec site. Above the man and woman seated on the left is a symbol of death. This could mean they are dead. The message being imparted was of the future upcoming End of the Age event and their expected resurrection unto eternal life.

Figure 34 – Galactic cosmology in the Izapan Ball Court. Copyright John Major Jenkins, www.Alignment2012.com

Nowhere is the Mayan 2012 cosmology event better symbolized than this image redrawn from one found in the Izapan ball court. The Mayan sacred ballgame is a cosmic reenactment of the future winter solstice sun alignment in 2012. The human head emerging from between the splayed legs represents rebirth or a resurrection on that date much as a woman gives birth to a child emerging from the vagina.

The ball game itself is the December solstice sun, and the goal ring is the "dark rift" transdimensional portal in the Milky Way. On the left is an upside down serpent head with the sun in its mouth, which represents the sun rising out of the mouth of the Ouroborus in 2012. When the game ball (Earth) goes through the goal ring transdimensional portal (dark rift), it enters the fourth dimension and was believed to be the end-of-the-world transformation (translation) of the Earth, a theme found in the Tzolk'in calendar. Even the "dark rift" of the Milky Way is shown in the sky background.

In volume 2, page 213, is found a picture of a ball game marker that once stood in a ball court in Teotihuacán, now preserved in the Museum of Anthropology in Mexico City. The statue depicts the wormhole opening above the Earth; the whole Earth will enter in 2012. As symbolized by the game marker, it is what the Mayan ball game was all about. When the ball (Earth) went through the ring (wormhole portal in the dark rift), Earth entered the fourth dimension. When the ball finally went through the ring, which is extremely difficult to do, the game was over. It is generally believed the winner, the one who put the ball through the ring, was sacrificed in honor of the upcoming 2012 cosmic event.

Figure 35 - Aztec Sun Stone

The famous Sun Stone of the Aztecs shows the sun god, Tonatiuh, in the center circle. Note, this illustration, by Roberto Sieck Flandes, is only a partial reproduction of the Sun Stone, as its outer ring is missing, but the center circle is the section of most interest to us at present. We chose this illustration because of the easily seen clarity of detail. The four squares around his face represent the four previous World Ages that were destroyed by cataclysms. According to their belief, the first age was destroyed by jaguars, the second age was destroyed by wind, the third age was destroyed by fire, and the fourth age was destroyed by water. The center circle represents the fifth epoch, called Nahui-Olin, meaning "Day of the Shaking Earth." Our present age is the fifth epoch and last age of Earth, which is destined to be destroyed by a cataclysmic earthquake.

It is incorrect to call the Sun Stone the Aztec Calendar Stone. When the relic was first uncovered, it was mistakenly thought to be their calendar because the outer ring contained the Aztec day glyphs. Later, it was learned that the Aztecs used two different calendars very similar to the Maya. The Aztecs were great borrowers (copiers). They borrowed Toltec technology, customs, and genealogies, and they borrowed the Mayan calendar. Basically, the Aztec calendar was similar but was more primitive and less precise; nevertheless it was accurate. However, it did correlate to the Mayan calendar in so much that the end of the Aztec fifth sun aligned exactly with the Mayan End Time date of December 21, 2012. Both cultures accepted the same date as the end of the world.

Your authors found a most interesting thing in the Mexico City Cathedral, when we visited Mexico in November 2005. In the back of the main apse of the cathedral is a very beautifully carved wooden altar. The front panel of the altar has the cardinal constellation points carved in large, bold relief. The four cardinal constellations are Leo, Taurus, Aquarius, and Scorpio. Leo was represented as a lion, Taurus as a bull, Aquarius as a man, and Scorpio as an eagle. Each figure is winged. The message in the symbolism was quite clear to those who understood Precession End Time meaning during the AD 1600–1800 usage of the Mexican cathedral, when the belief was commonly known. It was interpreted to mean when the four cardinal constellations align on December 21, 2012, to form a Grand Cross in the sky, it marked the end of the Precession Great Year or Aeon of 26,000 years, when the "harvest of the righteous" in the End Times and the resurrection of the dead was predicted to take place. The carved images on the front of the altar facing the congregation served as a constant reminder of the upcoming 2012 event.

Construction of the magnificent cathedral began in 1573 and was completed two centuries later in 1788. It is the largest colonial cathedral in the Americas. Apparently the doctrine of the "harvest of the righteous" and resurrection of the dead to occur at the end of the Great Year was believed and taught in the Mexican Catholic Church until the early 1800s; otherwise, why have the symbolism on one of their main altars? The once common knowledge now seems lost. The cathedral construction was finished when the Gregorian calendar was receiving acceptance in European countries. When it replaced previous, old calendars, the knowledge of the doctrine disappeared. Your authors have never heard this doctrine taught in any church today nor did any of our science classes mention

Precession.

Did other ancient civilizations know, as the Maya did, about the coming 2012 conjunction of the sun with the Galactic Equator of the Milky Way?

Yes, they did. Old world astronomy was closely related to the Mayans, ancient Egyptians, Chaldeans (Assyrians/Babylonians), Sumerians, Hindus, Tibetans, Greeks, Chinese, Israelites, and Jews observed, and to an important degree understood, the Precession of the Equinoxes. We know this because each of those civilizations knew and had a name for the constellation cardinal points, not to be confused with Earth cardinal points. Earth cardinal points are the true directions of north, south, east, and west. Heavenly cardinal points are the directional constellations of the zodiac used in measuring the movement of the ages and used as a sort of calendar to measure solstices and equinoxes. Alignment of the cardinal constellations at the end of the Great Precession Year will form a heavenly Grand Cross in the zodiac. It was understood when the heavenly constellation cross appeared, it marked the End of the Age and the end of the 26,000 year Precession of the Equinoxes or Great Year. In addition, the Maya, Egyptians, Chaldeans, Greeks, Hindus, Jews, and Christians, understood a cataclysmic earthquake would occur at the end of the Great Year.

In ancient times, early civilizations believed the heavens were sustained by four guardian pillars called the Pillars of Heaven. These four guardians of the heavens are sometimes represented as the four cardinal constellation points of a cross in the zodiac. To the Maya, these four guardians were called the Kan Bacab; the Egyptians referred to them as the four minor sphinxes, Chinese, Chaldeans, and Hindus called them the four Genii; Jews and early Christians referred to them as the four heads of the Beast, the four living creatures, or the four Cherubim/Kerubim (Revelation 4:6–7). Job 26:11, speaks of the "Pillars of Heaven" as "Supports of the Sky" and 2 Samuel 22:8, as "Supports of the Heavens."

Figure 36 - Ancient Egyptian hieroglyph for "Heaven"

Figure 37 - The Four Pillars supporting Heaven as crafted into the side of the Port Adelaide Masonic Centre.

ancientegypt.hypermart.net/freemasonry/index.htm

The "All-seeing Eye of Ra" is an Egyptian symbol of Precession. The "dot within a circle" is the pole of the ecliptic, the central point of the revolution of the signs of the zodiac and the Ages of the zodiac around the heavens, and signifies the fifth cardinal point. Other civilizations sometimes used the Earth as a fifth cardinal point. This is the origin of the sun wheel.

Figure 38 – All-seeing Eye Symbol. The dot within the eye is the Precession symbol.

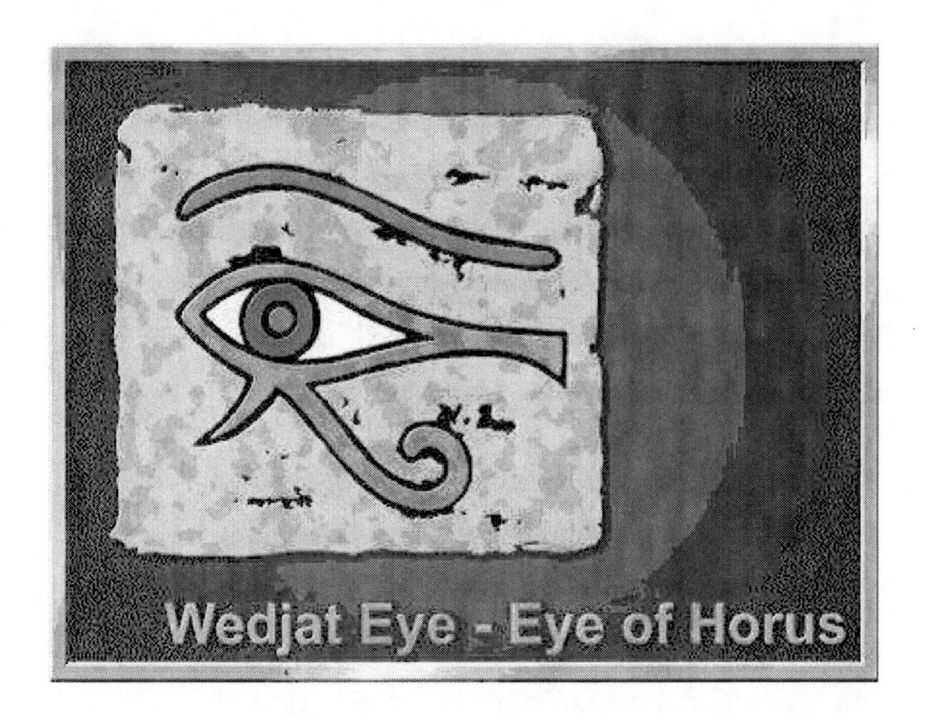

Figure 39 – Left Eye of Horus

The "All-seeing Eye of Ra" is also associated with the Egyptian god Horus, the sun god, who was originally a totally distinct god from Horus the son of Osiris the creator and Isis. Later, the two Horus gods were both confounded as one and the same god. It is the "third eye" of clairvoyance in the Hindu religion and the "Eye of Providence" on the Great Seal of the United States. A left eye image was used in Egypt to represent the moon and god Tehuti (Thoth). A right eye image, as above, could represent either Horus or Ra, and was a symbol of the sun. The dot in the circle was a symbol of Precession and believed to have magical powers for resurrecting the dead (Pyramid Utterance Text, Utterance 155).

The dot in the circle was a symbol of Precession noting the

time of the resurrection to occur at the end of the 26,000 Great Year, sometimes called the end of the Great Precession Year cycle. Assuming we are correct, then the two Babylonian sun symbols, previously pictured, are symbols of Precession, marking the time of the resurrection. Remember both had the dot inside a circle and one is found on the tomb of William Sinclair expressing the Templar belief when he expected to be resurrected.

Another Egyptian symbol, the hieroglyphic five-pointed star, has a dot within a circle located in the center of the star. The Egyptian priests called this symbol the *sha*. From earliest recorded times, the five-pointed star has always been the symbol for the feminine-gendered spirit Earth. It is note worthy to add that the entire temporal universe is male-gendered. Adding the Precession symbol, the dot within the circle, to this symbol demonstrates the role of the spirit Earth at the End of the Age as a symbolic reminder of its departure into the fourth dimension in 2012—a departure they called "the change." This was a symbol of highly esoteric spirituality. The same five-pointed star, divested of its encircled dot, is found in the Masonic Lodges of America. It represents the feminine, spiritual Earth.

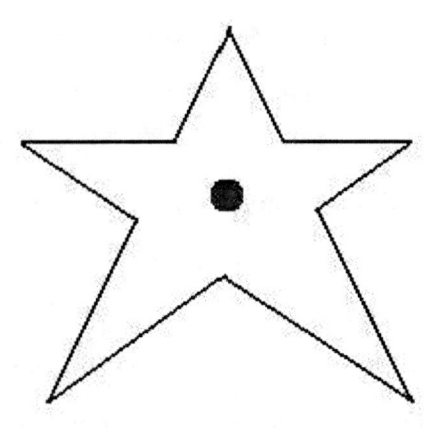

Figure 40 - Egyptian Sha Star: The feminine spirit Earth symbol used in Masonic Lodges divested of its encircled dot.

The Great Pyramid of Giza was constructed as a cosmic marker of Precession for future generations. The structure was symbolic of the Axis Mundi (Milky Way), part of the concept of Precession, and was built in the exact epicenter of the known landmass as a fifth cardinal point. It is believed by some that the missing capstone of the Great Pyramid had an "All-seeing Eye" symbol on it. The sum of the Pyramid's two base diagonals in pyramid inches equals the length of the Precession of the Equinoxes or the Great Year (25,827 years). The Great Pyramid also marks the time of the spring equinox. Due to the angle of the sides of the pyramid versus its latitude, it casts no shadow at noon on the day of the spring equinox. Functioning as a great sundial, its shadow to the north and its reflected sunlight to the south, it accurately marked the annual dates of both the solstices and the equinoxes.

All four sides align with the four cardinal points of the compass. Other pyramids in the world whose four sides align with the four cardinal points of the compass function the same as the Great Pyramid of Giza. These other pyramids are most notably found in Mesoamerica; however, they are found all over the world. The same can be said about Stonehenge and Avebury Henge as well as Native American stone medicine wheels. They were calendrical markers of both the solstices and the equinoxes and served as a cosmic marker of Precession. Another function of Henges, as documented in volume 1, was to predict impending cataclysms. If the ancients seemed somewhat obsessed with Precession, it was because they needed to know when the solstices and equinoxes occurred to time seasons of planting and harvest, plus they diligently watched the sky for the Suntelia sign to appear and the Grand Cross re-alignment of the cardinal constellations to occur so they would know the End of the Age had arrived, heralding the long-awaited Day of Resurrection. Another function of pyramids constructed like the Giza pyramid was to serve as vortex amplifiers of the Life Force energy that was previously documented in volume 1. Indeed, pyramids are amazing multi-functioning structures, which finally we are beginning to fully understand.

Figure 41 - Reverse side of Great Seal of the United States

The Masonic symbolism of the Great Seal Pyramid, found on the back of the U.S. currency one-dollar bill, has now become quite clear. This pyramid is identified with the Great Pyramid of Giza. The thirteen courses of stone represent "strength and duration" and the thirteen tribes of Israel (Jacob adopted Ephraim and Manasseh into the tribes, giving each a portion). The date on the base is the date of independence from Britain. America was believed to be the New Jerusalem or New Israel by its founding fathers. As established earlier, the pyramid is a symbol of Precession. Although little is found in their writings to indicate as such, much is found in Masonic symbolism to indicate that they did believe it.

Most all of the pilgrim emigrants acknowledged that they

were descendants of Israelites who came to the American wilderness to establish a new nation under God. In the Book of Revelation, Israel is found fleeing into the wilderness to a place prepared by God, a place where Israel would dwell in safety. The Pilgrims often referred to the first colonies on this shore as being in "the wilderness." Numerous books have been written on this very subject; we cannot do justice to it in one paragraph. However, it is believed by some that descendants of all the tribes of Israel are now represented in America, the resurrected New Israel, and comprise the majority of the population. Therefore, watching over the destiny of Israelites in America and the nation is the mystical eye of the God of Israel till the End of the Age (represented by the pyramid). At the bottom of the seal is the motto "Novus Ordo Seclorum" meaning "A mighty Order of Ages is born anew." A new nation, whose government, by the people, for the people, and under God, was born with individual liberty, justice, and freedom for all as its hallmark. Above the Seal is the motto, written in thirteen letters, "Annuit Coeptis," meaning "He hath prospered our undertakings." This refers to God prospering the people of America, the New Israel, whose greatness was prophetically assured.

Although a Greek name was given for the Ouroborus, the concept was understood by the Egyptians as early as 1600 BC and probably was known much earlier. They understood that when the Great Precession Year ended, it marked the End of the Age when they expected their god Osiris, the Bull of Egypt and god of the dead, to return from the netherworld and usher in the New Age of

Osiris or New Age of Horus. Egyptian kings expected to be resurrected or reborn unto eternal life at the End of the Age as their souls (Ka) had previously been carried to Orion, shortly after death, by the Four Sons of Horus to await the resurrection. It is by the power of Anubis, an Egyptian mortuary god, that the road to resurrection in the afterlife was opened and the deceased were ushered into the presence of Osiris (their creator) to await the resurrection and eternal life. This closely parallels events in the Bible, with only names and places changed to fit Egyptian ideology and beliefs most likely influenced by the Assyrian, Babylonian, and Sumerian cultures. The Mesopotamian influence is clearly shown on the zodiac below as the zodiac representations are of Mesopotamian origin rather than Egyptian.

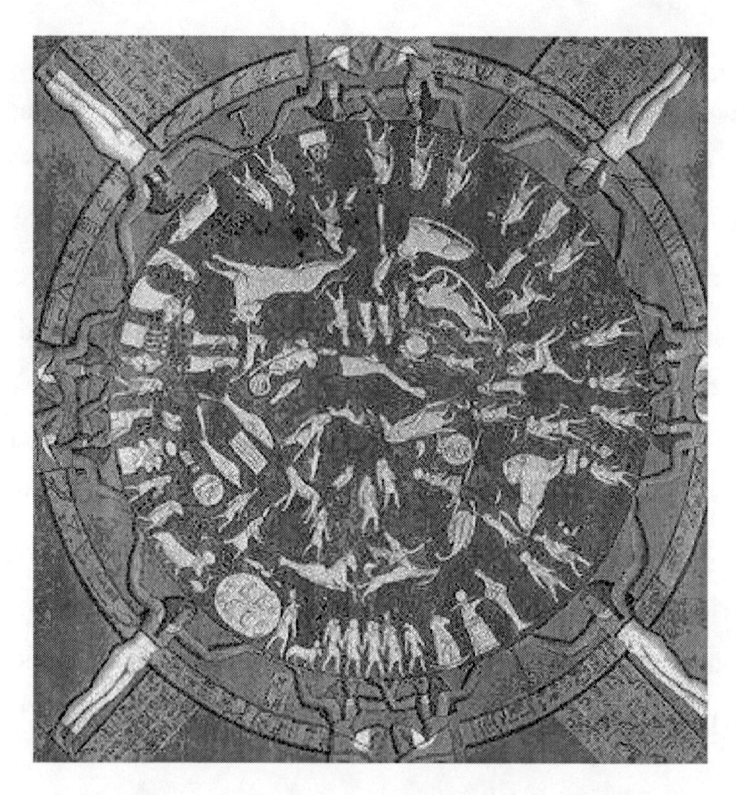

Figure 42 - Zodiac on Temple of Hathor ceiling at Dendera, Egypt, now in Paris Louvre (picture credit: *sunnyokanagan.com/joshua/Denderazodiac.html*-1k)

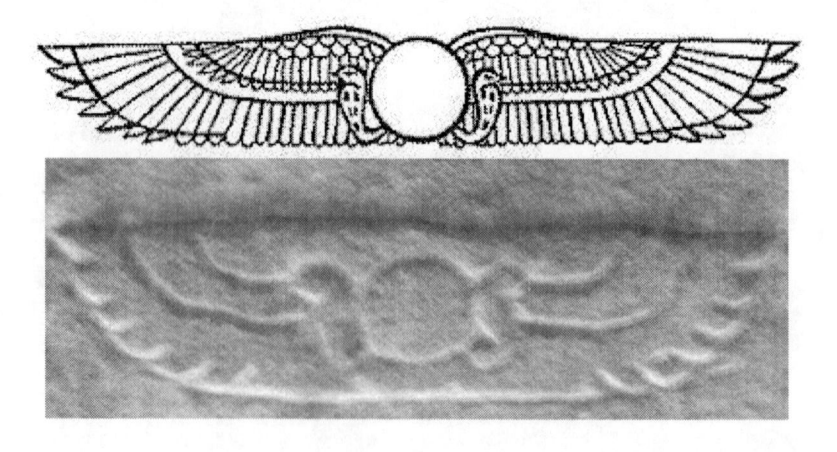

Figure 43 - Egyptian Winged Disk found at Philae, Egypt

As documented in volume 1, the Egyptian winged disk is a symbol of the Union of the Polarity. The disk itself has been wrongly identified as being the sun. Instead, our research indicates the disk represents the sacred gateway or portal into the higher universes; the portal through which the spirit Earth will pass in 2012. Of course, the Ouroborus portal is the "dark rift" in the Milky Way. This symbol was the ancient Egyptian way of explaining what was believed to take place at the End of the Age, which corresponds to the 2012 End Time events.

Figure 44 - Within the sacred gateway is to be found the emblem of the Royal Arch Masonic Chapter above the door of the Port Adelaide Masonic Temple: the triple tau within a triangle, within the winged disk.
ancientegypt.hypermart.net/freemasonry/index.htm

To the trained eye, Masonic symbolism in the above image is easily read and is there for all to see and for the wise to understand. As previously documented, the pyramid is both a Precession symbol and a tetrahedron Earth symbol, to be discussed later in another chapter, "The Tetrahedron." Within the pyramid triangle is a triple tau symbol. The symbol of a "tau" means a "holy or sacred opening or gate."

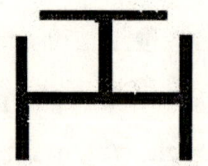

Figure 45 - Triple Tau symbol

The triple tau is a symbol of the Jerusalem Temple that is also considered a "sacred opening, gate or portal" into a higher universe. One trained in esoteric wisdom would read the symbolic message as: "At the end of Precession (represented by the pyramid triangle) the sacred Ouroborus portal is opened (represented by both the triple tau and the winged disk)." The tetrahedron triangle also represents the Earth. Even the position of the triple tau triangle within the circle or winged disk reveals further esoteric meaning that is interpreted by us as the passage or gate through which Earth enters into a higher dimension at the End of the Age or end of Precession. Earth, represented by the triangle, is shown passing into the "dark rift" opening of the disk. Truly, the old saying, "A picture is worth a thousand words" is fulfilled by the above winged disk images. A modern version of the Egyptian winged disk depicting the cosmic event of the spirit Earth passing through the disk Ouroborus portal into the fourth dimension is pictured on the front cover of this book. Although not pictured on the cover as such, the spirit Earth's land masses will be configured as it was in the beginning.

Figure 46 - Egyptian Tree of Life Picture credit:
goroadachi.com/etemenanki/endgame-4-p2.htm

The Egyptian Tree of Life is redrawn from an image found on the granite Sphinx Stela Monument located between the front paws of the Great Sphinx of Egypt. Thutmose IV, in about 1423 BC, placed the monument there during his reign. Clearly, it is an Egyptian Tree of Life being guarded by two sphinxes, the Egyptian version of cherubim or possibly the Nephilim god, Nergal (son of Marduk). A priest on the right appears to be offering or pouring Living Water into a raised bowl by his left hand or appears to be receiving Living Water in a small bowl held in his raised left hand, Osiris being the source of the Living Water. The other figure appears to be a person of high station (prince?) making what appears to be an offering to the sacred tree. The winged disk acts as the serpent bar, and the disk itself represents the Ouroborus portal into

101

heaven. The position of the disk midway and top of the cross represents 2012, when the sun conjuncts the galactic equator intersection of the Milky Way, marking the End of the Age. The roots of the tree (Milky Way Axis Mundi) extend down into the underworld region of the dead. Symbolically, the Axis Mundi is the path leading the resurrected dead to the portal of heaven that opens in 2012. What a find! **The monument leaves no doubt as to the meaning of the winged disk.**

The story recorded on the stele of a dream Thutmose IV had while still a prince is as follows: While on a hunting trip, the prince took a noonday nap near the buried Sphinx. The Sphinx spoke to him in the dream, promising Thutmose the kingdom if he would clear away the accumulated sand around him. He did so, and shortly became a Pharaoh upon the death of his ruling brother, who suddenly died under mysterious circumstances. The stele shows Thutmose paying homage and tribute to the sphinx sun god who spoke to him. The Egyptians received the knowledge of Precession and of the resurrection to occur at the End of the Age from the Babylonians/Sumerians/Assyrians; only they replaced the God of Noah with their own sun god. To Thutmose, his sun god was coming for the resurrection at the End of the Age; that belief is expressed and symbolized on the tree of life stele.

Because zodiac wheels first appear in ancient Sumeria/Babylonia, your authors feel Precession was also known early on, maybe as early as 10500 BC. From whence did this knowledge come? As written previously in the first two volumes, the knowledge can only come from three sources:

1. The Nephilim before and after the 9500 BC cataclysm

2. The Shining Ones and the pre-mortal Christ after the 9500 BC cataclysm

3. Noah's race. We suspect the knowledge came from all three sources at different intervals.

And, the biggest surprise was to find Precession knowledge linked to the End of the Age resurrection of the dead from earliest times of conception, which clearly indicates that the teachings of a resurrection unto eternal life at the End of the Age came from the pre-mortal Christ and the Shining Ones who traveled to ancient Sumeria. The doctrine of a universal resurrection was known and taught from the beginning as found in Moses 1:39. Ancient Sumeria was the birthplace of recorded history; however, Adam was taught this doctrine from the very beginning, and that doctrine was passed down through Noah's race.

It was not by coincidence that the pre-mortal Christ and the Shining Ones appeared on the scene apparently around the same time the Nephilim Anunnaki were present. The Nephilim Anunnaki countered the teachings of the pre-mortal Christ and the Shining Ones with teachings they dictated in the Sumerian texts to fit their own agenda. For example, they taught men of this planet that they were their creators. Perhaps they conjured up the missing planet Nibiru, better known as Planet X, to counter the End Time events taught by the pre-mortal Christ because the arrival of Nibiru back to our solar system is predicted to be catastrophic and due to cause havoc around the End Time date of 2012.

Because the Nephilim Anunnaki are pawns of Lucifer, we view them as evil corrupters of men and not to be trusted; therefore, in that light, we feel the Sumerian texts are not sufficiently reliable to say everything written in them are factual accounts. But, we emphasize again, it appears the doctrine of a universal resurrection was known and taught from the beginning (Moses 1:39).

According to the records of the Assyrians, Babylonians, and Sumerians, the Nephilim god Nergal, son of Marduk, was considered the deity represented by the zodiac sign of Sagittarius. He was often depicted as a lion with a human head and was the god of the dead, war, famine, and pestilence. An Akkadian poem describes his fall from heaven to the underworld to become the god of the netherworld by marrying the goddess of the underworld.

In the Hellenic Period, Nergal was identified with the god Hercules. In the astral-theological system, he becomes the planet Mars, emblem of bloodshed, while in ecclesiastical art he is represented as the great lion-headed colossi serving as guardians to the temples and palaces. In Mesopotamia he was worshipped from ca. 3500–200 BC. Current thinking is the Great Sphinx of Egypt may have been built in commemoration of Nergal. Facing due east on latitude 30 degrees N, its gaze is fixed on the Milky Way exactly where the sun will conjunct the galactic equator in 2012. In fact, this is the best viewing seat in the world to witness the event. As the Mesopotamian god of the dead, he stands guard over the stargate portal when the resurrected dead will depart his kingdom and pass into eternal life in 2012. Another clue: Cairo after all means "Mars." According to the Old Testament, the worship of Nergal originated in Cuth (2 Kings 17:30).

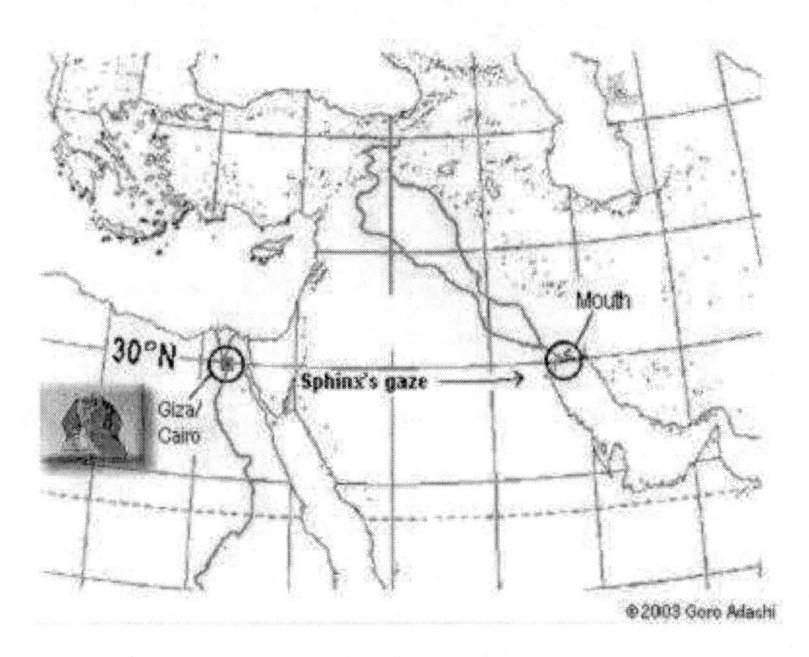

Figure 47 - Illustration from Book, *The Time Rivers,* by Goro Adachi (used with permission from Goro Adachi)

Your authors like the above illustration because on the right-hand side is a heavenly "reflection" or mirror image of the Milky Way as seen by the Sphinx's gaze. The round mouth circle is the exact midpoint where the sun will conjunct the Milky Way's galactic equator. However, your authors note that our idea for the illustration is different from the idea presented in the book *The Time Rivers*, authored by Goro Adachi.

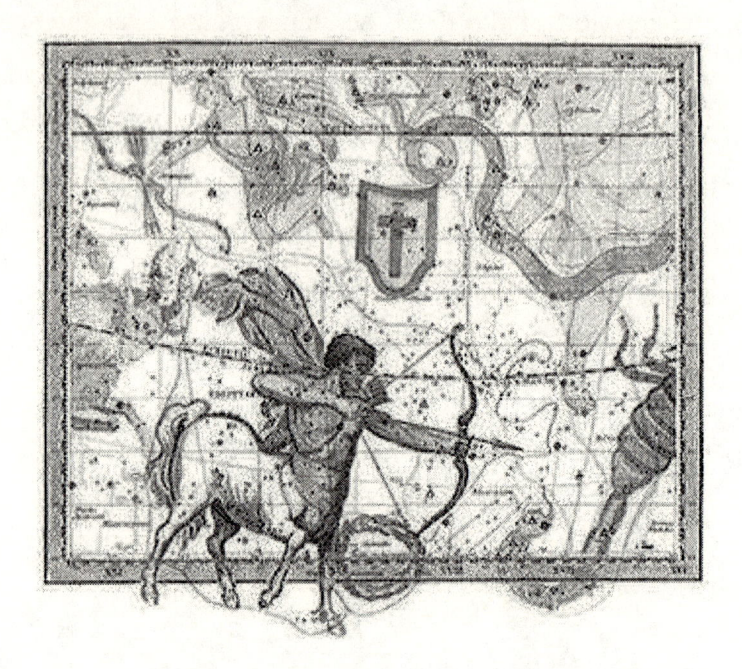

Figure 48 - Sagittarius Centaur

Figure 49 - Sagittarius pointing his arrow at the sign of the Suntelia Aeon—the End of the Age—on December 21, 2012

From a heavenly vantage point, the 2012 alignment is best viewed from the constellation of Sagittarius because the "dark rift" is located in the constellation. In 2012, the arrow of the centaur will aim directly at the sign of the Suntelia in the mouth of the Ouroborus (signs in the sky). If the centaur could release his arrow, it would fly into the midpoint of the galactic equator striking the exact place where the sun will conjunct the Milky Way on December 21, 2012. Is this a coincidence? Not hardly.

Ancient Sumeria constructed the Sagittarius constellation as a symbolic reminder of the coming sign of the Suntelia that marked the End of the Age and expected resurrection. A resurrection has always been associated with the End of the Age, even before the advent of the mortal Christ. It started in ancient Sumeria, spreading all over ancient Mesopotamia, Egypt, India, and Mesoamerica. Different countries then applied their religious ideology. An example from the Vedic Puranas:

Vishnu, it is said he will appear again soon, as Kalki, a white horse, destined to destroy the present world and take humanity to a different, higher place.

Terminology has changed throughout the centuries. In ancient times the term "resurrection" was expressed as a transformation, a return to life, the harvest, or higher plane of existence, but the meaning was the same as the more modern term of "resurrection" used today.

Figure 50 - Celtic crosses silhouetted at sunset. This is an accurate depiction of the Milky Way World Tree with four cardinal constellations forming a Grand Cross alignment.

Besides being symbols of the Union of the Polarity, ancient crosses were symbolic or served as a reminder of the end of the Great Precession Year or sign of the Suntelia, when the resurrection was prophesized to occur. Light coming through the four holes of the crosses represent the four cardinal constellations forming a Grand Cross alignment at the End of the Age. The cross structure itself represented the World Tree.

Figure 51 - Celtic sun cross. Notice the Precession *dot* in the center of the circle representing the sun conjoining the Milky Way galactic equator in 2012.

Precession is clearly represented on the above fifth-century Celtic solar or sun cross. The dot inside the center circle is the symbol for Precession, and by being located in the center of the cross it symbolizes the sun's conjunction at the midpoint of the galactic equator to occur on the Sign of the Suntelia in reminder of the resurrection day. The horizontal arm would represent the path of the ecliptic (sun's path) such as that demonstrated by a serpent bar in Mayan art. The cardinal constellations (four holes) are aligned to form a Grand Cross. At the top of the cross is the feminine *yin* symbol denoting the spirit Earth returning to heaven. These cross designs were popular gravestone markers, a reminder to grieving families of the coming Day of Resurrection.

Figure 52 - Celtic Cross with lines continuously knitted together denoting the Union of the Polarity.

Another fifth-century Celtic cross of interest. Lines continuously knitted together are symbols of the Union of the Polarity illustrating the two worlds firmly knitted together. In the center of the cross the circle marks the Suntelia sign. In Ireland there are many styles of Celtic crosses, both Christian and pre-Christian, clearly sharing the same theme to remind us of the approaching End of the Age. Indeed, research studies prove the ancient Celtics were highly advanced in astronomical observation, particularly in the construction of calendars.

Figure 53 - Tibetan Stupa resembles a Tesla coil. This one in Shigatse is constructed from 4,300 pounds of gold and more than 10,000 jewels. A stunning representation of the World Tree.

The Shigatse Stupa pictured above is more than sixty feet tall. The cocoon holding the interned bodies of the sixth, seventh, eighth, and ninth Ponchan Lamas is opened so that the pilgrim can see that the Tibetans believe that these holy men will be resurrected on the 2012 date. There is an inner layer of sapphires that may serve some electromagnetic purpose. Notice the rays of energy emanating from behind the likeness of the Ponchan Lamas. These touch what your authors believe is a representation of the serpent bar. At the peak of the serpent bar are placed two onyx stones representing the winter solstice date of December 21, 2012. This is supported by the careful placement of two Ouroborus symbols in the body of the cocoon.

The Ouroborus on this Stupa are swallowing their tails, indicating the End of the Age Suntelia Aeon. When this sign appears in the sky, the stargate portal, shown clearly on the ceiling exactly over the reflector of the Tesla coil behind the cocoon, will open. The coil may hold the energy to hold the portal open, or to help focus the opening to this specific point. This design was built in the seventh century. Tesla's coil was designed in the nineteenth century.

Tesla obtained the energy for his coil from the Earth itself. The two dragons on the base of the Tibetan Stupa represent the Life Force energy in the Earth. The stargate below is perhaps the most crystal-clear representation of the multi-dimensional aspect of the human soul and its many dwelling places of anything left behind by ancient cultures.

Figure 54 - Photo of the Stargate Mandala taken by the author in 2007.

The outer circle of the mandala represents the crust of the Earth. The next layer on the inside, with the four stars at 2, 4, 8, and 10 o'clock positions, represent the four key constellations lining up. The blue ring may represent the actual round opening of the Ouroborus stargate. The four cardinal directional points at north, east, south, and west indicate the exact alignment relative to the Earth. Each square represents a dimension, one inside the other. It could mean a progression into eternity, but mostly likely they each represent a dimension. There are nine dimensions shown in this stargate mandala.

Figure 55 - Images of four saints in Chartres Cathedral

The second saint image from the left holds a solar cross Precession symbol. He is probably the apostle Matthew. Again the center dot represents the conjuncture of the sun, denoting the End of the Age when the expected resurrection would occur. These statues are thirteenth-century and found on the central portal, north façade of the cathedral. With symbolism such as this, how could we have lost the message? He is telling everyone who walks beneath his feet exactly when the resurrection will occur.

Figure 56 - Chartres Rose Window in North Transept

Figure 57 - The Last Judgment Rose Window Chartres Cathedral France Picture credit website: History of Gothic Architecture Cathedral, Chartres no. 27

The famous Gothic stained glass Rose Window in the west façade of the Chartres Cathedral was created in the twelfth century. Most early Rose Windows typically have twelve major divisions (representing twelve Ages), and are intersected by the four cardinal constellation points, forming a cross that leads into the center circle,

.which usually has a picture of Christ within it or themes of the Virgin Mary with Christ child. Sometimes the apostles are depicted. The center circle (dot within the circle) would represent the conjunction of the sun's path with the galactic equator to occur in 2012. A few Rose Windows (e.g., Notre Dame Cathedral in Paris) even display signs of the zodiac and the cardinal constellation points. Do you see the symbolism represented? When the cardinal constellation points are aligned to form a Grand Cross in 2012, the expected coming of Christ or the resurrection occurs. It is a message for all to see and for the wise to understand.

John 6:40, 44, 54 all state, "…and I will raise him up at the **last day**." Up until the 15th–16th century this "last day" was understood by Christians to be the *last day* of this Age, the Suntelia Aeon, or December 21, 2012, when the resurrection of the righteous would take place. The words of the sister of Lazarus echo that belief: "I know that he will rise again in the **resurrection at the last day**" (John 11:24).

The magnificent artwork and Rose Windows displayed in cathedrals were for the benefit of the unlettered faithful at the bequest of the sixth-century Pope Gregory the Great. His bequest was reiterated in 1025 to embellish the cathedrals with works of religious art, for "this enables illiterate people to learn what books cannot teach them."

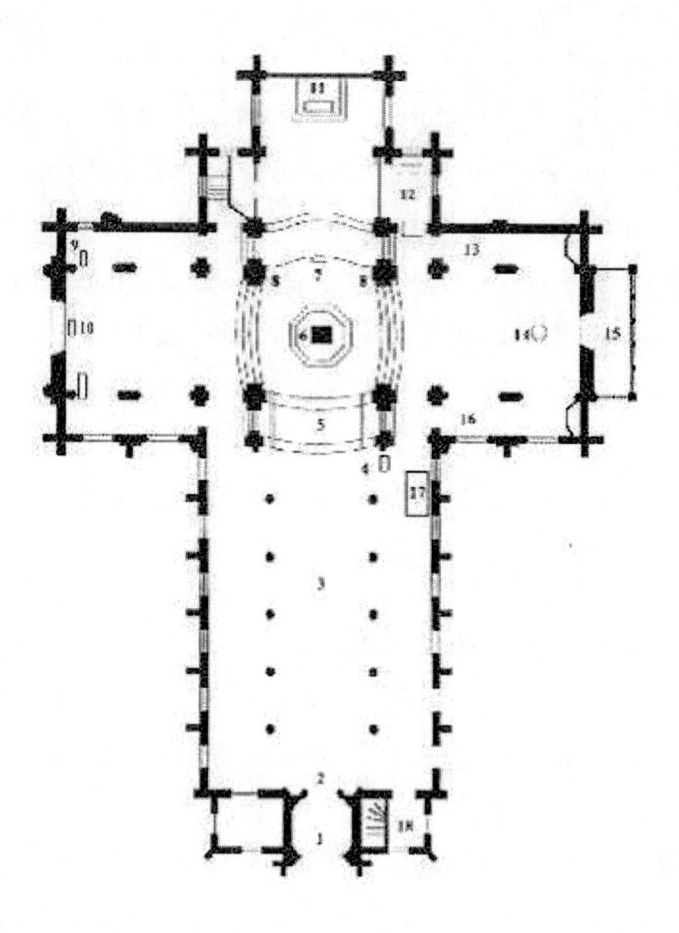

Figure 58 - Typical cathedral floor plan

Above is a typical floor plan of cathedrals, which are usually built in the cruciform plan, that is, in the form of a cross. The cathedral was the medieval Christian version of the Milky Way Tree of Life. The crossbar (same as Mayan serpent bar) is the transept (usually called the north and south transepts), and the eastern arm is where the choir usually sat. Cathedrals were positioned so their congregations would face east to the rising sun and were built as a representation of Precession and the coming resurrection at the End of the Age as previously discussed with cross symbolism. In the center of the transept is a stage with pulpit symbolizing the conjunction date of 2012. Medieval congregations were mostly illiterate, but they could understand the meaning of the cruciform floor design whenever they entered the building to worship. We can conclude with certainty that the cross, in all its many forms, represented the Tree of Life that was always associated with the Union of the Polarity. Cathedrals and gravestone cross markers were the Christian symbols of the Tree of Life, Axis Mundi, World Tree, or Milky Way. They symbolically measured the Precession 2012 End of the Age events and served as a reminder of the long-awaited coming Day of Resurrection set to occur at the End of the Age.

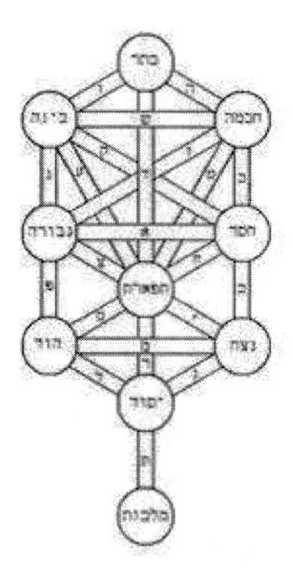

Figure 59 - The Sephiroth; a ten-dimensional diagram of human consciousness.

The Sephiroth image above was the Jewish Kabbalist

representation of the Tree of Life. Its meaning, however, was adapted to Jewish ideology that taught the symbolic twenty-two paths to heaven. The ten concentric circles make up the Tree of Life, and when added to the twenty-two paths, the number becomes thirty-two Kabbalistic Paths of Wisdom that corresponds to the thirty-two degrees of Freemasonry. In simple terms, the Sephiroth, represented by the ten circles, symbolize the ten attributes that God created through which he can project himself to the universe and man. More on this symbolic meaning will be discussed in "The Grand Finale" chapter.

Figure 60 - Hendaye Cross Monument to the End of Time.
Picture credit: *users .glory road/-bigjim/hendaye.htm*

Figure 61 - Base of the Hendaye Cross. The four A's probably represent the cardinal constellations forming the solar cross at the End of the Age, the cross being a representation of the path of the ecliptic and conjunction of the sun with the galactic equator in 2012. *zelator.topcities.com/hendaye.htm*

Figure 62 - Another side of the base of the Hendaye Cross showing the face of an angry sun at the End of the Age as represented by the cardinal constellations (stars).

Figure 63 - Crescent moon side of base of Hendaye Cross. The fourth side has a picture of an eight-rayed single star (not pictured) but probably represents the dual-tetrahedra that formed an eight-pointed star when they united in the Union of the Polarity (read chapter "The Tetrahedron").

Located in the southwest of France, on the town square of Hendaye, the famous Hendaye Cross is late seventeenth century. Its symbolism on the base and top has been the source of several books. Your authors believe it is just another symbolic representation of the solstice sun/galactic equator conjunction in 2012 (represented by the cross on top), as previously discussed. The column represents the Axis Mundi, World Tree, or Milky Way. It is just another reminder of the coming resurrection and earthquake destruction in 2012.

Figure 64 - The Farr Stone in Scotland. Picture credit:
www.celtarts.com/cross3.htm

This Pictish stone is found on the north coast of Scotland at old Farr Church at Bettyhill in Sutherlandshire. Over two feet wide, it stands 7.5 feet high. Its markings are not found on any other ancient Celtic carvings and have remained a mystery until this writing. An analysis of the stone clearly shows a yin-yang symbol in the center of the cross, denoting the Union of the Polarity. The Greek key designs on three of the ends of the cross are also Union of the Polarity signs. The cross itself stands as a Milky Way World Tree. Part of the cross reaches into heaven (the square box at the top of the cross). At its base the yin-yang symbol (representing the two Earths) is now shown as two swans with their necks intertwined, pulling apart as the two Earths are separating in the "dark rift" of the Milky Way. The "dark rift" is the upside down U shape (coded 2012 date) containing the two swans with necks intertwined, which represents the two Earths coming apart during the three-day transit of Earth through the "dark rift" in 2012. Swans are a perfect representation of the two Earths as one Earth will "fly away" into the fourth dimension and the other, temporal Earth will simply continue "flying on her wings" in this universe. The base of the cross extends further down into the netherworld. The horizontal bar of the cross represents the serpent bar or path of the sun. It conjuncts or intersects at the center of the cross, denoting the winter solstice in 2012 when the separation of the two Earths is slated to take place.

As in other solar crosses, the holes represent the re-alignment of the four cardinal constellations at the End of the Age. What a marvelous find! Its message is literally carved in stone and was meant to last until the End Time generations were born so they could be reminded of the upcoming 2012 date so as to "prepare" for the event, lest they be caught off guard.

Figure 65 - Tymphanum of St. Trophine. Picture credit:
www.sangraal.com/AMET/prologue.html

Saint Trophine is a twelfth-century Romanesque-style church located in Arles, France. Above the front entry door for all to see is Christ surrounded by the four beasts or cardinal constellations. The message for all to see and remember is: when these cardinal constellations align to form a Grand Cross at the End of the Age, the resurrection occurs on the last day, that is, December 21, 2012. It is the last day for the spirit Earth in this dimension but not the last day for the temporal Earth.

On the highest hills outside of Florence, Italy, stands the Basilica di San Miniato del Monte, a medieval, twelfth-century church famous for its remarkable thirteenth-century zodiac floor. In front of the church, above the main altar, is a large painting of Christ surrounded by the four cardinal constellation signs. Later Christian doctrine represented each one of the four apostles as a cardinal sign.

Symbolically, Mark is a lion, John is an eagle, Luke is a bull, and Matthew is a man. However, this is later doctrine symbolism. Originally the four beasts were those who surround the throne of God (Revelation 4:6–7), which are symbolized as one of the four cardinal constellations. One can certainly see the symbolic message of Christ returning at the End of the Age when the four cardinal constellations are aligned to form a cosmic cross. The cardinal constellations are time measurements of the zodiac. Beneath the picture and in front of the main altar is the zodiac floor inlaid in marble. What more do you need? The evidence is right before your eyes. In spite of this, there are those who associate the zodiac floor of the ancient basilica with paganism. What fishlike absurdity.

Figure 66 - Picture above altar in San Miniato Basilica. Picture credit: *www.fuka.com*

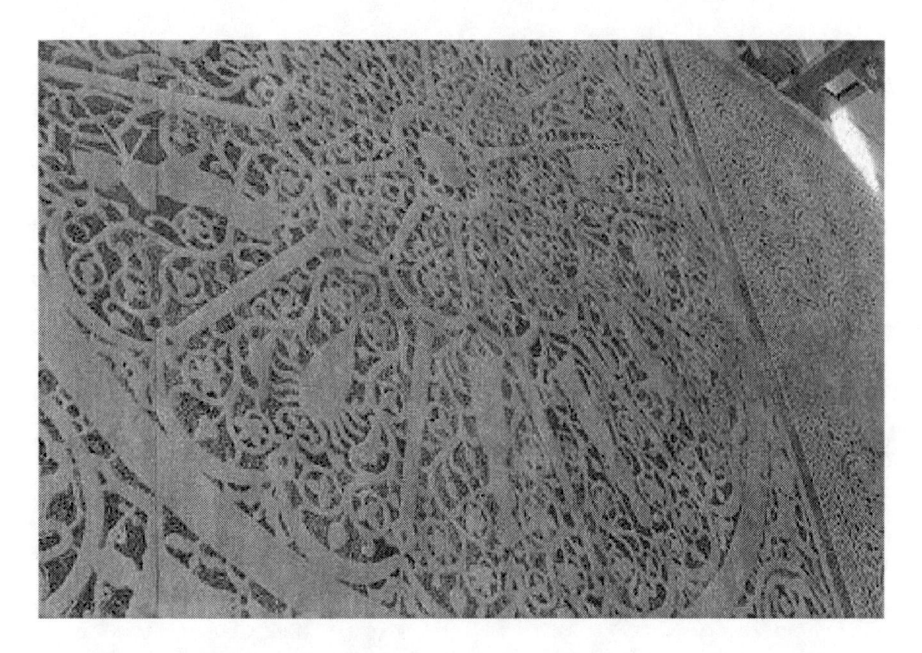

Figure 67 - Zodiac floor. Picture credit: *www.fuka.com*

The sixth century Beth Alpha Synagogue, located at the base of Mt. Gilboa in the Valley of Jezreel is noted for its intact zodiac mosaic floor. The mosaic covers the entire nave area and has inscriptions referring to the zodiac in Hebrew and Greek. Similar zodiacs have been discovered in seven ancient synagogues. Rabbinical tradition asserts that the signs of the zodiac have represented the twelve tribes since antiquity. It would be reasonable therefore to conclude that the Jewish synagogue zodiacs had nothing to do with the second coming of Christ or Precession but rather a symbolic representation of the twelve tribes. According to Jewish tradition, Moses lined up each tribe according to their zodiac symbol and order of position in the zodiac to start the Exodus,

The exodus out of Egypt was one huge zodiac. Precession

was known by Jewish astrologers; however, we do not believe they associated it with a resurrection at the End of the Age—at least we haven't been able to find any evidence as such, although the doctrine of resurrection is found in Ezekiel 37. This does not mean that they didn't know of the belief but rather they most likely considered it pagan and rejected the teaching since Egypt and the Babylonians believed their god was returning for a resurrection at the End of the Age. The Israelites, being held in bondage by both the Egyptians and Babylonians for long lengths of time, surely were aware of their captors' beliefs but perhaps elected instead to await their promised messiah and deliverer.

Figure 68 - Beth Alpha Synagogue sixth-century zodiac mosaic floor Picture credit: Wikipedia, the free encyclopedia, Zodiac

Figure 69 - St. Peter's Square, Rome. Note the eight rays represent the sides of the star tetrahedron passing through the Earth.

Designed by Giovanni Lorenzo Bernini, St. Peter's Square was completed in 1667. The thirteenth-century Egyptian obelisk from Heliopolis was already in place when Bernini was commissioned to build a public plaza, the Piazza San Pietro. This was a phenomenal act of engineering to accomplish, as there were no cranes in those days. At risk to both the obelisk and human life, it was moved on rollers with nothing but muscle power. The message portrayed by the architecture was worth it.

In 1817, circular stones were set to mark the tip of the obelisk at noon as the sun entered each of the signs of the zodiac, making the Piazza a gigantic sundial. A bronze globe and cross sit on top of the obelisk located in the center of the Piazza. It is evident that Bernini used Precession symbols to mark the coming 2012 End of the Age resurrection in his design, common knowledge in his day.

He used the obelisk as a representation of the World Tree. There is one remaining question. Why was that particular obelisk moved to that location? Could it be the immanent role Rome would play in the End Times described by your authors? Further emphasis on Precession was added later with the addition of the zodiac symbols. One can see the cardinal constellation points and the cross laid out on the square, the horizontal bar of the cross representing the serpent bar that conjuncts with the World Tree obelisk (dot inside a circle) marking the End of the Age in 2012.

Figure 70 - The Freemason Royal Arch

Did the seventeenth–eighteenth-century Freemason founding fathers of America know about Precession and the 2012 End Time date? Although we have not found anything in writing stating as such, there is however an abundance of evidence that perhaps they did believe in it because they left symbolism all over Washington, D.C., in plain view for all to see both in and on public buildings, monuments and memorials. Precession symbolism is found on the arch of the Masonic Royal Arch Degree shown in the above illustration.

The Royal Arch (serpent bar) is another representation of the ecliptic path of the sun and is really the arch of the zodiac, marked with seven signs of the zodiac, from Aries to Libra. The keystone represents the sun's conjunction with the midpoint of the galactic equator at the End of the Age on December 21, 2012. Located on the keystone is the sigil for Cancer, the sign through which spirit descends into matter or the Union of the Polarity. Since it is used in connection with the End Time date, it represents the time of separation of our two planets. Rebirth and resurrection are also associated with the constellation of Cancer, which is also called the Beehive Cluster. The Beehive Cluster is often portrayed in Masonic symbolism on ceremonial Masonic aprons as a beehive surrounded by bees. The arch is supported by two Pillars of Heaven representing the World Tree that are also drawn to look like the columns of Solomon's temple. Noticeably, the column on the right resembles the Apprentice Pillar in Rosslyn Chapel, further proof that Rosslyn Chapel was a Freemason chapel. On the Corinthian-like capitals on both columns are two five-leafed floral designs. Each leaf represents an Age of 5,125 years. The five-leafed floral design is a representation of the Babylonian Tree of Life.

We are in the fifth and last Age. Between the two posts is a shield with the four cardinal constellations aligned to form the cosmic cross at the End of the Age. Below the floor rests the coffin of Hiram Abif, the Master Mason builder of Solomon's temple. An acacia bush identifies the coffin as that of Hiram Abif, who was buried by his murderers next to an acacia bush. Traditionally, he is said to have been reburied under the floor or porch of Solomon's temple as shown in the illustration. Symbolically, Hiram is awaiting the coming Day of Resurrection and ascent into heaven slated to occur at the End of the Age as depicted by the keystone on the Royal Arch. It appears that our founding fathers did know about the slated time of the resurrection and incorporated the knowledge into their rites.

Figure 71 - Masonic apron

The Masonic symbolism found on this apron is quite evident. Notice the Ouroborus in the center with wheat sprigs underneath. Look under these symbols to the left at the pyramids and the Beehive Cluster. Moving to the bottom center are the temple columns of Masonry. Through symbolism the apron tells us the following message: At the end of Precession (represented by the pyramids and temple columns) the End of the Age occurs (represented by the Ouroborus serpent swallowing its tail) when the resurrection of the dead into eternal life and ascent into heaven occurs (represented by the skull and crossbones and sprigs of wheat that symbolize eternal spiritual life). The Beehive Cluster represents the Union of the Polarity separation, or translation of the Earth, and the transformation of humans into spiritual, or higher-dimensional, beings called "the rapture," both of which will ascend through the Ouroborus at the End of the Age into eternal life. Masonry tools of the Creator used in creating the cardinal constellations have formed the Grand Cross that occurs at the End of the Age. Above, on the left, is the spirit Earth with its transformed, "raptured" inhabitants actually depicted passing through the Ouroborus "dark rift" circle into the presence of God, the Creator and architect of the universe (the radiant face on right), thus entering into eternal life.

Figure 72 - Copyright© 1996–2000 Grand Lodge Of Pennsylvania *pagrandlodge.org/tour/mtemple.html*

One can easily see the modern representation of the Royal Arch in the above picture. Clearly Precession symbolism (dot in circle) is evident in the arch (serpent bar) and solar window (cross). This particular arch rests on four Pillars of Heaven. We can conclude, with some certainty, that Masonry indeed has retained much of the End Time knowledge that is incorporated into their rites, although the actual understanding of the meaning may have been lost by them.

> "The purpose of Masonry is to train a human being so that he will reconstruct, through the body of change and death that he now has, a perfect physical body that shall not be subject to death. The plan is to build this deathless body, called by modern masons Solomon's Temple, out of material in the physical body, that is called the ruins of Solomon's Temple."
> —Harold Waldwin Percival, *Masonry and Its Symbols in the Light of "Thinking and Destiny"*

Adding to the above statement, ancient Egyptian Masonry believed this perfect body was a perfected physical body, capable of living in a spiritual domain and worthy to enter into eternal life at the End of the Age. Modern Masonry rites are patterned after the ancient Egyptian rites. It seems that the Egyptians were not fixated on the afterlife, as thought by early Christian translators, but were focused on creating a higher type of human when the "change" would occur at the End of the Age.

Joseph Smith, who was a 33rd Degree mason, patterned a little of the Egyptian Masonry into modern-day LDS temple rites. When LDS saints receive their ordinances in their temples, they are in essence perfecting themselves according to the celestial law. This can be compared to raising their vibrational level.

The raising of one's vibrational energy does seem to bring an ability to see light and even joy where beings who maintain a lower, or darker, energy cannot. The primary focus of teachings designed to raise human consciousness is that of mastering one's fear. Fear is much more powerful at manifesting reality than love. Replacing fear with love is the challenge all humans face in this metamorphosis. It is said many times in the ancient writings that when Jesus returns, those beings who are like him will be able to see him. Those who are not of this higher vibrational state will see nothing. There will simply be a mass disappearance, often called the "rapture."

According to the "Calendar in Stone" of the Great Pyramid that describes the so-called "Phoenix Cycle" of our galactic orbit, the present time period ends (converted to the Gregorian calendar) in the year 2012 with a cataclysmic "change." The "change" will quicken (translate) the resident life forms to the next evolutionary phase, prior to exodus from the womb planet (the temporal Earth).

From the above statement, it is apparent that the ancient Egyptians were aware of the Precession End Time knowledge and the term "change" is none other than the transformative change some modern religions now call the "rapture." As consulters of the Tzolk'in calendar, the Egyptian astronomers were aware of its prophecies, as were the Maya.

Have the Masons retained this knowledge into their rites today? That is difficult to say with certainty but there remains much symbolism to suggest that that they do to some degree. For instance, Masonic Temple lodges usually have the pillars of Boaz and Jachin on either side of their front doors leading into the temple and always include a representation of them inside the lodge as well. Most of the pillars have a globe resting on top of their chapters or pillars. One globe, the terrestrial globe, represents the Earth and the other globe, the celestial globe, represents the zodiac Precession movement.

The pillars themselves represent the World Tree or Axis Mundi, the axis around which the galaxy rotates, which probably meant the zodiac rotation around the vault of heaven to the ancients. Symbolically, the Royal Arch with its keystone and the two columns with their globes are still used in temple rites.

To the trained eye of students of esoteric wisdom, the true meaning is quite clear. Also, it is quite evident that Masonry meaning continues to change or evolve somewhat according to the times and varies with lodges. Some of the true meaning has been lost and gradually replaced with new meaning; however, the esoteric symbolism remains unchanged and has become somewhat of a "mystery" even within their own ranks as they strive to understand it. No doubt, the city planners of Washington, D.C., and our founding fathers understood the true meaning because the entire city celebrates Precession End Time knowledge of the coming resurrection. It is there for all to see and for the wise to understand.

Figure 73 - The entrance, or porchway, to the Port Adelaide Masonic Building. The Gateway of the Sun. The Temple of the Sun.

Figure 74 - Pillars of Boaz and Jachin. Note the dot in the eye represents Precession.
ancientegypt.hypermart.net/freemasonry/index.htm - 28k

Zodiacs are considered one of the mysteries of the city of Washington, D.C., that may be solved with this writing. What did the Freemason founding fathers of America leave for all to see as a remembrance of the up-coming End Time event? They left more than twenty-three complete zodiacs in public government buildings and one thousand more zodiacal symbols on monuments and room interiors. We mention only a few below but it is evident that the zodiacs have hidden cosmological symbolism that symbolizes the upcoming 2012 End Time belief of a resurrection to occur on that date, common knowledge believed up until the early eighteenth century before the teaching was lost.

Figure 75 - The Zodiac Floor in the Great Hall of the Library of Congress

In the Great Hall of the Library of Congress the zodiacal twelve constellations are inlaid in the marble floor and are arranged in a square with alternating rosettes at the center of which is a radiant sunburst, marked with the cardinal points of the compass. Painted on a dome, another circular zodiac is found in the ceiling of the Pavilion of the Elements, an upper room of the Library of Congress. Ornate stucco decorations frame the zodiac, which includes sixteen five-pedaled flowers, each petal representing an Age. An attempt to link the two zodiacs together lies in their very design.

Figure 76 (a&b) - Taurus and Sagittarius Rosettes in the Zodiac Floor of the Library of Congress

The lower square zodiac represents the physical creation (in Masonry the square represented the Earth) and the upper round zodiac painted on a dome, representing the heavens, is the spiritual creation (in Masonry, the circle represents the spiritual element).

Linked together as the spiritual descent into the physical reality, it is the artist's rendition of the Union of the Polarity, and at the same time it reiterates the oft quoted phrase from the Zohar, "As above, so below." In the past, these words have been mistakenly attributed to Hermes Trismegistus; they originate from the much older Zohar.

Figure 77 - Library of Congress window arches with the Babylonian Tree of Life symbol in the *keystone* position indicating the 2012 End Time date. There are a series of windows like this on the outside of the building. Note the serpent bar arch.

In the main rotunda of the Library of Congress is a zodiacal clock. Standing on the top of the clock is a figure of Saturn, the Roman god of harvest, holding his sickle. Behind him are a group of mosaics representing six more of the zodiacal signs. The symbolism becomes quite clear in the illustration below of Saturn, the Roman god of harvest holding an Ouroborus in his left hand.

Figure 78 - Roman god Saturn holding the Ouroborus in his left hand and surrounded by symbols of Rome and agriculture produce.

The Ouroborus represents the End of the Age and Saturn, the Roman god of harvest, symbolically fulfills Fenton's translation of Matthew 13:39–40, "the harvest is the End of the Age." This illustration, found in Johann Bode's 1801 atlas, *Uranographia,* is further proof of the belief in a resurrection at the End of the Age in earlier times. In ancient times, the word "harvest" meant resurrection of the dead, when used in biblical context or depicted with an Ouroborus. Therefore, the library clock is measuring time till the End of the Age when the resurrection takes place. If you look at the clock face and its encasement, you will see the serpent bar that represents the path of the sun. Above the clock face, midway at 12 noon, is a cross-like marker denoting the End of the Age.

Figure 79 - Zodiac Clock in Main Reading Room of Library of Congress. Roman god Saturn holding the sickle of the 2012 harvest. Note the serpent bar over the top of the clock slowly measuring time till the 2012 *harvest*.

The signs of the zodiac are shown from the ceiling of the Great Hall of the National Academies of Sciences. The Federal Reserve Board building has a beautiful 1937 Steuben glass ceiling lamp depicting the zodiac. President Garfield's memorial statue has both astrological signs and planets on the pedestal. The Mellon Memorial fountain's rim is decorated with all twelve signs of the zodiac, and the Dirksen Senate Office Buildings' interior contains twelve zodiacs. The Academy Building also has twelve bronze, stylized zodiacal characters on the south entrance hall door.

Overlooking Constitution Avenue, on the central pediment of the Departmental Auditorium, is a naked woman with a sheaf of corn (corn represents a resurrection), seated on a bull (Taurus), sculpted in 1935 by Edgar Walter. This part of the detail is meant to represent the Earth signs. Three other elements of water, fire, and air are also represented in the same pediment on the other side.

Figure 80 - Woman on bull in DC with sheaf of corn representing resurrection.

Another sculpture found on the pediment of the Interstate Commerce Commission Building on Constitution Avenue was sculpted in 1935 by Edward McCartan. It is a naked woman with a sea horse, surrounded by dolphins, which symbolically is intended to represent the water signs of the zodiac, which are Cancer, Scorpio, and Pisces.

Figure 81 - Woman with sea horse in DC with zodiac water signs of Cancer, Scorpio, and Pisces represented.

Sherry Fry sculpted a naked woman with an urn overflowing with an abundance of food, next to a ram, on the pediment of the former Department of Labor Building, overlooking Constitution Avenue in 1935. The sculpture represents the fire signs of the zodiac of Aries, Leo, and Sagittarius.

Figure 82 - Woman on Ram with Urn in DC with zodiac fire signs of Aries, Leo, and Sagittarius represented.

On the same building is another pediment, sculpted by Albert Stewart in 1935, of a naked man with a sheaf of corn (representing a resurrection), sitting on a rock, and leaning against a bull. Taurus, Virgo, and Capricorn are the zodiac Earth signs represented. Capricorn is the Earth sign when the resurrection occurs on the winter solstice.

Figure 83 - Man in DC with zodiac Earth signs Taurus, Virgo, and Capricorn represented.

The Mall between the Washington Monument and the Capitol was meant to portray the path of the sun, the ecliptic, through the zodiac. Constitution Avenue, which runs parallel to the Mall, has zodiac markers on either side of it and on the other end of the avenue are three more zodiacs.

When the Capitol building was laid out on Capitol Hill, it was oriented so that the East Wing received the first rays of sunlight, then the sun progressively moves in an ecliptic path through the zodiac placed around the Mall until the sunset occurs over the western rim of the city. The dome of the Capitol building was set in the center of the horizon to symbolically represent the Royal Arch of Freemasonry.

The Charles Bulfinch dome (built 1820–22), pictured below, is a squatter version of today's dome; however, the symbolism of the Royal Arch is more readily seen than in today's dome. Both are meant to symbolize the same theme: the Freemason Royal Arch. The flat space in Bulfinch's dome represented the keystone of the Royal Arch or the End Time date of 2012. The front porch pillars supporting the dome represent the Pillars of Heaven upon which heaven's vault rests (the Royal Arch).

Figure 84 - Bulfinch's Dome as depicted in this historical model. Note the Freemason symbols of Precession.

Today's Capitol dome is topped with the Statue of Freedom but she represents the keystone position and symbolically has the same meaning. In addition, twelve stars, which represents the zodiac, surround her eagle headdress, and she stands on a globe, representing the Earth, encircled with the original national motto, *E Pluribus Unum,* the Latin for "One from many." She is the **symbol** of freedom and not a pagan goddess of freedom.

Figure 85 - Statue of Freedom is the keystone of 2012 atop the dome on the Capitol building.

Situated on the highest elevation in the city, the silhouette of the Capitol's dome is there for all to view as a reminder of the End Time date and upcoming events of 2012. America's capitol building is one of the world's most recognized structures. How fitting to incorporate the End Time knowledge into its design as a silent, almost reverent, testimony of the coming 2012 day of resurrection. It is both fitting and proper that Freedom, a divine principle, represents the *keystone* on the Capitol Dome serpent bar. And, if that were not enough, there is even more hidden esoteric symbolism that few know about. When the architects laid out the city plan over two hundred years ago, they engineered a play of light to occur only one day each year. On that day a triangle of light touches a triangle of Earth on Capitol Hill, over the western rim of the city, at sunset, to form a Union of the Polarity. In David Ovason's book, *The Secret Architecture of Our Nation's Capital,* he states the Earthly triangle is what now is called the Federal Triangle, and the stellar light triangle is comprised of the three main stars of the constellation Virgo: Spica, Arcturus and Regulus. Originally, the Earthly triangle was composed of three points: the Capitol building, the Washington Monument, and the White House. The stellar triangle of stars reflects the Federal Triangle points. Arcturus falls on the White House, Regulus falls on the Capitol, and Spica falls on the Washington Monument. When the sky triangle is measured against the Earth triangle, the correspondences between the two are almost exact. He concludes that the stellar event occurs on August 10 (other writings say about August 15) of each year and states because of Precession, as the years pass, *the visual impact of this cosmic triangle will become more and more powerful.* On that day, shortly after sunset, the stellar triangle literally hangs over the Earthly Federal Triangle, to the south of Pennsylvania Avenue.

Because the three main stars of the constellation of Virgo

form the stellar triangle, the image of the zodiacal Virgo Virgin is found all over the city, in or on public and government buildings. Most all of the public zodiacs emphasize the role of Virgo in one way or another. Her image dominates the city of Washington, D.C., because she is the arcane symbol denoting the annual Union of the Polarity cosmic play of light.

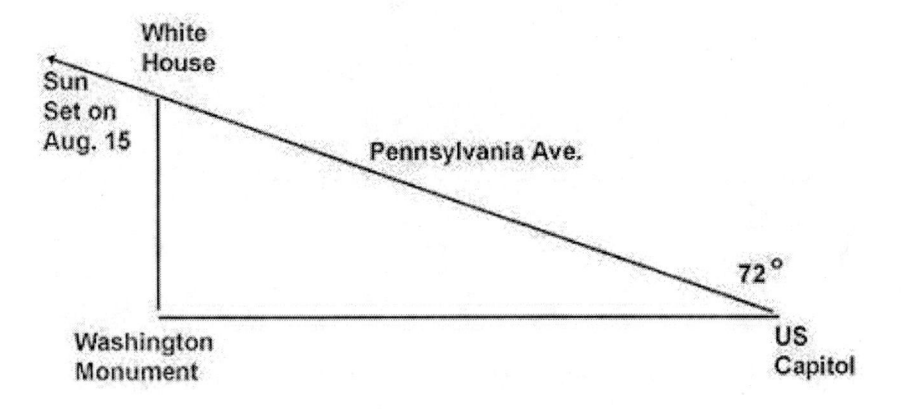

Figure 86 - Sun Triangle in DC

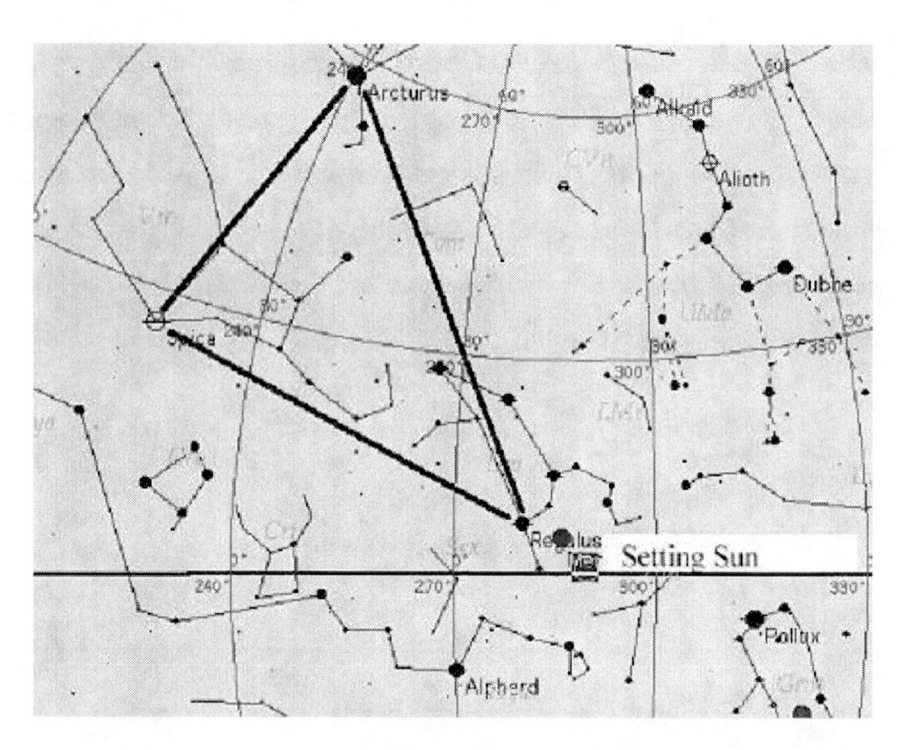

Figure 87 - Cosmic Star Triangle formed by the setting sun in DC on August 15 of each year.

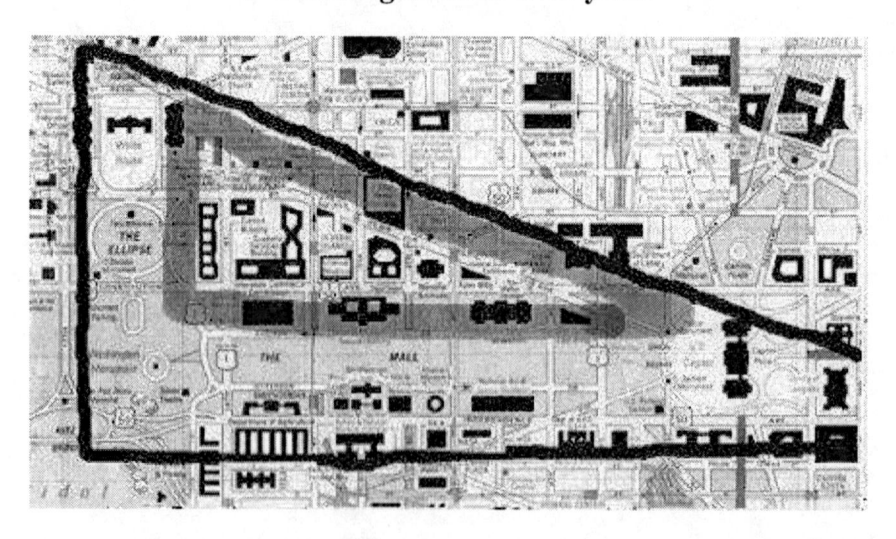

Figure 88 - Federal Triangle. Small triangle as it exists today but originally as large triangle

Several books have been written on pagan symbolism in Washington, D.C., and if you surf the web you will find sites of that same mentality depicting the Freemason founding fathers as steeped in paganism and satanic worship. They would have you believe that America's government was founded on evil symbolism and democratic principals not found in the Bible, and therefore it is not a nation founded on Christian principals as commonly held. Nothing could be further from the truth; in fact, it is just the opposite. We believe we have established proof to the contrary in this chapter. Democratic principals, as such, may not be found in the Bible but it was found in God's own handbook called The Divine Book of Wisdom, The Flying Scrolls, or Adam's Book as documented many times in volume 1 and volume 2 of this book.

Figure 89 - The Andrew Mellon Memorial Fountain in DC with the signs of the zodiac around the rim bowl.

Figure 90 - The ram of Aries and the rim bowl of the Andrew Mellon Memorial Fountain

The Mellon Fountain is located at the tip of the Federal triangle shown above. The image of Virgo is oriented along

Pennsylvania Avenue, as she dominates many of the zodiacal symbolism in the city. Aries, which faces due East, is one of the twelve signs designed by Sydney Waugh. The sun's rays strike the image of Aries on the fountain rim bowl in the early morning of each day. The zodiac was not laid out in order of months, but rather in the order the sun travels through the constellations in the Precession.

Washington D. C. is truly a national treasure chest filled to the brim with symbols of Freemasonry, Freedom, Democracy, and Precession End Time knowledge.

Figure 91 – The authors standing at the Side Entrance to Rosslyn Chapel Scotland. Note the symbol of the Union of the Polarity in the stained glass window with the central point of the cross being the 2012 End Time date. A serpent bar arch representing Precession frames the door.

Above the side door of Rosslyn Chapel, a fifteenth-century, medieval Gothic building, is a splendid example of a solar cross window symbolizing Precession and the upcoming 2012 event. Light streams through the four cardinal Grand Cross constellation alignment for all to see and remember the End of the Age event to come. The horizontal bar of the cross itself represents the path of the sun crossing the galactic equator in the exact center of the cross that is due to happen at the End of the Age on December 21, 2012, heralding the Day of Resurrection. Framing the side door is the serpent bar arch, its top peak representing 2012. William St. Clair modeled Rosslyn Chapel after Solomon's Temple. At either side of the side door entrance are representations of the two famous columns, Boaz and Jachin, of Solomon's Temple. There is an almost overwhelming abundance of hidden, esoteric symbolism found both within and without the Templar Chapel.

We are fortunate the ancients left carved monuments for us to decode, and that they have survived the decay of centuries, so we can know exactly what they prophesied and believed about the 2012 End Time date. We have presented some of what is "out there" as evidence. If one could visit all the old cathedrals of Europe, we are sure much more could be found. The same could be said for the many archeological sites that we didn't mention. The irony is most of this "evidence" has been right under our noses all along. We have taken the "evidence" at face value, never questioning the meaning, and consequently nearly lost the hope and contemplation of the Ages, looked forward to by nearly all who preceded us in countless years past.

Remote viewers can apparently see past the 2012 date. They report *seeing* a cataclysmic destruction but do not know what caused the destruction. One third of the world's population appears to have been killed. The Horizon Project is investigating this phenomenon to try and find out what exactly has happened in 2012. One of your authors, Dr. Agnew, participated in their research project and got a chance to present some of our views as presented in *The Ark of Millions of Years*, volume 1 and volume 2. The show was taped and available for sale on Dr. Agnew's website, X-Squared Radio. Later, *The Horizon Project* will air on the History Channel sometime in the future.

Even the "sleeping prophet," Edgar Cayce, foresaw the event as found in the Great Pyramid Timeline reading as follows:

> "...there began the building of that now called Gizeh....the Hall of the Initiates....this, then, receives all the records from the beginnings of that given by the priest....to that period when there is to be the **change in the Earth's position and the return of the Great Initiate** to that and other lands for the folding up of those prophecies that are depicted there." [Bold type added for emphasis]

Last but not least, there is at least one person in modern times who has retained this knowledge. That person is the architect of the Casa Magna Marriott Hotel in Cancun, Mexico, which was opened in 1991. The entire hotel was constructed to symbolize Precession and 2012. There is absolutely no doubt that the architect understood the End Time events and purposefully designed the hotel to reflect the End Time knowledge as a beautiful reminder to its guests.

Figure 92 - The Casa Magna Marriott Hotel logo, representing the twelve Zodiacal Ages positioned inside a serpent bar arch.

Figure 93 - Lobby view at Casa Magna in Cancun, Mexico. There are twelve arches down each wall to the front main entrance representing the twelve Ages. Inside, the rays of the sun light up the arches as the sun slowly moves in its daily path, representing its movement through the zodiacal Ages.

Figure 94 - The Babylonian Tree of Life symbol is above each arch of the Casa Magna Hotel in Cancun, Mexico

Figure 95 - The Babylonian Tree of Life is located in the *keystone* position of each arch, denoting the 2012 End Time date.

Figure 96 - Angel in the lobby of Casa Magna Hotel holding the Zodiac Wheel of Ages measuring the time of 2012.

Figure 97 - Babylonian sun symbol with eight rays, a representation of Precession and polarity union, above the doorways in the Casa Magna Hotel lobby. Note the Babylonian style serpent bar.

Everywhere you turn in that hotel, the symbolism can be seen. There are at least thirty-one huge arches in the lobby and meeting rooms alone, not counting all the arches on the back side of the building that surround the restaurant and pool. The outside arches would represent the path of the sun. The inside arches represent the 2012 End Time events. The grandest of the arches is the front entry into the hotel lobby. This architect understood the End Time events because he or she used the Babylonian Tree of Life symbol on the keystone of practically every arch as pictured and explained above. Perhaps the architect is a modern-day Mason?

Figure 98 - The Casa Magna Hotel in Cancun, Mexico. Outside, the sun slowly moves across the arches each day, carefully representing its movement through the zodiac. The large arch in center square has the serpent bar with a circle dot above in the exact center denoting 2012. **Heaven's vault rests on pillars.**

In conclusion, from the evidences presented in this chapter, there was almost a universal knowledge of Precession starting from earliest recorded times in ancient Sumeria. With this knowledge was the teaching of the return of the Creator who would usher in a new Golden Age and resurrect the dead to eternal life at the End of the Age, marked by the sign of the Suntelia and the cardinal constellation Grand Cross. Most assuredly these teachings came from the pre-mortal Christ and the Shining Ones who accompanied him to ancient Sumeria and to other places throughout the world. Different civilizations applied their own religious ideology to the teaching but basically the main story theme remained the same.

Another common thread was the belief that the world would be afflicted by a series of natural disasters in the End Times that would culminate in a great destructive earthquake leaving few survivors. It appears that the users of the Tzolk'in calendar in ancient Mesoamerica were the only ones who retained the knowledge of the Earth actually departing this physical universe to enter the fourth spiritual dimension at the End of the Age, although some symbolism still remains in Scotland on the Farr Stone, the Egyptian winged disk and references made to the "coming change" of Earth in various texts.

Other civilizations referred to this event simply as a transformative change from the material to a spiritual existence, a rise to a higher level of consciousness, a rebirth, a quickening, a time of refreshing, the removal of Earth, the translation of Earth, the transition, etc., a new Golden Age, or a renewal of the Earth. Apparently this knowledge was slowly lost when the Gregorian calendar came into acceptance in the fifteenth century.

The common man could now track time with a simple day calendar rather than relying on astronomers watching Precession and reckoning time by the Ages. Unless you are an astronomer, who today knows about Precession and tracking time by the Ages? Over time, Precession and End of the Age symbolism used in the cathedrals of Europe and Mexico lost its true meaning by the mid-1800s. This is because the meaning was understood by the masses of illiterate people and never written down, only symbolized.

Perhaps the biggest factor contributing to the loss of this knowledge was a translation error that occurred in either the 1611 translation or one of it's later revisions of the King James Version of The Holy Bible, wherein Matthew 13:39–40 was mistranslated. We are mystified how a key piece of scripture, telling in Christ's own words when the resurrection or "harvest of the righteous" was to take place, was simply translated as "the harvest is the end of the world" in the KJV. It should translate to read ***"the harvest is the End of the Age"*** as found in Ferrah Fenton's 1908 translation of the Bible, which is recognized today as the most accurate translation in the world.

With the almost universal use of the KJV by Christians today, the teaching that the "harvest of the righteous" or resurrection would occur at the End of the Age or Suntelia Aeon was lost. Your authors see the fingerprints of Lucifer here. Another translation of the Bible, done in 1952, is called the Revised Standard Version (RSV), which we are happy to report, now has Matthew 13:39–40 translated correctly; however, the majority of Christians still use the KJV.

The facts remain that the pre-mortal Christ taught the doctrine in ancient times in Sumeria and wherever he traveled with the Shining Ones. In mortality he taught the same doctrine to his apostles as found in Matthew 13:39–40 in Ferrah Fenton's translation. His teachings were preserved in the many stone carvings in Mesoamerica and other civilizations as presented in this chapter. The Tzolk'in calendar, however, is a written pictorial record of the same events. The ancient calendar was perfected by the pre-mortal Christ/Quetzalcoatl during Mayan times. The evidence presented in this chapter offers conclusive proof of the Savior's doctrine concerning the End of the Age. It seems that Christ has always been with us physically on Earth until his ascension into heaven and then spiritually until 2012. Matthew 28:20 KJV reads, "and, lo, I am with you always, even unto the end of the world." Fenton's translation reads: "and then I am with you through all time, even until the completion of the age."

Opponents of the pre-tribulation rapture say the early church never taught this doctrine. They are wrong, as the correct translation of Matthew 13:39–40 does teach the doctrine. Opponents believe it originated with a Catholic Jesuit priest named Ribera in 1580 and is therefore a relatively new doctrine. Again they are wrong, because the doctrine originated in ancient Sumeria with the teachings of the pre-mortal Christ and the Shining Ones. It is not a new church doctrine but rather one of the oldest. Ribera merely resurrected the ancient doctrine.

If you are not very religious or spiritually minded, these findings may mean little or nothing to you. However, your authors know the Earth is going to make a three-day transit "sailing the cosmic sea" in 2012. That is a fact. It will be a voyage of cataclysmic destruction, and Earthlings need to prepare if they are to survive. A later chapter will be on how to prepare to survive the coming cataclysm...that is, if you want to survive it. Humans and animals have a natural instinct to flee danger and destruction, so it is only natural to seek protection in times of impending peril. The prudent and wise will take heed of the warning and will begin to make survival preparation immediately.

Last night (May 31, 2006), meteorologists on CNN News channel predicted the next few years to be those of intense storms and category 5 hurricanes. They said these weather patterns were not all being caused by global warming but something else was happening that for the present was unexplainable, something causing high winds. And the entire Gulf Coast was sinking at the rate of one inch per year. The question was raised as to whether or not to rebuild in those areas. Their findings support what we have written in volumes 2 and 3 concerning the weather patterns, only we know the true cause and why it is happening.

As natural disasters occur this year and up to publishing time of this volume, we will record the events at the end of this chapter. Please note only those natural disasters leaving ten or more persons dead in their wake will be reported. We will attempt to list all but please forgive us if a few are missed as it will not be intentional.

May 27, 2006: Central Java was struck by a magnitude 6.2 earthquake. Although the active volcano Merapi didn't cause the quake, its activity level increased after the shock. At last count the death toll had reached over 6,200 with at least 250,000 injured and more homeless. Indonesia sits on the

"Ring of Fire," marked by heavy volcanic and tectonic activity. The situation was further hampered by torrential rains.

June 22, 2006: Deadly floods and landslides following four days of torrential rain in the southern province of Sulawesi, Indonesia, killed 200 people with another 130 reported missing.

June 27, 2006: Storms and relentless rains flooded four Mid-Atlantic U.S. states. At least 13 dead and three were missing at latest report. Flooding washed out roads and bridges with widespread power outages. Towns were evacuated in Maryland and Pennsylvania, where 200,000 were forced to flee rising water. Pennsylvania's governor declared a disaster emergency in forty-six of the state's sixty-seven counties.

July 3, 2006: China's Meteorological Department reported the entire month of June brought disastrous, torrential rainfall to parts of China that triggered flash flooding and landslides, forcing thousands to flee their homes. At least 612 were killed and 208 reported as missing. Heavy rains continued to wreak havoc across the country.

July 17, 2006: At least 531 people died and 275 were reported missing when a tsunami triggered by an undersea, 7.7-magnitude earthquake smashed into the southern coast of Indonesia's Java Island.

July 20, 2006: The International Federation of Red Cross and Red Crescent Societies reported floods and landslides in North Korea left more than 100 people dead or missing. The floods damaged 11,524 houses and left more than 9,000 families homeless. In South Korea, at least 25 people died and 24 others were missing, according to the National Emergency Management Agency.

July 31, 2006: The U.S. and Europe baked under a July heat wave. Britain reported the hottest July temperature on record, which killed more than 48 in Europe. The heat was blamed for at least 231 deaths in the U.S. More than 35,000 head of cattle and 700,000 fowl died during the extreme heat in the U.S.

August 1, 2006: Typhoon Kaemi struck southern China, killing at least 55 and leaving 17 people missing. The typhoon season, which started unusually early in 2006, killed more than 1,460 people by August.

August 4, 2006: Tropical storm Prapiroon killed at least 31 people in Guangdong province, China, with 14 more missing. The storm destroyed 46,000 houses, leaving thousands homeless.

August 5, 2006: At least 60 people drowned in Mardan Pakistan, when monsoon flood waters swept away a bridge they were standing on watching the rising waters. In India, monsoon rains killed 42 people and displaced tens of thousands of others.

August 14, 2006: Typhoon Saomai slammed into China's crowded southeast, killing at least 214 with more than 100 missing. More than 50,000 houses were destroyed, more than 1,000 ships sank, and more than 1.6 million people were forced to flee from their homes. China's Meteorological Administrator, Qin Dahe, said, "The strength of typhoons is increasing, the destructiveness of typhoons that have made landfall is greater and the scope in that they are traveling is farther than normal." Saomai was the eighth major storm to hit China during an unusually violent typhoon season and the most powerful typhoon since their record keeping began in 1949.

August 15, 2006: Flash floods in Eastern Ethiopia killed over 600 people when the Dire Dawa and Dechatu Rivers swept through the town of Dawa and nearby villages. Thousands of Dire Dawa's estimated 250,000 residents were displaced by the flooding.

September 30, 2006: Typhoon Xangsane struck the Philippines, officially killing 526 with 720 missing however, the Red

Cross believes as many as 1,000 died in the thousands of homes buried under volcanic debris, mud and floodwaters. Most of the dead were drowned, buried by landslides, hit by fallen trees and debris, or electrocuted. The storm then swept over the China Sea and hit Vietnam, killing 69 more.

December 21, 2006: Two back-to-back, slow-moving blizzards dumped twenty-four to thirty-two inches of snow and ice over portions of six western states of Colorado, Wyoming, Kansas, Nebraska, the Oklahoma panhandle, New Mexico, and northern Texas. The storm left 5,000 air travelers stranded in the Denver airport and air traffic in a mess, closed major highways, and left tens of thousands without power during the Christmas holidays. Twelve deaths were deemed blizzard-related. The governors of four states declared the regions a disaster and asked for disaster aid particularly to farmers whose cattle were at risk from being without food or water in freezing temperatures.

December 25, 2006: Days of heavy rains triggered floods and landslides in the worst-hit area of Tamiyang in Eastern Aceh province of Sumatra Island of Indonesia. The death toll was at least 118, with dozens reported missing, while some 252,302 people were forced to flee their homes. The Forestry Ministry blamed illegal logging and deforestation for the devastating floods and landslides that occurred. Banda Aceh, on the same island, was where the tsunami struck in December 2004. The Tamiyang area was not affected by the tsunami.

January 6, 2007: Sao Paulo, Brazil. Fox News reported that after five days of torrential rain downpours in southeastern Brazil, at least 31 people were killed by mudslides and flash floods. Thousands were forced to flee from their homes.

February 1, 2007: Central Florida. Multiple tornados ripped through central Florida during early morning hours, killing at least 20 and leaving 1500 homes destroyed or damaged in the mega-storm's path of destruction.

February 14, 2007: United States. Monster snowstorm blamed for at least 15 deaths across the Midwest and Northeast of the U.S. The storm dumped huge snow piles, covered roads with ice, and left thousands without power.

March 1, 2007: Twenty reported dead from killer tornadoes that passed through Missouri, Alabama, and Georgia.

March 1, 2007: La Paz, Bolivia. Months of deadly flooding left 35 dead and affected some 72,000 families. The flooding drowned some 22,500 head of cattle and destroyed an estimated 404,000 acres of cropland. President Evo Morales officially declared it a national disaster.

March 3, 2007: Indonesia. Mud slides from heavy rains killed at least 32.

March 15, 2007: Madagascar reported at least 80 dead from a late-season typhoon that passed over the northern region of that island nation.

April 1, 2007: Solomon Islands. A magnitude 8.0 off-shore earthquake triggered a sixteen-foot tsunami that wiped out 900 homes and business structures along the coastal regions in the Solomon Islands. Thirteen were reported dead and many more missing or unaccounted for.

May 5, 2007: Greensburg, Kansas. Deadly tornadoes ripped through the area killing at least 10. Most of Greensburg was destroyed by a reported F5 tornado.

June 11, 2007: China. Torrential rains and flooding killed 40.

June 12, 2007: Bangladesh. Torrential rains and flooding killed 100.

July 15, 2007: Japan was struck by an earthquake 160 miles northwest of Tokyo along Japan's western coast, killing at least 10 persons. Japan's seismology agency put the strength of the quake at magnitude 6.8.

July 24, 2007: Europe. Europe battled floods and record temperatures. Extreme heat killed at least 30 from Austria to Romania over the past week. Temperatures exceeding 100 degrees Fahrenheit sparked forest fires in Italy, Greece, and Bulgaria and further damaged crops withered by drought. Britain was flooded by catastrophic rains. More than 2,500 homes and businesses were swamped and tens of thousands of people were without water and electricity. June was the wettest ever recorded in England. Warm temperatures the previous winter ruined Switzerland's ski season.

August 14, 2007: North Korea. An estimated 200 died following days of torrential rain and flooding that destroyed the nation's major railways, roads, bridges and crops, raising the specter of food shortages. Power supply and communication networks were severed.

August 15, 2007: United States. Torrential rains flooded the Midwest and Texas. At least 24 drowned. Rains and flooding continued while the southern and western states languished in the worst drought in 100 years.

August 16, 2007: United States. At least 50 deaths were blamed on a heat wave that baked the nation. August 2007 was the hottest on record for the U.S.

August 18, 2007: Pisco, Peru. Pisco, Ica, and Chincha, Peru, were rocked with an 8.0-magnitude earthquake. At least 540 people were killed and 1,000 wounded. Powerful aftershocks followed.

September 11, 2007: Indonesia. A series of tremors of 8.4-magnitude earthquakes stuck the regions surrounding Indonesia, near the island of Sumatra. At least 13 people were killed and 130 buildings collapsed. This ends our reporting of natural disasters as we prepare for publication.

Psalm 46

"God is our refuge and strength, a very present help in trouble. Therefore will not we fear, though the earth be removed, and though the mountains be carried into the midst of the sea; Though the waters thereof roar and be troubled, though the mountains shake with the swelling thereof."

The Oldest City in the Americas

Located on the northern desert coast, twelve miles inland in the foothills of the Andes, approximately two hours from the Peruvian capital city of Lima, in the Supe Valley, are the ruins of a city whose pyramids would rival those of Egypt, not in size but in antiquity. Its pyramids are contemporary with those of Egypt and the ziggurats of Mesopotamia. The ancient city of Caral (Chupacigarro Grande) was first discovered in 1905, but because the site yielded no ceramics or gold objects, it was quickly forgotten until it was rediscovered in 1994 by archeologist Ruth Shady, who has been excavating the site since then. She stunned the world when she announced in the magazine *Science* on April 27, 2001, that carbon dating of the site placed the age of the city to 2627 BC, making Caral now considered the oldest city in the Americas. But, what about Tiahuanaco in Bolivia—isn't it older? Archaeologist Arthur Posnanski, who studied Tiahuanaco for thirty years at the turn of the century, decided the city was from ten thousand to twelve thousand years old, and your authors are in agreement with him. However, traditional archeologists scoff at this idea because carbon dating of artifacts taken from the site only date to 1700 BC. Until more is found from Tiahuanaco to prove otherwise, Carel will hold the title as the oldest city in the Americas. There are twenty other, smaller sites in the area attributed to the ancient Caral-Supe culture that run almost linearly from Peru's central coast inland up the Andes, dating to the same time period as Caral; however, Caral is the largest site, covering 160 acres. Because Caral was larger, it may have served as the capitol city of the region. Dotted with pyramid temples, sunken plazas, densely packed housing complexes and even an amphitheater, the urban center demonstrates that it was a carefully planned city. The ancient original name of the city is for now lost in the sands of time; however, most cities were named after their king.

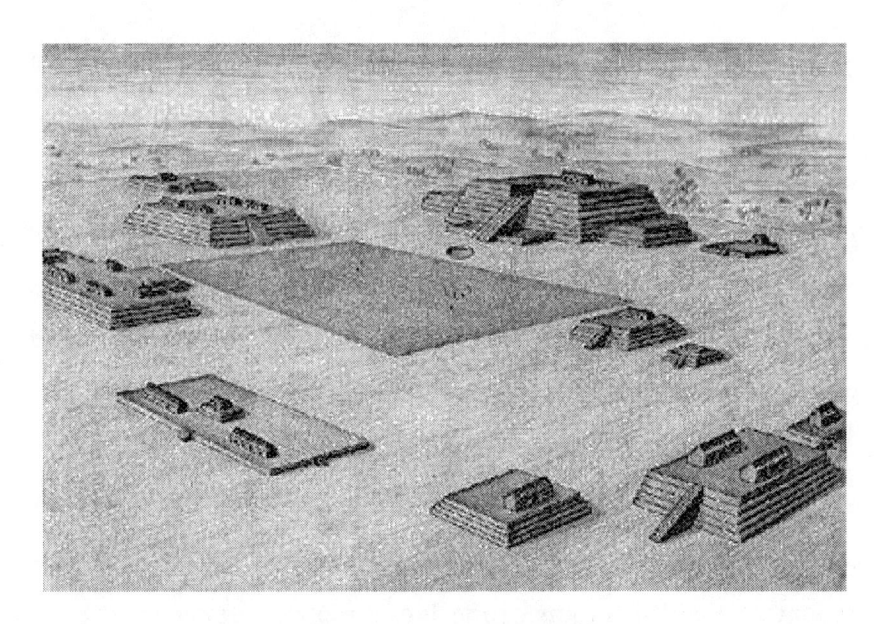

Figure 99 – Caral (picture credit *philipcoppens.com/carnal.html-12k-cached*)

It is estimated the city had a population of approximately three thousand people but if you take into consideration the other sites in the Supe Valley, perhaps twenty thousand people inhabited the area. It was possible to get a very precise and accurate carbon date because stones were carried in shicra grass sacks to construct the pyramid structures. These grass sacks were found at the site and were carbon dated.

Among objects found at the site were thirty-two flutes made from pelican and animal bones and thirty-seven cornets made of deer and llama bones that were engraved with figures of birds and monkeys of the Amazon, suggesting that this civilization perhaps extended to the Amazon regions of South America. Archeologists have found evidence of irrigation, domestic planting of beans, squashes and guava, and large-scale cultivation of cotton. In addition, bones of anchovies, sardines, and shells of mollusks and shrimp have been found, suggesting they either traded with coastal villages or were engaged in fishing themselves. Perhaps the most important recent find was a *quipu*. *Quipus* were a system of knotted, colored cords of various thicknesses, used to store and convey numerical information in a positioned decimal system, a sort of early calculator similar in function to the abacus. A *quipu* could have as many as two thousand cords of stored information. *Quipucamayocs* (called *Tahuantinsuyu* in old spelling Quechua) were the imperial accountants and historians of the Inca Empire. They were the ones who created and deciphered the *quipu* knots and were capable of simple mathematical calculations such as addition, subtracting, multiplying and division. *Quipus* could also be used to store historical data, events, and stories, by years, to be recalled in later times by the year; events and stories were recalled by memory associated with the year. Battle years and birth and death dates of all citizens were recorded in the same way, so a great responsibility rested on the memory of the *quipucamayocs*, who never let the *quipu* leave their fingers while awake. In fact, so great was their responsibility that they were exempted from paying tribute and exempted from any other form of service. The significance of this information is that it appears that the Incas and perhaps a few other northern South American tribes may be descendants of the earlier Supe Valley inhabitants, some of whom were the builders of Caral who apparently had or developed the first *quipu* technology in the Americas.

Your authors became quite excited over the carbon dating of Caral because the date corroborates the history of the Lords of Totonicapan, who wrote a document in 1554 called the *Titulo de Totonicapan*, which told the origin of their ancestors (vol. 1, 360). Their written history closely follows the written accounts of the Mexican scholar, historian, and Catholic priest Fernando de Alva Ixtlilxochitl (AD 1578–1650) (vol. 1, 360–367). These two records closely parallel the ancient Toltec/Book of Mormon record, giving an account of a group of different peoples who left the Tartary section of the Orient and Babylonia about 2800 BC, traveling together in ship-like barges and arriving in the Americas around 2700 BC (vol. 2, 77–78). The Totonicapan record and Ixtilxochitl's writings both relate that, upon arrival, they settled in the northern part of the land, named themselves collectively Chichimecas after the name of their first king, and built a city. Did they land off the northern coast of Peru, having traversed the Pacific, travel inland a few miles and build Caral? Current thinking among some LDS scholars is they landed off the coast somewhere in what is now called Central America, so northern Peru is very close. The time frame suggests the inhabitants of Caral could have been this group of settlers, plus it is impressive that we have three written accounts, written independently of each other, essentially telling the same story. If Caral was settled by the Chichimecas, then its ancient name would be Chichimecatl, named after their king. It could have been spelled Xhixhimecatl or another variation of the name in ancient times.

We wrote in volume 1 that in a few years, various families, having multiplied, left to settle other areas and build their own respective cities suiting their culture. The archeology record supports this because traveling northward into what is now coastal areas of Central America, the Olmecas/Jaredites had settlements, most notably coastal areas of Costa Rica, Guatemala, and regions of Honduras. Eventually they built cities or dwelt in settlements in Izapa, in the state of Chiapas, Mexico, settled many areas of central and lower Mexico, and built cities along the coastal areas of Veracruz, Mexico. Other non-related families probably migrated later into Honduras and still others into Guatemala, becoming the ancestors of various Chichimeca Quiche Maya tribes, as is supported by the migration records of the Popol Vuh. These records say as tribes multiplied they would break away to form another tribe, take a different name, elect their own king, and build a city. It is safe to say the Chichimec Zapotecs were one of these early break-away tribes. According to the Totonicapan and Mexican Ixtlilxochitl records, the Toltecas, now called the Chichimec Toltecas, wandered for 104 years to finally arrive and settle a place they called Huehuetlapallan (ca. 2607 BC), which Mesoamerican scholars generally agree is located in southern Veracruz, Mexico. Later these early Chichimec Toltecs multiplied and migrated into northern Mexico, even into what is now New Mexico and Arizona. In time, a few of the Nahuatl-speaking tribes migrated further northward into

North America and became the ancestors of Nahuatl- or Uto-Aztecan-speaking western Indian tribes. It is interesting to note that when the Nahuatl-speaking Aztecs migrated back into Mexico to found Tenochtitlan, they, on occasion, referred to themselves as the Chichimec Aztecs. There is much disagreement among linguists as to where the Nahuatl language originated. Some contend it was carried from North America into central Mexico, but if they would study the written records of the Lords of Totonicapan and the writings of Ixtlilxochitl, they would discover that some of the 2700 BC first settlers, who called themselves the Chichimecas, spoke Nahuatl and were identified as the Nahuales. These same three written records disclose two other additional languages the first settlers spoke, which were the languages of U-Mam and the pure Adamic language that we identified in volume 2 as being archaic Sumerian. Although the records mention three different languages brought to the New World, there may have been more as the first settlers were a diverse group from different areas. Some were Orientals and some were Middle Easterners.

Mitochondrial DNA studies were done on five thousand American Western Indians, who are descendants of the early Nahuatl-Uto-Aztecan speaking tribes. Their mitochondrial DNA blood samples confirm their ancient ancestors came from Asia.

The Mississippi mound builders also built cities very similar to Caral. Their city ruins are found along the Mississippi from the Great Lakes to the Gulf of Mexico and extend into the Ohio River

Valley. The question is, were they influenced by the Mesoamerican culture? Most archeologists have now generally discounted this idea. The mound-building cultures are complex because many different tribes are involved over roughly three eras: 1. Archaic era (ca. 2500–1000 BC) 2. Woodland period (ca. 1000 BC–AD 1000) 3. Mississippian Culture (ca. AD 900–1000). Here again, your authors do not fully agree with archeologists because we feel the Mesoamericans could have easily had contact with some of these peoples. All they had to do was follow the Caribbean coastline in their trading canoes to the Mississippi Delta and up the river. The Maya had southern water trade routes well established to Peruvian ports, why not northern ports as well? Besides trade, there was some intermarriage between Peruvians and the Maya, because Maya traditions relate how a Peruvian prince came to their lands to marry a Mayan princess. Therefore we cannot discount the possibility of intermarriage occurring with tribes of the Mississippian Culture too. Could it be they all were distant cousins? The similarity of many of the mound builders' cities to those of Mesoamerica is in our opinion the main clue of connection, plus the Mississippian Culture shared the Life Force feathered serpent religion, a point often overlooked by researchers. Few researchers realize that most of their temple mound platforms were built over or near caves where the spiraling Life Force energy vortexes were strongest, the same practice found in Mesoamerica (vol. 1, 278). Temples and mounds built over a vortex served as an amplifier of the Life Force energy as vortexes are simply the 'earth chakras' or 'power points' ("The Union of the

Polarity" in vol. 1 and "The Spiraling Life Force" in vol. 2). Coincidental? Not likely.

Even at one's first glance at the picture of Caral, one can see it was the prototype of future cities built in Mesoamerica, Mississippian Culture cities in North America and Andean regions. Later cities differed in that they were usually larger in size and had bigger pyramids with more grandeur, but the style of architecture and layout of their urban cities was usually very similar. Because the first Chichimeca settlers came from Babylonia and the Tartary areas of the Orient, their city was built in the manner of or very similar to Babylonian cities. The records indicate that twenty-four families came in the first migration to the Americas around 2700 BC. The Popol Vuh gives the genealogies of twenty of these families, and the Toltec/Book of Mormon records the activity of one of these families, namely the family of Jared. Where are the other remaining three families? Could it be that they remained in the northern regions of South America and became the ancestors of many Andean tribes?

For unknown reasons, Caral was abandoned rapidly after a period of five hundred years (ca. 2100 BC). Drought is the preferred theory as to why the people left the region, it forcing them to search for fertile plains elsewhere. The Supe-Caral culture was succeeded by the Chavin culture ca. 900 BC. The Chavins laid the cultural foundation for the other Peruvian civilizations to come. If, however, the Supe-Caral culture proves to be the landing place of the

Chichimecas, then history will have to be rewritten again to include the cultural foundation of Mesoamerica and some of America's Native American Indian population as well. Peru's National Culture Institute is actively promoting the site as a tourist and educational destination.

The Tetrahedron

When the Knights Templars went to Jerusalem under the guise of protecting Christian pilgrims, they actively engaged in exploring the ruins of Solomon's Temple, searching for two things: the Ark of the Covenant and the "flying scrolls" of Adam or as they were later called, the Jerusalem Scrolls. It is in Templar tradition that they did find these items and brought them back to France to the abbot Bernard de Clairvaux, who became the protector of the relics. Hugues de Payens was a cousin to Bernard de Clairvaux and was one of the Poor Knights of Christ/Knights Templars who found the relics in Solomon's ruined temple.

The Poor Knights of Christ/Knights Templars were warrior monks who were first organized by the abbot Bernard de Clairvaux for the explicit purpose of searching, finding and returning the sacred relics to him. Bernard was probably the first serious "Indiana Jones" Ark hunter (vol. 1, 247–249, 317–321, and "The Ark of the Covenant" in vol. 2).

According to traditions, the "Jerusalem Scrolls" were none other than many loose manuscripts that formerly comprised an ancient text called The Divine Book of Wisdom, which was preserved by Noah on his Ark. Volume 1 contains many detailed accounts of The Divine Book of Wisdom as to its origin and whereabouts today. The Knights Templars, or should we say abbot Bernard de Clairvaux, was interested in the "flying scrolls" because it was believed these scrolls contained the alchemical formula to turn base metals into gold. Indeed, the scrolls apparently yielded up the formula, because the Knights Templars became very wealthy in a short period of time. In the process of translating and searching through the scrolls for the alchemical formula for gold, Bernard and the Knights Templars learned of four more important things; one turned the tides of history, another revolutionized architecture, the third changed navigation knowledge, and the last is fulfilling prophecy in the last days.

If you have read volumes 1 and 2, then you know the first is democracy. The Jerusalem Scrolls taught that the principles of governmental democracy were divinely inspired and instituted by God. Included were a set of instructions on how to form democratic governments based on freedom of the people. The Freemason founding fathers used these instructional guidelines to draft the Constitution of the United States. E. J. Clark recently had the opportunity to talk to a Sinclair descendant who confirmed that items his Templar ancestors possessed were carried to the American colony Freemasons from Rosslyn Chapel Scotland. Although he didn't know what these items were, he knew his ancestors deemed them to be important. No doubt, among these items were copies of the Jerusalem Scrolls.

The second item Bernard and the Knights Templars discovered was the knowledge of sacred geometry. Evidently the scrolls revealed the architect and creator of all things in the temporal universe was God, the son, who acted under the direction of God, the father ("The Temporal Creation" in vol. 1, 122) who is the Supreme Architect of all creation. Using the principles of geometry, God, the son, designed, created and measured all things on Earth and in the universe with geometric tools. Proof is offered in the evidence of his geometric designs found in all things on Earth and in the heavens. Geometric designs are circles, squares, rectangles, and triangles in all their many forms, such as plane, solid and platonic solid geometry. These designs are drawn with instruments of geometry—namely the square, the compass, and the rule—which became the symbols of Masonry known as the Mason's Mark. The G in the center can stand for either God or geometry. Because God implemented these designs in creation it became known as sacred geometry.

Figure 100 - Masonic symbol

Figure 101 - The Great Architect of the Universe Illumination from Bible Moralisee ca. 1250 (Picture credit: *rosslyntemplars.org.uk/Rosslyn_Symbolism.htm*)

Knowledge of sacred geometry revealed in the scrolls resulted in an explosion of cathedral-building throughout Europe that revolutionized architecture. Using the principles of sacred geometry, the Knights Templar symbolically recorded the polarity union and the coming 2012 events in their cathedrals for all to understand, especially as a reminder to the End Time generations in fulfillment of End Time prophecy. Of course, many other biblical events were pictured in their stunning stained glass windows. One might say it is the Bible retold in stone and glass imagery.

Sacred geometry knowledge, however, was known in more ancient times by Noah and his sons, who possessed and protected The Divine Book of Wisdom manuscripts. It is safe to say that the Star of David originated from sacred geometry knowledge found in the sacred scrolls. Apparently the scrolls revealed new ideas of how the universe was created using sacred geometry, employing in particular the five platonic solids. An earth was conceived as being designed as a tetrahedron. The tetrahedron is a four-sided geometrical figure whose sides are equilateral triangles having 60-degree angles at all three corners, as shown below.

There are five convex regular polyhedra, known as the Platonic solids,

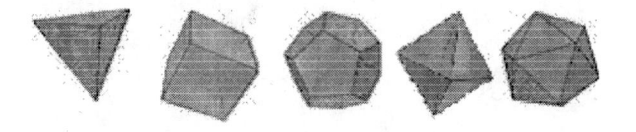

Figure 102 – Five regular polyhedrons

and four regular star polyhedra.

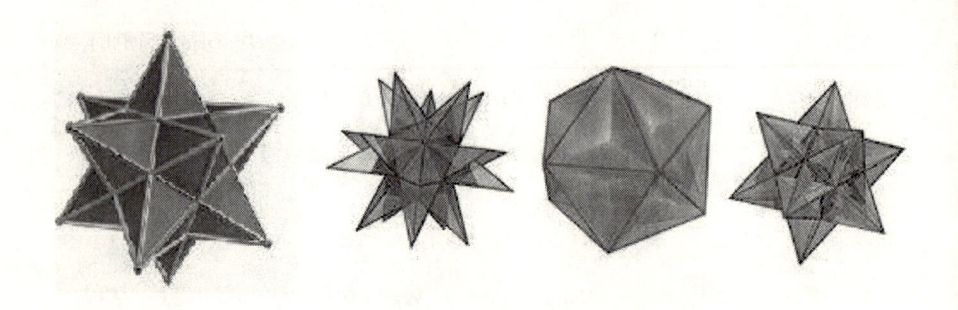

Figure 103 – Four regular star polyhedrons

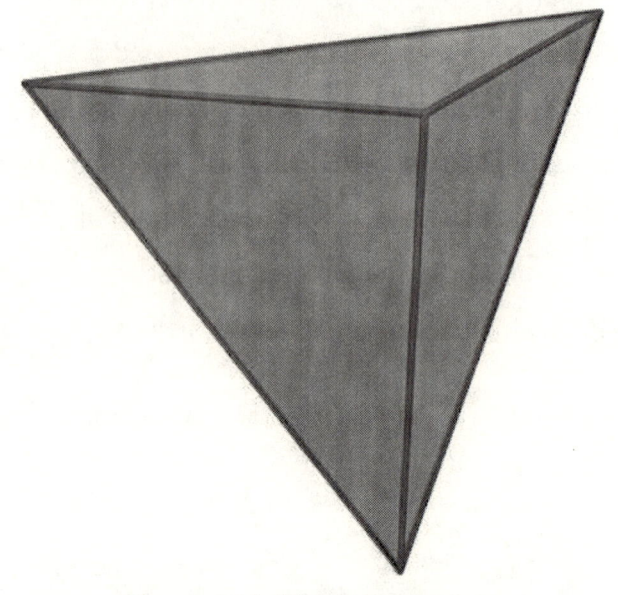

Figure 104 The Tetrahedron

Next, picture the tetrahedron inside a sphere (figure 105), representing a planet. Once you know what it represents, you'll begin noticing it everywhere. When you re-examine ancient art or architecture, this universal symbol of life energy within the sphere of Earth will make itself known to you.

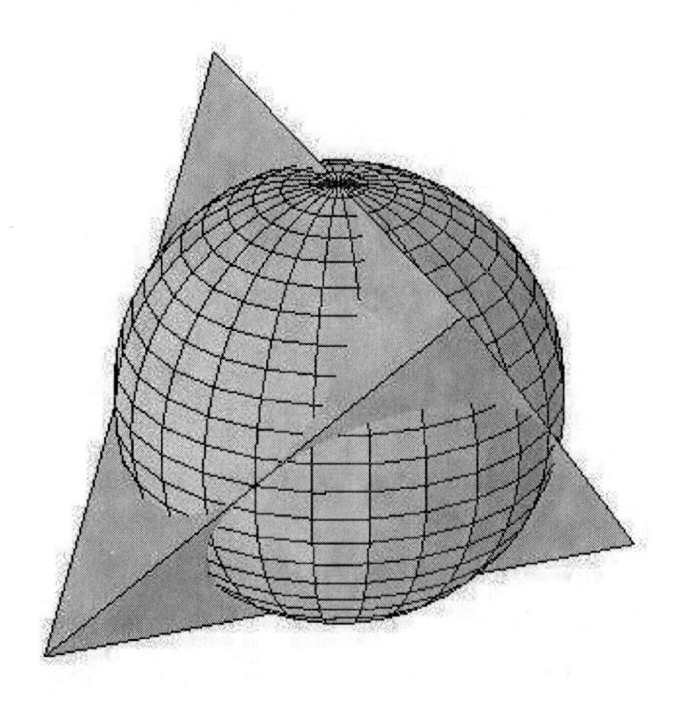

Figure 105 Tetrahedron inside a sphere

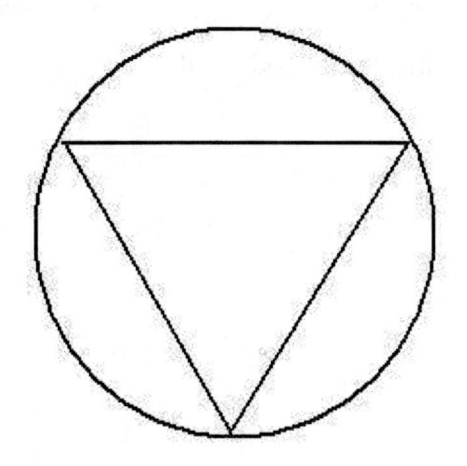

Figure 106 - Spirit Earth Tetrahedron with point down

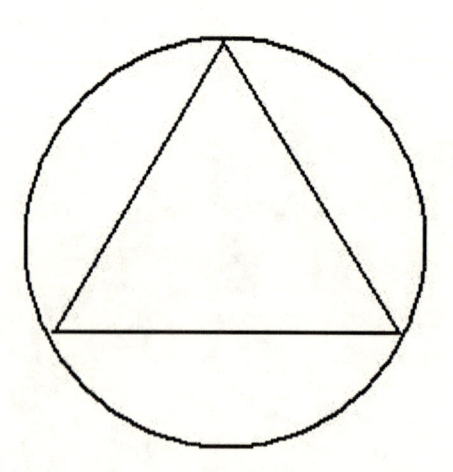

Figure 107 - Temporal Earth Tetrahedron with point up

When the Union of the Polarity occurred, two tetrahedra united to form a dual stellar or star tetrahedron, also called the Star of David, pictured below. A stella octangula is another name for two interpenetrating tetrahedra (tetrahedra is the plural of tetrahedron). Few people realize a separate spiritual dimension infused into our reality making our planet a co-dimensional sphere. In essence we are living in two different worlds at the same time. This means we are multidimensional beings because we co-exist in two different realities at the same time. The three-dimensional version of a two-dimensional, six-pointed Star of David visually clarifies the Union of the Polarity. The three-dimensional star tetrahedron now has eight points, whereas the two-dimensional Star of David has only six points.

In the first chapter of this book, remember the famous Hendaye Monument, called a Monument to the End of Time?

Carved on one side of the monument's base is an eight-rayed star representing Earth's star tetrahedron. The builders of the cross monument were imparting knowledge of the Union of the Polarity as a reminder of its role to be played out in the 2012 events. A large star tetrahedron hangs down from the ceiling vault, near the main front altar, in Rosslyn Chapel. It also serves as a reminder of the Union of the Polarity.

Figure 108 - Two-dimensional Star of David

Figure 109 - Star tetrahedron three-dimensional Star of David
(*kalarhythms.com/theory/th.dimensions.htm*)

Figure 110 - Duel star tetrahedron inside a circle representing an Earth

Plato (ca. 427–347 BC) thought the triangle to be the building block of the universe. In one of his books, the *Timaeus*, he presented that idea and others on how the universe was created to resemble a geometric progression, using what are now called Platonic Solids. Even though Platonic Solids were known since Noah's time, Plato was able to revive and assimilate the ancient knowledge into an understandable theory of the geometric creation of the world, described in his *Timaeus* treatise. Plato's love of geometry was such that the Platonic Solids bear his name.

Essentially, the ancients believed that all physical matter is made up of the atoms of the Platonic Solids, much in the same way that all matter is made up of combinations of atoms. The mechanism of Platonic Solids has proven to be so perfect at explaining the building blocks of matter that their concepts might be more evolved than our present knowledge of the atom model. Sacred geometry is an ancient science that is being rediscovered again by modern scientists because it seems to be the key to a new quantum physics that better explains the existence of the zero point energy fields. Hyperdimensional quantum physics is the new science that has emerged as a revival of the nineteenth-century ether physics, which emerged from sacred geometry knowledge.

In theory, the new science conceives of multiple dimensions sharing the same space but at the same time remaining independent of and separate from each other by utilizing different energy frequencies. On the other hand, the ancient Hebrew texts and Mayan

Codices describe the universes or dimensions as being multi-layered, one on top of the other, as envisioned by E. J. in volume 1.

The truth of the matter probably lies somewhere in-between, with some interpenetration of dimensions as described in the Union of the Polarity but not necessarily involving entire dimensions at the same time, in the same space. There is agreement that energy frequencies determine the reality of each dimension. As stated above, the new science is really an old science that is trying to be understood with today's knowledge of physics. It is written in the Doctrine and Covenants that "all things will be revealed in the millennium" in case we fail to find the answers prior to 2012 (Doctrine and Covenants 101:32).

In ancient times, the Egyptians used sacred geometry to explain the creation, since they were learned in esoteric truths taught in the "mystery schools." As previously discussed in chapter one, the five-pointed star was the symbol of the feminine-gendered spirit Earth. They placed the five-pointed star inside a triangle to represent it as a tetrahedron spirit Earth. Jewish Star of David necklaces often place the dual, two-dimensional tetrahedron star inside a triangle for the same purpose, symbolizing planet tetrahedron unity or polarity union.

Figure 111 – Star tetrahedron in two dimensions is often worn as jewelry

Everyone agrees Freemasonry is the legacy of the Ancient Egyptians. The five-pointed star appears on their ceremonial clothing, inside their lodges and on their temple walls. The ceiling vault of Rosslyn Chapel, a Templar structure, is covered with thousands of five-pointed stars, representing the invisible feminine-gendered spiritual worlds. In chapter one, there were two Babylonian sun symbol images shown, to which we gave new interpretation. One of these images is found on William Sinclair's tomb. Both images are eight-rayed symbols having a center dot inside a circle. It appears to be a Precession symbol rich with hidden, esoteric knowledge. Additionally, the eight rays represent the three-dimensional star tetrahedron imposed on the sun's path of the ecliptic, symbolized by the dot inside of the circle, which represents Precession End of the Age knowledge that will affect both spiritual and temporal creations in 2012. Here is found the perfect example of the old saying "a picture is worth a thousand words."

It appears with utmost certainty Noah knew and understood how he arrived to this planet through the Union of the Polarity. If he lacked any understanding, the Jerusalem Scrolls would have clarified everything. Even from the earliest days of Sumeria, the importance of preserving the knowledge from these scrolls was recognized, but preservation wasn't enough; it had to be taught to the adepts in generations to come. This was the origin and purpose of the "mystery schools" that started in Sumeria and spread to the Babylonians, Assyrians, Egyptians, and Greeks. Jewish "mystery schools" taught the knowledge as Kabbalah and have in recent times preserved the teachings through the many Kabbalah texts. The teachings are found in Gnosticism, Hermeticism, Buddhism, and the Masons. In fact, bits and pieces of the knowledge have crept into all the major religions. In ancient times, only the adepts studied the teachings; however, it was prophesied that in the last days, the general population would come to the knowledge of it as well. For the reading public of today, *The Ark of Millions of Years* trilogy has restored the knowledge of the Union of the Polarity in fulfillment of that ancient Jewish prophecy. For the adepts of today who are seeking further light and knowledge, there are various schools of Kabbalah one might attend, seminars on spirituality are in abundance that include Yogi, meditation and spiritual healing, and of course there are the Masons and the Eastern Stars. On top of that, it is available in bookstores, on CDs, DVDs, videos, and the Internet. As a popular television commercial starring David Carradine points out, seekers of knowledge no longer have to make a pilgrimage to Tibet to speak to a llama adept to find answers. They need only to refer to YellowBook.com to find their path. The "path" being a directory to find various schools, bookstores, and organizations.

Students of Yogi know the star tetrahedron is formed within the first eight cells of life and remains fixed at the base of the spine throughout one's life. In Jewish Kabbalah, the star tetrahedron is referred to as the MerKaBa or light body, described as a counter-rotating energy field that affects both spirit and body. Light bodies have the ability to connect us to other dimensions. MerKaBa is a Hebrew word meaning "chariot." In ancient Egyptian, **Mer** means rotating fields of light, **Ka** means spirit, and **Ba** means soul.

The key to understanding how to move from a single dimensional level to another begins with the MerKaBa. In fact, disciples of Kabbalah understand everything in the universe has a MerKaBa field around it, even a planet. The MerKaBa, soul or light body, of the temporal Earth is the spirit Earth. It will depart from the temporal Earth on December 21, 2012, to enter into the fourth dimension. Using Platonic Solid imagery to explain, our dual-tetrahedron Earth is losing one of its tetrahedra. When the two tetrahedra fully separate, the term used by New Agers and Spiritualists defining the separation of the two planets is "the change" or "the transition," and the term used by Christians is "the rapture." The process of tetrahedra separation is the cause of most of the End Time natural disasters such as earthquakes. The tetrahedra of the two earths are held together by harmonic vibrations of energy fields, a view held in quantum physics and many Eastern mystical religions.

Excess negative vibratory energy is forcing them apart because the dual tetrahedra are both energized as never before with this type of low-density, Life Force energy. This process may be softening the ocean bottom, allowing more magma to heat the ocean floor and warm the two-mile deep ice caps at the bottom rather than the top, causing large ice chunks to fall off. Siberia's permafrost is melting in a similar situation. If this is proven true, it would be considered another aspect of global warming. According to the Bible, one of the signs of the End Times is an increase in earthquake activity such as we are experiencing now. For the first time, we can understand the heavy black lines on *The World Grid Energy Network*, pictured in volume 2, page 119. These energy lines are being naturally generated by the energized eight points of the star tetrahedron. In simpler terms, the energized points of the star tetrahedron are supplying the energy along the heavy black ley lines. The circular, star-like vortex points on the grid match perfectly to the points of the star tetrahedron projecting to the outside of the Earth.

Envision the eight tetrahedra of our dual star tetrahedron as mighty rocket engines and the spirit Earth as a space shuttle sitting on the launch pad of the temporal Earth with these engines fired up (four engines on each tetrahedron). The countdown for lift off has begun (one second equals one year till 2012). At the last second these engines will rev up and kick into high gear, launching the spirit Earth into space. Once free and clear of the temporal Earth's gravitational pull, she will use her four remaining mighty tetrahedron engines to propel her through the Ouroborus portal into another dimension. Temporal Earth's four remaining tetrahedron engines will then shut down, gradually cooling off over a period of time. As of this writing (Sept 25, 2007) we are five seconds from lift off. Our planet Earth is a co-dimensional planet, and the heating up of the dual tetrahedra will take the spirit Earth out of this dimension. The process has already begun. At the last second which begins on the onset of the year 2012, the "kicking into high gear" of the tetrahedron engines will cause natural disasters to occur as never before seen in recorded history.

Two schools of theory exist concerning the nature of the departure of the spirit Earth. One theory holds to the new science of quantum physics; proponents think the spirit Earth will merely change dimensions and will not necessarily physically move. Dr. Agnew holds to that view. The other theory views the departure of the spirit Earth as a physical move through the Ouroborus wormhole portal into another dimension as held by the ancient world. E. J. holds to the latter theory. In reality the physics of how the spirit Earth departs doesn't matter other then to help us to understand the nature of the event; just know the change will occur. The symbolic *harvest* at the end of the age will separate the wheat from the tares; the wheat (good people) will be "raptured" and tares (bad people) left behind to be burned at the second coming following the tribulation.

Spiritualists also believe that everyone possesses their own MerKaBa or light body "chariot." The adept masters claim it is possible to have an out-of-body experience (OBE) and to travel to other dimensions in their MerKaBa chariot. This method of inter-dimensional travel is called "riding the chariot" or "astral travel" and is believed to be the method of travel Old Testament prophets used to transport themselves to heaven and back, a condition they described as "being in the spirit" (2 Corinthians 12:2).

Figure 112 – Tetrahedron crop circle

Crop circles are using sacred geometry to send us visual messages. This one appeared June 1, 1997, in Winterbourne Bassett, a village in the English county of Wiltshire. Study it closely. By now the symbolic message should be easy to read. It is a tetrahedron inside a circle. The circle is symbolic of the "dark rift" Ouroborus portal (the Egyptian winged disk) with the spirit Earth tetrahedron (triangle) passing through it into the fourth dimension, represented by the smaller circles off the points of the triangle. If you look at these smaller circles, they are made up of four triangles each, which represent the fourth-dimension destination of the spirit Earth tetrahedron. The circle or dot inside the triangle is a Precession symbol denoting the End of the Age on December 21, 2012, when this event will happen. It is a warning to "prepare" for the time is at hand. This crop circle appears to be extra-terrestrial in origin because until the interpretations were explained in this book, previously no one understood its symbolic meaning. It is not simply a pretty, random design but is an encoded message that is readable because we just read the message.

Perhaps no phrase in Scripture has been so controversial as the phrase, "the four corners of the earth" as found in Isaiah 11:10-12, Ezekial 7:1, and Revelation 7:1. Isaiah 40:22 makes it quite clear the Earth is a sphere. How can a spherical earth have corners? Could it be that the biblical prophets understood the spirit Earth's four tetrahedron points to be its four corners as illustrated in figure 105? We can say with certainty that the biblical Israelites, Jews, and ancient Egyptians understood the concept of planets being tetrahedrons in design, as symbolized by the Star of David.

The Union of the Polarity was not easy for the ancients to understand, and neither is it fully understandable in our time.

However, the use of sacred geometry tetrahedron images visually clarifies the concept in a simple manner. Like the Knights Templars and Plato, we have also revived sacred geometry in the form of Platonic Solids to help visually explain the Union of the Polarity to our readers, further fulfilling End Time prophecy. It is a rare thing to actually see prophecy unfolding before your very eyes, but it is to be expected in the last days. Remember, most prophecies are fulfilled in very subtle ways. Those who are spiritually awake will "see," with their third or spiritual eye of wisdom, and will "prepare" for the time is at hand. Those who are spiritually asleep simply are "blind" to the truths and remain as lost sheep wandering in the desert.

The Other Worlds

We sometimes have sat outside on a warm, clear summer night to gaze at the stars and watch the full moon rise over the horizon. During these moments our soul can be captivated by the moon's awesome beauty and the realization of the vastness of our universe. In quiet inner reflection our soul questions its own mortality and the purpose of life. We wonder at the timeless structure of the universe and ask the most asked questions of all "Are we the only humans in the universe?" "Do other worlds like Earth exist, or are we alone?" Something about a starry, moon-filled night stimulates us to ask those questions almost as if we were programmed to do so. Perhaps it is a reminder that man is nothing more than a man to keep us humble.

Moses too asked these same questions, and God revealed to him the existence of other worlds as recorded in the Book of Moses, chapter 1, verses 29, 33, and 34:

> "And he beheld many lands; and each land was called earth, and there were inhabitants on the face thereof."
>
> "And worlds without number have I created; and I also created them for mine own purpose; and by the Son I created them, that is mine Only Begotten."
>
> "And the first man of all men have I called Adam, that is many."
>
> Moses was humbled by these revelations and he said unto himself:

> "Now, for this cause I know that man is nothing, that thing I never had supposed" (Moses, 1:10).

Even the prophet Enoch received revelation concerning other worlds in the upper and lower universes in the following scripture:

> "And were it possible that man could number the particles of the earth, yea, millions of earths like this, it would not be a beginning to the number of thy creations; and thy curtains are stretched out still;" (Moses 7:30).

According to these writings, our Earth is just one of many earths created in the temporal and spiritual universes. Furthermore, they are peopled with inhabitants like us. In "The Dual Creation" chapter, volume 1, there are various writings that attest our temporal universe was patterned after a higher, spiritual universe. An oft quoted phrase found repeated many times over in the Zohar, "as above so below," reflects this belief. What is contained in the higher, spiritual universes is also contained in the lower, temporal universes, the only difference is the lower universes and worlds are less perfect than the upper ones they are patterned after. The purpose of these worlds is to bring about the eternal salvation of men.

After the Great War in heaven, Lucifer, the son of the morning, and his followers were cast down onto our Earth in the lower universes. Among his followers were a class of angels called the Watchers, who fell, but not all Watchers fell. Those Watchers who did fall or come to the lower universes were called Nephilim. According to Jewish writings our temporal universe is considered to be one of the lower hell universes. Just being in a temporal state, versus the spiritual state, was considered a hell. In order to survive in the temporal universes, the great fallen spiritual beings had to lower their vibrational levels or else these lower universes and worlds within would be destroyed, described in the Zohar as "the worlds could not endure them." Likewise they could not endure living here, continuing on in the Zohar as "…and neither could they endure the worlds." This change to lower vibrational levels prevents them from returning to the higher, spiritual universes forever, unless permission is granted from God. Having no other choice, these great fallen spiritual beings have made the lower temporal universes their home forever in this eternity. After his fall from glory, Lucifer became known as Satan, or "the accuser of our brethren," the devil, the father of lies, to deceive and to blind men, and to lead them captive at his will, even as many as would not hearken unto the voice of the Lord (Revelation 12:10 and Moses 4:4).

It appears that all Earths inhabited by humans in this universe undergo the same process that our Earth is undergoing. It is first born spiritually, falls to this universe and unites with a temporal Earth, and later is "raptured" back. The same thing happening to our Earth is being repeated over and over in other worlds. Brigham Young best explains the planetary process repeated throughout our universe:

> "Earths…are continually coming into existence, and undergoing changes and passing through the same experiences that we are passing through. Sin is upon every earth that ever was created…and every earth, and the people

thereof, in their turn and time, receive all that we receive, and pass through all the ordeals that we are passing through" (Brigham Young, July 10, 1870, JD 14:71).

Literally, the phrase "worlds without end" can now be understood because the work of creating earths will continue forever and ever throughout all time and eternity, even into the limitless eternities of time and space (Doctrine and Covenants 76:112).

There is some scientific evidence to validate that worlds are being created and destroyed elsewhere in our universe by the following news article: "Deep in space on December 14, 1997, an explosion was received on Earth from deep space. From an area about the size of Texas, about 12 billion light years away, an explosion occurred that, based on $E=3Dmc^2$, would have required all the known and visible matter in the universe to release that much energy. It would have been equivalent to one thousandth of a second after the original Big Bang. Over 2,000 of these explosions have occurred since the first one."

The Bible gives us little insight as to why Lucifer and one third of the hosts of heaven rebelled against God. We must first understand just who Lucifer was before his fall from glory. He was a great and noble spiritual being, an "angel of God who was in authority in the presence of God" (Doctrine and Covenants 76:25). Having incredible beauty and being highly intelligent, he was called a "bright star" or "son of the morning." No doubt he possessed a charismatic personality to match his physical attributes, because he had obtained a widespread following among the hosts of heaven

(Abraham 3:28). Being full of pride, he became angered when God rejected his proposal to be a redeemer of mankind in favor of Jehovah (Moses 4:1–2 and Abraham 3:28). At that day, many followed after him. Thereafter Lucifer and his followers openly rebelled against the plan of the Father, against the Only Begotten Son and against the Grand Council of Gods. Fueled by ambition, pride and revenge, he coveted God's own power and sought to take over heaven as reported in Isaiah 14:13–14:

> "For thou hast said in thine heart, I will ascend into heaven, I will exalt my throne
> above the stars of God: I will sit also upon the mount of the congregation…I
> will ascend above the heights of the clouds; I will be like the most High."

The revolt caused war in heaven. Lucifer led one third of the host of heaven in war against the armies of God captained by the archangel Michael. Revelation 12:7–9 tells us God's armies defeated Lucifer's armies; as punishment for their crimes, they were cast out of the highest heaven into the Earth by God.

So great was Lucifer, in spite of his rebellion and eviction, the remaining two thirds of the host of heaven cried out over their loss,

> "How art thou fallen from heaven, O Lucifer, son of the morning! How art thou cut down to the ground!" (Isaiah 14:12).

And

"The heavens wept over him—he was Lucifer, a son of the morning" (Doctrine and Covenants 76:26).

It is impossible to determine the time when the war in heaven took place because it happened in the highest spiritual heaven, located in another dimension. It's another time and another place due to time difference between dimensions. By the same token, it is impossible to estimate the number of the one-third fallen host of heaven, but it could be in the millions if not billions. If God's plan of salvation extended to only this earth, the number would probably be in the millions. If, however, this same plan included other earths, the number would be in the billions. It appears to your authors that this plan included other earths as well, for reasons to be discussed later in this chapter.

Prior to being cast out of heaven, Lucifer knew of God's plan to send a redeemer into the temporal universe to ransom the fallen worlds within, only he did not know what world he would be born into or when he would come. In revenge for not accepting Lucifer's offer to be that redeemer, Lucifer and two hundred Watchers conceived a plan to corrupt the seed of man on the spirit Earth, in order to stop God's plan, which resulted in the destruction and fall of that creation and brought the arrival of Noah to this planet by the process we call the Union of the Polarity.

After the flood of Noah, the flood of Deucalion, they instituted the same plan of action, with an attitude of unprecedented hatred and vengeance toward God, in the temporal universe, to defeat God's plan of redemption on this planet and other fallen worlds that had human inhabitants. If they were successful in this endeavor, these fallen worlds would remain forever in their hands for this eternity. The captive inhabitants would then be subject to Lucifer's rule with ultimate loss of their agency to choose for themselves. They would become willing workers and slaves for their "gods," worshipping and serving Lucifer instead of their creator. All hope of their eternal progression toward salvation would be lost. In addition, Lucifer held an upper hand advantage in that he knew the location of the other worlds in the temporal universe, knowledge he had prior to his fall, as he probably played a role or was at least an observer in their creation.

Such was the case and situation our planet found itself in sometime after modern man made his appearance (150,000–215,000 years ago). The Nephilim, under orders from Lucifer, came to this planet and represented themselves as gods and as men's creators. Men accepted and worshipped them as their gods. They willingly "slaved" for them in the building of their temples and in the mining of the most sought after precious gems and ores. Giants were produced when the Nephilim mated with mortal women. Not only was the seed of men corrupted by their DNA but the animal and plant world as well. Monsters and all sorts of strange deviant creatures were created.

They were deliberately undoing the works of God's hands in order to prevent the redeemer from being born on our earth. Then, the unthinkable happened. From the deep inner depth of our galaxy, a cosmic interloper was on a collision course with our solar system. Sent by God, its mission was to destroy the Nephilim giants and all the corrupted works of the creation. It was the day the Earth nearly died, 9600 BC, when an estimated ninety percent of all life perished. Thereafter the event was remembered as the Flood of Ogyges ("The Brave New World" in vol. 1).

It is a misconception to believe when Lucifer and the fallen host of heaven were cast out to the Earth, they were confined only to this planet. The fallen Watchers or, as they were later called, the Elder Gods, by use of their "seer stones" actually foresaw the coming 9600 BC disaster by several hundred years and left the planet. Several thousand years later, they did return to help restore civilization and re-corrupt the seed of the survivors. Arriving back, around 8000 BC, they took on human form and were visible to mankind, who accepted them once more as gods. Though they were in human form, they lacked a body of flesh and blood as we possess. By lowering their already lowered vibrational rate, they could materialize or disappear into thin air without a trace.

Your authors picture them as the "Darth Vaders" of our universe using *Star Wars* technology. They seek out other worlds to corrupt and rule. As Brigham Young stated, "what our planet undergoes, other earths pass through the same experiences." The only difference is our planet was chosen as the birthplace of the redeemer. As written in volume 1, page 416, John 3:16 somehow became twisted in translation because in the original Greek, the word for *world* is the Greek word *cosmos*. The Greek word *cosmos* refers to anything and everything that is in this universe, therefore the entire universe would be redeemed by Christ's atonement. If this earth were the only fallen planet, it wouldn't have been necessary to redeem the entire universe. Christians here are fortunate to know the atonement took place on this planet.

Christians living on other planets have to believe the atonement took place somewhere in this universe in another world. Each earth has its own Adam and maybe different tempters, but it appears they all have the same redeemer. If this is correct, then God's plan of salvation extends to these other worlds too. God, the son, working under the direction of his father, is the creator of this universe, and was the rightful heir chosen to be its redeemer. In order to save his creation, Christ, in an unprecedented act of love, was willing to die for it as an infinite atonement for the sins of all men. The effects of this infinite atonement covers all men, the Earth itself and all forms of life thereon, other worlds with their many life forms, even reaching out into the endless expanses of eternity.

Jesus acknowledged Lucifer as "Lord of the Earth" (Matthew 4:8–10, John 12:31, and John 14:30). The apostle Paul called him "the god of this world" (11 Corinthians 4:4). Here is food for thought: God rules over the lands called heaven and Lucifer rules over the lands called hell. We are living in a land or planet ruled by Lucifer located in a lower universe, referred to by higher beings as a hell universe, a place prepared for them from the beginning (Doctrine and Covenants 29:38). Despite Earth's delights, it is "hellish" compared to the heavenly "above." Hell is wherever Satan and his angels are found. Because of this, there are people who believe we, as mortals, are living in hell. When you stop and think about it, it does explain a lot of things. Life on this planet can be harsh, cruel, unfair, and at times unbearable. Latter Day Saints refer to these life experience adversities as "the refiner's fire" sent to test and purify our souls in the form of trials and tribulations. The "refiner's fire" is the same as hell fire that forges and hammers souls into perfection. It, however, is not the same type of fire we know as combustible fire. Prayer and repentance are the vehicles of relief from sin-stained souls undergoing hell-fire purging wrought-up by the wiles, temptations and buffering of Satan. Apparently, the mortal experience is a necessary part of salvation to see if we will choose the good over the evil and to see what god we will follow…the god of this world or the God of heaven. These are sobering thoughts, to say the least.

As written in volume 2, page 200, Fenton's Holy Bible in Modern English translation of the "lake of fire and brimstone" reads as "the fiery Lake burning with Divine anger." Apparently there is another region of hell reserved in the end for Satan and his angels, the Antichrist, and the false prophet. According to Latter Day Saint doctrine, included in this list are those who absolutely will not repent and those who blaspheme the Holy Spirit. Those souls cast into this region face the full fury of God's anger and are tormented and purged with relentless divine fire, a fire more awful and terrible than hellfire, for eternity. Just where this region is located has not been revealed. Maybe it is in a lower hell universe beneath ours but most likely it is somewhere in another spiritual dimension.

Without a redeemer to perform atonement for the fallen worlds and for its fallen habitants, the gates of heaven into the higher spiritual dimensions would remain shut. There would be no resurrection, and our souls would remain forever trapped in this hell universe. Jesus broke the bands of death, permitting resurrections to take place. He redeemed worlds and people from their fallen state, which permits them, if worthy, to leave this "hell" by process of resurrection or translation into a higher, spiritual heaven. He was the only being in the universe capable of entering this process into the Akashic records for us to access. There was no capability in all the mortals who ever lived on the Earth to do this on our own. Jesus never said he was God. **He said he was the *way*.** Entry is by way of one of the many portals that have now been opened through his work.

That is the message of the World Trees encoded in symbolism for all to see and for the wise to understand. Jesus taught the day of the *harvest* or "rapture" for this world would take place at the End of the Age, that is, December 21, 2012. The sign of the Suntelia Aeon marks the event in the heavens, when it was in ancient times believed the Ouroborus portal in the "dark rift" was opened to allow the "transition," "rapture," or "rolling back" of the

Earth into the fourth spiritual heaven or dimension ("The End Times" in vol. 2). Each civilization had another name for Jesus, which has created confusion and lack of understanding of the meaning of the World Trees. We have wrongly assumed these symbols were pagan when in fact they were carved in stone as reminders to future generations of the coming 2012 event. Having said all of the above, we hope you can now view the atonement in a more grand, eternal sense, while at the same time feel a personal debt of gratitude toward the savior of the worlds and all mankind. It is difficult to fully grasp the implications and impact this one act of atonement had upon eternity.

The Book of Revelation states that Satan knows his time here on this planet is short and in spite of all his efforts to subdue this world, he will be defeated. Haven't you wondered, if Satan already knows the predicted outcome, why doesn't he just wave a white flag and give up? We speculate it is because he has already persuaded a number of other worlds to follow after him. He has won many trillions of souls to follow his lower-dimensional glory. Their scriptures probably said the same thing as or something similar to the Book of Revelation; however, the ultimate outcome depends on men's free agency to choose whom they will follow. In fact, those worlds may not have had as much removed from their scriptures as we have, so they may have had an even clearer picture of the process. However, they did not have Christ live his mortal life on their planets, so the task of corruption may have been easier. It is a quandary as to who had the greater challenge: to live on the same world as Christ, with greatly emasculated scriptures, or to live on the world with pristine scriptures and a belief that Christ lived on a distant world. The fact that Lucifer has won ground across the universe is what encourages him and his staff of loyal Nephilim to continue working on our world. Look how much he has already won from you.

God does not force men into heaven. In point of fact, God cannot control anything. Were he to take control of the free will of any matter or spirit, the entire universe would collapse. The realization that you are a sovereign being with the entire universe rolled up inside of you is key to understanding how you can ascend in a single lifetime. This process is also called *translation*, the same process by which Enoch and his people left this planet before the flood.

Another factor is that the pure Adamic bloodlines called the *Holy Seed*, the same bloodlines as the redeemer, are still on this planet, and the righteous portion of them are given divine protection until the end of the world. Satan's intense hatred for this race of people fuels his already perverted thinking into believing if they are exterminated he has a good chance of keeping dominion of this world. For over two thousand years the Jews have been driven out of countries, persecuted relentlessly, and massacred, because Satan stirs up the hearts of men to do his "dirty work." The peak of this all out extermination happened in 1933 when Hitler killed an estimated six million Jews.

Ishmael, the son of Abraham, was the ancestor of the Arab nations. They too have some of the same "divine portion" because they are descendants of Noah and of the Adamic Race; however, the Arabs may not be as racially pure as the Jews because they permitted outside marriages with other tribes. For centuries different Arab tribes have been at war with each other. Each would like to exterminate the other, particularly in Iraq in today's times. Lucifer stirs them up to kill each other. The war economy has been flourishing on Earth at the time of the writing of this book for well over three hundred years. The weapons systems are much more powerful and sophisticated, but fairly balanced across the world, strangely, so that all people can remain at war without one side winning a clear and total victory. Terrorism, the act of inflicting fear in your enemy, is at its pinnacle of power in your day.

In its guise of "civil war," the extermination method being used by Lucifer is quite effective. The danger therein is it could spread into other countries. Do you not see factions from Iran and Pakistan entering into the conflict? Similar situations exist in Lebanon and Palestine. If this is allowed to continue, without resolution, eventually other countries will be drawn into their conflict.

Those people caught up in these barbarous conflicts probably yearn to escape from this world of pain and fear, desiring instead to live on another planet in peace and harmony. It is wishful thinking because other worlds are undergoing similar situations as our planet

Earth. In reality, the grass is not greener there because wherever Lucifer reigns, there is hell. The key to happiness is not to allow that fear to grow in your heart.

Neither scientists nor astronomers have been able to locate another planet that has human life forms. **SETI (Search for Extra-Terrestrial Intelligence)** is the name for a number of organized efforts to detect extraterrestrial life. A number of efforts with "SETI" have been organized, including projects funded by the United States government. The general approach of SETI projects is to survey the sky to detect the existence of transmissions from a civilization on a distant planet, an approach widely endorsed by the scientific community as hard science (see, *e.g.*, claims in *Skeptical Inquirer*).

There are great challenges in searching across the sky for a first transmission that could be characterized as intelligent, since its direction, spectrum and method of communication are all unknown beforehand. SETI projects necessarily make assumptions to narrow the search, and thus no exhaustive search has so far been conducted. Many Discovery Science documentaries have featured SETI. In spite of all efforts by SETI, thus far no communications have been established with any other worlds.

However, remote viewers all claim that the nearest planet with human life forms is located somewhere in the Pleiades star system. It is called Earth 2 because it is very similar to our planet. Bear in mind, this finding is not scientifically proven. The Pleiades star system is about 440 light-years from Earth, a fact confirmed by the Hubble telescope's measurements.

Remote viewers also claim there are many different intelligent life forms other than human. For example, there are the intelligent insect beings that are an ancient race of evolved beings who live incredibly long life spans and who are allegedly one of the original species of the Pleiadian Federation, a Federation located in a higher dimension, that is made up of six hundred planets. Supposedly, they are the ones who designed the black triangle spacecraft that flew over Belgium.

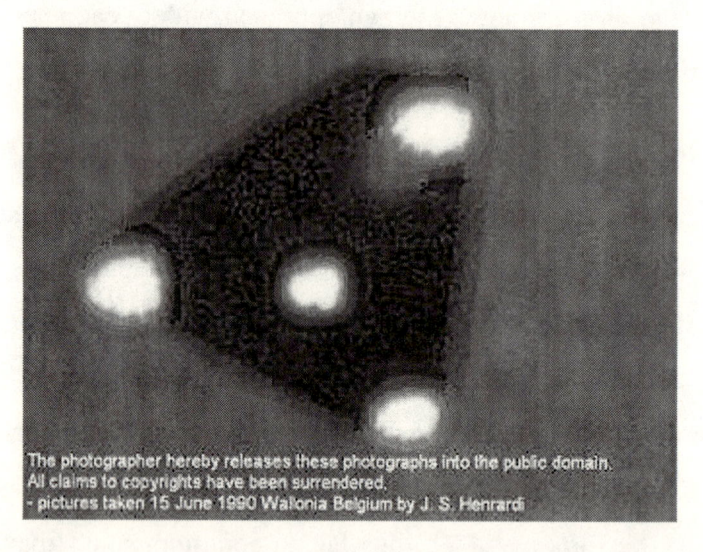

Figure 112 – Ground photo taken in Belgium and released to public domain of a black triangle craft that eluded F-16s with no problem.

As incredible as this all seems, they may be the ones mentioned in the Sumerian texts as there exists a carved Sumerian panel picture depicting them with insect bodies, like those of a locust, but with heads and arms of those of men. In that panel picture, they are shown paying homage to the sun god, Shamash. Sorry, have not been able to find an Internet image of that panel; however, the panel does exist. An alien abduction case described another intelligent insect creature as looking like an eight-foot tall praying mantis–type creature. It could be that the praying mantis–type beings are the same ones described in the Sumerian texts but in their ideology were shown as part men and part insect to indicate that they were advanced, intelligent beings. After all, the lower locust like body is very similar to that of the praying mantis. But, more than likely, they are two different groups of intelligent insect beings because the Sumerian texts indicate that Enki created the mantis insect creatures from the praying mantis about 100 sars ago—that is, approximately 360,000 years as one sar equals 3,600 years. The other insect creatures appear to have evolved naturally over a long period of time and were not created by spiritual beings in the process of corrupting the seed of praying mantis insects.

Now, here is where it gets interesting. Remote viewers say our planet Earth is due to be transitioned soon into the Pleiadian Federation (2012?). It will not be the physical Earth, but its co-dimensional counterpart that is none other than the spirit Earth. If this is the case, then the Pleiadian Federation exists in the higher, fourth-dimensional universe. From time to time, remotes viewers have been in contact with a woman admiral, who is second in command to his majesty, the Admiral of the Defense Department of the Pleiadian Federation. She apparently is a perfected physical/spiritual being similar in form and appearance to us.

Of course, most everyone has heard of the alien abductions where two types of gray aliens were involved. There are the small, large-headed, hairless grays and the much taller, large-headed, hairless grays. Both are described as having large, black, insect-like eyes, two holes for a nose, and a slit for a mouth. It is the consensus of most abductees who had encounters with these beings that the beings are emotionless, biological androids who work for others.

Then there are the Reptilians described as green-skinned, yellow-eyed lizard men. They may not be intelligently superior, but they possess great body strength inherited from a long line of warrior ancestry. It is said had our dinosaurs survived the global disaster that destroyed them, they would have evolved into these Reptilians. It appears that the grays, Reptilians, and insect mantis beings work collectively with others in some sort of pre-arranged scientific work agreements.

Regardless, none of this has ever been scientifically proven but has remained the "food" for various science fiction screen writers who with movie producers have thrilled us with the visual effects of the *Star War* epics, awed us with *E.T.* and *Close Encounters of the Third Kind,* and held us in our movie seats spellbound with the hair-raising *War of the Worlds.* Such is the stuff science fiction is made of, and its fans can't seem to get enough of it!

Nevertheless, a few religious paintings by the old masters and unknown painters have vimana-type spaceships being piloted by human-like beings painted into their backgrounds. One example, shown below, is from a thirteenth-century fresco work titled *The Crucifixion*. The scene is taken from the upper left of the work. There is an identical UFO pictured opposite on the upper right hand side. In the center of the fresco, Christ is hanging on the cross. Clearly, it is a UFO being piloted by a human-like being witnessing the crucifixion.

Figure 113 - The Crucifixion painting. Notice the airships in the sky

The following is a list of early paintings that have UFOs painted into their backgrounds that can be looked up on the Internet and viewed closely. These are only a few as they are too numerous to list and we want to make mention that literally thousands of UFO art examples exist on cave walls, cliff walls, coins, pyramids, and temple walls.

1. Summer's Triumph 1538 tapestry

2. Glorification of the Eucharist 1600

3. The Baptism of Christ 1710 Flemish artist Aert De Gelder

4. Mary the Magnificat tapestry

5. Crucifixion of Christ seventeenth-century Svetishovoli Cathedral, Mtskheta, Georgia

6. Windsor Castle 1783

7. Basel, Switzerland 1566

8. Theatrum Orbis Terrarum

9. Annalas Laurissenses Crusaders 100s

10. Saucer at the Tomb of Jesus

11. Nuremberg 1561

12. The Crucifixion Fresco 1350

13. The Miracle of the Snow

14. The Madonna with Saint Giovannino fifteenth century by Dommenico Ghirlandaio

In addition the British Museum houses statues of the Reptilians dating to 5000–4500 BC.

The point we want to make or perhaps we should ask is… where did these UFOs come from? Before any assumptions are made, read the following ancient writing:

> The Hakatha (Laws of the Babylonians) states quite unambiguously: "The privilege of operating a flying machine is great. The knowledge of flight is among the most ancient of our inheritances. A gift from 'those from upon high'. We received it from them as a means of saving many lives."

More fantastic still is the information given in the ancient Chaldean work, The Sifrala, which contains over one hundred pages of technical details on building a flying machine. It contains words that translate as graphite rod, copper coils, crystal indicator, vibrating spheres, stable angles, etc. (Childress, D. Hatcher, "Ancient Indian Aircraft Technology," *The Anti-Gravity Handbook,* Adventures Unlimited Press)

It appears from the above writings that flying machines were a gift from 'those from upon high' who were none other than the Nephilim, and furthermore they came with a building instruction manual. So, we can conclude with a certain amount of certainty that at least some of the UFOs in ancient times were of man-made, earthly origin. Perhaps these are the ones drawn into the backgrounds of so many paintings? Maybe that is the way King David came into possession of his 'flying car' that was passed down to his son, King Solomon, who gave it as a gift to the Queen of

Sheba. It seems the Vedic Indians retained most of the technology to build them as there are literally a hundred or more Indian writings giving building instructions of engines for these 'flying machines' they call vimanas. One 800 BC writing, titled *Encyclopedia of Machines*, allegedly written by Maharshi Bhardwaj, describes three types of vimana as those that travel from place to place, those that travel from country to country, and those that travel between planets.

Figure 114: Vimana carved in the ceiling support by Seti I at Abydos, Egypt

We suspect most terrestrial 'flying machines' were of the first two types. It however remains a mystery as to how this technology was lost and even worse not one shred of tangible evidence of them survives. Had this technology survived, we would all be flying around in George Jettson–style personal flying automobiles.

Besides the Nephilim and Noah's entourage, has there ever been any other extra-terrestrial contact with our planet? There is mounting evidence that perhaps from time to time Earth has been visited by ETs and still continues to have visits. Whether or not governments are involved in cover-ups or sharing technology with them, we cannot say with certainty. What we do know for sure is that a few people involved in alien abductions claim they still continue, animal mutilations still occur, sightings still happen, and mysterious, intricate crop circles appear overnight.

In recent times, the most compelling evidence occurred during a full solar eclipse on July 11, 1991, over Mexico City. While thousands witnessed the event, a large, luminous, spherical UFO appeared and hovered silently in the sky for about forty minutes. At least seventeen people videotaped the incident. Unbelievers and skeptics were converted on the spot. This event fulfilled an ancient Mayan prophecy found in the Dresden Codex that foretold the eclipse would herald the emergence of the Sixth Sun of the Quetzalcoatl. In addition, the Tiger Sun, born of the total solar eclipse, would mark the beginning of Earth changes and bring "cosmic awareness brought about through encounters with masters of the stars." The prophecy was cast 1,200 years ago in AD 755. Since the eclipse, the Mexico City area has remained the hot spot for UFO sightings of not only singular craft but, on occasion, fleets of them.

But, the story doesn't end there, not by a long shot. Remote viewers claim they have made contact with the UFO pilots over Mexico. Your authors actually witnessed a session of remote viewing when contact was made with them. During the session it was learned the UFO pilots are Mayan. They left this planet (your authors presume with the Nephilim in their interplanetary spacecraft) in the year 750 BC from a little town in ancient Mexico no longer in existence. When they left, they promised to return during the July 1991 solar eclipse and birth of the Tiger Sun. When they returned during the solar eclipse, they were disappointed that there were no celebrations or greetings waiting for them. Since no one greeted them, they decided not to make any contact with Mexican leaders, electing instead to establish a base in nearby surrounding mountains. Remote viewers asked if 2012 would be catastrophic to this planet. They replied, yes. When asked why they had returned to Earth, they revealed they had come for the Maya to save them. Remote viewers then asked, when will this take place? They answered, 2008.

Naturally, your authors were skeptical about the information being received until it was learned that remote viewers everywhere are receiving the same message. Since the Yucatan has nearly five million Maya, not counting the Mayan populations in Belize and Guatemala, we asked the remote viewers, how could the UFOs save that many? We were quickly informed that one large UFO could hold a million people! As fantastic as this story may seem, in view of all that has been presented in other chapters pertaining to 2012, the year 2008 bears watching to see if the Maya are taken to other worlds, presumably to another planet somewhere in the Pleiades. If this does occur then another ancient Aztec prophecy will be fulfilled, one that says:

> "The sons of the Sixth Sun will be the first to journey to new worlds in the stars."

As none of this can be scientifically proven, perhaps the prudent thing to do is take the position of "wait and see." It is after all only six months, as of this writing July 8, 2007, until the year 2008. We reason, if in fact this does occur, it would be a gradual removal of the Maya over the entire span of a year.

Recently, on July 15, 2007, CNN television interviewed several UFO researchers. Included in the group was the former Republican Arizona Governor Fife Symington, whose statements marked a dramatic turnaround from previous statements made ten years ago concerning the "Phoenix Lights" that appeared over Phoenix around 8:15 p.m. on March 13, 1997.

He was on the program because he wanted to make amends to his constituents and set the record straight. On that night a big, black, triangular or delta-form UFO silently drifted very low directly across metro Phoenix, including the central downtown area and Sky Harbor International Airport. It was seen by hundreds or thousands of people, some of whom videotaped the event that was visible for at least forty minutes. The delta-shaped object had lights defining its shape that appeared to be as large as two miles in span!

The governor said, "It was enormous and inexplicable. Who knows where it came from? A lot of people saw it, and I saw it too. It was not of this world. It was dramatic. And it couldn't have been flares because it was too symmetrical, as it had a geometric outline, a constant shape."

He further said that he called the commander at nearby Luke Air Force Base, as well as the top general of the Arizona National Guard, and he checked with the head of the Arizona Department of Public Safety and the State Police Agency about the huge, mysterious flying object. They were "perplexed" and offered no explanation. Since then, many more UFO sightings have been seen in the area.

Could it be that this huge, triangular or delta-shaped UFO is one of many based in the Mexican mountain ranges awaiting the 2008 removal of the Mayans? Perhaps it was out surveying large cities near to Mexico that might have a Mayan population living there as well? We will know shortly, as 2008 is practically in the door.

As for the 1947 Roswell crash, your author E. J. Clark and her brother Phil H. Clark were witnesses to this incident as children when we were traveling in a car crossing the plains at night. After this book is published, another book is planned describing what we witnessed on that night. We believe we are the only persons living who can give an eye-witness account of the incident; furthermore we can pin-point the exact date and time of the event. Until that book is published, we are "lying low" and not saying much about it so as not to have a visit from the MIB (men in black).

When the last spirit Earth of other worlds in this universe returns to the fourth dimension, it may mark the end of a temporal eternity that may be one of many temporal eternities. Our definition of a temporal eternity would be a vast period of incomprehensible time pertaining to our temporal universe. The Buddha is reported to have recovered the memories of eighty-four past world-periods, an immense stretch of time almost impossible to comprehend. In this sense, the Buddha's definition of world-periods is the same as our definition of temporal eternities. The temporal eternities are a vast measurement of time in our universe, but they are temporal, having a beginning and ending. Therefore, they are not eternal as being unending forever, as in a higher, spiritual universe. It could be that our universe will expand to its limit and then contract or return to near nothingness, maybe even imploding on itself in an act of self-destruction in order to return once more to one point of singularity where all matter and space is compressed into a state of incredibly high temperature and pressure to await another "Big Bang" that will bring forth another new temporal eternity. The "Big Bang" was an explosion of space, not one in space. The oscillation theory is supported by the Vedic, Buddhism, and Jainism, along with Brahmanism, views that hold that our present universe is only one in a beginningless series, reappearing and disappearing from time to time.

According to the old serpent religion belief, at the end of time, the Twin Sons (yin and yang) reunite as their father/mother and become one again with the Primal or Fire Serpent. When this occurs, the universe is thrown out of balance, resulting in full-scale destruction called the destruction phase. An excerpt taken from Mark Pinkham's book, *The Return of the Serpents of Wisdom*, states "In the blink of an eye the Primal Serpent in the form of a colossal Fire Serpent consumes all life in its path and reverts all material forms back to pure Life Force or cosmic fire."

"The Hindus refer to this final consumptive phase as 'flames belched forth from the fangs of Shesha' that incinerate all material forms in the universe. The ancient Egyptians of Heliopolis alluded to the universal dissolution as 'the end of time (when) the world will revert to the primary state of chaos and Atum (the Creator Dragon) will once again become a Serpent (pure Life Force).'"

Christians can equate the Supreme Being (God) to that of the Primal Serpent, who brought forth the Word or Logos to that of the Serpent Son…the Word moving like a breath (the serpentine or spiraling Life Force) through space and the universe, causing the substances to vibrate and glow with the Serpent Fire friction. In a unique concept, the message remains the same whether the Serpent Son or Christ is the creator of the universe.

From the Milky Way Cosmic Tree standpoint, the final destructive phase culminates in the ascent of the Serpent up the cosmic tree. There is little information to be found concerning the

Serpent's ascent up the Cosmic Tree during the destructive phase or even the Serpent's descent down the Cosmic World Tree during the creative phase. What we present next is mostly our interpretation of the Serpent's symbolic meaning of descending and ascending the Cosmic World Tree or Milky Way World Tree during the creative and destructive phases.

According to the Babylonians, Egyptians, and Maya, the Earth and universe undergo cycles of creation, preservation and destruction, some that are major cycles and some that are minor cycles. The 26,000-year Precession of the Equinoxes or Great Year is classified as a minor cycle of time. A major cycle of time is one of 104,000 years, called a Sun Year. The Precession cycle of a Great Year is one-fourth of a larger, 104,000-year cycle. Thus, four Great Years make up a Sun Year. At the end of a major cycle of time, a grand phase of destruction and transformation takes place. According to the Mesoamerican calendar, we entered the grand phase of destruction and transformation on August 16, 17, 1987, which will culminate in the year 2012 and 2013. In fact, many cycles of time come to a completion in 2012. The 13,000-year (half of a Great Year) minor cycle of the Phoenix started with the destruction of Atlantis and ends on December 21, 2012. A 52,000-year cycle (midpoint of the 104,000-year cycle) resulted in the first destructions of Lemuria and Atlantis. We are nearing the end of the following half of the 52,000-year grand phase, parts of which end in 2012 and 2013, which according to prophecy, holds the greatest potential for destruction and transformation. According to this particular prophecy, it is the end of the Fourth Sun. Other prophecies say it is the end of the Fifth Sun, depending on the tradition.

Draco, Latin word for "dragon" (Serpent), is a constellation in the northern part of the sky. It is a faint constellation twisting, like a serpent, around the north celestial pole and lying between Ursa Major and Cepheus. The ancients viewed Draco as a representation of the creator-destroyer. Draco has a star called Alpha Draconis or Thurban that formally was the Pole Star that sat at the top of the World Tree (World Tree Bird of Paradise). When Draconis was the Pole Star, the ecliptic would have coincided with the equator. Days and nights would have been equal year-round, resulting in a year-round, perpetual spring, a Golden Age. After the 9500 BC cataclysm, the axis of the Earth was tilted. Draconis was cast down from the top of the Milky Way World Tree, and a new Pole Star, Polaris, moved up to take his place at the top of the Milky Way World Tree. Symbolically, the "dragon" had descended the World Tree, following a catastrophic destruction, and a new phase of creation began with the survivors of the cataclysm and the Union of the Polarity.

Earth now is physically drooping on its axis instead of being polarized upright, symbolizing paradise lost. The great charge of man, in particular, is to re-instate the world to its upright position, by righteousness (positive energy), to restore Paradise.

On December 21, 2012, a great destruction of Earth is foretold to be followed by a return to the Golden Age. Symbolically, it will be the "dragon" ascending the Milky Way World Tree during the destructive phase. During the ensuing predicted cataclysm, we wrote in chapter one, the Earth could tilt more or even right itself. According to this belief, Earth will right itself and Alpha Draconis will once more resume its place at the top of the Milky Way World Tree as a Pole Star. Symbolically, the "dragon" will then dive into the cosmic sea for a period of planetary rest. Of course, the true Earth—that is, the spirit Earth—will be transitioned or "raptured" into the higher, spiritual fourth dimension to begin its Golden Age or renewal creative phase. After the tribulation years and the return of Christ, the physical earth, its axis now righted, will start its Golden Age in a renewal or creative phase.

This particular prophesied destructive phase, slated to take place in 2012, is a planetary one. It could also mean, after the millennium, when the temporal Earth dies, our cosmic solar system will explode like the explosions previously mentioned. However, if our spirit Earth is the last one to leave this universe—noting there is no way of knowing—then, a universal destruction could occur at the end of the Golden Age of the temporal Earth when this planet dies ("The End Times" in vol. 2). Therefore the destructive phase could be planetary, cosmic or universal, or perhaps a destructive phase includes all three as a process of destruction over a lesser cycle of time. The Bible implies it could be a universal destruction because death is destroyed and Satan, his demonic followers, the condemned lost souls of mortal men, and the fallen angels are cast into the "fiery lake burning with Divine wrath," the location thereof not disclosed but probably somewhere in a spiritual dimension. Will their punishment be endless and forever?

We don't know but it is conceivable that eventually the condemned lost souls of mortal beings cast there, over a thousand-year period of time, will be purified by the divine fire sufficiently to repent and the wages of sin will be paid up to the uttermost farthing, maybe to inherit a kingdom of telestial glory (Doctrine and Covenants 76:81–112 and Revelations 20:5, 21:8). As for Lucifer and the fallen angels, ancient Mesoamerican prophets declare, "they cannot be redeemed according to God's justice; and they cannot die, seeing there is no more corruption" (Book of Mormon Alma 12:17–18). Another name for God is *Endless...Endless is My Name* (Moses 1:3). Therefore, *Endless punishment* is God's punishment (Doctrine and Covenants 19:10). It is only he who can decide when enough punishment is enough. These scriptures suggest perhaps there is hope for the lost souls of mortal men to eventually be redeemed from the "fiery lake."

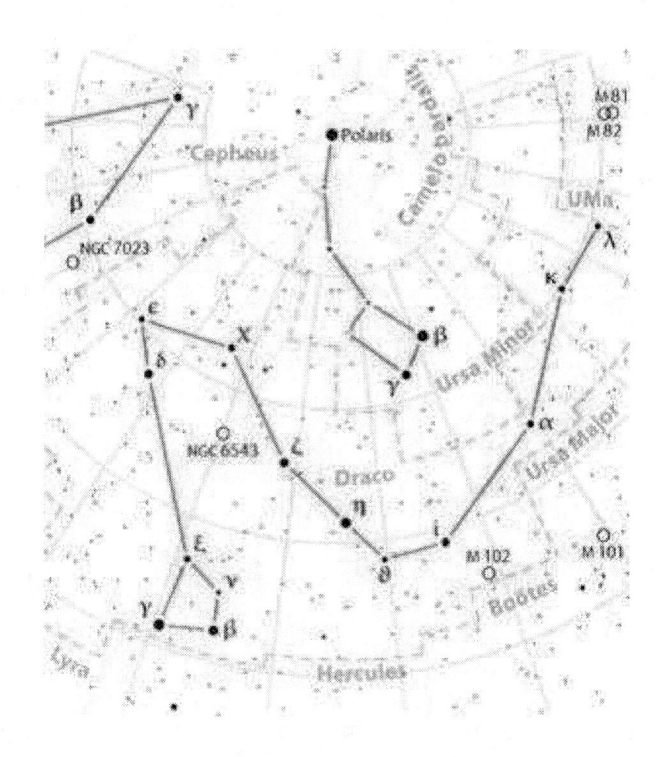

Figure 114 - Draco Constellation

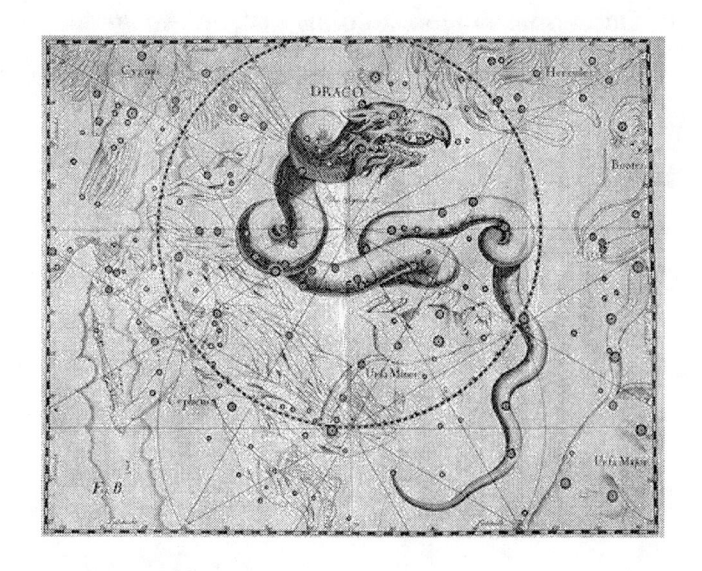

Figure 115 - Draco

Pralaya, in Hindu cosmology, is a period of the cycle of existence where activity does not occur. It is a period of repose, whether planetary, cosmic or universal. According to computations of the Brahmans, this period lasts 4,320,000,000 years. During Pralaya, the sleeping god (Narayana or Vishnu) sleeps on the coiled form of Shesha, the seven-headed Serpent (seven aspects of God), floating on the universal ocean. When the sleeping god awakes, the creative cycle begins again. Whether the cycle is universal, cosmic or planetary will determine what kind of creative process will take place. If it is universal, then another "Big Bang" will take place. If it is cosmic, then solar or star systems will be created. If planetary, then a restoration will take place, probably in a much shorter time frame than allotted by the Brahmans. They were probably giving the figures for a universal Pralaya repose. As symbolized in ancient times, the Ouroborus dragon holding just the tip of his tail in its mouth expressed the cycles of creation and destruction as one endless round.

Figure 116 - Pralaya cycle represented as Shesha, the seven-headed serpent with sleeping god (Mark Pinkham, *The Return of the Serpents of Wisdom*, page 313)

The Cataclysm Survival Plan

In volume 2's "The End Times" chapter, we wrote of how to become spiritually prepared in order not to be "left behind." Since we do not know for sure whether or not we are worthy enough to be translated into the fourth dimension, it would be the wise and prudent thing to prepare as if we were one of those who could be "left behind." We know from the ancient writings and the Tzolk'in calendar that the earth will make a three-day transit "sailing the cosmic sea" starting December 21, 2012; this transit was prophesied to be one of cataclysmic destruction by earthquakes that would kill most of the world's population. Besides the earthquakes, there are other factors to consider. Energy being emitted from the monstrous, spinning black hole may affect the sun's corona, causing it to send super solar flares of plasma energy into space. These super-size solar flares of plasma energy could scorch the earth in minutes, primarily affecting the northern hemisphere. In addition, tectonic plate movement could cause a pole shift. Should a pole reversal happen, hurricane-force winds of 300 three hundred miles per hour combined with solar flares of plasma energy could sweep across the planet to become the firestorm from hell. Because we do not know exactly what to expect, except for three days of darkness, earthquakes, heaving seas, torrential rainfall, and raging tempests, all things must be taken into consideration in order to survive (Revelations 6:12–17 and Doctrine and Covenants 88:87–91). Preparation should be made for a worst-case scenario. It is better to be prepared and not need it than to need it and not have adequate preparedness. Preparedness is the key to survival. That one statement, if heeded, can save millions of lives. As we approach the 2012 End Time date, it will quickly become apparent that the "signs of the times" are manifesting as prophesized, and survival is going to be everyone's priority. It is necessary to be both spiritually and temporally prepared. Both are addressed in this book. This chapter will help you to prepare temporally and *The Grand Finale* chapter will help you to prepare spiritually.

Is there a way you can prepare to survive the coming cataclysm? Yes. Your authors have carefully thought this out and would like to submit the following survival guide plan, recognizing that each person or family may have to make adjustments to fit their survival needs. Some adjustments will not be easy to make but thinking in terms of survival will help to make difficult choices easier. We emphasize that survival depends mainly on **YOU** making your own preparation. Do not depend on your government to do this, because even with all government preparation possible, it will save only a small percent of the population. Therefore, we recommend building private, underground shelters and stocking them with emergency essentials. Because the following is merely a guide, we recommend reading books on emergency preparedness. Most of the emergency preparedness books discuss the various types of underground shelters, giving the pros and cons of different models, size and cost. They also recommend how and what kind of emergency essentials to store in the shelter. Our guide plan's purpose is to make our readers aware of what is involved in preparedness for the coming cataclysm so they can start making survival plans immediately. To make the survival guide plan easier to follow, we will break it down into topics.

Location

Move away from coastal areas and low-lying ground around coastal areas. Sea-level ground, even if fifty miles inland, will not be safe. Sea level will not be safe ground anywhere. Remember, the higher the better. This will apply to those who live on islands. It would be better to move off islands. If this is not feasible, then at least move to higher ground. Most islands have mountains. If your island is flat, such as Grand Cayman, move off the island to somewhere else.

Move away from low-lying river areas. Some people live below dams. Move, because these dams will not hold; neither will riverbank levees hold.

Why move from these areas? Because, just before the "great shaking" of the Earth occurs at the End of the Age, the seas will heave themselves out of their bounds accompanied by raging thunder, torrential rainfall, high winds, and electrical storms (Doctrine and Covenants 88:90). All coastal cites and low-lying coastal areas will be inundated with water, either from the seas or flooded from deluges of torrential rainfall like unto the days of Noah. This will start to occur about two weeks or so prior to December 21. If it is impossible for you to move from coastal cities because of employment, then consider making a safe survival place inland where you can flee to for safety. Do not take shelter in high-rise buildings. Go to high ground. This cannot be emphasized enough. A fifty-foot or higher wall of seawater could sweep inland, globally wiping out everything in its path. Furthermore, the water will remain. All low-lying coastal areas will be flooded with deep water. Torrential rains will flood other low-lying areas not in a coastal plain. Even after Earth makes the three-day transit, raging thunder, high winds, electrical storms, and torrential rainfall will continue maybe for two to three weeks afterwards, until the Earth is completely clear by moving out of the area of the energy paths of the monstrous, spinning black hole.

Move away from earthquake fault lines and known tectonic plate lines. Earth movement will occur along these "seam lines" as these are the weak points of the Earth's crust. Remember, the weakest stress points always fail first. Land masses around the Pacific "ring of fire" areas should be vacated. Move away from volcanoes, even inactive ones. Stay clear of Yellowstone National Park as it is a super-volcano just waiting to explode. When Yellowstone does blow, geologists predict that every living thing within six hundred miles is likely to die.

Shelter
Underground Family Bunkers

The only way to truly be safe is to go underground. An underground bunker will give you a fighting chance at survival in a worst-case scenario. It is not necessary to go deep underground, but deep enough to cover an underground shelter with five feet of dirt. In the 1960s, many people built underground bunkers in their back yards as bomb shelters. These shelters can be reopened and used. Underground tornado shelters can be used; however, most are small and lack a chemical toilet. You will be holed up for at least three days, more likely thirty days; therefore, plan accordingly. There are companies who make underground shelters in custom sizes and in various different materials in all price ranges. Check them out online. Some are made of fiberglass, concrete, and prefabricated steel designed to withstand an F-5 tornado and exceed FEMA standards. Prices usually include installation but not always.

In planning a shelter, remember you will be in it for at least three days during December 21–23 as the Earth makes the three-day transit through the "dark rift" of the Milky Way. Plan for thirty days because of terrible weather conditions both before and after the three-day transit. You certainly will need a chemical toilet, enough room to sleep all members of your family, water, a light source, and a three- to thirty-day supply of food—at a minimum. Underground shelters should be placed in open clearings, eliminating the danger of trees or buildings toppling over and blocking your exit ways.

Where you live will determine whether or not to build a long- or short-term shelter. Warm climates, short term. Cold climates, long term. Long-term shelters need to be larger in size, a sort of underground mini-home. These are the bare-bone basics. Tent houses (yurts and yomes) could be erected after Earth's three-day transit and used in combination with either long- or short-term shelters in the event your house is gone with the wind or lying in a pile of rain-soaked rubble. Otherwise it will be camping outside during daylight hours and sleeping underground at nighttime.

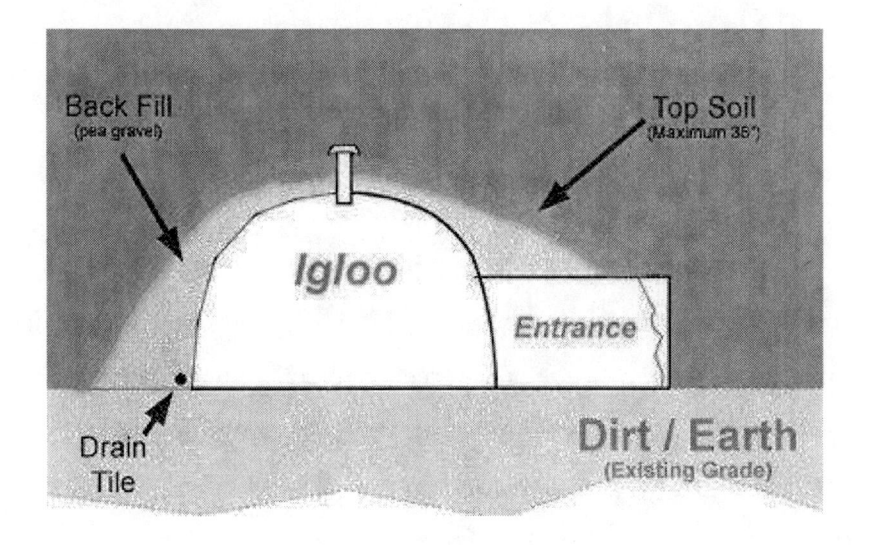

Figure 117 – Top-of-ground igloo shelter

Figure 118 – Underground igloo construction (*fiberglassigloos.com*)

Basement Safe Rooms

A good underground basement can be used with some modifications. It needs to be enclosed into one room with four thick walls and a strong, thick, reinforced cement ceiling. Incorporated into the design should be an airshaft and a blast entry door made of metal mounted with heavy-duty latches, lift cylinders, and hinges. Basement shelters are more economical to install, but unless you have a thick concrete insulating ceiling you are in danger if your house catches fire. The same companies who make underground shelters also make basement shelters. Most are made of prefabricated steel. With proper insulation from heat, they could work.

Build your own underground shelters

Books are available with instructions on how to build your own root cellar underground shelter. Certainly a good carpenter could make his own basement shelter with careful planning. Check with FEMA or visit their website for free plans to build your own underground shelter or safe room.

Underground community shelters

Families and friends could invest together and build collectively a large underground shelter. Each family would own their own bedroom and share a kitchen, bath, and living room. The advantages are that the shelter is roomier and more cost effective as the cost of building is shared, like buying an underground condo. In other words you get more bang for your bucks. A few companies do build these custom underground shelters.

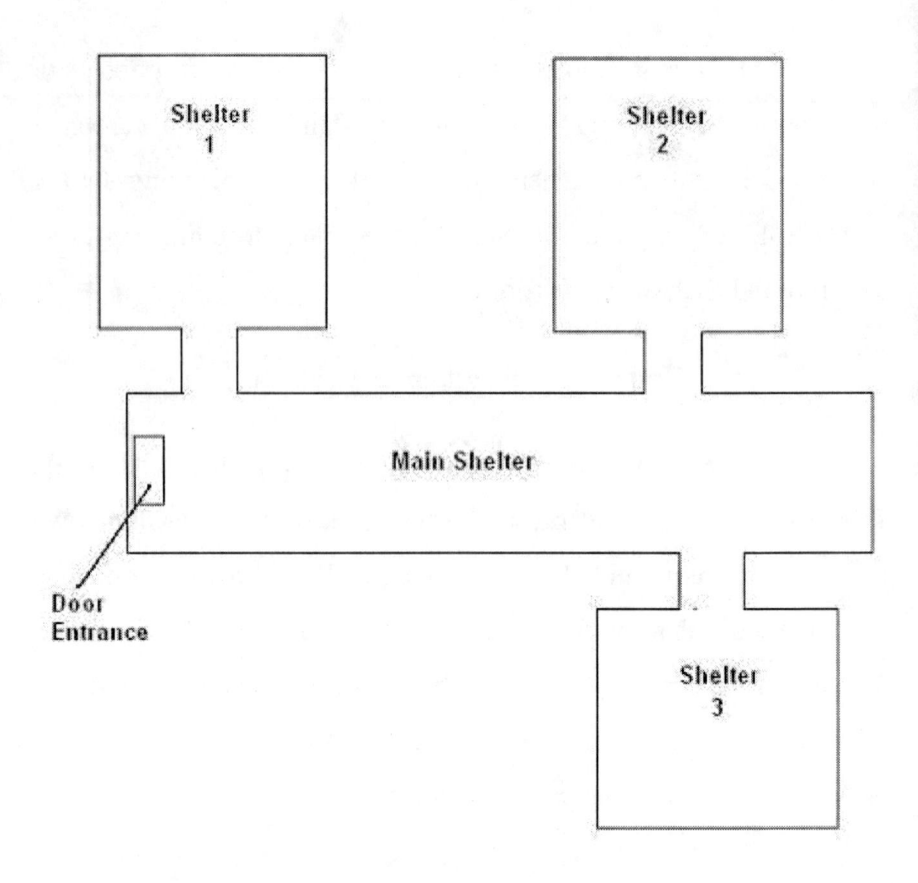

Figure 119 – Shelter design capable of housing a small family
(f5shelters.com)

At least one community is already prepared. North of Yellowstone, there is a place called Paradise Valley where there are about thirty big underground shelters capable of housing an entire community. The main shelter consists of three floors with forty bedrooms, each individually furnished by families who own them. The long corridors are packed with dehydrated food, beans, lentils, and oatmeal. A well-stocked clinic and a big community kitchen is included. There's even an auxiliary shelter for pets. The complex is self-contained with three diesel engines and enough fuel to power a community for a long time. These shelters were built in the 1980s when nuclear war was a threat. They have never been used and are well maintained in the event of a disaster.

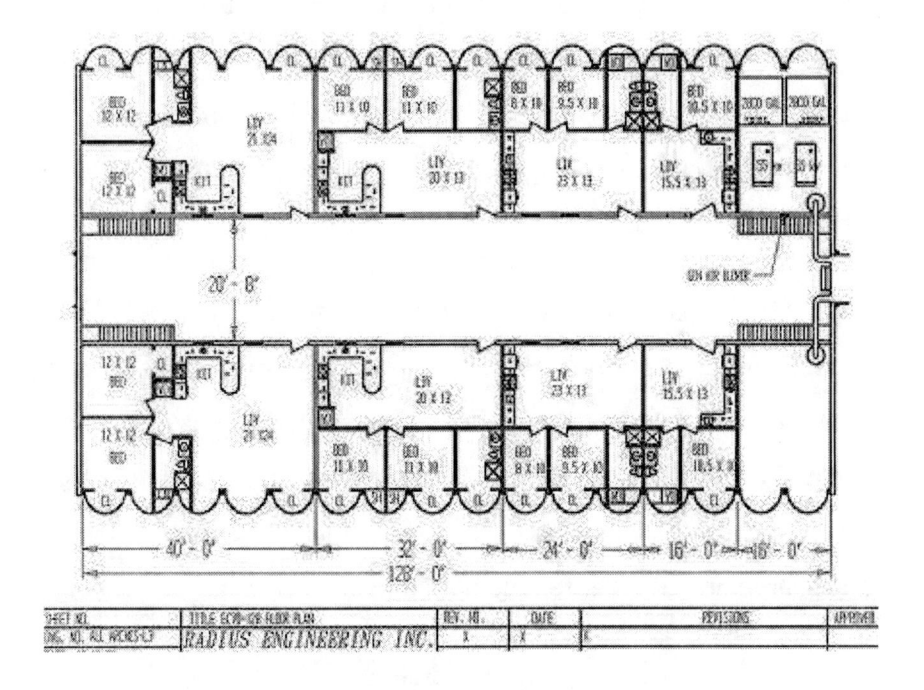

Figure 120 - Sample plans for an underground community shelter designed by *Earth.com*

Tunnels

Above-sea-level cities that are fortunate enough to have an underground subway system could open up their tunnels to serve as a mass shelter. An entire city population could find safe refuge for three to thirty days. With a little planning, a repeat of the Superdome scenario in New Orleans during hurricane Katrina can be avoided. Hospitals should consider making makeshift emergency rooms, operating rooms, and delivery rooms in the tunnels as well.

Highway and railroad tunnels could serve as a mass three-day shelter. Simply pull in a tractor-trailer-load of porta-potties, a tractor-trailer-load of food, a truckload of water, and install several giant fans operating from generators supplied with a truckload of fuel to circulate air and provide light. Sandbag the ends of the tunnels, leaving air space at the top. Those seeking refuge would be required to bring camping gear such as sleeping bags, cots, air mattresses, and personal hygiene items.

The Swiss have a long highway tunnel that they have outfitted with a blast door, ventilation, emergency power generators, sanitation, stored beds and supplies to accommodate seven thousand people. In fact, the Swiss can shelter its entire population of 7.5 million citizens in blast-hardened, well-stocked shelters on short notice, a remarkable feat for any nation to accomplish.

Fall-out Shelters

Fall-out, air raid, or Civil Defense shelters were built decades ago by most U.S. cities and communities. Bright yellow and black Civil Defense signs indicating a shelter are still visible if one looks for them. Communities built these underground shelters beneath banks, libraries, fire halls, and churches. If you are an American citizen, perhaps you know of one of these relics in your community. As bomb threats diminished years ago the Federal Government cut off funding for the maintenance of these shelters. Many still exist but are sealed off or being used as storage areas. These shelters can be reopened, refurbished, and updated. Dallas,

Texas, was one of those cities who built a model air raid shelter. Reportedly, it is sealed off.

Russia has built underground shelters that can house seventy percent of their civilian population.

Beijing, China, has an immense, eighty-five-square-kilometer underground city, a subterranean complex built as a bomb shelter in the early 1970s during the Sino-Soviet conflict. This complex is now used for shops, theaters, hotels, restaurants, roller skating rinks, markets, etc. With some modifications it could serve as an underground shelter for thousands of people.

Japan has five underground "cities," and all are shopping malls.

Montreal, Canada, has an underground city with thirty kilometers and more of connecting areas, passageways, and hubs beneath the downtown. The underground city has theatres, cinemas, restaurants, shops, museums, and other entertainment venues.

New Delhi, India, has an underground shopping center by the name of Palika Bazaar at the center of Connaught Place.

The Republic of China (Taiwan), Finland, Hong Kong, and Kish, Iran, all have an underground system of connecting tunnels that house a number of retail shops.

Of course, most people are aware of Lebanon's and Israel's underground bomb shelters.

Many U.S. cities have tunnels that connect into a series of underground passageways that link to office towers, hotels, restaurants, retail stores, etc.

We have mentioned only a few of the world's underground cities, tunnels, and connecting passageway systems. With very careful planning, all could be used for mass shelters as long as they are above sea level.

Caves and mine tunnels

Caves and mine tunnels are places of last choice but better than nothing. Earth movement could cause them to collapse, burying their occupants alive. In-ground shelters and safe rooms are best because the walls are reinforced.

Missile silos

A few people have bought missile silos, no longer in use, from the U.S. government and converted them into underground homes. These should work nicely as they are well constructed with reinforced concrete. Provision should be made for emergency lighting and ventilation, with backup generators operating from a stored fuel source.

Bermed underground homes

These are not a good choice because part of the homes are exposed to the outside. However, one could make a safe room in the most protected underground section. Follow plans for making a safe room.

Basement shelters in multi-storied buildings

Do not create safe rooms in basements of multi-storied buildings as there is a danger of building collapse into the basement entrapping you with no hope of rescue.

Government secret bunkers

It is no secret that governments have built secret and often lavish underground bunkers to protect government officials. A few are no longer secret; the one in Greenbrier, West Virginia, is now open as a sort of historic museum for tourists. This bunker has been well maintained. With a few modifications and restocking of food, this underground shelter could house perhaps several hundred souls.

Submarines

This could work, if you stay submerged deep enough and away from tectonic plate edges. You will not have a GPS guidance system, so plan to navigate the old-fashioned way. It is risky to say the least.

Food and Water

A three-day supply of food is the bare-bones minimum. What if you survive the cataclysm only to starve to death afterwards because of food unavailability? For this reason, we recommend having a year's supply and preferably two years' or more of food on hand. Store foods that have long shelf-life such as wheat, dried beans, rice, oat groats, powered milk and eggs, MRE's, and various freeze-dried and dehydrated foods. There are companies who make camping gear, campers' dehydrated meals, and survival foods for food storage. Some of the dehydrated meals even come with their own flameless heat source that would be ideal for the three to thirty days underground. These meals are quite tasty. Take into consideration special diets such as for diabetics, if any family member is a diabetic. Babies will need baby food and formula. Pets will need pet food. Plan your food storage to fit your family's needs.

Unless you have built an underground bunker large enough to store a year's supply of food for each family member, a separate, smaller underground bunker installed next to your main underground shelter for food storage is really the only safe option. Another alternative is to dig a root cellar into a bank. Root cellar building plans are available. Seal the recessed entrance with a heavy metal door.

The following is the recommended one-year, basic long-term food storage plan for one adult, noting that the list is nothing fancy but only survival food to sustain life.

- Grains: 400 pounds per year or about 33 pounds per month (wheat, oat groats, corn, pearl barley)

- Rice: 24 #10 cans per year or 2 #10 cans per month

- Legumes: 60 pounds per year or 5 pounds per month (dried beans, lentils, and split-peas)

- Quick oats: 12 #10 cans per year or 1 #10 can per month

- Macaroni: 12 #10 cans per year or 1 #10 can per month

- Sweeteners: 60 pounds per year or 5 pounds per month

- Non-fat dry milk: 16 pounds per year or 1.5 pounds per month

- Fats: 10 quarts of oil per year or .83 quarts per month

- Salt: 5 pounds per year or ½ pound per month

Children under the age of twelve will require a full adult portion and those over age twelve will require 150% of the recommended adult amount.

After you have stored the above basic recommended foods, then gradually add dehydrated and freeze-dried fruits, vegetables, meats, soups, condiments, butter, cheese, peanut butter, crackers, eggs, freeze-dried dinners, desserts, MRE's, popcorn and pastas. You can even get freeze-dried ice cream. Include books on cooking with stored foods to your emergency essentials food list.

Water

Enough drinking water should be stored in your shelter to last at least three days for each person, and preferably enough water for thirty days. Provision needs to be made for more in case utility district water lines are broken. Farmers who still have the old-fashioned hands pumps on wells are truly fortunate as electric pumps will not work because of no electricity, unless an electric pump is powered by a generator. In the event of no water, drinking water will have to be collected from springs, rivers, lakes, ponds, and rain collectors, then purified before drinking.

A high-performance water filter, such as made by Katadyne, is needed to eliminate bacteria, protozoa, and *giardia lambda*. It will pump one liter of water in thirty-six easy strokes with a single cartridge filtering up to two hundred gallons. It is used by hikers, the military, and the International Red Cross, along with many other relief and government agencies world-wide. The device is strictly for making water safe to drink. The same company makes Micropur brand water purification tablets, which can be used in lieu of a water filter. The tablets make water safe to drink but do not remove impurities such as sediments that make water cloudy. Bathing will be limited to warm weather, the majority of baths to be taken in rivers, creeks, and lakes; alternatively, you may use a camper's five-gallon solar-heated shower. Laundry will have to be done the old-fashioned way of pounding clothes on a river rock or using a laundry washboard and tub, preferably galvanized tubs. Water containers of various sizes are handy to have for water transport and storage.

After Earth's three-day transit is completed, a water source will have to be found to provide addition drinking water and water for cooking, limited cleaning, laundry, and bathing. For this reason, availability to water should be a factor in choosing a shelter site.

Water purification

Water also can be made safe to drink by boiling it for ten minutes or by adding laundry bleach in the amounts listed below and letting it sit for thirty minutes before drinking, or you can add twelve drops of tincture of iodine per gallon of water, mix and let stand for thirty minutes. This, however, will not remove any foreign material or dirt particles. It is recommended after purifying water by one of the above methods to then use a mechanical purifier to filter out these substances, gases, and bad taste.

CLEAR WATER	**BLEACH**	**CLOUDY WATER**
1 quart	2 drops	4 drops
1 gallon	8 drops	16 drops
5 gallons	1/2 tablespoon	1 tablespoon

To preserve water for water storage it is recommended to do the following:

1. Add 1/2 to 1 tablespoon of household bleach, such as Clorox, to each five-gallon bucket (almost all bleaches, no matter what brand, have 5 1/2% Sodium Hypochlorite, which is the purification chemical).

2. Add 1/2 cup of bleach to a fifty-five-gallon barrel. Add 1/3 cup of bleach to a thirty-gallon barrel. (Putting more than the recommended amount will not injure the water.) Water stored in this manner will last for seven years.

For water storage the following containers are recommended:

1) The best containers are five-gallon buckets or larger plastic barrels, (thirty- or fifty-five-gallon sizes) If you use the larger barrels make certain that they carry a DOT (Department of Transport) approval certification. This means that they have met standards for strength and durability.

2) Smaller containers can be:

   a. Clean, empty glass jugs. (May break during earthquakes.)

   b. Empty Clorox bottles. Leave a few drops of Clorox in the bottle.

   c. Clean two-liter soda bottles.

How much water should you store? Allow at least two gallons per day per person for drinking, cooking, and limited hygiene.

Survival Supplies

1. A year's supply of matches stored in waterproof box.

2. Pots, pans, metal mixing bowls, cast-iron skillets and a cast-iron Dutch oven.

3. A large, heavy-duty metal grill to place over a camp fire to support skillets, pots, etc.

4. Sleeping bags for your climate with liners (twin sheets).

5. Additional blankets for extra needed warmth.

6. Folding sleeping cots.

7. Pillows with pillow cases.

8. Folding chairs and a folding table.

9. Kitchen utensils for cooking such as ladles, spoons, spatulas, knives, forks, cutting board, etc. Include measuring spoons and measuring cups.

10. Towels for bathing and cooking.

11. Chemical LED flashlights that use no batteries.

12. Assortment of tools such as hammers, saws, shovel, spade, metal garden rake, hoe, axe, nails, screw drivers, levels, wrenches, etc.

13. Assortment of garden seeds suited for your growing region.

14. A camper's dining kit for each person that includes eating utensils, bowls and drinking mugs or camper's metal dining ware. No glass or plastic.

15. Clothes line rope and clothes pins for hanging clothes to dry.

16. Galvanized laundry tubs (two) with wash board, one for laundry and one for rinsing.

17. A Coleman Black Cat flameless catalytic heater with year's supply of fuel canisters for heating your underground shelter.

18. Two hurricane oil lamps with year's supply of wicks and lamp oil. The Aladdin oil lamps are best because they provide enough bright light for reading. You will need extra globes and wicks. The Petromax lantern burns lamp oil and kerosene; however, it will burn about thirty-two ounces of oil in eight hours. Like the Aladdin lamp, it gives off a white, bright light suitable to read by. Use no candles. Paraffin lamps can be used but you will need a year's supply of them, noting one lamp will burn for one hundred hours. Remember, your bunker will be in pitch-black darkness, so a lamp needs to be burning at all times.

19. Two metal pails and one large metal dish pan.

20. A hand-cranked short-wave solar radio (just in case a radio station or emergency band does survive).

21. A chemical toilet with adequate supply of toilet tissue and chemicals.

22. Several large bottles of hand sanitizer to save water (can't have too much on hand).

23. One camper's shower for outside use later.

24. One broom, dustpan, and mop. If bunker floor is carpeted, a non-electric push vacuum.

25. Katadyne water filter with extra cartridges and supply of water-purifying tablets.

26. A manual can opener.

27. A wood folding rack for drying clothes inside your bunker.

28. A mechanical water filter with at least three spare cartridges.

29. Plenty of plastic garbage bags.

30. An alcohol stove with year's supply of denatured cans of alcohol.

31. Texsport campfire tripod.

32. A fire extinguisher for your shelter.

33. Food storage cookbooks.

Other outdoor options are campers' cooking stoves and Jetboils. Just remember these require fuel canisters, and a year's supply is needed. Gas and charcoal grills are for outdoor use only. They are certainly OK to use, but storing them during the cataclysm can be a problem due to their size. Plus, extra gas cylinders may be difficult to store. Just remember, any device requiring propane fuel canisters to operate are for outdoor use only because of carbon monoxide danger. For limited indoor cooking (heating water for dehydrated meals and hot drinks), use alcohol countertop stoves. A small wood-burning cast-iron heating stove can be installed with a flue in your bunker for long-term use both before and after the cataclysm. Just make sure the stove has adequate ventilation to prevent smoking. Of course, a supply of wood cut in small logs to fit the stove is necessary. Such a stove would also alleviate your cooking problems. It doesn't take much to heat a bunker that has seven feet of dirt over it, because in most climates the underground temperature stays at sixty-five degrees Fahrenheit. In the far northern latitudes, the underground temperature will be a constant forty-five degrees Fahrenheit.

Toilets are a big issue. A chemical toilet will suffice for short-term use in the underground bunker, but for long-term use you have two options: (1) dig an outhouse hole and later, after the cataclysm, build the little outdoor Johnnie over the hole. It is more politically correct to refer to the outdoor Johnnie as a self-composting outdoor toilet. Or, a self-composting toilet can be installed in your bunker. Chemicals keep the odors from forming. (2) install a waterless, chemical-less, no-septic-tank-required toilet such as used in third world countries where there is no electricity and water is unavailable. This type of toilet has to be vented to the outside. An example where they are used are is safari tents for tourists in Africa. Flushing toilets require too much water, plus septic tanks can crack and septic lines can disconnect in earthquakes, creating a septic waste back-up nightmare in your now overflowing toilet.

Survival commodities

Note: Adjust the list to allow for a two-year supply on hand for most items.

1. Laundry soap and liquid dish detergent.
2. Soap for bathing.

3. One camper's mirror for grooming, shaving, etc.

4. Disposable diapers for babies.

5. Hand-cranked grist mill for grinding stored grains.

6. One lever for opening large plastic pails with lids holding stored grains, etc.

7. Feminine hygiene products (tampons, Kotex).

8. Toothbrushes and toothpaste, denture cleaner and adhesive.

9. Deodorant.

10. Disposable razors.

11. Cooking oil or shortening in small containers to prevent them going rancid after opening.

12. Salt, pepper, and food spices, sugar or sugar substitutes.

13. Vitamin C tablets or powder to prevent scurvy. The powdered fruit drink, Tang, will supply vitamin C but is high in sugar.

14. Shampoo and conditioner, baby shampoo, baby powder, baby oil.

15. Q-tips.

16. Small sewing kit with scissors, safety pins, thimbles, etc.

17. Hair-cutting or barber scissors, combs, brushes, and hair twisters.

18. Body lotions.

19. Pet supplies such as dog and cat food, cat litter, brushes, sleeping pads, feeding and water bowls, medications, shampoos, etc.

20. Extra light bulbs should you have an operating generator for electricity.

21. Paper towels.

22. Manicure kits.

Medical commodities

1. Store large bottles of aspirin and Tylenol for a two-year supply.

2. Have a two-year (if possible) supply of any prescription medications you take on hand that are necessary to sustain health (heart medications, blood pressure medications, insulin with syringes and needles, diabetic glucose monitoring supplies, thyroid medications, allergy medications, birth control pills, etc.).

3. Store a basic first aid kit.

4. Have several tubes of neomycin on hand.

5. Have an assortment of band-aids available.

6. Store an oral thermometer.

7. A manual blood pressure cuff, monitor, and stethoscope if you have hypertension. A battery-operated cuff can be used—just remember to have extra batteries. The same for battery-operated glucose monitors.

8. Update all your vaccinations with boosters prior to the cataclysm (diphtheria, tetanus, small pox, measles, chicken pox, mumps, polio, etc.).

9. If you are a wearer of contact lenses, a two-year's supply of cleaning solution and lenses.

10. Four bottles Kaopectate or any anti-diarrhea meds (Imodium).

11. Chap stick.

12. Vitamins.

13. Extra pairs of eyeglasses, reading glasses, contact lenses, and sunglasses.

14. Several jugs of Clorox for disinfecting and water purification (can't have too much on hand).

15. Poison ivy and poison oak medications.

16. Calcium tablets with Vitamin D.

17. Tincture of iodine for water purification (Clorox may be used instead).

18. Store plenty of sunscreen.

19. Hydrocortisone cream.

20. Antihistamine capsules.

21. Other non-prescription drugs you may take on a regular basis, e.g., Advil, Aleve.

22. Instant chemical ice and heat packs.

23. Fish oil capsules.

24. Tend to dental needs about one year prior to December 21, 2012. Nothing worse than a toothache with no hopes of seeing a dentist.

25. One metal leg and one metal arm splint in case of broken bones. You may have to set or splint your own fractures. Include plenty of gauze rolls and ace elastic bandage wraps to secure splints.

26. Skin care products.

27. Scabies and lice lotions.

Those who have serious medical problems need to find hospital shelters as care may be non-existent elsewhere after the cataclysm. If at all possible, avoid becoming pregnant with delivery dates near to December 21, 2012. Better yet, avoid having any babies at all in 2012 as there may not be any health care for infants after the cataclysm. The stress of survival is bad enough without having an infant to care for. Those who have babies under a year old in 2012 will be at risk for high infant mortality rates due to epidemic outbreaks, pneumonia, etc.

Clothing

Clothing should be determined by the climate you live in.

1. Durable pants (jeans): four pair per person.

2. Long-sleeve shirts for winter: four per person.

3. Short-sleeve shirts for summer: four per person.

4. One pair of insulated coveralls per person if you live in cold climates.

5. Shorts for summer: four pair per person.

6. One stadium-length all-weather coat or heavy winter coat per person.

7. One pair waterproof insulated boots for cold climates per person.

8. One pair hiker's-quality shoes either high or low tops with extra shoe laces per person.

9. One pair durable athletic shoes with extra shoelaces per person.

10. Socks: six pair per person.

11. Gloves, scarves, hats, and caps for cold climates and caps, hats, and visors for summer protection.

12. Rain ponchos.

13. Underwear: six pairs each per person.

14. Long-handled underwear if in cold climates.

15. Store clothing and shoes in larger sizes for growing children, or children may have to go barefoot.

16. Hiker's durable sport sandals with lug soles for summer (e.g., Murrell or Attack sandals).

Clothing should be of durable material such as for camping and for rugged outdoor use. No dresses, please. Think in terms of survival clothing suitable for outdoor living. Those who live in cold climates already have clothing on hand fitting for their climate.

Optional miscellaneous items

Pop-up screen canopies can be stored and used later. They are handy for warm-weather outdoor living. The 8x8 and 10x10 are the most popular sizes and usually sell for about $100. Catch one on sale at the end of the season.

Yurts and Yomes are tents assembled on wood platforms. They are designed after the Siberian nomad felt tents. Felt panels can be added to these tents for year-round use. These tents are durable and sturdy, lasting for at least fifteen years. Your climate will determine which model is best suited for your area because whether you get heavy snow or are in a cold, damp, rainy climate are all factors in determining what model is best suited for you. Storing one of these tents and erecting it later could solve your housing problem, especially if used in conjunction with your underground bunker. They come in different sizes, makes, and models. **FEMA tents** as used in Afghanistan could work, although they are not as roomy or nice as a Yurt or Yome.

Bicycles may become the best mode of transportation. Roads may be impassable with vehicles. Consider storing one or two with a hand air pump for inflating tires.

Solar battery charger with assortment of rechargeable batteries. You can charge AAA, AA, C, D, and seven different sizes of specialized NiCad and Ni-MH batteries.

Hand-cranked washing machine (Wonder Clean Washer) is a small, hand-turned washing machine designed for campers. With the addition of hot water and detergent, the device will efficiently clean sheets and small loads of clothing with a few cranks of the handle.

Solar camper's oven (Global Sun Oven) is a directional reflector of solar sun rays. The deluxe model will bake or cook meals at 360–400 degrees Fahrenheit without cooking over a flame. It works outside in full sun.

A compass might come in handy.

Fishing poles with well-stocked tackle box may be useful in areas near rivers, streams, and lakes.

Chain saw will no doubt be useful if you have room to store fuel cans outside of your bunker.

Rifles and ammunition for hunting wild game such as deer, boar, turkeys, quail, pheasants, rabbits, and squirrels, etc. depending on where you live.

Important Documents and items

These items need to be placed in a water-tight storage box and taken inside of your bunker: driver's license, passport, birth certificate, social security number, marriage certificate, citizenship papers, health insurance cards, deeds to your property with any surveys, bank records, tax records, house and vehicle insurance papers, diplomas, and stock holdings.

Family pictures and genealogies need the same type of storage. Save your genealogy on CDs and also make a print-out because it could be a long time before computers are back.

Take good jewelry (diamond rings and necklaces) and other small heirloom pieces (sterling silver place settings and sterling silver serving pieces) into storage.

Take a copy of your sacred records (Bible, Book of Mormon, Qur'an, Torah etc.) into your bunker. Include any favorite books and reading material you might like to save.

Store a battery-operated clock with additional batteries. Take a calendar, writing tablets, pens, pencils, and a non-electric pencil sharpener.

Store "How To" books such as books on how to make soap, how to make lye water, how to grow a garden, how to cook over a camp fire, how to dry foods, how to identify wild plants for eating, etc. The Fox Fire series of books are a good example but there have been many other good books on survival as well.

Consider storing highway maps of your area and perhaps an atlas.

Items of entertainment

Consider taking a deck of playing cards and games played on game boards (checkers, chess, monopoly, and scrabble) into your shelter to prevent boredom.

Walkmans, iPods, and battery-operated CD players may be the only access to recorded music. Players of small musical instruments (flutes, guitars, banjos, violins, harmonicas, etc.) may want to take their instruments into the bunker to entertain themselves and others.

If you have room, consider taking home-schooling material and equipment for children into the bunker. This may be the only way to educate your children for several years, at least in the basics of reading, writing and arithmetic.

Money and assets

In the event of a global cataclysm, it is doubtful if money will be of any value, especially if governments collapse. For that reason, we recommend selling off your assets gradually (stocks, CDs, large houses, boats, planes, etc.) and converting the money into gold. Buy small homes and build an underground shelter in the back yard. Store your gold in the bunker with you. If after the cataclysm, your find your small home has been destroyed, it will not be the financial loss of a larger one. It, however, will be a complete financial loss because insurance companies will be out of business. However, we still recommend saving insurance papers, deeds, bank and tax records, etc. just in case some areas fare better than others. As stated before, we are dealing with the unknown in certain areas.

Farm animals certainly can be saved with effort. It will require the installation of a ventilated metal Quonset hut partially underground and covered with five feet of dirt. Close the structure with a heavy metal door. Stalls can be made for horses and other types of animals. Of course, food and water will have to be stored in the shelter. The animals will be in complete darkness for three days or longer. High winds, raging electrical storms, and torrential rain may make it impossible for them to leave the shelter for thirty days and may make it equally difficult to attend to these animals. At present we do not recommend substituting this type of shelter for an underground shelter however, it is the best that can be done for farm animals.

That concludes our list. Perhaps there are other things we could have added but each family has different circumstances so emergency survival items have to be individualized to fit you and your family's needs. At first glance, the list may seem daunting, but there are many items you already have. Will building shelters be expensive? Yes. That is why we recommend downsizing into smaller, less expensive homes and taking your profit to build an underground shelter in the back yard. Are emergency essentials expensive? Some are. That is why we recommend preparation now in order to take advantage of sales. Furthermore, the task will not be easy because you may be ridiculed for taking seemingly extreme survival measures, just as was done to Noah when he told the people a great cataclysmic flood was going to happen. You cannot wait for the last minute to prepare. If you do, when the word gets out, emergency shelter builders will be swamped with back orders. The sooner you build your underground shelter and begin stocking it, the better. What you take into your underground shelter is all you will have to survive on for at least one year and most likely two years.

Remember there are only five years left. Are your authors going to heed their own advice? You betcha. One of your authors has already moved to a safer area and downsized his home. Although these are events leading to the separation of the two Earths, and most people hope to ascend with the spirit Earth, there will be a need to survive long enough to help as many people as possible understand what is happening. E. J. will stay put, but plans to build an underground shelter on their farm by next year.

Remote viewers have already seen people hiding in underground shelters as did the prophets of old. Revelation speaks of "men hiding in caves" during the End Time commotion on earth, which could be interpreted to mean underground shelters. All young people around twelve to thirteen years old or younger who ask for a reading from remote viewers, in order to find the best occupation suited for them to study in college, receive the same answer from the Akashic Record. "They have no occupation or career." Because so many people are seen hiding in underground shelters by remote viewers, two things have had to transpire: either your authors have sold millions of books and the readers have heeded our advice, or something else has happened that we haven't heretofore discussed and perhaps now should.

History tends to repeat itself. There is a good possibility that first contact will be made somewhere between 2008 and 2010 by alien off-worlders. Their mission will be to try and save the population from the coming cataclysm. These aliens are none other than the Nephilim still working under the direction of Lucifer and his sons. As they did before the 9500 BC cataclysm, so they may again do before the 2012 cataclysm. In ancient times they dug tunnels and caves to hide and save some of the populace as written in "The Brave New World" chapter of volume 1. Why would they do this in today's times? For the same reason they did in ancient times—to save some of the populace, "for what good is a kingdom without subjects?" Lucifer plans to keep this planet. He needs it populated with people to worship and serve him. In the guise of aliens from another world, they might work with governments to build mass underground shelters. New technologies will be introduced to expedite the worldwide building of the underground shelters. What ordinarily would take ten years to accomplish, they will do in two to three years max. At that late date, the world really will have no choice but to accept their help.

After they have helped governments to build underground shelters in safe areas, the off-worlders will likely depart as they have in times past until after the End Time cataclysm. Having previously established a friendly working relationship with earthlings, they will undoubtedly find that those who survive the cataclysm will readily accept their help when they return to restore civilization. Most survivors on earth will view them thereafter as an advanced race who came to protect them and who cared enough to return in order to restore civilization. Some of the survivors may even accept them once more as gods.

The world has been prepared to expect a first contact through the media. Will they come? Well, someone obviously has built lots of underground shelters, seen by remote viewers, in a short amount of time. Do the Nephilim build them, or will our book series go on to become the all-time best sellers of 500 million books, spurring the population to build the shelters? So far, we are the only authors who have correctly identified the nature of the cataclysmic destruction predicted by the Maya to occur on the Tzolk'in End Time date of 2012; therefore it is either them or us. Only time will tell. In the meantime, start survival preparation now rather than waiting till the last minute, because by then, the unprepared will be in a state of mass hysteria, making it difficult to get things accomplished or even to find necessary supplies. The store shelves will be picked clean.

Truly, in this instance, it is the early bird who gets the worm. It is still possible to buy all of these items. When the cataclysm becomes imminent, these items will no longer be available.

The Grand Finale

Volume 3 of the *Ark of Millions of Years* completes the trilogy. There will not be a volume 4 mainly because, having written three books on the subject, we have exhausted our knowledge pertaining to the missing "key" of creation and Precession End Time events set to occur on December 21, 2012.

The purpose of these books is to restore the lost, ancient "key" in order to understand the creation correctly and its ultimate destiny in the End Times. Whenever possible, documentation from reliable sources has been used to support our findings. In many instances our findings left us no other choice than to break away from traditional thought. Correctly understanding the creation from the standpoint of the missing "key" piece of knowledge, which is the Union of the Polarity, changed almost everything we have traditionally accepted as the absolute truth. It was the "key" that unlocked the true meaning of the Mayan Tzolk'in calendar and the "key" to correctly understand the symbolic meaning of the World Trees. It was the "key" to understand much of the symbolism used in Freemasonry and the "key" to understand symbolic meaning in old European cathedrals. The "key" unlocked the symbolic meaning of ancient monuments, the Pyramids and old-style gravestone markers popular in England and Ireland. Each turn of the missing "key" unlocked more and more Precession End Time knowledge pertaining to 2012. The symbolic wonders of Washington, D.C., were laid bare by the ancient "key." But most of all, the "key" unlocked the meaning of prophetic words of Mesoamerican and Old Testament prophets, especially the words of Isaiah. In doing so, the "key" literally fulfilled the prophetic words of Nephi, an ancient Mesoamerican prophet, who declared the words of Isaiah would be understood in the End Times. Because the "key" has unlocked so much knowledge and has opened the eyes of our understanding, even to understanding the words of the prophets in fulfillment of prophecy, we feel the Union of the Polarity did happen. The 2012 Precession End of the Age events can now be understood if correlated to the Book of Revelation.

Your authors have done our best to present and interpret what we have found pertaining to the End Times in regards to the "change or transition" of Earth, commonly called in today's times, the "rapture." Did we get everything one hundred percent correct? Probably not, but it is close. Because our books are about the creation and not about religion, it was never our intent to preach religious doctrine. However, much of what we document is taken from sacred and religious writings because the answers are found there. The Union of the Polarity "key" piece of knowledge changed almost everything pertaining to Earth's early history and our understanding of its destiny. We think that we have proved the doctrine for a pre-millennial "rapture" in this book. Furthermore, we prove the knowledge of a resurrection and "rapture" was known and taught from the very beginning of historical time, 3000 BC, in ancient Sumeria. And, even the dates for these upcoming events were known in ancient times. Christianity in Mesoamerica existed prior to the arrival of the Spanish conquerors, and Pakal was indeed a giant king and we have found evidence of the knowledge of the Union of the Polarity as late as the eighteenth century AD.

Having said all of the above, we are now asking for church leaders and religious theologians to read and examine our books. Because of the doctrinal differences of the many Christian denominations, complete agreement may not be possible but it may be possible to find some common ground to at least warn their congregations to "prepare" for 2012, both spiritually and temporally.

Some of our writings may seem contrary to traditional Christian belief, but the knowledge of the restored "key" we call the Union of the Polarity has dramatically changed our traditional views. This becomes more evident in our views toward the millennial Golden Age for both earths. Prior to the knowledge of the Union of the Polarity, we traditionally thought of only one earth being "renewed"; now we have two. We want to emphasize that even though the spirit Earth has been "changed," "transitioned," or "raptured" into a spiritual fourth dimension, it is not heaven as we traditionally think of heaven. Rather, it is an intermediate, terrestrial spiritual place preparatory for its "raptured" and resurrected righteous souls to receive further light and knowledge pertaining to their eternal salvation. A thousand years could easily pass before the expected arrival of Christ occurs to begin his thousand-year millennial reign on the spirit Earth.

After all issues have been settled and after the one-thousand-year millennial reign of Christ is completed, a final formal judgment will take place that will involve every living soul. This judgment follows several, earlier, partial judgments. All souls shall stand before God, the books will be opened, and the dead will be judged out of those things written in the books, according to their works (Revelations 20:11–15).

Some Christians believe those righteous living souls who came through tribulation on the temporal Earth will join those on the spirit Earth for an undetermined length of time, to give them time to receive their ordinances necessary for eternal progression before the last great, final judgment takes place sometime after the millennial reign.

Those who abide the celestial law will inherit a celestial glory (the third heaven). Those who abide a terrestrial law will inherit a terrestrial glory (the second heaven), and those who cannot abide by either a celestial or terrestrial law will inherit a telestial glory (the first heaven). Each will receive the glory where they are the happiest for eternity.

Only those who follow and live the celestial law will be permitted to remain on the spirit Earth to be "transitioned" or "rolled back" into the highest spiritual heaven, the universe where God resides. Soon after arrival into the highest spiritual heaven, in a twinkling of an eye, the spirit Earth will undergo yet another change into a celestial earth paradise, the place we traditionally think of as heaven. But also remember, in essence the spirit Earth is our future heaven, and it is on the temporal Earth today as heaven and Earth united. When we speak of Mother Earth we are referring to the spirit Earth. That is why the ancients always held Mother Earth as a sacred world.

On the temporal Earth, during the millennial reign of Christ on the spirit Earth, the remnant of Israel will remain to repopulate the earth for one thousand years. During this thousand-year period, the temporal Earth will experience a Golden Age of peace and righteousness. Following this period of one thousand years, Satan is loosed for a "little season," presumed to be another one thousand years of time, to try the Golden Age's later generations. Again Satan will stir up and deceive the nations of the temporal Earth to rise up against Israel and Jerusalem.

Once more, war will cover the land, climaxing in the post-millennial Gog and Magog invasion. Satan and his armies are finally defeated when fire descends out of heaven and devours them. The last to be resurrected and judged are the wicked and non-believers, but the final day of formal judgment follows sometime later. When the spirit Earth receives its celestial glory, the temporal Earth, in its telestial state, will be consumed and destroyed by fire; the planet dies. Some believe that the temporal Earth will also be resurrected, translated, and reunited with its spiritual counterpart in the celestial kingdom. Perhaps this brief review of the millennial events will clarify some points we failed to make in the "End Times" chapter in volume 2.

The above review is in accordance with the **original** beliefs of both Old Testament Jews and New Testament Gospel writers. In order to understand the Biblical scriptures, it is necessary to understand the early Jewish and gospel writers' beliefs from their standpoint in order to get the correct meaning and intent thereof. Many Gentile churches have failed to do this. Whenever you have seeming contradiction in Biblical scripture, it is usually the result of one or more of the following three; a mistranslation, missing scripture or misunderstanding of intent.

This certainly seems to be the case in our understanding of heaven because we have failed to understand the Jewish Biblical concept of heaven. To the Biblical Jews the Kingdom of Heaven, the Kingdom of God, or heaven is the upper Earth or spirit Earth (vol. 1, 234). According to their belief as expressed in the Zohar, the upper or spirit Earth was first created in the third or highest heaven, the place where God dwells, fell as the result of Adam's transgression to this lower physical universe to unite with the temporal Earth, and will eventually return to its birthplace to become the Kingdom of Heaven or **Kingdom of God** for those worthy of a celestial inheritance. There it will join other celestial worlds and become one of the many footstools of the Lord. The apostle Paul speaks of the third heaven in 2 Corinthians 12:2. Where there is a third heaven, there is also a second and first heaven. A brief review of the chapter

"The Heavens" in volume 1 gives an account and description of these three heavens called kingdoms of glory. Now we can fully understand the following Biblical scripture:

> *"Except a man be born of water and of the Spirit, he cannot enter into the **kingdom of God**"* (John 3:5). [Bold type added for emphasis.]

Thus, water baptism is necessary for entrance into the Kingdom of Heaven or Kingdom of God to be located on the upper or spirit Earth when it eventually returns or "rolls back" into the third heaven to receive its celestial glory after the millennial reign of Christ.

The Apostle Paul taught that immortality is a free gift of God and comes without works or righteousness of any sort; all men will come forth in the resurrection because of the atoning sacrifice of Christ, as found in the following scriptures:

> *"For by grace are ye saved through faith; and that not of yourselves: it is the gift of God: Not of works, lest any man should boast"* (Ephesians 2:8–9).

> *"For as in Adam all die, even so in Christ shall all be made alive"* (1 Corinthians 15:22).

In this light, the resurrection is a form of general salvation meaning that believers are thereby saved from death, hell, the devil, and endless torment. It is salvation by grace and faith alone. But, salvation in the celestial Kingdom of God, however, is not salvation by grace and faith alone. Rather, it is salvation by grace and faith in addition to living in complete obedience to the *celestial laws.*

Briefly those laws are faith in Jesus Christ, repentance, baptism, receiving the sanctifying gift of the Holy Ghost by the laying on of hands and enduring in righteousness to the end of mortal life. Failure to live the celestial law will result in living in a lower kingdom of glory, namely the second or first heaven.

Biblical scripture is missing concerning the second and first kingdoms of glory but through modern-day revelation revealed in the Doctrine and Covenants, we can learn of these lower kingdoms of glory ("The Heavens" in vol. 1, 36). The laws one accepts or abides determines the type of body one receives to live in on one of the three kingdoms of glory. Different bodies probably have different vibrational levels to endure each type of spiritual existence at the various levels of the kingdoms of glory. In the following verse Paul, with his vision of the kingdoms of glory revealed to him by the Lord, teaches in his First Epistle to the Corinthians that the different kingdoms of glory are not just a comparison of the sun, moon and stars with earthly bodies, but also a reference to the fact that there are three different major levels of glory to which a body can be resurrected:

> *"There are also celestial bodies and bodies terrestrial: but the glory of the celestial is one, and the glory of the terrestrial is another. There is one glory of the sun, and another glory of the moon, and another glory of the stars: for one star differeth from another star in glory. So also is the resurrection of the dead."* (1 Corinthians 39–42)

Origen (ca. AD 185–254) was an early Christian scholar and theologian and one of the most distinguished of the early fathers of the Christian Church. He revealed that the early Church interpreted this passage in essentially the same way:

> *"Our understanding of the passage indeed is, that of the apostle, wishing to describe the great difference among those who rise again in glory, i.e., of the saints, borrowed a comparison from the heavenly bodies, saying, 'One is the glory of the sun, another the glory of the moon, another the glory of the stars.'"* (Origen, De Principis 2:10:2, in Ante-Nicene Fathers 4:294)

Many believers receive the type of bodies for entry into one of the three kingdoms of glory at the resurrection as was determined by the type of life they lived while in mortality. This principle is taught in the General Epistle of James in the following scripture:

> *"Yea, a man may say, Thou hast faith, and I have works: shew me thy faith without thy works, and **I will shew thee my faith by my works**. Even so faith, if it hath not works, is dead, being alone."* (James 2:17–18) [Bold type added for emphasis.]

Simply stated, this scripture says how you live your life in mortality determines where you will spend eternity. **Your faith is demonstrated by how you live.** We will be resurrected to the degree of glory consistent with our faithfulness (1 Corinthians 15:40–44).

Others will receive their body types later during the millennium as spiritual progression continues there too.

All men are saved by the grace of God through the atoning sacrifice of Christ. The free gift of eternal life is given to all, both good and evil and both believers and nonbelievers of Christ. It is because of the light of Christ that righteousness prevails in that all men know good from evil and enjoy the guidance of what is called conscience. Choosing good over evil or doing that which is right is righteousness. These are they who possess the attributes of wisdom, truth, charity, and love for their fellow men. Charity is best defined as the pure love of Christ. Good, righteous men, if through no fault of their own they never hear of the gospel or deny Christ while in mortality at the time of the "rapture," will have the opportunity to learn of the gospel in the millennium because they were living in obedience to the *terrestrial law*. Remember, the righteous souls living on earth that are "raptured" or translated have not tasted of death but are preserved in this state until after they have the opportunity to hear the gospel and be resurrected in their perfected bodies at a later time according to the law they are obedient to. The light of Christ leads to salvation, if not in mortality then later. The Mesoamerican prophet Alma taught the principles of righteousness in the following verses:

> *"Therefore, my son, see that you are merciful unto your brethren; deal justly, judge righteously, and do good continually; and if you do all these things then shall ye receive your reward; yea, ye shall have mercy restored unto you again; ye shall have justice restored unto you again; ye shall have a righteous judgment restored unto you again; and ye shall have good rewarded unto you again. For that that ye do send out shall return unto you again and be restored;...."* (Book of Mormon Alma 41: 14–15)

The same message is found in Paul's Epistle to the Galatians as follows:

> *"Be not deceived; God is not mocked: for whatsoever a man soweth, that shall he also reap. For he that soweth to his flesh shall of the flesh reap corruption; but he that soweth to the Spirit shall of the Spirit reap life everlasting. And let us not be weary in well doing: for in due season we shall reap, if we faint not. As we have therefore opportunity, let us do good unto all men, especially unto them who are of the household of faith."* (Galatians 6:7–10)

Before we continue, a brief review of the laws of the kingdoms of glory, as understood by the biblical Jews and gospel writers of the New Testament, will be helpful as follows:

Celestial Law is that law by obedience to which men gain an inheritance in the kingdom of God in eternity. It is the law of the gospel, the law of Christ, and it qualifies men for admission to the celestial kingdom because in and through it men are "sanctified by the reception of the Holy Ghost," thus becoming clean, pure, and spotless. In essence, by sanctification, you are privileged to "walk with God." The law requires faith in Jesus Christ, repentance, baptism, receiving the gift of the Holy Ghost by the laying on of hands and enduring in righteousness to the end of mortal life. Those who live this law will inherit the Celestial Kingdom of glory or Kingdom of Heaven in the third heaven, which is compared to the sun in the firmament. Even this kingdom is divided into three further levels of glory.

Terrestrial Law consists in living an upright, honorable life, but one that does not conform to the standards whereby by human souls are sanctified by the Holy Ghost; rather they "walk in the Spirit of God or light of Christ." The second comforter, the Holy Spirit of Promise, can lead those living the terrestrial law to accept and live the celestial law. According to Joel's promise, this light of Christ is the Spirit that is being poured out upon all flesh in the last days (Joel 2:28–29). Those who live this law will inherit the Terrestrial Kingdom of glory, which is compared to the moon.

Telestial Law is the law of the world. People who are obedient to this law are those who refuse to worship the true and living God, who are unclean and immoral, who are proud and rebellious, who walk in paths of wickedness, who are carnal and sensual, who do not maintain standards of decency, uprightness, and integrity. Liars, adulterers, sexual perverts, homosexuals, murderers, rich who will not help the poor, and those who cannot cease from sin are included in this list. Those who live this law will inherit the Telestial Kingdom of glory, which is compared to the stars in the firmament of heaven. Even this kingdom is apparently divided into different levels of glory defined "as one star differs from another star in glory, even so differs one from another in glory in the telestial world" (1 Corinthians 15:41), meaning that all who inherit the telestial kingdom will not receive the same glory.

Clement of Alexandria (ca AD 150–211/216) was one of Alexandria's most distinguished church teachers. Down to the seventeenth century he was venerated as a saint. He also expressed belief in the three degrees as follows:

> *"Conformably, therefore, there are various abodes, according to the worth of those who have believed....These chosen abodes, that are three, are indicated by the numbers in the Gospel—the thirty, the sixty, the hundred. And the perfect inheritance belongs to those who attain to 'a perfect man,' according to the image of the Lord.....To the likeness of God, then, he that is introduced into adoption and the friendship of God, to the just inheritance of the lords and gods is brought; if he be perfected, according to the Gospel, as the Lord Himself taught."* (Clement of Alexandria, Stromata 6:14, in Ante-Nicene Fathers 2:506)

Clement also preached that the three gradations of glory are procured by virtue of three types of actions:

> *[Clement of Alexandria] reckons three kinds of actions, the first of that is....right or perfect action, that is characteristic of the perfect man and Gnostic alone, and raises him to the height of glory. The second is the class of....medium, or intermediate actions, that are done by less perfect believers, and procure a lower grade of glory. In the third place he reckons sinful actions, that are done by those who fall away from salvation.* (Ante-Nicene Fathers 2:506)

This doctrine goes back much further than Origen; however Irenaeus preserved the same tradition. Irenaeus (b. second century d. end of second/beginning of third century) was bishop of Lugdunum in Gaul, which is now Lyon, France. His writings were formative in the early development of Christian theology, and he is recognized as a saint by both the Eastern Orthodox Church and the Catholic Church; both consider him a Father of the Church. He was also a disciple of Polycarp, who was said to be a disciple of John the Evangelist. Unlike many of his contemporary Christians, he was raised in a Christian family rather than converting as an adult.

Irenaeus was the first Christian to list all four of the now-canonical Gospels as divinely inspired and was the first to assert that the Gospel of John was written by John the Apostle and that the Gospel of Luke was written by Luke, the companion of Paul. (The Gospels themselves are anonymous.) This tradition Irenaeus preserved supposedly came from the elders who knew the Apostles. He writes:

> *"And as the presbyters say, Then those who are deemed worthy of an abode in heaven shall go there, others shall enjoy the delights of paradise, and others shall possess the splendour of the city; for everywhere the Saviour shall be seen according as they who see Him shall be worthy. [They say, moreover], that there is this distinction between the habitation of those who produce an hundred-fold, and that of those who produce sixty-fold, and that of those who produce thirty-fold; for the first will be taken up into the heavens, the second will dwell in paradise, the last will inhabit the city; and that was on this account the Lord declared, 'In My Father's house are many mansions.' For all things belong to God, who supplies all with a suitable dwelling-place; even as His Word says, that a share is allotted to all by the Father, according as each person is or shall be worthy. And this is the couch on that the guests shall recline, having been invited to the wedding. The presbyters, the disciples of the apostles, affirm that this is the gradation and arrangement of those who are saved, and that they advance through steps of this nature; also that they ascend through the Spirit to the Son, and through the Son to the Father, and that in due time the Son will yield up His work to the Father, even as it is*

> *said by the apostle, 'For He must reign till He hath put all enemies under His feet. The last enemy that shall be destroyed is death.'"* (Irenaeus, Against Heresies 5:36:1–2, in Ante-Nicene Fathers 1:567)

The apostle Paul's Epistles are for the most part letters written to churches that he had founded or visited. These churches had many new Jewish and Gentile converts who had questions concerning his doctrines on the resurrection, kingdoms of glory, and baptism for their dead who had died without knowledge of the gospel. His letters, or epistles, in response to the various churches are full of expositions of what Christians should believe and how they should live. He brought the gospel of Jesus Christ first to the Jews and then to the Gentiles.

The First Epistle of Peter teaches that Christ went and preached the gospel to the dead spirits in prison that sometime were disobedient in the days of Noah (1 Peter 3:18–20). This scripture was in response to Peter's question as to why was the gospel being preached to those who are dead. (1 Peter 4:6). The fact that Christ went and preached to these disembodied spirits indicates that they must have the ability to hear and understand. A few verses later in the same epistle, the apostle Peter refers back to this very event:

> *"For for this cause was the gospel preached also to them that are dead, that they might be judged according to men in the flesh, but live according to God in the spirit."* (1 Peter 4:6)

In more simple terms, the gospel is preached to the dead so that they can be judged by the same standard that will be used to judge those who hear the gospel in mortality.

While deceased souls are being taught the gospel in the spirit world, they have need of baptism if they accept the gospel. Not having a physical body results in a dilemma of how to accomplish baptism. How else but by proxy baptism performed by the living in their behalf? This same question was delivered by Paul to the early converts:

> *"Else what shall they do that are baptized for the dead, if the dead rise not at all? Why are they then baptized for the dead?"* (1 Corinthians 15:29)

Paul further asserts in reference to the dead: *"They without us cannot be made perfect..."* (Hebrews 11:40). We can conclude baptism for the dead is necessary in order for them to be perfected.

Paul cited this practice to support his argument for the resurrection; noting there was no disagreement, it seems clear that he as well as the Corinthians must have viewed baptism for the dead as a valid ordinance. The *scripture* suggests that ancient Christians were evidently already practicing baptism for the dead.

The early Christian writer Hermas definitely provides evidence that baptism for the dead was a Biblical and Christian concept. His writings were even revered as scripture by some early Christians, though they are not part of the modern canon. In the apocryphal Third Book of Hermas, Similitude 9, verses 150–160, Herme's angel messenger is explaining that the pre-Christian dead—"who had fallen asleep"—were also baptized. This is followed by the explanation that the New Testament priesthood bearers had been baptized again (acting as proxies) to make this possible. The plainest point he makes is that after death the "Apostles and teachers" continued their missionary labors in the spirit world, adding the dimension that preaching to the dead continued after Christ. Another point Hermes makes is that he defines the Seal of the Son of God as baptism by water. Concerning the dead, Hermes states the following in verse 159:

> *"They died in righteousness and great purity, and this seal was the only thing they lacked."*

Epiphanius (ca. AD 310/320–403) was a Jewish church father who was a strong defender of orthodoxy, known for tracking down deviant teachings during the troubled era in the Christian church following the Council of Nicea. At the beginning of the fifth century he reports:

> *"From Asia and Gaul has reached us the account (tradition) of a certain practice, namely that when any die without baptism among them, they baptize others in their place and in their name, so that, rising in the resurrection, they will not have to pay the penalty of having failed to receive baptism, but rather will become subject to the authority of the Creator of the World. For this reason this tradition that has reached us is said to be the very thing to that the Apostle himself refers when he says, 'If the dead rise not at all, what shall they do who are baptized for the dead.'"*

A scriptural example of a possible Old Testament foreshadowing of baptism for the dead is found in the prophetic statement by Zechariah:

> *"By the blood of thy covenant I have sent forth prisoners out of the pit wherein there is no water."* (Zechariah 9:11)

Obviously, the pit is the spirit world but what waters are necessary to free one of captivity? Why, the waters of proxy baptism—how else?—a doctrine taught by Paul.

In the Sayings of Jesus, Christ further indicates the dead will receive salvation in the spirit world sufficient for entry into heaven as follows:

> (as resurrected beings) *"Even as my Father raised me from the dead, so you too, will rise again and be received into the highest heaven."*

One of the requirements for entry into the highest heaven, the Kingdom of God, was baptism. Those who have not had a fair chance to hear and accept the gospel in mortality will have their **first chance** to hear of it in the spirit world. This is because God is a just, fair and loving God. He is not a respecter of differences in people but rather loves all his children equally; therefore, he must give equal opportunity to all to hear the gospel of his son. Those who hear and reject the gospel while in mortality do not get a second opportunity to accept the gospel plan of salvation in the spirit world.

Paul also cites the antiquity of baptism within Judaism as related in his words found in 1 Corinthians 10:1–4, where in addressing his "brethren," Paul refers to the passing of *"our ancestors through the sea, and all were baptized in Moses."* He also mentions that the "supernatural rock" that followed the ancestors (out of Egypt) was Christ.

The Gnostic churches of the Sabaean Mandaeans of Iraq and the Christian churches of the Coptics of Egypt have practiced the doctrine of baptism for the dead for centuries and continue to do so today.

Many cultures have practiced rites similar to Christian baptism including the ancient Egyptian, the Hebraic/Jewish, the Babylonians, the Mayan, and the Norse cultures.

The Old Testament Jews practiced total immersion in water for purification under Mosaic Law. The laws of impurity required cleansing oneself in Living Waters from springs, cisterns, rivers and oceans. These are waters charged with the Life Force or spirit of God. It had to be total body immersion in not less than eighty gallons of water. Mosaic Law was strict, demanding ritual purity regularly after various events, according to regulations laid down in the Torah and always performed before offering a sacrifice. They called this ritual "baptism" a bath (Mikvah), or washing for uncleanliness and for removal of sin. Under Mosaic Law this type of Mikvah was not permanent and had to be repeated often. Jews today still perform ritual cleansings in the Mikvah. It looks exactly like a baptismal fount. An observer watches to see if total body immersion is accomplished; even hair cannot be braided. Under Mosaic Law this type of "baptism" bath was acceptable unto God for purification and removal of sin.

In Mesoamerica, Christian converts were baptized by water as attested to in the ancient Toltec record known in today's time as the Book of Mormon. Catholic priests also confirmed that the indigenous people practiced baptism before the arrival of the Spanish and that their rites of baptism followed Christian rites of baptism in the same manner.

Baptism by water to remove sins is an ancient Egyptian motif where Osiris takes upon himself "all that is hateful" in the dead. That is, he adopts the burden of his sins, and the dead receiving baptism are purified by the typical sprinkling of water. Therefore, baptism for the dead was practiced in ancient times before New Testament times.

Figure 121 – (left) Egyptian baptism was done by sprinkling with water long before Christian times. Thoth, son of Marduk, and Horus are administering this ordinance of cleansing of sins. (vignette from Champollion's Monuments of Egypt and Nubia, vol. 1, p. xiii) (right) The baptism of Horus carved on wall at Philae, Egypt.

Rev. J. P. Lundy, author of *Monumental Christianity*, made ancient religions a special study. He writes:

> *"Baptism for the remission of sins goes back 2400 or so years before the Christian era to Sumerian times. Such baptism doubtlessly existed in the neighboring Canaanite culture as well; it certainly was practiced in Palestine prior to Christ's advent"*

> *"The sacred annual bathing of Palestine pilgrims in the River Jordan is the same now as it was in John the Baptist's time; and precisely the same as it is and always has been in the sacred rivers of Hindustan. It is a custom far older than Christianity, and universally prevalent. John the Baptist simply adopted and practiced the universal custom of sacred bathing for the remission of sin. Christ sanctioned it, the church inherited it from his example."*

Lundy's research and our research arrived, independently of each other, to the same conclusion; a conclusion we have several times previously written to the effect that…**it all started in ancient**

Sumeria when the pre-mortal Christ and his twelve Shining Ones (pre-mortal apostles?) made their first appearance in ancient Sumeria (ca. 3000 BC). They came to counter the Nephilim and Lucifer's teachings with the true message and gospel of Christ. Our statement is supported in the Sumerian Tablets of Maklu that reveal Enki (Lucifer) was importing water to his city of Eridu from the Nile (Living Water) for use as a spiritual cleansing agent, as in baptism. It appears Enki was teaching his own brand of salvation that needed to be countered with the true plan of salvation that was delivered by the pre-mortal Christ and his twelve Shining Ones.

In the Sumerian texts, Enki (Lucifer) portrays himself as the "good guy." It was at his urging that Adam and Eve eat of the fruit of the Tree of Knowledge of good and evil. It was his half-brother Enlil who drove them out of the Garden of Eden. Enki saved a few good men from the flood sent by Enlil, who hated humans. It was Enki who took credit for the creation of this world and the universe. He took credit for the creation of men on this planet and claimed to be able to raise the dead. He was everything Enlil was not. Just remember that both Enki and Enlil were fallen sons of God, the Nephilim who were the source of the Sumerian text stories. Mortal men of Sumeria recorded the stories as told to them by the Nephilim in what is now called the Sumerian Texts. These stories are what the Nephilim would have mortal men to believe concerning the creation and their creation as well. They, therefore, in our opinion, are not reliable texts.

Ancient Sumeria was a mixture of some of the descendants of Noah who didn't scatter, various ethnic tribes who moved into the area, Babylonians, the Nephilim gods and of course Enki. Common men were probably illiterate; language certainly was a barrier. In order to deliver the gospel message these obstacles had to be overcome. This was accomplished by the brilliant use of the universal language of **pictorial symbolism. The evidence is found in the pictorial symbolic teachings of the World Tree.**

World Tree symbolism first appeared in ancient Sumeria (ca. 3000 BC). The first World Tree was probably a simple, unadorned cross. Through use of the cross symbol, the pre-mortal Christ taught of his coming atoning sacrifice and crucifixion by being nailed to a tree cross. Christ also used the Milky Way World Tree or Axis Mundi to teach of the kingdoms of glory that exist above the earth. The topmost branches of the cosmic World Tree represented the *celestial* kingdom, the trunk would represent the middle or *terrestrial* kingdom, and the roots reaching down into the watery abyss represented the lowest or *telestial* kingdom. All true World Trees have three divisions incorporated into them, and they are considered sacred because the pre-mortal Christ used them to teach his gospel, called the plan of salvation.

Baptism was taught as a necessary part of the plan of salvation; note that baptismal rites first appear in ancient Sumeria. Like the New Testament apostles, the converts wanted to know when he would return for their resurrection, and he told them he would return for *"the harvest at the End of the Age."* The horizontal bar of the cross represents the serpent bar or the ecliptic path of the Sun. Christ used the cosmic Milky Way World Tree to teach the End of the Age by use of the horizontal or serpent bar. When the Sun's path crossed or conjoined the galactic equator in the center of the Milky Way World Tree, the sign of the Suntelia Aeon would appear (sun rising out of the mouth of the Ouroborus), denoting the End of the Age. The Maya were able to incorporate all of Christ's teachings on their stylized cosmic World Tree crosses. We believe the Sumerians did too. As a book can have several pages, so could there be several different types of World Tree symbols to teach the gospel message. For example some World Trees only have people eating or picking of the fruit of the tree (this one is easy to read). They are eating or partaking of the fruit of gospel knowledge. Most of the cosmic Milky Way World Trees are guarded by Kerubims (see Stele 5, first chapter). They are guardians of the gate into heaven, the "dark rift" Ouroborus portal, which is scheduled to be opened at the End of the Age in 2012. They also guard the portals from one dimension into another. Other cosmic Milky Way World Trees have a serpent guarding the tree. The serpent (Lucifer) makes the path of ascent through the upper kingdoms of glory difficult by sending many trials, temptations and tribulations. Those who embrace the gospel fully, by obedience to the celestial law, will inherit the highest kingdom of glory (the Holy Grail) and receive a Crown of Righteousness.

John Duncan understood the teachings of the World Tree as shown in his 1911 work titled *The Riders of the Sidhe*. In the painting, Celtic fairies celebrate the Feast of Belenus, the Celtic symbol for Christ carrying the World Tree. The serpent on top of Christ's head identifies him as a creator god. Riding beside Christ is a fairy that has achieved spiritual perfection by living in obedience to the celestial law and has inherited the Holy Grail or highest kingdom of glory where she has received a Crown of Righteousness that glows like a halo. Note the World Tree shown in the hand of Christ has three divisions and even has a serpent bar on the top level with the bird of paradise (a representation of God) directly above the curled up end of the serpent bar. Through use of pictorial symbolism, this painting teaches the three degrees of glory and the End of the Age time of the "rapture" called the "*harvest*." It shows that Christ is the messenger teaching by use of the symbolic cosmic World Tree, and it teaches those who accept his gospel and achieve spiritual perfection by obedience to the celestial law will inherit the highest kingdom of glory represented in the painting as the *Holy Grail* and will receive a Crown of Righteousness. It appears that John Duncan was an Irishman who knew the Celtic legends of Christ (Belenus, the name he was known to the Irish) teaching his gospel through World Tree symbolism to the Celts.

Figure 122 – Jesus with the fairy. *The Riders of the Sidhe*

It also appears the entire gospel of Christ was taught in ancient times through use of the World Trees by pictorial symbolism. Like the transparent skin and rings of an onion, the esoteric meaning is multi-layered. The more you peel, the more you find. In the first chapter of this book we showed how World Trees were used to teach of Precession and the End of the Age resurrection, but like the rings of an onion the esoteric symbolism was much deeper than we had ever previously imagined because World Trees were also used by Christ to teach his gospel.

Enki (Lucifer), not to be outdone by the teachings of Christ, immediately countered the teachings of Christ by designing his version of the World Tree. Like the cosmic Milky Way World Tree, his World Tree also stood at the center of the universe near his ancient city of Eridu, so named for him, located at the mouth of the river Euphrates. Its white crystal roots penetrate the primordial waters of the abyss, which was guarded by the Nephilim Kerubim. The god of wisdom, Ea, was the source of the waters of life that made the plains fertile. Ea was the Babylonian name of Enki. Enki was his Sumerian name. Therefore Enki was also the source of the Living Water of the Euphrates much like the God of Christianity is the source of the Living Waters that flow from beneath his throne. Here we see Lucifer imitating or counterfeiting God.

The foliage of the sacred tree was the seat of Zikum, the goddess of the heavens, while its stem was the holy abode of the Earth goddess Damkina (wife of Enki) and her son Dumuzi (Sumerian name). His Babylonian name was Marduk. Enki's version of the World Tree is one without the three divisions as pictured on page 226 in volume 2 and on page 366, Figure 149, in this book. All World Trees used by Christ had three divisions. If our interpretation of Enki's World Tree is correct, then the picture on page 226 of volume 2 and on page 363, Figure 149 in this book is evidence of two different religious followings in Assyeria associated with World Trees; followers of Christ and followers of Enki. Including both religious viewpoints certainly is a very clever ploy used by rulers to keep their popularity and maintain religious peace among their subjects. We see the same evidence in Sumeria where Ziggurat temples were built in honor of Enki, other Sumerian Nephilim gods, and in honor of the true God, which shows there were different religious followings in the region. Just remember Enki's World Tree lacked the three divisions and the true World Tree, used by the pre-mortal Christ to teach his gospel, always had the three divisions.

Figure 123 - **Kerubim Watchers guarding a Sumerian World Tree with three divisions. This appears to be the first representation of the pre-mortal Christ's World Tree.**

Figure 124 - Close-up of Sumerian World Tree showing the three divisions used by the pre-mortal Christ to teach his gospel to the Sumerians.

According to many legends, oral traditions and scripture (Book of Mormon 1 Nephi 1:8–11), the pre-mortal Christ and his twelve Shining Ones left Sumeria and traveled to Tibet for an undisclosed amount of time, then afterwards traveled over parts of Asia and the Middle East and later came to South America, Mesoamerica, the Pacific islands, and lastly North America. In each of these places he taught his gospel using the same World Tree symbolism as was taught in Sumeria. The pre-mortal Christ apparently was like a translated being (for lack of a better word) as he was not mortal and had not experienced a mortal birth but came down to Sumeria directly from heaven with his Shining Ones. He came three thousand years before his advent into mortality and traveled the world with his Shining Ones, teaching his gospel, until his birth into mortality. Wherever he went, he lived with the people and taught them many other things pertaining to improvement of their living situations, such as agriculture, astronomy, medicine, etc. When asked who he was, the pre-mortal Christ answered, "you may call me by the name of your choosing." Therefore, he was known by many names throughout the world. For some unknown reason, researchers of ancient religions have been blind to this fact.

J. P. Lundy wrote:

"Present day Christians are under the erroneous and grave belief of that the tenets and beliefs of their religion are unique. In reality, nothing could be further from the truth. What is unknown to the believers today is that the world has known countless other crucified saviors who were: Born from a virgin mother in a cave or underground chamber on or near Christmas Day—each led a life of sacrifice for mankind, were called by the names of Light-bringer, Healer, Mediator, Savior and Deliverer. They were vanquished by the powers of darkness, descended into hell or the underworld, each rose again from the dead and became the means for mankind to enter the heavenly world. They founded communities of saints and churches into which disciples were received by baptism—and they were commemorated by Eucharistic meals. Thus, every element of

modern-day Christianity was present in the pagan world prior to the advent of Jesus."

Buddhism and Christianity share many similarities, enough to mystify religious researchers. Most of these researchers now believe that Buddhism influenced the early development of Christianity, but your authors believe that it is the reverse. The roots of Buddhism and many other Eastern religions are deeply embedded in Christianity. These truths were taught by the pre-mortal Christ and his Shining Ones. There is also strong evidence that Jesus traveled to the East to learn and teach these principles between the ages of twenty-two and twenty-nine years of age. His gospel was taught by pictorial symbolism and never written. In time, many of his teachings were adopted into their religious ideology, thus the similarities. Egypt did the same thing.

It is possible that Buddha was taught by the pre-mortal Christ. According to the teachings of Buddhism, the first Buddha, Siddhartha Gautama, received "enlightenment" by sitting under the sacred Bodhi Tree 2,500 years ago. As founder of Buddhism, he is considered the Supreme Buddha. Maybe the sacred Bodhi Tree was the World Tree of Christ as it was also considered sacred. Christ could have used the Bodhi tree as the working substitution for the World Tree as it too was considered sacred, was a tree that Buddha was familiar with, and was one he could associate to the symbolism being taught. The evidence is again found in the **World Tree**. In chapter one of this book is a picture of a Stupa in Tibet. The World Tree knowledge is built into its design, even to the 2012 End Time date and the opening of the Ouroborus. From whence cometh this knowledge? The evidence points conclusively to the pre-mortal Christ and his pictorial symbolic World Tree.

The Supreme Buddha was not Christ but the first Buddha taught many of Christ's sayings and accepted many of his teachings as evidenced in the Stupa construction. Another point: in Buddhism, anyone who is an "enlightened one" is considered a Buddha. In this context, the pre-mortal Christ was considered a Buddha and would be addressed as Lord Christ Buddha. Both Buddhism and Christianity proclaim man's responsibility for his actions and the freedom of moral choice; both teach retribution for all deeds and believe in the perfectibility of the individual. *"You must be perfect as your Father in Heaven is perfect,"* says Jesus (Matthew 5:48)

The Tibetan Stupa also has the exact proportions and design parameters of a Tesla Coil right down to the number of coils and the stylized lightning streaming down each side of the tower. The only difference is that the Tibetan model was made out of more than 4,300 pounds of gold and more than ten thousand jewels. Gold is a natural collector of energy, while jewels resonate at specific frequencies. Sounds like they saw something like it perform a fantastic function. It was great enough to instantly become a core symbol of Tibetan Buddhism in the seventh century.

Summarizing the essence of his ethics, in the words of the Buddha:

"To shun all evil, to practice what is good, to cleanse one's own heart that is the teaching of the Enlightened Ones."

Jesus summarizes the essence of his ethics in his words:

"So in everything, do to others what you would have them do to you, for this sums up the Law and the Prophets." (Matthew 7:12)

Figure 125 - Buddhist Tree of Life depicted on a Laotian Buddhist Temple tile enclosed in a lotus blossom symbol of eternal life. It has three distinct divisions. Confirms Bodhi tree was the World Tree.

The Bhavishya Purana is a Hindu religious text, written in Sanskrit, dating back to 3000 BC. It consists of eighteen major Puranas or Tales of Ancient Times. One of the Puranas describes the coming of Jesus to India and the Himalayas and gives a concise overview of his mission centuries before his advent into mortality. In the text, he is referred to specifically as Isha Putra—"The Son of God." How did the tale of Jesus appear in one of India's most ancient texts? It was because the pre-mortal Christ and his Shining

Ones were there teaching the gospel in ancient times. It was Christ who told them of his coming mission on earth.

The Bhagavad-Gita, meaning "Song of the Divine One," is the main religious text of India and contains many concepts compatible with Christianity; Krishna, the god of the Gita, closely parallels the life of Christ. Christ comes from the Greek word Christos, and Christos is the Greek version of the word Krishna. These findings have made religious researchers question if perhaps Hinduism influenced Christianity when, in fact, your authors again believe it was Christianity that influenced Hinduism. The sayings and some teachings of the pre-mortal Christ are reflected in Krishna, the god of the Gita, as expressed in Hindu ideology. So impressed were the writers of the Gita of the teachings of the pre-mortal Christ, the Hindu god Krishna carried his name. Expressed in another way, Krishna is the personification of Christ. Written in Sanskrit, the Gita is a text from the Bhishma Parva of the Indian Epic, the Mahabharata. For those who wish to read the text, it is posted on the Internet; just Google Bhagavad-Gita.

Krishna was born of a virgin. His birth occurred in his native city while his parents were paying taxes to the king. He was born in a cave and visited by three wise men bearing gifts. A star heralded his birth. The king sought his life, causing his parents to flee with him in infancy. Krishna was crucified at noon; the skies were darkened. After death, he descended into hell and raised the dead. He brought back from hell two boys, the sons of a high priest. Note, the apocryphal Gospel of Nicodemus relates the same two boys' account. Krishna is the second person of the Hindu Trinity: (1) Brahma (2) Vishnu (3) Siva. Krishna is the incarnation of Vishnu.

Christian missionaries to India could not believe this story pre-dated the advent of Christ by many centuries. They said that it had to be after the advent of Christ and forced the Indians to change the date of the text to around the first century BC. The truth of the matter is the text does predate the advent of Christ by many centuries. Researchers of ancient religions have overlooked the stories of the pre-mortal Christ and his Shining Ones and have not understood or associated the verses in 1 Nephi to these thirteen heavenly, shining, spiritual beings who *"came down and went forth upon the face of the earth."* Once more the evidence is found in the pictorial symbolic World Tree. Hindu scripture describes a celestial tree having its roots in heaven and its branches in the underworld, similar to the one pictured below. Symbolically, this World Tree teaches the source of Living Water, milk and honey that water the earth, comes from the God in heaven. It is an excellent example of the different World Trees the Lord used in his teaching methods. This is a reversal of our usual World Tree; however, it would still have three divisions: the roots, the trunk and the branches. In India and Malaysia the Gunung Merta tree literally means the Tree of Life.

Figure 126 - Upside down World Tree

In ancient Persia, now Iran, the religion of Mithra took root about 1400 BC, others say 600 BC. Researchers of ancient religions assert that the figure of Mithra has many commonalities with Jesus, too common to be coincidence. His life shared many of the same themes of those of the Hindu god, Krishna, listed above. Again, your authors believe it was because the pre-mortal Christ visited the Persians in ancient times and taught them his gospel. Maybe Christ was known as Mithra to them or they applied the teachings of the pre-mortal Christ to their ideology. Rome's Vatican was built upon the foundation previously devoted to the worship of Mithra. Orthodox Christian hierarchy is nearly identical to the Mithraic version. Rome adopted the miter, wafer, water baptism for removal of sins, altar, and chants or hymns of praise used in religious services from Mithraism. All religious Vatican symbolism came from the religion of Mithra that subsequently was the prototype of later rituals used in Christian church worship. The evidence is found in the Tau Cross World Tree, the symbol of Mithra.

Figure 127 - Tau Cross World Tree symbol of Mithra

As previously written in the past two volumes, the pre-mortal Christ and his twelve Shining Ones came to the Andean and most of the Pacific coast regions of South America, ca. 3000–2000 BC. They were accompanied by three boatloads of faithful grandsons of Noah, as well as Votan, another grandson named specifically. It appears that during the 3000–2000 BC time period the entire group traveled together. The pre-mortal Christ was known as Viracocha in South America. The evidence found in those regions is the same cross symbol used in Mithra, the Tau Cross World Tree.

During Mesoamerican times, it appears that the pre-mortal Christ traveled alone; however, Votan is remembered as sailing up the Huehueton River, where he built a temple and deposited the "national records." Other traditions say he (Votan) returned to

Babylonia several times, each time returning to Mesoamerica. He is traditionally credited with being the founder of the ancient settlement of Palenque. If Votan returned to Babylonia several times, this indicates all of the shiploads of faithful grandsons and possibly the Shining Ones and the pre-mortal Christ accompanied him crossing the ocean. This could explain how the pre-mortal Christ was seen in Sumeria, Tibet, Asia, South America, and Mexico, seemingly in a fifteen-hundred-year time span from 3000–1500 BC. Returning, he and his Shining Ones visited Persia. After his advent into mortality, according to oral traditions, as written in volume 1, pages 480–481, the resurrected Christ visited the people of the Pacific Islands and the various Indian tribes of North America, including some Canadian tribes. It is said that the Canadian Yakima tribe named their highest mountain Tacoma to honor his name—Tia-acomah meaning Lord Miracle Worker. The evidence found in Polynesia is their sacred World Tree, the coconut palm, which they believed was the pathway leading to heaven and to other worlds. For many North American tribes, the evidence found is their sacred spruce World Tree.

The pre-mortal Christ was known by many different names in Mesoamerican times. Probably the most well known name was Quetzalcoatl, and the second most recognized name was Kukulcan He had the same attributes, themes and identical life story as the Hindu Krishna and the Persian Mithra. He taught his gospel to the Mesoamerican people. As documented in volume 2, one of the visits of the pre-mortal Christ is recorded in the Toltec/Book of Mormon record probably around 100 BC (Book of Mormon Mosiah 27:7). His visit may have lasted 15–20 years as he stayed long enough to prosper the Zapotec/Mulekite nation of King Mosiah. Prosperity doesn't happen over night, so we reason he stayed with them a fairly long period of time in accordance to oral traditions that Quetzalcoatl traveled and lived among his people for various periods of time. Adding to the confusion, there were several Toltec kings who took upon themselves the name of Quetzalcoatl who were not the pre-mortal Christ Quetzalcoatl. This fact has been overlooked among many researchers. His pre-mortal last appearance in ancient Mexico was around 100 BC. The evidences found in Mesoamerica are the stylized Palenque World Tree Crosses (see chapter one) and the Olmec (Jaredite) World Tree, pictured below.

Figure 128 - Olmec World Tree. Note the three divisions of the cross and the serpent bar. The portal into heaven is marked by the all-seeing "eye of God" that is also a Precession symbol.

The top figure represents God in heaven. The two-headed serpent is the Union of the Polarity symbol and since it is entwined on the cross probably represents Lucifer guarding the Tree of Life and acts as the ecliptic path of the sun as well. The End of the Age is definitely encoded. This Tree is deep and multi-layered in symbolic meaning, some of which we are unable to interpret.

Figure 129 - The Crucifixion of Quetzalcoatl (From the Codex Borgianus)

Figure 130 - The Crucifixion of Kukulcan

The Maya of Copan took it one step further as they carved stela of their kings dressed up as the pre-mortal Christ/Maize God in very elaborate World Tree costumes pictured in chapter one. It wasn't until now that the carved stela images in Izapa, Mexico, of the pre-mortal Christ began to make full sense. He taught his gospel and of his coming crucifixion and then of the coming resurrection at the End of the Age to the Mesoamerican people. They in turn carved pictures of him symbolically teaching his message. In two of these images the crucified Christ had been mistakenly identified as the First Father by historians. These images are also found pictured in chapter one of this book. Again, these carved images are further proof of Christianity in Mesoamerica and, as we now believe, have been misidentified. Correctly interpreted, it is now possible to read and fully understand the messages of these carved pictures.

In author L. Taylor Hansen's book, *He Walked the Americas,* legends tell of the pre-mortal Christ traveling on a ship north from Brazil through the Caribbean and Gulf of Mexico, docking at sea ports along the way. Here he received one of his many names—Hurukan—when he calmed the winds of a deadly storm sweeping the land. His stay with the Toltecs in Tollan lasted many years. It is thought that the Temple of the Sun at Teotihuacán and the sacred pyramid at Cholula were his special shrines where he taught the priesthood and people his gospel. According to the book, legends say that Christ/Quetzalcoatl would go to Mount Popocatepetl often to pray. It is said that during one of his visits to pray upon Mount Popo he received a vision of the year 2039, when the land would be reborn for the millennial age. This legend is in agreement with our writings, as we wrote that 2039 was the probable date for the end of tribulation and the second coming of Christ; at that time the temporal Earth would begin its golden renewed millennial age. The book also says that Christ/Quetzalcoatl returned twice to Peru to visit his temples and teach more of his gospel. According to the book, the Peruvians of Paracas erected a monument of sorts by incising a geoglyph in the sand hill facing the sea north of the Paracas peninsula to commemorate his visits as evidenced below.

Figure 131 - Known today as the "Candelabra," "Three Crosses," or "Trident" the Nazca drawing has never been identified as to its true meaning by archeologists. It is another World Tree used by the pre-mortal Christ to teach the ancient Peruvians his gospel. Note the three divisions. Peruvians believe it marks the crucifixion of Christ and the two thieves.

The book discloses that when Christ/Quetzalcoatl departed from Mesoamerica, he did so from the now island of Cozumel as in those days it was still connected to the mainland by a land mass. He departed on a large, wooden, Roman-style sailing ship returning to his place of sailing origin, Tla-Pallan, which is believed to be an ancient sea port in Babylonia. And the book mentions that Mount Wakoyama in Japan is said to be named for a white God who taught there in ancient times.

About twenty-five miles outside the city limits of Mexico City, lay the magnificent ruins of Teotihuacan (200 BC-AD 750). New research from the Tree of Life and plan of salvation standpoint indicates the city may have been designed to reflect the plan of salvation. The Temple of Quetzalcoatl may have been a representation of the telestial glory, the Pyramid of the Moon a representation of the terrestrial glory, and the Pyramid of the Sun a representation of the celestial glory. In ancient times, the Chichimec Toltecs may have built the city in stages to serve as their capitol city, although the Aztecs say the city was built by the Totonacs. If the Totonacs were the original city builders, they were displaced later by the Chichimec Toltecs. Many researchers speculate it was the fabled, ancient city of Tollan (Tula). Tollan was the favorite city of Quetzalcoatl. He spent much time there teaching his gospel plan of salvation. It is quite obvious to visitors of these ruins that it was once a great religious center that honored Quetzalcoatl. Teotihuacan fits the criteria to be the proposed ancient city of Tollan, also spelled Tullan and Tula for short.

Jacob of the Old Testament saw the plan of salvation ascension as a ladder reaching into heaven; Moses experienced it in the form of a mountain. Some ancients thought of the plan of salvation as three worlds or kingdoms stacked one above the other. Spanning these three worlds was a rope descending from the highest kingdom bringing connection to the lower worlds (see chapter one, Quetzalcoatl descending from heaven on a rope). The Jews of King David's time understood that each of the three worlds was tied to a rope by a knot, and the knot was fastened with a nail (Vav). The temple is a knot symbolizing the connecting place between the worlds. Each level of temple worship has an altar that represents the Vav or nail in that world. David's tabernacle and Solomon's temple were constructed to represent the three worlds or kingdoms of glory. Often the Jewish Menorah is depicted with the candles aligned as a Tree of Life.

Figure 132 - Jewish Menorah Tree of Life

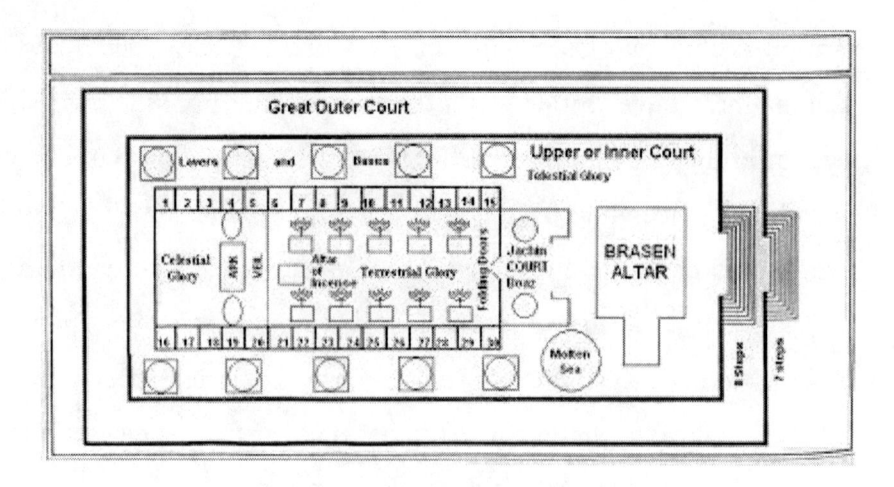

Figure 133 – Floor plan of Solomon's Temple showing the relationship to the three degrees of glory

The earliest texts that describe the Tree of Life, outside the Torah, are the Bahir, Sefer Yetzirah, Sefer Raziel Hamalach, and probably the most influential, the Zohar. These books describe a Kabbalist Tree of Life, sometimes referred to as the Sephirothic Tree of Life (see illustration first chapter). The circles or spheres are called Sephiroth. This Tree of Life is embedded with much hidden, esoteric wisdom. Its teachings are deep and complex, but in the same context the Tree can potentially be applied to any area of life, especially the inner, spiritual side of man. It can be compared to a sort of "Jacob's Ladder" or journey of return to God by stages or thirty-two paths of spiritual wisdom by ascension through the Sephirothic worlds. It is the perfecting of the soul to achieve the ultimate Holy Grail or Kether.

By the same token, another "Jacob's Ladder" is the Yoga Tree of Life. Yoga means "union with the Divine" and is a group of ancient spiritual practices originating in India. The goal of Yoga is spiritual perfection and enlightenment attained through meditation. There are seven main chakra wheels and numerous smaller chakras, all inter-connected. Through meditation techniques, the Serpent Power Life Force or Kundalini, located at the base of the spine and the seat of all knowledge, can be awakened to ascend the spinal column and trigger the awakening of the upper chakra wheels. When the "third eye of wisdom," located in the forehead (number six chakra), is awakened, spiritual enlightenment will burst out of the top of one's head like a ray of light. This is called a crown of enlightenment, similar to a halo crown of righteousness. Attaining this crown of enlightenment is through the power of Kundalini, defined as absolute purity, chastity, auspiciousness, self respect, pure love, concern for others, detachment, and the finding of infinite joy and inner peace. In ancient times the Life Force was equated to the powers of the Holy Spirit (Spirit of God), defined as the spirit of intelligence given to the spirits of men for understanding (vol. 1, 134, 124–125). Spiritual enlightenment is the "understanding" of higher principles. It is a path of spiritual perfection culminating in a temporary union with God as a feeling of "oneness."

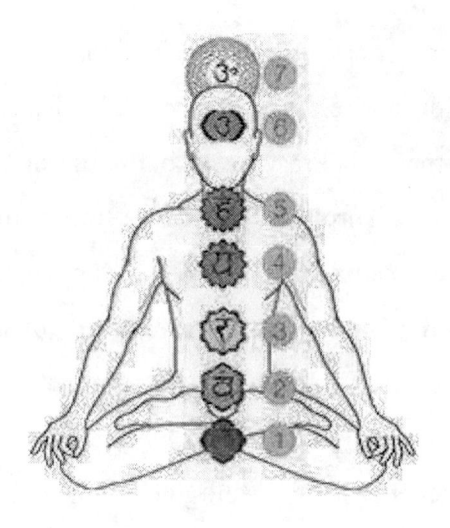

Figure 134 - Yoga Tree of Life

Essentially the Sephirothic Tree of Life and the Yoga Tree of Life teach the spiritual principles necessary to gain eternal life through ascension of the tree. The lower levels could be compared as living the telestial principles, the middle levels compared to living terrestrial principles, and the highest level to living the celestial principles. Because these spiritual journeys were never described in ancient times in written terms, your authors believe the true meaning has been lost.

Mani (AD 216–277) was a Persian apostle who founded the religion of Manichaean. Mani was a title of respect rather than a personal name; his true name is unknown. At one time there were ten million members reaching far beyond Persian borders into Syria, Iraq, Egypt, Africa, Spain, France, Northern Italy, Northern India, West China, and Tibet. Although persecuted, this religion thrived for one thousand years until persecution intensified. Mani was imprisoned, and many of his apostles and church members were brutally massacred until finally in the thirteenth century the religion became extinct. The influential early Christian writer Augustine of Hippo was a Manich for ten years before his conversion to Christianity.

Manichaean is based on Gnostic teachings of the Apostle Mani. Its teachings are Christian-based but rely on the words of Christ found in the Gnostic scriptures (Nag Hammadi) rather than the Bible. In ancient times this religion taught the concept of the three spiritual worlds by the same names: the celestial worlds, the terrestrial worlds and the lower worlds of darkness (telestial). Their Tree of Life was very similar to the Kabbalistic Tree of Life, and they used their Tree of Life to teach the paths leading to these upper, spiritual worlds. In 1981, there was a resurgence of belief, and the religion was reorganized under the name of the Manichaean Orthodox Church. Since most of the original writings of Mani have been lost, the present church may not teach the original doctrine.

The Essenes were a religious community consisting of both Jews and Gentiles, and men and women, whose purpose was to prepare for the coming of the Messiah. The term Essene is not mentioned in the Bible. According to the Jewish historian Josephus, the Essenes flourished from the second century BC to the first century AD. Many scholars today argue that there were a number of separate but related groups that had in common mystic, eschatological, messianic, and ascetic beliefs that were referred to collectively as "Essenes." These include the Nasoreans, the Nazarenes, the Nazoraeans, and the Sampsaeans. These groups may have been separated by nationality. Their communities were located in Syria, Egypt, and Israel. Essenes were early sects of Jewish Disciples of Christ who held orthodox or Gnostic Christian views. The term Nazarene was a common name for all early Christians until the term Christian was applied in the Syrian city of Antioch (Acts 11:26).

Pliny (AD 23 –Aug. 24, 79), an ancient Roman author, describes the Essenes as:

> "*A race by themselves, more remarkable than any other in the world.*"

The Jewish historian Josephus (AD 37 –after 100) describes the Essenes as:

> "*...they show more love for each other that do others and live a more moral life. Rightly do they deserve to be called an example for the life of other people.*"

Philo (20 BC–AD 50), a Hellenized Jewish philosopher writes:

> "*They live each day in constant and unalterable holiness.*"

The most startling disclosure of the Essene documents (The Dead Sea Scrolls) is that the sect possessed, two hundred years before Christ, a terminology and practice that have always been considered uniquely Christian. They practiced baptism and shared a liturgical repast of bread and wine presided over by a priest. They believed in redemption and immortality of the soul. In ancient times, their most important teacher was a mysterious figure called the "Teacher of Righteousness." Your authors believe the "Teacher of Righteousness" was probably the name given to the pre-mortal Christ who visited and taught them his gospel centuries before his advent. The evidence to be found is in the Essene Tree of Life that was instituted by the "Teacher of Righteousness." An Essene Tree of Life usually has one "Teacher of Righteousness" pictured in the center of the tree's truck. It has seven branches and seven roots. The top seventh branch represents heaven or God, and the center root represents nature. The Carmel/Alexandria manuscript is full of references to the Tree of Life and Sevenfold Peace. The tree below doesn't have a figure of the "Teacher of Righteousness" in its trunk but the style is the same.

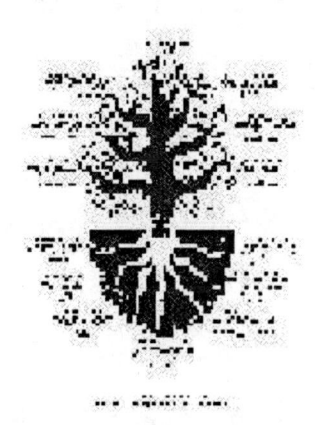

Figure 135 – Essene Tree of Life

Bro. Nazariah, D.D., a modern-day Essene writes:

"In the ancient Essene manuscripts used by our church, Jesus predicted his enemies would altar his teachings after his crucifixion and his church would become corrupt. He was right. Jesus was crucified, His church taken over by his enemies, and his true followers were executed as 'heretics.'"

Archdeacon Wilberfore of Westminster said, *"That after the Council of Nicea, AD 325, the manuscripts of the New Testament were considerably tampered with."*

Professor Nestle in his *Introduction to the Textual Criticism of the Greek Testament* tells us that certain scholars, called correctors, were appointed by the ecclesiastical authorities and actually commissioned to correct the text of the scripture in order to correct their meaning in accordance with the views just sanctioned by the church meeting at Nicea in AD 325. The correctors were present at the meeting.

Many truths were removed from the Bible by the correctors at that meeting. That is why so many verses leave you questioning logic and reasoning. The important parts explaining the doctrine of baptism for the dead and the doctrine of the kingdoms of glory were removed at that time. Only traces of it remain in the New Testament. Surprisingly, Bible theologians estimate nearly one-third of the original text was removed.

Yes, as J. P. Lundy wrote: *"The world has known many countless other crucified saviors..."* (at least sixteen crucified saviors), but your authors believe they were either the pre-mortal Christ, called by another name of their choosing, or the personification of the pre-mortal Christ. It is interesting to note that after the advent of Christ into mortality there have been no more new stories to crop up of another crucified savior.

Around AD 1119, the Knights Templars were organized and sent to Jerusalem, under the pretense of protecting pilgrims visiting Holy sites. Their true mission was to locate the fabled *"flying scrolls"* repudiated to contain the alchemical formula for turning base metals into gold. Finally, after seven years of searching through the ruins of Solomon's Temple, they found the scrolls hidden inside the hollow bronze columns known as Jachin and Boaz located on the front porch entry of the Temple. Collectively these scrolls were called The Divine Book of Wisdom, The Book of Adam or The Jerusalem Scrolls and nicknamed the "flying scrolls" because they flew out of Adam's hand in the Garden of Eden.

Upon returning to France, the Templars began building magnificent European cathedrals using new architectural methods apparently revealed in these scrolls. Moreover, the scrolls yielded many mysteries of God. Due to the inquisition of the Holy Roman Church, the Templars were unable to teach these new findings in church doctrine under penalty of death; therefore they built the teachings as symbolic messages into the structures themselves.

What were these symbols for all to see and for the wise to understand? First of all, all true cathedrals are laid out in the shape of a cross, the Christian World Tree. In addition all true temples are patterned after Solomon's Temple. In the Templar-built cathedrals, they used some of both, which became the prototype for future gothic cathedrals. Like Solomon's Temple, there usually is a small altar on entry into a cathedral. The main altar will sit in front of the representation of the Holy of Holies that is always located at the front of the cathedral. Lesser altars may line both sides of the interior wall and represent the inner room of Solomon's Temple. The World Tree, as you know by now, has layers of hidden, esoteric symbolism. When one enters the front door of a cathedral and walks down the long aisle toward the main altar, one is walking up the World Tree. In addition, the magnificent stained glass windows visually repeated the themes. Messages of the Union of the Polarity, Christ's birth, the crucifixion of Christ, the resurrection of Christ, the End Time resurrection date, baptism, receiving of the Holy Ghost, kingdoms of glory, hell, Judgment Day, Christ visiting the dead, the four beasts, the apostles, the Tree of Life, Adam and Eve, Precession knowledge, and the zodiac were all incorporated into these cathedrals.

It was the Bible told in pictures and symbolism so the illiterate could read and understand the Biblical messages. Most of the plan of salvation, the part removed by the correctors at the church council meeting in Nicea, was symbolically restored in the cathedrals unbeknownst to and right under the nose of the Holy Roman Church. The meaning of the symbolism was taught secretively "underground" as whisperings and bywords. It was understood but never written. The evidence can also be found in the World Tree emblem of the Queen's bodyguard of the Yeomen of the

Guard for Scotland, the Royal Company of Archers, founded in 1676. Their real historical origin dates to the bodyguards of the Plantagenet kings of eight hundred years ago (AD 1207). Although the crown represents the rulership of England today, it draws its symbolism from more ancient roots embedded in the teachings of Christ, as the crown above the tree represents the crown of righteousness gained upon entry into the celestial kingdom.

Figure 136 – Yeomen of the Guard emblem.

Figure 137 – Byzantine Tree of Life with Christ in the branches. Note that all the true World Trees have three branches.

Byzantium or Byzantine Empire is the term used since the nineteenth century to describe the Greek-speaking Roman Empire of the Middle Ages (fifth–fifteenth century). The Byzantine Church today is known as the Greek Orthodox Church. This Church has some of the most beautiful iconology in the world that symbolizes many of their early teachings. Apparently, even as late as the fifth century AD, they knew of Christ using the World Tree to teach his gospel. The evidence is found in their World Tree of Christ. This World Tree leaves no doubt as to who is teaching the Christian gospel and that it is the plan of salvation symbolized by the three branches of the tree trunk. Pictured in the branches of the tree are eleven of the original twelve apostles.

Figure 138 - Mohammad on his night flight down the Axis Mundi at the jeweled tree (Cook p. 126).

It appears Mohammad entered heaven via the portal of the Axis Mundi and came close to the Garden of Eden. Note the World Tree has three jeweled divisions, suggesting he perhaps knew something of the kingdoms of glory described in the Qur'an as the celestial world (heaven), paradise (the terrestrial world) and hell (telestial world).

Even until the eighteenth century, the World Tree knowledge was around, and then suddenly it just vanished completely. The evidence found is an eighteenth-century World Tree below.

Figure 139 - Eighteenth-century World Tree

This World Tree pictured above shows the palm tree or path to heaven firmly rooted in the physical Earth. There are the three worlds of the kingdoms of glory above the physical Earth. The black world is the lowest kingdom of glory. Above it is the terrestrial kingdom of glory, and the white world is the celestial kingdom of glory. Above the celestial world is another circle with a triangle or spirit Earth tetrahedron passing through the circle into the fourth dimension (the dimensions are the circles inside the triangle).

Whenever the plan of salvation or fullness of the gospel is reintroduced, persecution starts upon the person or organization reintroducing the knowledge. As in the past, many persons teaching these principles met with death, even centuries before the advent of the twelve apostles of Christ, most of who were also martyred. This is Lucifer's way of guarding the Tree of Life. The Knights Templars were no exception; because Phillip the Fair persecuted them almost into extinction. Almost, but not quite, as they reorganized under different names known today as the Knights of Columbus, the Order of Christ, the Rosicrucians and the Freemasons.

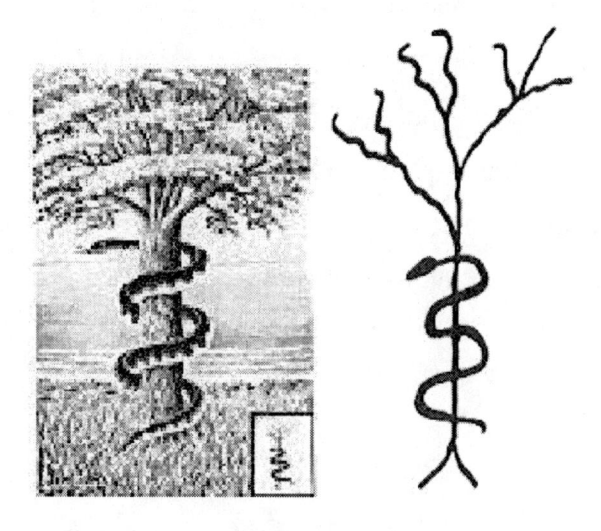

Figure 140 – The serpent guarding the World Tree

Freemasonry is not a religion, but they do practice perfecting the soul and physical body in preparation for the coming "transition of Earth." Their method of perfecting the initiate is similar to the Sephiroth World Tree of ascending through thirty-two steps to heaven, only they call the steps "degrees." There are steps like Jacob's ladder within the degrees that lead to perfection of mind, soul, and body. Below is a good illustration of Freemasonry degrees. The Roman god of *harvest*, in the guise of Father Time, is shown holding a sprig of the acacia bush, a symbol of the resurrection of the dead. The hourglass is measuring the time to the End of the Age when the first resurrection of the morning or *harvest* is scheduled to take place and the sickle is ready to begin the *harvest*. Father Time is standing on the platforms labeled the three degrees. They symbolically represent the three levels of the Tree of Life known as the telestial, terrestrial and celestial levels or degrees of glory. The fourth degree represents the highest level within the celestial worlds. Over time, much of the true meaning of the symbolism has probably been lost and new meaning applied. As previously written in chapter one, the city of Washington, D.C., was designed by the Freemasons to symbolically teach of the Union of the Polarity and of the coming day of resurrection at the End of the Age.

Ravages of Time

Luke 2:46
And it came to pass, that after three days they found him in the temple, sitting in the midst of the doctors, both hearing them, and asking them questions.

Figure 141 - Freemason Tree of Life

The Rosicrucians are an offshoot of the Knights Templars who date from the fifteenth century. They preserved much of the same esoteric and alchemical knowledge of their parent organization in art and symbolism. Below (figure 142) is pictured an oil painting, artist unidentified, from their organization depicting much of their understanding of the Union of the Polarity and of the Tree of Life.

Figure 142 - The Rosicrucian Tree of Life

Figure 143 – Michael with spirit Earth in his hands (view 1. Notice the tiny cross on top of the globe.

Figure 144 – Michael with transparent spirit Earth (view 2)

What a marvelous find! In the first painting above (figure 142) is the spirit Earth with the waters of the flood merging or coming to the waters of this planet. Note that the spirit Earth is transparent. Wrapped around the spirit Earth is the zodiac band from which the Tree of Life springs. On top of the cross Tree of Life are three fruits, possibly date clusters, which represent the three kingdoms of glory or plan of salvation, the knowledge of which is being guarded by the serpent Lucifer. Not only is Lucifer guarding the knowledge of the plan of salvation, but he is guarding the knowledge of the Union of the Polarity. This knowledge has been deliberately hidden from the world because of Lucifer guarding the Tree. He is the one responsible for the loss of the ancient missing "key" piece of knowledge we call the Union of the Polarity, the loss that resulted in a major stumbling block for many, leading to their unbelief and accepting the Bible as a collection of myths. We accused him of this in the first chapter of this book and in our previous books. This painting is proof that he did so.

If you notice on the far left lower side of the painting is the Egyptian ankh that we identified in volume 1, page 235, as the Egyptian symbol for the Union of the Polarity. We were right, as it is used here again to denote the Union of the Polarity. Because the cross is springing from the zodiac band, the cross represents all the things previously written as to the meaning of the End of the Age and Precession events marking the time when the End of the Age occurs. As an offshoot branch of the Knights Templars, the Rosicrucians preserved the Union of the Polarity knowledge in their order. Obviously, the Knights Templars found this knowledge in the Jerusalem Scrolls taken from Solomon's Temple. It is the most convincing piece of evidence found so far that indeed the Union of the Polarity did happen. Your authors are convinced that it did happen. What further proof do you need?

Pictured below figure 142 are two more marvelous pictures of the spirit Earth (figure 143 and figure 144). These are Byzantine fifth century paintings found in Greece, in a Greek Orthodox Church. These paintings express an early belief among the Greeks of the Union of the Polarity which was most likely learned from the New Testament apostles.

Figure 145 - Alchemical Union of the Polarity

The Rosicrucians believed that the Union of the Polarity was an alchemical process as illustrated above. It was their way of explaining how the two planets came together. Just as the ancient Jews struggled to understand this "mystery" in the Zohar, so did the Knights Templars and the Rosicrucians struggle to prove planetary union to their followers. In the center of the zodiac ring is a laboratory flask showing the Union of the Polarity occurring as a result of a chemical process. Above the neck of the flask are the twin dragon symbols of the Life Force creative powers of God. Appearing at the bottom of the flask is the Egyptian symbol for the Union of the Polarity. In our opinion, these pictures are conclusive proof the Union of the Polarity did happen because the Rosicrucians expressed the ancient belief that it did happen in their paintings. The pictures certainly support the ancient belief that indeed the two planets did merge together in the days of Noah.

Persecution occasionally comes in subtle ways, ways the average Christian would deem unthinkable. In 1611, the long-awaited King James Version (KJV) of the Bible was first published. Since then, over the years, it has undergone fifteen more revisions. As previously discussed in chapter one, as beautifully written as the text is, it has major translation problems in the most critical areas. Since it is the most widely read and accepted version in use by Christians today, it appears we have valued its poetic beauty at the cost of accuracy in translation. Ferrah Fenton was one of the first to recognize the translation problems and subsequently did a new translation that was published in 1908. His Holy Bible in Modern English is regarded as the most accurate translation in the world. Other translations, such as the New American Standard Bible, have followed suit. The KJV translated the New Testament Gospels from the Textus Receptus Edition of the Greek text. Modern English Bibles and the New American Standard Bible declined to translate from that Greek text, opting instead for what modern scholars feel are more reliable critical editions. What did we lose in translation? Five things come to mind, noting there are others, all of which we have addressed in the first two volumes and in this volume too. First was the confusing of the two creations in Genesis; second was how Noah arrived on this planet; third was the scattering of Noah's children after the flood as cited in the table of nations (first volume); fourth are the problems concerning the confounding of the languages at the Tower of Babel (second volume); fifth is the designated time of the first resurrection (second and third volumes); the last being the most important.

These translation errors have created major stumbling blocks for some and nearly caused the faithful to miss the Savior's announced time of the first resurrection of the morning, one of the most awaited events for Christians since time immortal! One would not think that Lucifer would actually persecute Bible translations but your authors see his fingerprints everywhere. Indeed, he guards the Tree of Life well.

It appears much of the symbolic teachings of Christ's gospel were slowly forgotten over time, and new symbolic meanings were applied. This occurred mainly because the teachings were understood and never written down. Of course, translations errors and the removal of text at the council meeting in Nicea didn't help matters either. After the deaths of the apostles, Christians were persecuted and many suffered martyrdom for their beliefs. Christianity passed through a time of "spiritual apostasy" so bad that it has never been forgotten and since then has been remembered forever more as the "dark ages." By the beginning of the eighteenth century Christ's teachings of the symbolic Tree of Life had all but vanished; only the image of the Tree of Life remained. Fortunately, the times were changing: people were receiving some education, and many could read and write. Christianity was flourishing, and the time was right to re-introduce the gospel in its fullness for the last time in this dispensation.

The gospel in its fullness is the gospel the pre-mortal Christ taught using the symbolic World Tree that is called the plan of salvation. After his advent into mortality, he taught the same gospel to his twelve apostles. Some Biblical references are made to the World Tree as believers are called "trees of righteousness" in Isaiah 61:3, and "branches" in John 15:5. As stated before, the fullness of the gospel was removed by the correctors at the council meeting in Nicea. Only traces of it remain in the Old and New Testament today.

Modern-day revelation restored the fullness of the everlasting gospel through the Prophet Joseph Smith and it is contained in the Doctrine and Covenants. It is part of the sacred scriptures used by the Church of Jesus Christ of Latter-Day Saints (vol. 1, 5–6). The Doctrine and Covenants was first published in 1876. Latter-Day Saints are not Catholic nor are they Protestant but refer to themselves as members of the Restored Church.

Even from the earliest beginnings of this Church, Lucifer has lashed out and directed all his fury toward it. All manner of persecution began culminating in the martyrdom of its leader, Joseph Smith, and his brother Hyrum on 27 June 1844. Under heavy persecution from angry mobs, church members left Kirkland, Ohio, to settle in Far West, Missouri. Not long after their arrival, in 1838, a series of calamities led to trouble and strife between church members and those of another faction resulting in much bloodshed and the destruction of property. This action led to a mid-winter expulsion of the entire Mormon community of twelve thousand souls from the state. The people immigrated into Illinois and built the city of Nauvoo. After Joseph Smith was slain, the persecution intensified to the point it became apparent that the Saints would have to leave. Enemies of the church had hoped the death of Smith would be the death of the religion, but it survived under the leadership and genius of Brigham Young. Believe it or not, the persecution of the Mormons was officially sanctioned by at least two different state governments. The decision to leave Nauvoo started the greatest exodus of people to the Rocky Mountains in the history of the United States. Other Saints from many nations, traveling by foot, on horseback, and by boat, joined with the Saints on the long, perilous journey to the Rockies and Salt Lake Valley.

Many died along the way. Church headquarters were established in Salt Lake City. Since that time, the Church still experiences persecution, although not as severe as in the early years; however, it remains the most persecuted religion in the United States. Despite anti-Mormon persecution, the Church has prospered and grown into a worldwide Church.

Why didn't the Lord reveal these teachings to other Christian Churches? Actually he tried through Joseph Smith, but the church leaders of Joseph Smith's time would not listen. Instead they branded him a heretic, and he soon became the object of much persecution and reviling in his neighborhood. Eventually the Lord directed Joseph Smith to organize a Restored Church whose mission was to restore the teachings found in the original Christian Church that were lost soon after the deaths of the apostles. Joseph Smith organized the church on April 6, 1830. As in the past, wherever and whenever this knowledge was re-introduced, heavy persecution followed. So it is with the Church of Jesus Christ of Latter-Day Saints. It is Lucifer guarding the Tree of Life, for he desires the souls of men for himself and does not want men to find salvation through God's plan. Since Lucifer's eviction from heaven, there has been ongoing spiritual warfare between the sons of darkness and the sons of light, competing for the souls of men.

When one partakes of the fruit of the Tree of Life, one by means of symbolism can understand the plan of salvation. Then, one who eats from the Tree of Life (*understands the plan of salvation*) is given *(if obedient to the plan of salvation)* eternal life. That is the true meaning of the Tree of Life or World Tree. Through modern-day revelation found in the Doctrine and Covenants, access to the Tree of Life has been restored again.

Does this mean only Mormons will go to heaven? No. The Lord will not punish churches for not possessing missing New

Testament scripture, but at the same time he has decreed that only those who live in obedience to the celestial law can be admitted into the Kingdom of God, regardless of their particular religiosity. Each individual human being will judge himself by his own vibrational state. Light will go to light, and darkness will go to darkness. There are dimensions and aspects to love that many do not understand. The thing that lowers the frequency of a sentient being faster than anything is judging another being.

What your authors present next is strictly our viewpoint. After much thought and careful analysis and taking into consideration the division of the two earths during the millennium, we are presenting a possible order of the resurrections. We hope by doing so, it will attract and stimulate the interest of others to examine our findings, noting that we have not tampered with, added to, taken away, or changed any of the Biblical text. As the resurrections do affect the destiny of this planet, we feel we should also address them. The very concept of the resurrection may have become so distorted after centuries of religiosity that it is impossible to have a clear understanding except through personal prayer and meditation. Many churches preach that Jesus was the first to be resurrected. With that we do not argue. Establishing ascension in a single lifetime had never been done before Jesus. Perhaps his performance of the ordinance established the pattern in the Akashic record so that others, perhaps even you and we, could pass the same way.

Next, let us first review a few known facts before we present our views. As written in volume 2, Isaiah and the Old Testament prophets understood the true Earth, the original creation, to be the spirit Earth. In this light, most of Isaiah's prophecy's concerning the Earth are speaking of the spirit or true Earth and not the physical Earth. If the Biblical prophets understood this, then most likely John the Revelator did too. Isaiah tells us the spirit Earth is going to be removed during a cataclysmic event. This event may take place at the End of the Age or December 21, 2012. In ancient times this event was referred to as the "transition of earth," or the "removal of earth," known today as the "rapture." Furthermore, the ancients, the prophets and the apostles knew the scheduled expected time the event would take place: at the End of the Age, which calculates to December 21, 2012, when the sign of the Suntelia Aeon appears. It is also known that text is missing from the Biblical manuscripts and that many translation errors are in the KJV.

According to the Doctrine and Covenants, resurrected beings come forth with the bodies suited to the glory they will inherit. Those inheriting the celestial kingdom will be resurrected first, those inheriting terrestrial bodies will come forth second, and those inheriting telestial bodies will come forth last. Paul expresses it as *"But every man in his own order"* (1 Corinthians 15: 23). Bodily perfection will come to all men as a free gift in the resurrection as well as the free gift of immortality that comes by grace alone. However, any of the spiritual blessings that flow from gospel obedience are not free gifts. All rewards gained in the eternal worlds must be earned. The perfection sought by believers is both spiritual and temporal and comes only as a result of full obedience to the plan of salvation.

This principle is found in the Book of Revelation as *"He that is unjust, let him be unjust still: and he that is filthy, let him be filthy still:"* These are those who lived the telestial law. *"and he that is righteous, let him be righteous still:"* These are those who lived the terrestrial law. *"and he that is holy, let him be holy still."* These are those who lived the celestial law. The following verse then says that Jesus will then reward them according to the work, meaning the law they abided as written: *"And, behold I come quickly; and my reward is with me, to give every man according as his work shall be."* (Revelations 22:11–12) The clarifying parts of these scriptures were removed by the correctors but those familiar with the plan of salvation can readily interpret their true meaning. In ancient times, the pre-mortal Christ taught these same principles using the World Tree or Tree of Life symbolism.

Now, we will proceed with our interpretations of the resurrections, taking into consideration the End Time knowledge, separation of the two earths and the plan of salvation.

Therefore:

There may two types of people "raptured" from the living. People already living in obedience to the celestial law and people who are living the terrestrial law stand to be "raptured." Those living the terrestrial law are those who are good, charitable and righteous, regardless of religion (vol. 2, 204). If you are "raptured" from the living, you will undergo a translation to endure living on the spirit earth in another dimension. When you are a translated being, you are still considered a mortal because you have not tasted of death. Translation is a temporary state and not eternal, although it could last several thousand years.

Those living the terrestrial law will have the opportunity to hear of the fullness of the gospel on the spirit Earth and will have the opportunity to gain the fullness of salvation through the receiving of necessary ordinances. All they lack is the sanctifying Seal of God. Those who are living the celestial law may not have had enough time to complete all their necessary ordinances and therefore will be afforded enough time to do so.

Both groups of people are still mortal; they will be active in performing proxy baptisms and other necessary ordinances for their dead and for others yet to be resurrected at a later time. They will have until the end of the millennium to finish this task. At the end of the millennium, those who have complied with the celestial law will receive their celestial bodies. In order to receive their celestial perfected bodies, they too must taste of death but their bodies do not have to await the grave as they are changed at the moment of death into celestial perfected beings in a twinkling of an eye.

At the "rapture," part of the first resurrection of the *morning* or resurrection of the just occurs for those who have lived the celestial law while in mortality and for those who have accepted the fullness of the gospel hearing it for the first time while in the spirit world of the dead and who have received all ordinances by proxy necessary for salvation in the celestial kingdom. This group of people will be resurrected in their celestial bodies.

When the second coming of Christ happens at the end of tribulation, approximately thirty-nine to forty years of Earth time (could be one thousand years in the fourth dimension due to time difference in dimensions) after the "rapture," those who are "caught up" to meet Christ in the clouds, both living and the resurrected dead, will be those who have not received the mark of the beast during tribulation. They will accompany Christ to the spirit Earth to usher in the millennial reign. Apparently tribulation will sanctify this group sufficiently to be included in the second part of the resurrection of the just or resurrection of the *morning* (Revelation 7:13–17). During the millennium they will complete the necessary ordinances required in the plan of salvation described in Revelation as *"washed their robes in the blood of the Lamb."* During the millennial reign of Christ on the spirit Earth, all who reside there are priests and kings unto God (Revelations 5:9–10).

There could be another resurrection of the just or resurrection of the *morning* toward the end of the millennial reign. These will be resurrected in celestial bodies, having received all the necessary ordinances by proxy by those "mortal" translated beings on the spirit Earth during the millennium. We think this because the kingdom of the dead is so vast that it is not possible to complete this work on Earth before the "rapture" and before the second coming of Christ; therefore most of the work for the dead will be done during the millennial reign of Christ. This proxy work for the dead will also be going on during the millennium on the physical Earth as those living on the physical Earth will be living the celestial law. At their moment of death, they also will be changed in the "twinkling of an eye" into celestial beings and will join those on the spirit Earth.

At the end of the millennial reign, the *afternoon* of the first resurrection will most likely happen. Those coming forth at that time do so with terrestrial bodies and are destined to inherit a terrestrial kingdom of glory in eternity.

When the thousand years of the millennial reign are expired, the time Satan shall be loosed out of his prison for a season will be the most likely time for the first part of the resurrection of the unjust to occur. Those coming forth will be the "spirits" of men who are be judged and found under condemnation. These are the rest of the dead, and they live not again until the thousand years of Satan's season are ended, neither again until the end of the Earth. They apparently suffer the wrath of God in hell until the last resurrection.

These are the ones who will inherit telestial bodies, ones whose final destiny is to receive a telestial kingdom of glory. If any refuse to repent, and those who deny the Holy Ghost, and thus commit the unpardonable sin, having spent one-thousand years in *hell*, they will not inherit any kingdom of glory but are cast into a region called "outer darkness." Origen taught that the wicked in "outer darkness" would be devoid of intelligence, and will possess bodies stripped of all glory. Similarly, both the Gnostic Christian Gospel of Philip and the Pastor of Hermas describe the souls of men cast into "outer darkness" as those who have made a conscious and specific choice to rebel against God.

Near to the end of the thousand years of Satan's season, the second part of the resurrection of the unjust, the sons of perdition or those who "remain filthy still," shall come forth from their graves to be cast into the "fiery lake of Divine wrath" to an everlasting destruction.

Besides the two coming future resurrections, there was a resurrection of the righteous dead who lived from the day of Adam to the time when Christ broke the bands of death in his resurrection (Doctrine and Covenants 133:54–55). When Christ was resurrected, the graves were opened of the righteous saints and they came forth and went into the holy city, and appeared to many (Matthew 27:52–53). These came forth with celestial bodies and will have an inheritance in the celestial kingdom (Doctrine and Covenants 88:96–102).

It is a general consensus among those familiar with the plan of salvation that the majority of people of this earth will receive a telestial kingdom of glory. We can find some comfort in the knowledge that even the lowest telestial kingdom of glory is far better than the physical Earth on which we now reside.

Essentially the plan of salvation was the belief of the Biblical Jewish writers of the Old Testament, the gospel writers of the New Testament, and the Mesoamerican prophets. If Christians accept the doctrines of the New Testament gospel writers, they must accept their concept of heaven as well. The part not clearly defined, only alluded to, in Biblical scriptures is the knowledge of the spirit Earth being the location of the Kingdom of God or heaven as we think of it. It is the missing "key" to correctly understand the creation and to correctly understand the scriptures; the "key" we call the Union of the Polarity.

For those who are currently living the terrestrial law, it is most important to be found possessing the virtue of charity. Clement, not to be confused with a later Clement of Alexandria, was a disciple of Peter, and afterwards Bishop of Rome. He wrote the First Epistle of Clement to the Corinthians, which was excluded from the Bible. In chapter eleven of this epistle he wrote of the effects of true charity, which is a gift of God obtained only by prayer. The following verses 4–11 and 13 in chapter eleven read as follows:

"Charity unites us to God; charity covers the multitude of sins; charity endures all things, is long-suffering in all things. There is nothing base and sordid in charity; charity lifts not itself up above others; admits of no divisions; is not seditious; but does all things in peace and concord. By charity were all the elect of God made perfect: Without it nothing is pleasing and acceptable in the sight of God. Through charity did the Lord join us unto himself; whilst for the love that he bore towards us, our Lord Jesus Christ gave his own blood for us, by the will of God; his flesh for our flesh; his soul, for our souls. Ye see, beloved, how great and wonderful a thing charity is: and how that no expressions are sufficient to declare its perfection. But who is fit to be found in it? Even such only as God shall vouchsafe to make so. Let us therefore pray to him, and beseech him, that we may be worthy of it; that so we may live in charity; being unblamable, without human propensities, without respect of persons. Happy then shall we be, beloved, if we shall have fulfilled the commandments of God, in the unity of love; that so, through love, our sins may be forgiven us."

Additionally, the following quote in Matthew 22: 37-40 says:

*"Thou shalt love the Lord thy God with all thy heart, and with all thy soul, and with all thy mind.
This is the first and great commandment.
And the second is like unto it,
Thou shalt love thy neighbour as thyself.
On these two commandments hang all the law and the prophets."*

Charity is the pure love of Christ. It is not enough to simply believe in Christ, we must become like him----Christ like. It is well known that the *devils* believe and still tremble. There is a *knowing* that comes to life inside us as we bring our vibration or Life Force energy to match that of the Christ. It is also well known that when He returns to Earth, we will see Him because we will be like Him.

The purpose of the trilogy of *The Ark of Millions of Years* is to restore the missing "key" back to Earth and to restore the knowledge of the End Time date in fulfillment of End Time prophecy. The Doctrine and Covenants restores the plan of salvation or the gospel Christ taught. Because the *Ark* trilogy was written and published in the End Times and contains information primarily pertaining to the End Times in fulfillment of prophecy, they qualify therefore to also be among the books called *The End Time Books,* thus fulfilling the prophecies made by Joseph Smith, Jr.

December 21, 2012, marks the End of the Age. It marks the end of Precession or the 26000 Great Year. It marks the end of the Piscean Age and the beginning of the Age of Aquarius. It marks the end of the Mayan long-count calendar and the end of the Mayan and Aztec Fifth Sun. It marks the end of the 104,000-year major sun cycle and several other minor cycles of time. These findings are significant and cannot be over-stated. All evidence leads to the conclusion that we are the End Time generation and if permitted to live another five years until 2012, we will witness the End Time events and "rapture." In a sense, the "rapture" is a second coming of Christ too, albeit we think of the second coming, according to Biblical scripture, happening after the tribulation. The "rapture" is a resurrection for some and a temporary translation for others. Biblical scriptures indicate there are multiple resurrections to occur at different times; it is a process. Perhaps the Mesoamerican prophet, Alma, states it best in the following verse:

> *"Now whether there is more than one time appointed for men to rise, it mattereth not; for all do not die at once, and this mattereth not; all is as one day with God, and time only is measured unto men."* (Book of Mormon Alma 40:8)

We make no apology if this chapter "rings" of religion because the chapter literally wrote itself even down to and stopping at our views on the resurrections. We had little control over it as it simply dictated itself to us, the scribes. Seemingly it had a mind of its own that took charge whenever we sat down to write this particular chapter. If we deviated from that which was being dictated or tried to take control, our minds would go blank.

In order to get back on track, all we had to do was hold our fingers on the keyboard, in quiet submission, and slowly the words or directions to locate documentation would come. From the very onset, we quickly learned it is how the chapter wanted to be written or else we would have permanent writers block resulting in no final chapter for this book and even extending into the inability to write future books. As to World Trees being used to teach the gospel plan of salvation, we would have never conceived of the idea by ourselves, although we knew World Trees were used to teach of the End of the Age resurrection date as written in chapter one. We had no idea as to where the chapter was taking us and were just as surprised as you may have been at its ending. The Union of the Polarity pictures were icing on the cake. We had no idea pictures existed illustrating the ancient belief and yet, the chapter found them for us. Some things just cannot be explained; certainly the writing of this chapter was one of those things. Even so, with some reluctance we confess we can only take full credit for being the scribes. Therefore, it stands as written and declared by us as finished.

Next we want to thank our readers for purchasing our books. If you like these books or have any comments, please email us on the address on the back cover. Last, but not least, please spread the message of these books to your family, friends and neighbors. Give the trilogy set as gifts for birthdays, Christmas, Easter or just for the gift of giving to someone special.

Perhaps after reading this book, whenever you see a cross, or a Rose Window, or an arch with a keystone, or a solar window, or a solar grave marker, or the nation's capitol dome, or Father time holding his sickle, or the zodiac, or a Tree of Life…you will view it differently as we do and will be reminded of the coming End of the Age *"harvest."*

Now that you know the actual date of the "rapture," will it change your life in any way? Are you spiritually "prepared" or do you need to "prepare" for this great event? Introspection of one's soul is never pleasant but is a necessary step toward repentance and "getting right with God."

Figure 145 - Today's Christian Tree of Life or World Tree

The Trees of Life

Figure 146 Assyrian Cylinder

Here is early evidence of Biblical teachings in Assyria, whose kingdom was a product of earlier kingdoms—namely the Babylonians and Sumerians. The Tree of Life pathways, symbolized by branches, are being guarded by two kerubim. Two winged Watchers are guarding the gate or portal into heaven, symbolized by the Assyrian winged disk seated on top of the tree. Later the Egyptians adopted the winged disk symbolism from the Assyrians. Ancient Semites (Noah's race) formed the Assyrian nation.

Figure 147 - The Assyrian Winged Disk

Figure 148 - A Stylized Egyptian Tree of Life. Note the three white chevrons cut into the trunk. These represent the three levels or kingdoms of glory. The very top of the tree is heaven. The palm leaves represent the serpent bar. Where they meet at the top center of the tree is a representation of the End of the Age or 2012.

Egyptian hieroglyphs telling the story of human DNA, Enki (Osiris) working his science, resulting in the Tree of Life. (photo at Phillae Temple, Egypt).

Figure 149 - Mesopotamian or Enki's Tree of Life.

tau CROSS

from Sacred Mysteries Among the Mayas and the Quiches by Augustus LePlongeon

Mexican MS. in British Museum.

Figure 150 - Mayan Tree of Life. The Tau Cross tree represents Christ and the fruit his gospel. Eating of the fruit leads to eternal life in heaven represented by the Bird of Paradise. The flowered branch is the representation of the serpent bar denoting the End of the Age and Day of Resurrection. Further evidence of Christianity in Mesoamerica.

Figure 151 - Navajo Tree of Life wall hanging. Very ancient pattern. Note the three divisions.

Figure 152 - Amur Russian Tree of Life motif on garment with three divisions.

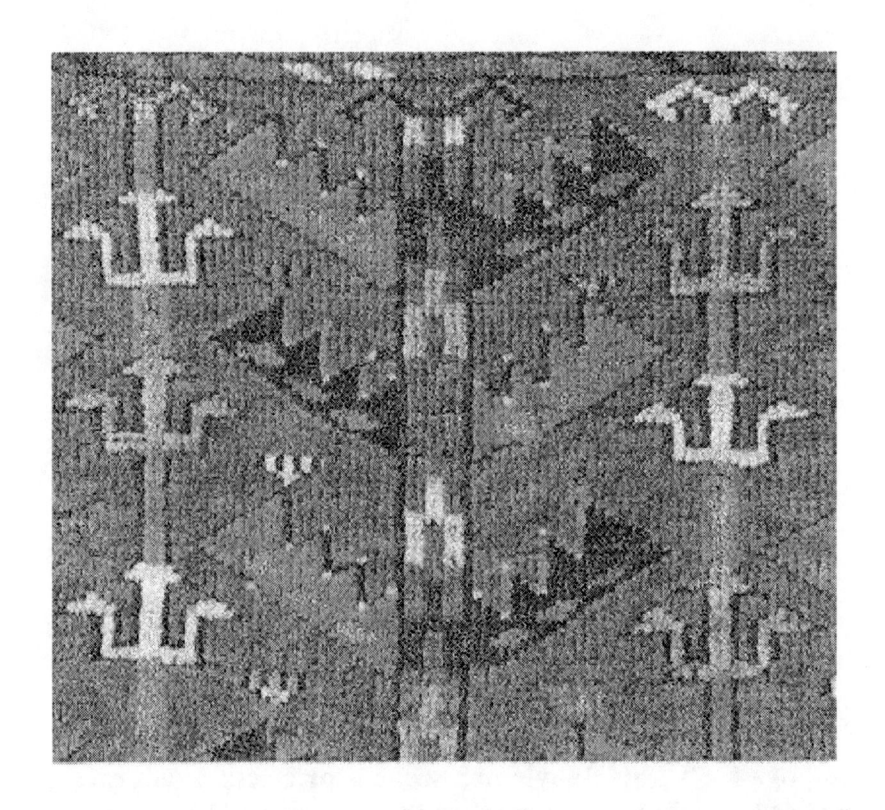

Figure 153 - Turkish Tree of Life rug design with three divisions

Figure 154 - Ulebord Dutch cast-iron Tree of Life with three divisions and serpent bar denoting the End of the Age resurrection.

Figure 155 - This Babylonian scene is priceless. It appears a teacher is teaching the three degrees of glory by World Trees on either side of an altar, suggesting the teacher is a priest. Note the three divisions of the trees growing out of pots. Above the teacher are symbols of the sun (celestial glory), the moon (terrestrial glory), and a triangle tetrahedron (spirit Earth). The physical Earth is represented by the square cube or altar. It may be the teacher is explaining the nature of the spirit Earth departure at the End of the Age. Stars on either side of the triangle represent the telestial glory.

Figure 156 - Flag of Chuvashia, Russia, with stylized Tree of Life. This is an old, traditional emblem. It has three divisions and three stars representing the worlds within the kingdoms of glory.

Figure 157 - The Norse World Tree is a giant ash tree called Yggdrasill. It has three divisions with the serpent Lucifer guarding its trunk.

Figure 158 – Avalokiteshavara, the thousand-armed and eleven-headed god of compassion. The Chinese World Tree of Quan Yin. It is patterned after the Tibetan Stupa.

Figure 159 - Irminsul is the name of the Germanic World Tree venerated by the Saxons.

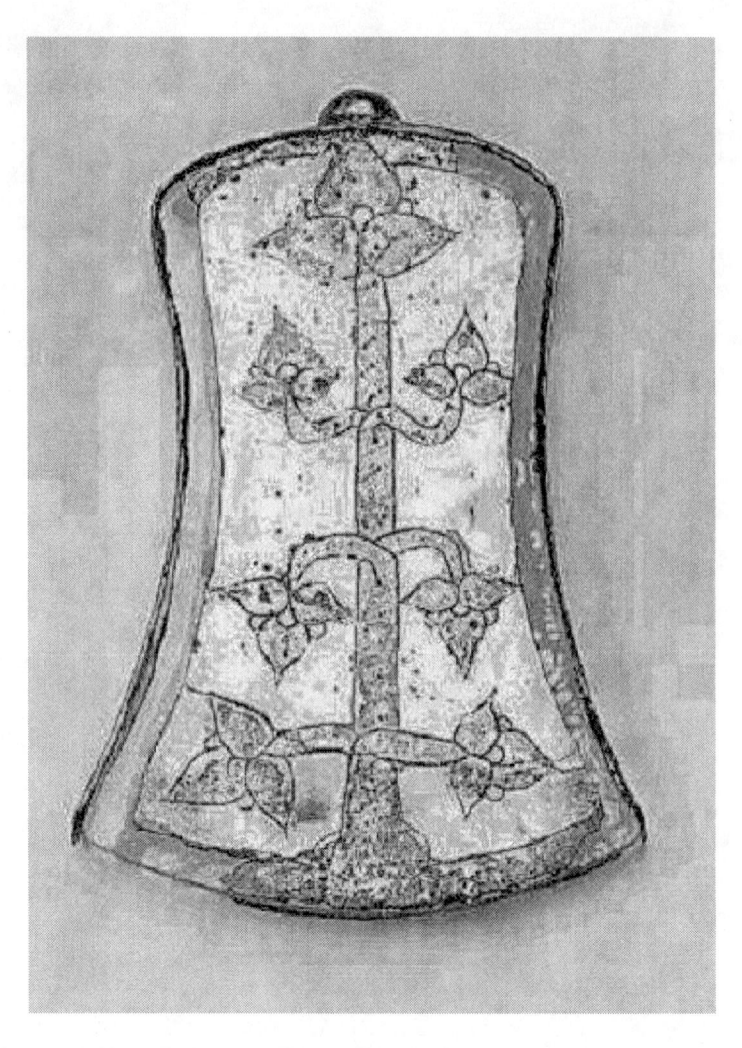

Figure 160 – Oriental Tree of Life as captured in a very old piece of jewelry.

Figure 161 - This is the Persian version of the Egyptian winged disk, now called the Faravahar or Farohar, that was adopted by the Zorastrians as their symbol. The three layers on the garment of the Wise Lord/Christ indicate he is the source of the teachings of the three kingdoms of glory or plan of salvation.

This Faravahar or Farohar symbol first appears in Assyrian times usually seen floating over Sumerian-style Trees of Life. A picture of this symbol floating over a Sumerian style Tree of Life is found on page 226 in volume 2 and figure 149 of this chapter. Although that Tree of Life doesn't have three divisions, the flowers surrounding the Tree may indicate progressive steps toward spiritual perfection. The twelve ages of the zodiac are represented by a Babylonian fan-style plant at the top of the tree; each leaf represents an age. This may be the first evidence of the teachings of the pre-mortal Christ from Sumerian times.

The Egyptians adopted their style of the winged disk from the Assyrians but essentially the symbolic meaning was the same. Later the Persian Zoroastrians adopted this symbol into their religion. The current interpretations of this symbol found on websites are all modern, twentieth-century. Clearly one can see the

Precession symbols, the dots in the circles on the representation of the serpent bar, linked to the circle Ouroborus indicating the End of the Age (2012) when the Wise Lord/Christ (figure inside the circle Ouroborus) will return. The three layers of feathers on the wings of the Ouroborus represent the three kingdoms of glory or plan of salvation. The three layers on the garment of the Wise Lord/Christ indicate that he is the source of the teachings found on Trees of Life. In his left hand the Wise Lord/Christ is holding a large, gold ring that symbolizes eternal life. This symbol is the Assyrian adaptation and later the Persian Zoroastrian adaptation of the Tree of Life. It is to remind one to live in such a way that the soul progresses spiritually through the plan of salvation to be reunited, "raptured," or resurrected unto eternal life with the Wise Lord/Christ at the End of the Age in 2012. Placing this symbol over a Tree of Life, as the Assyrians did, emphasizes the meaning and purpose of the Tree of Life.

Update

In volume 2, page 144, we wrote of the Nephite (Toltec) destruction as a nation occurring in AD 385 as recorded in the Book of Mormon. This destruction was the result of warfare following a long process of extermination by their enemies. E.J. will make some additional comments following her new Mesoamerican research.

It appears the Nonoalca Maya are the candidates best fitting the description of the Book of Mormon Lamanites. The archeological records indicate the Nonoalca, who lived near the Toltecs, were constantly at war with the Toltecs as early as 500 BC. It appears they were the ones who finally defeated the Toltecs in AD 385. Around AD 700–800 the Chichimec Toltecs, not to be confused with the Toltecs, reached their zenith as the most powerful nation in all of Mesoamerica. Their empire controlled most of central Mexico, the Yucatan peninsula, the Gulf coast, Chiapas and the Pacific coast as well. Trade was established as far away as what is now the Mexican states of Veracruz, Puebla and Zacatecas; as far north as the U.S. states of New Mexico and Arizona; and as far south as Guatemala and Costa Rica. These Chichimec Toltecs had a reputation of being fierce, militaristic and barbarous. They were descendants of the first settlers who came to the Americas around 2700 BC and bear the name of their first king as written in the chapter "The Oldest City in the Americas." I proposed in volume 2 that there were two sets of Toltecs, defined as the Chichimec Toltecs who were descendants of the first settlers and the later Toltecs (500

BC) who were the best candidates for the Book of Mormon Nephites.

The Nonoalca Maya are also referred to as the Huaxtecs and the Mazatecs. In ancient times they occupied an area near the Gulf of Mexico, Huaxteca, and on both sides of the Panuco River. Today their descendants occupy two parts—the Huaxteca Veracruzanna and the Huaxteca Potosina. The former are located in the state of Vera Cruz and the latter in the state of San Luis Potosi.

In time, struggles and tension emerged, most likely over the rapid expansion of the Chichimec Toltec Empire taking the lands of the Nonoalca Maya, and over religious disagreements. Most likely this erupted in warfare between the two groups, probably resulting in the downfall and defeat, coupled with drought, of the Chichimec Toltec capital city of Teotihuacan (Tollan) ca. AD 750. Around 600 BC, the city had already begun to experience decline. Consequently the Chichimec Toltecs moved about fifty miles northwest of Teotihuacan and shortly after founded their new capital city of Tula. These Chichimec Toltecs reigned supreme for several centuries. Nevertheless it appears that there arose a great Chichimec Toltec priest-king ruler and leader of Tula around AD 975, who of all things had Nonoalca roots in his genealogy. (Note: there is much disagreement among archeologists and historians as to the exact years these events took place.) This leader was Ce Acatl Topiltzin, who later took on the revered title of Quetzalcoatl. Topiltzin apparently lived up to his name as he was reputed to have lived a saintly life and instituted the teachings of Quetzalcoatl to his people. It is possible that he was a disciple of Quetzalcoatl and knew him personally because he built temples in honor of Quetzalcoatl, did away with human sacrifice, took on the name of Quetzalcoatl and was beloved of his people. Although revered as a god, he never claimed to be a god. His lineage and kingship of the Chichimec Toltecs apparently solidified the two factions for a period of time, but internal problems arose from religious beliefs. It seems the Nonoalca chose to follow the god Tezcatlipoca while the Chichimec Toltecs chose to follow the god Quetzalcoatl. Apparently the straw that broke the camel's back was when Topiltzin expelled the pagan Nonoalcas out of Cholula, the sacred city of Quetzalcoatl.

Tezcatlipoca, the god the Nonoalcas worshiped, was called the Lord of this World, appeared as a tempter urging men to do evil; possessed mysterious powers like those of a magician; could resurrect men; was god of all material things, of night, of robbers, of rulers, of warriors, of deceit, and of war; and was an opponent of Quetzalcoatl. He carried a magic mirror that gave off smoke that killed his enemies, earning him another title "God of Smoking Mirror." With some certainty it appears Tezcatlipoca and Lucifer were one and the same, or he was one of the Nephilim gods.

It is difficult to fully construct the story accurately due to the many myths mixed with undocumented facts surrounding the fall of Tula, but it appears that the Nonoalca Maya wanted to reinstate the human sacrifices done away with by Topiltzin. As both gods of

Tezcatlipoca and Quetzalcoatl had shrines in Tula, the Nonoalca worshipers of Tezcatlipoca apparently overpowered Topiltzin and forced him to leave. When he left, his Chichimec Toltec followers who believed in his teachings left with him. Those who didn't depart with Topiltzin were later forced out. Legends say some of these departed in ships to parts unknown. Another group went to Cholula and resided with the Olmeca-Xicalanca until the twelfth century when the Chichimec Toltecs drove the Olmecas out. Under their control Cholula flourished once more and became Tollan Cholollan, the site of a very important sanctuary temple complex dedicated to the god Quetzalcoatl. Topiltzin and his followers traveled to the Yucatan, where they apparently were assimilated into the Mayan city of Chichen Itza and made it their new home. I don't think the city was captured but that they were allowed to live amid the Maya, perhaps in exchange for new knowledge or maybe for added military advantage.

This is evident because the Toltecs added a new building complex of the most splendid Toltec design to the older city, and new research has revealed the Yucatan Maya always occupied the city. Maybe it was because of Topiltzin's Nonoalca Maya bloodlines and his respected reputation that he was welcomed as a close cousin and he and his followers were invited to make a new home for themselves in their midst. Here Topiltzin built the now famous Temple of Kukulcan, also called El Castillo, over an older Mayan temple. This is an important point to consider as apparently the teachings and worship of Kukulcan replaced the old Mayan gods of the city, symbolized by the building over of the older temple. It is not clear if the Maya of the city continued their human sacrifices after the arrival of Topiltzin, who clearly continued his teachings of Quetzalcoatl/Kukulcan, perhaps converting many of the Maya.

There is a possibility that Topiltzin may have converted the entire city to the teachings of Quetzalcoatl/Kukulcan, especially if Quetzalcoatl had visited the area. I propose this because the centerpiece and most striking feature of Chichen Itza is the Temple of Kukulcan, suggesting his religion was the city religion. If so, then human sacrifices would have stopped with perhaps the exception of the ball game beheadings. Apparently each faction respected the other, and they were able to live in harmony. There is evidence that other Yucatan cities such as El Tajn, which is the site of a mural that was previously pictured in chapter one supporting the presence of Christian teachings, followed suit and converted to the new religion.

What is certain is that Chichen Itza became the capital of a very powerful, multi-ethnic regional state whose rulers forged alliances with other Itza dynasties in centers like Mayapan and Izamal. By the 1200s the decline of Mesoamerican civilizations was well under way, probably from civil warfare as many of the Yucatan cities were walled cities built for fortification against attack. It is a fact that by AD 1200–1250 the monumental center of Chichen Itza showed signs of pillage and abandonment.

Fray Servando Teresa de Mier, a late seventeenth-century Creole priest, in his formal farewell letter to Mexico in 1821 said:

"'Mexico' with a soft x like the Indians pronounced it means: 'where Christ is worshiped,' and 'Mexicans' is the same as 'Christians.'"

De Mier believed and preached Mexico had been Christianized prior to the Spanish Conquest. He paid dearly for his unorthodox preaching by being publicly denounced and repeatedly imprisoned, because without the pretense of evangelization the Spaniards were wholly without excuse for the atrocities they had inflicted on the Native American populations. Our findings agree with those of de Miers, as it appears parts of Mexico were indeed Christian prior to the time of the arrival of the Spanish. In truth, the Spanish didn't recognize Christianity in the Mesoamericans' language, writing, and liturgy, which tragically resulted in the deaths of many thousands of Christian Mesoamericans at the hands of the Christian Spanish.

The Christian Mesoamericans practiced the Plan of Salvation as taught them by Quetzalcoatl using cross symbolism. All knowledge of these teachings were again wiped out with the Spanish conquest. Millions were killed, codices were burned, and survivors were persecuted into accepting another version of Christianity. Lucifer was guarding the Tree of Life exceptionally well during Mesoamerican times.

It appears many take the Toltec/Book of Mormon record lightly, even regarding it as a fictitious work, as some do the Bible, or refer to it as the Smith myth. Next I would like to present some facts, known to be true in the Mesoamerican civilization, that are documented in the Toltec record. These facts were not known until recent times and therefore could not have been known in Joseph's day when he translated the Toltec record into what is now called the Book of Mormon.

Fact: Research by archeologists confirms the first settlers in Mesoamerica were the Olmecs, a name given by archeologists to this group of people, who date back to 2700 BC.

Finding: This finding is validated in the Book of Mormon as it tells of a group of people who crossed the ocean in ships to the "Land of Promise"—interpreted as the Americas—shortly after the confounding of languages at the Tower of Babel ca. 2800 BC and arrived in Mesoamerican ca 2700 BC. Joseph Smith was once asked in an interview as to where the Book of Mormon lands were located. He answered, "They lived about the narrow neck of land, that now embraces Central America, with the cities that can be found." This of course was Mesoamerica in ancient times. (Book of Ether)

Fact: Archeologists have found Mesoamerican writing dating to 500 BC.

Finding: This finding is validated in the Book of Mormon as it says a system of writing was brought to this region in 500 BC by the Nephites who we propose to be the Toltecs. In fact, this is the only region in the Americas that had a system of writing dating to 500 BC. (Mormon 9:32–35)

Fact: Archeology records indicate the Zapotec and Toltec cultures had a close relationship because Toltec cities had living quarters for Zapotec visitors and Zapotec cities had living quarters for Toltec visitors.

Finding: The Book of Mormon states the Mulekites, who we theorize partly integrated with the Zapotec culture, and the Nephites, who we theorize were the Toltecs, united to form one nation, possibly around 300–200 BC. (Mosiah 25:4)

Fact: Archeologists have found many walled cities in the Yucatan, Belize, and Guatemala indicating these were for protection against attack.

Finding: The Book of Mormon states the Nephites (Toltecs) built walled cities to protect them from enemy warfare. (Alma 48:8)

Fact: Archeologists do not know what happened to the Olmec culture because by 400 BC all hallmarks of the culture had vanished within Olmec sites and elsewhere, except for Cholula and Cacaxtla.

Finding: The Book of Mormon records the destruction of the first civilization (Jaredites) who are believed to be the Olmecs ca. 236 BC. (Mosiah 8:5–14)

Fact: Mayan scholars confirm the Toltecs made a revision or adjustment of their calendar system in AD 6, when a mass planetary conjunction occurred.

Finding: This calendar adjustment is found in the Book of Mormon wherein it states nine years after the birth of Christ (4 BC), the people adjusted their calendar system, the beginning of AD 6 or the end of AD 5. (3 Nephi 2:7–8)

Fact: The genealogy of Kan B'ahlam, the son of the giant King Pakal of Palenque, is found engraved on the Tablet of the Cross. Among the names of Kan B'ahlam's royal ancestors are found what may be the full name of King Kish—U-Kish Kan, an ancient king of the Olmec (Jaredite) culture. His date of death is given as Wednesday, March 8, 993 BC.

Finding: In Ether's account in the Book of Mormon, a Jaredite (Olmec) monarch, King Kish, who lived about the same time period, is mentioned. No other information is given other than his name, the name of his father, and the name of his son, along with a genealogy of fourteen generations further back. (Ether 1:18–19; 10:17–19)

Fact: On the Palenque Temple of Inscriptions are found Mayan glyphs that translate as "and it came to pass" recorded in the passage three times.

Finding: This same phase is mentioned in the Book of Mormon 1,381 times.

Fact: Evidence now exists showing that there were horses in Mesoamerica prior to the Spanish conquest of 1519–21. In the Maya room of the National Museum of Anthropology in Mexico City there is a display of four horse bones discovered in the caves of Loltun near the Maya ruins of Uxmal in the Yucatan Peninsula. These bones were discovered at about the same depth as Mayan pottery fragments that appear to date to the Classic period of AD 200 to 900. The bones were those of a six- to eight-year-old mare, weighing about eight hundred pounds, a rather small horse by U.S. standards. The curator of the Maya room, also an anthropologist, stated that the museum's objective was to present the total picture of the ancient Mayan history and seemingly there was no doubt in her mind about horses existing in Mesoamerica before the conquest.

Finding: Horses are mentioned fourteen times in the Book of Mormon. The first mention is about 592 BC. Opponents of the Book of Mormon said the horse never existed in Mesoamerica prior to the arrival of the Spanish.

Fact: The 16th-century Catholic priest named Bernardo de Sahagun wrote a detailed, comprehensive analysis of the history, beliefs, and customs of the Mexican people. He wrote, "And then they hunted out men of fair hair and white faces; and they sacrificed them to the Sun." (Sahagun 7:36) He also commented on horses as follows: "And they removed each of the deer which bore men on their backs, called horses." (Sahagun 12:69) Sahagun tells us not only were the white Indians destroyed but their horses as well.

Finding: The Book of Moroni, chapter 1:1-4, records the Nephites (white Indians), that will not deny the Christ, were put to death. Moroni, a Nephite, states he wanders whithersoever he can for the safety of mine life.

Lastly, the final update is the addition of three more prophecies that have been fulfilled since volume 2 was published. On pages 203-204 of volume 2, there are ten prophecies listed that have been fulfilled. We would like to add the following additional three prophecies to that list as follows:

11. The knowledge of the Union of the Polarity has been restored in the End Times.

12. Isaiah's prophecies are being understood in the last days.

13. The *End Times Books* have come forth (you are reading one of them). There may be more to come as thousands of people receive the information from the universe through intuition, dreams, and visions.

Part Two

Reaching
Ever reaching into nova spawn
Seeking knowing;
Moving forward,
Back to memory's home
Of Is.

The Spirit Race

We returned to March 25, 2007, to begin the Spirit Race, a term coined by Ken Payne of Tell City, Indiana. Although he is acknowledged here for this idea, he did not participate in the writing of this book. The race is designed to inspire humans to feel a sense of urgency to awaken and become enlightened to their full potential. It is grand and daunting to think that an entire human race must be awakened and enlightened. It is possible, though. When we looked back into time to select the optimum time to begin the Spirit Race, we chose March of 2007 because it was the point at which certain people had reached their ascension and were ready to lead the world to the next level. In every age there are a few humans who can master everything. In ancient times they were shaman. At the end of medieval times, they were called Renaissance men. In modern times we called these people X-Factor humans.

We discovered that in the social structure of societies, it takes only a small percentage of people to adopt a concept before it explodes into global acceptance. If this fraction includes X-Factor humans, then only a very small number of people may be needed to turn the world away from the precipice of self-destruction. The universe can fully be affected by taking action early enough.

The *Source* of the universe exists in each of us. We have memories in our very souls that are older than creation itself. We have other memories as well.

Genetic Memories

There are genetic memories. Information coded into a series of amino acids making up DNA is passed from one descendant to the next, perhaps over hundreds of generations. Not only are the propensities of the parents inherited by the offspring, non-congenital traits can be passed along as well.

For instance, healthy mice treated to develop diabetes will give birth to offspring that spontaneously develop diabetes. There are numerous studies that show that people often have behavioral traits of their ancestors.

Still an emerging science, the study of genetic memory is gaining many supporters. The idea that an ancestor could learn a skill or a personality trait that is somehow encoded onto the DNA, and then that DNA is passed to a descendant, is theoretical. However, the ability to play music, throw a ball, paint pictures, or even leadership traits passed down from one generation to the next are well documented, even in case studies where the child was adopted and did not have any exposure to the biological parents.

Light Memories

There are light memories. Light itself is just a form of energy. Each photon is a particle without mass that carries information. When left to travel through space unfettered, a photon displays properties of a wave. This wave will last forever, unless it runs into something. This information is transferred to the target that is impacted by that photon. Normally, photons are sent in a beam of information that leaves the source. The distance between the two electron shells is absolutely mated to the frequency of that photon. That is to say, a molecule of potassium that is volatilized in a flame will generate photons in the red color band. Those photons can be detected by a solid-state device and identified as potassium without any doubt.

There are also patterns of photons that provide information. Our eyes are designed to respond to photons that strike specialized cells called rods and cones. Those inputs are deciphered by our brain and turned into images that very closely resemble our world. Photons outside of the sensitivity of those cells, or outside the experience of the brain, will not register to humans. For these photons we humans might need something else. We might need an instrument to detect these photons. We might need training to allow our brain to see something that is happening around us. There are most certainly energies in the form of waves or particles around us that are hitherto undetected by us. As soon as the particle's spin in observed, however, it immediately drops out of being a wave and displays properties of a particle.

Niels Bohr's **Principle of Complementarity**, in essence, states that there may be more than one accurate way to view natural phenomena. The idea that light displays characteristics of both a particle and a wave took physicists many years to agree upon. Bohr argued that even if observations may appear to be in conflict, both viewpoints are needed in order to form a more complete understanding of an object or event. As he once explained:

Figure 162 – Niels Bohr 1885–1962

"The opposite of a correct statement is a false statement.

But, the opposite of a profound truth may well be another profound truth."

Bohr was a visionary in the field of quantum mechanics. His ideas of the structure of the atom are still standard instruction in chemistry and physics. He once had a healthy argument with Max Planck. Niels offered a hypothetical condition of a bucket hanging from the ceiling by a rope. The bucket was filled halfway with water, and then the rope was wound up by rotating the bucket by hand. When the rope had about one hundred turns on it, the bucket was released to unwind. The question was this: "What does the surface of the water appear to an observer inside the bucket?"

The answer is that the surface of the water will curve due to the centrifugal force of the spinning bucket, as the water catches up to the bucket that is spinning while the rope unwinds. Max agreed, but then made an even more startling observation. The observer on the water in the bucket actually sees the bucket standing still while the room revolves around the bucket. So Max posed another question: "How does the surface of the water appear if the bucket is stationary, and it is in fact the room that is spinning?" The answer is that the water would curve exactly the same way.

You see, it is the relative difference between the bucket and the room that makers the water curve. It is therefore a very solid assumption that our universe is curved based on the idea that it may be spinning relative to another universe outside of our own. Like a balloon around a balloon, the two universes have curving effects on each other. This is important to remember, as we compare our own souls to others around us.

In 1799, Thomas Young initiated his medical practice in London. His primary interest was in studying sensory perception, and while still in medical school, he discovered how the lens of the human eye changes shape to focus on objects at different distances. While pursuing his interests in the function of the human eye, Young discovered the cause of astigmatism in 1801, which was about the time that he began his study of light.

Figure 163 – Thomas Young 1773–1829

In 1801, Young began a series of experiments with light pattern interference. He observed that when light from a single source is separated into two beams—like when a flashlight shines on a dark piece of paper with two slits cut into it—and the two beams are recombined onto a screen a few feet away, the combined beams produce a pattern of light and dark fringes. Young concluded that these fringes were the result of the beams of light behaving as waves with their peaks and troughs either constructively or destructively interfering with each other. When this occurred, alternating lines of light and dark resulted.

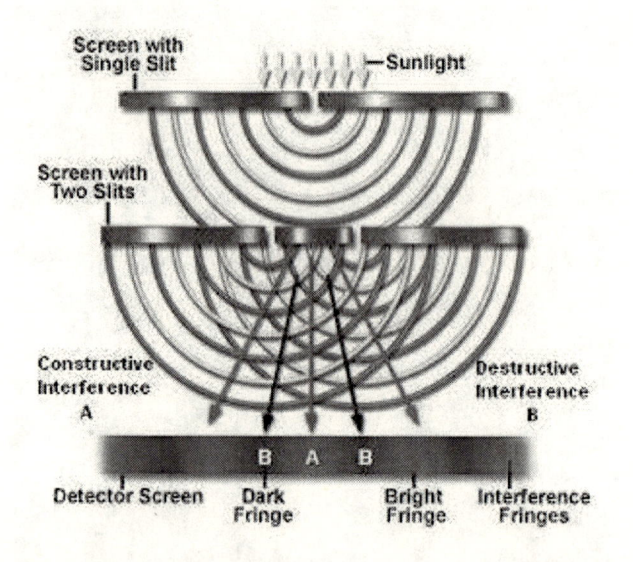

Figure 164 - Thomas Young's double slit experiment

What became apparent, in Young's conclusion, was that different light waves interacted with one another in and out of phase to either annihilate one another to darkness, or add to one another for greater brightness. When two energy signals come together, they either constructively interfere with each other, thus adding to the power making them brighter, or they destructively interfere with each other, causing a cancellation of the signals making them darker.

The dark fringes are a visual version of what noise-cancellation headphones do for room noise. The small microphones on the outside of the headphones pick up the room noise. The tiny amplifier inside the headphones makes an equal and opposite sound, and plays it along with the music you want to hear. The room noise is magically reduced to almost nothing, because the two opposite sounds cancel one another out.

Oh that we could have small microphones that pick up the tiny positive energies around us and collect them into a single signal. Then we could shift the phase of that positive energy and then overlay it upon our negative life energy. The result would cancel out any negative signals in our lives. In the future, we see that many people bringing their positive energies together have a mighty effect, even on the very structure of matter itself. Whether it is water, tissue cultures, or the health of a human being, the constructive interference of positive signal has a great effect for good. Likewise, collecting and echoing the negative energies in the world have the expected effect.

Our suggestion is that from the year 2007 on, you turn the television news programs off. Every hour, the media cranks the negative stories out to your living rooms, adding a resonance to your lives that is negative. Do not let their need for ratings perpetuate and breed the negative energy that tears down all the good done in the world. Nikola Tesla proved through his resonance experiments that a small amount of energy added precisely to a metal beam rebounding from a previous input would cause that metal beam to fail eventually as if overloaded by a much larger weight. This constructive interference with a very small weight at the exact right moment made the metal beam look like it was being bounced upon by an eight-hundred-pound gorilla, when in actuality the weight was only a few ounces.

The dark fringes in Young's double slit experiment are not the source from which to draw happiness. The bright areas resulting in light added upon light are the most likely places for positive energy to be found.

There are also atomic memories laid into us at birth and added to as we consume matter for food, and as our cells are replaced with new matter from that food. That matter may contain particles that are entangled with sister particles possibly created by the same ancient super-nova.

These particles act like molecular transmitters of our intention across space and time. Sister particles may exist in other humans alive on the Earth now, souls embodied on distant worlds now, or even as parts of other worlds now. The common thread is that these particles are entangled always in the *now*. There is no future or past to consider. Every effect, one way or the other, is exactly in the *now*. It is not that a future or a past does not exist. It is that these energies, like photons, are massless and exist independent of time. They may be multi-dimensional in nature, so that they are not limited or slowed down by a requirement to satisfy three-dimensional physics as we know it.

All humans emit energy into the universe. Most people do this in an unconscious manner. They think their thoughts, and act on those thoughts, unaware of the effect they have on the universe. Most of these people function out of fear. That is to say, the energy they generate is not based on love, but rather on fear. One person has an effect. One billion people in the same state of fear have an unimaginable effect on the entire universe.

Where did these entangled particles and energies come from? The belief that the universe came into being from a single big release of energy from super-compressed matter is fairly common. The observation that humans can comprehend the smallest quantum energy and particle, as well as the birth of solar systems, lends power to the idea that we may have been, and yet still are, involved in creation itself.

Energy, raw and chaotic, tends to wind down like a clock. As energy moves away from its point of release, emanating in all directions at once like a sphere, we calculate that the rate of dissipation is the square of the distance traveled.

If a firecracker exploded in the middle of a football field, persons standing at the forty-yard line would hear much more volume than those standing at the goal line. Besides the sound source expanding at the square of the distance, the very air molecules that allow the sound to travel to our listeners also reduce that energy to the point that the sound pressure is completely absorbed. Three hundred yards away, that firecracker may be completely inaudible. The sound expanded out in all directions with a fixed original energy. As the volume of space increased, the amount of energy available to go into your ears was reduced by the square of the distance. This energy moves through space in little packets.

Each individual packet of energy, called quanta, can change state almost at will. Whose will? Great question. Hopefully, the answer will light a fire inside of you. What is meant by changing state? Energy can exist in one of two states that we will consider.

One state is called a wave, or a vibration. The other state is called a particle, like a proton, electron, or photon. There are even smaller particles, but in our spacetime they exist for perhaps a millionth of a second before disappearing. These states are important to understand, so here we go.

There is an event in the universe that occurs randomly that releases immeasurable amounts of high energy. It is called a supernova. This is one of the stages in the death of stars of a minimum mass. We don't really know how large a collapsed star mass can be to form a super-nova, and we are surprised when they occur. We suspect that they have to be at least 1.4 times the size of our own sun in order to display this stellar death sequence. We are also very happy all super-novas have occurred very far away from Earth, so far. When a star that mass or larger loses its explosive drive, gravity begins to tip the natural balance between blowing up and collapsing completely. Now, there are a couple of forces at work here, so here they are.

Figure 165 – A super-nova can turn entire solar systems into pure energy and give birth to higher order elements. It may be the source for entangled energy and particles.

When an ice skater begins to spin, and then draws her arms in tightly against her body, the speed of her spin increases incredibly. She can spin so quickly the TV cameras can't capture the movement with anything better than a blur. This principle is called conservation of momentum. There is a certain amount of energy contained in her diameter and spin. If she decreases the diameter, then the rate of spin must increase to balance the equation. The same thing happens with shrinking suns.

As gravity compresses the size of the sun, now no longer exploding, its revolutions increase. For example, if our sun were to reach the point where it was collapsing, the revolutions would speed up from about twenty-eight days to hundreds of revolutions per second or more. Nevertheless, the same mass of this massive sun would occupy a smaller and smaller space as it collapses further and further. Then a moment occurs with that massive sun that is rare and remarkable.

The electrons that used to exist predictably in probability clouds around hydrogen protons, which are now helium nuclei, can no longer remain in their quantum probability clouds at a likely and safely reactive distance. The inter-molecular gravitational force becomes so great that the electron is pulled down onto the proton. The proton is neutralized by the electron, forming a neutron. At first, this happens a few atoms at a time. As the collapse continues, more and more neutrons are formed. Sort of like rope that is stretched to its limit by a heavy weight, first a few fibers snap, then a few more. Finally, a point is reached when the remaining fibers can't hold the weight, so the rope completely fails. During this chain reaction all the remaining electrons fall into protons in an instant.

This event creates a tremendous explosion called a super-nova. The remaining atmosphere of the star is sheared off, and the most powerful radiation imaginable shines out into space, converting entire solar systems into raw energy as it blasts into space. This energy is single in source, providing enough power to form higher elements well beyond the molecular weight of iron. If it were not for super-novas in the universe, eventually all matter would become cold and lifeless iron. This is apparently a creative event that replenishes the upper-order elements throughout the universe.

The important thing to remember here is that the energy it took to form these higher elements was singular in source and synchronized all the matter in its creative path. It is believed by most physicists in our day that super-nova events happen all over the universe.

It is also possible that medium *bangs,* as opposed to *big bangs,* resulting from the Higgs processes and causing black holes to explode occur on a fairly regular basis in the void at the outside of the universe. It is known at this time that these structures are mathematically extremely stable, and that thus it takes something anomalous to make the black hole explode into the void. A Higgs condition is a little like balling up Velcro. The little hooks get caught up in the little fibers, resulting in a sort of rubber-band backlash if they ever get a chance to come loose. This may be the little rip in the somewhat seamless fabric of a black hole. These energy events release enough energy to create whole galaxies, much of which contains these entangled particles and entangled energy. Hold that thought.

Entangled Particle Theory

There is a principle called the *theory of entanglement* that we mentioned in the beginning of this chapter. This term can involve energy or particles. For some reason, as yet still unexplained, pairs or groups of particles can demonstrate a remarkable property. We will discuss the experimental treatment of this later. Experimentally, two small particles can be "picked" off of a large particle and separated by incredible distances.

At first, the distances were a few millimeters. Then, in 1999 they were separated by eleven kilometers. In the year 2015, we use beryllium ions as switches in the BIM's for deep space communication. BIM's are Beryllium Ion Modems, capable of transmitting binary data instantaneously across any distance without any loss of power. The latest generation of Mars rovers uses these for communication. It greatly reduces the power needed for transmission and uploaded instructions, as well as the bandwidth. The high-definition video coming back from these rovers allows far better efficiency with the mission. The folks at Cornell University were very happy when the BIM's became available on deep-space programs.

Here is how it works, generally speaking. Each particle has a spin quality. Like a little planet, each one spins on its tiny axis.

Some spin in a fashion we call plus one-half, and some spin in a fashion we call minus one-half. Typically, a given electron cloud on an element will have a nearly even number of each, called the Pauli Exclusion Principle. The spin of one particle can be changed by a technician through small, electromagnetic pulses. Instantaneously, the sister particle—called an entangled particle—changes spin as well. As it turns out, it is at least thirty times to speed of light…perhaps much faster.

The most incredible aspect of this repeatable process is that it does not matter how far these particles are separated. Instantaneously, these particles change spin identically. The reason is unknown. The effect is irrefutable.

The importance of this *switching* action is that it acts just like a binary code. One spin direction is zero (0), and the other spin direction is one (1). Plus one-half and minus one-half are good discrete values that can be used in binary code. This means that with a small bank of these ions, and a spin modulator, a modem can be designed. In the year 2015, we call them BIM's, named after the original Beryllium ions that were used to make the first deep-space modem.

Now, back to the thought. Energies, and thus particles, are entangled across the universe. What affects a particle in one part of the universe affects its sister particle the same, even across parsecs of space and time, instantaneously and without any loss of power. This exchange of energy is an exchange of information. Yes, energy transfer is the same as the exchange of information. Like genetic code passed from parent to offspring, or electricity applied to one end of a copper wire from one telephone to another telephone, the movement of energy is the exchange of information.

There are some really fascinating things we discovered that you need to know. Humans are capable of generating strong magnetic fields. These fields are normally in a nice, symmetrical star tetrahedron around the human body. This three-dimensional geometry is shaped like this:

Figure 166 - The star tetrahedron

This energy pattern is that of human consciousness. It is also the life energy pattern around the Earth, not to be confused with the Christ Grid. It is called the MerKaBa. It is part of the Christ Grid, and when it is energized through human intention, it connects human beings to the grid. This connection may be the connection to Source through which *downloads* of various inspirational content comes forth. We will learn more about this later. These fields can be programmed with the intent of the individual. If the human is angry, then the field can be very distorted and energetically chaotic. If the person is very sad, then it can be nearly motionless and the points of the tetrahedra can be misshapen and actually not symmetrical.

In truth, the human geometrical magnetic field is a good reflector of the energy of the human being. Without getting into details beyond the scope of this book, we want you to know that these fields can be manipulated by the individual to great levels of power. They can also be left idle in ignorance. The effect on the particles and energies of the human is measurable and profound.

You see, the three-dimensional body of a human being is made of cells. Each cell is a living thing in need of its own nutrients and waste management. For a human body, this respiration process is done as a very complex system or physiology. Each cell needs a fresh supply of oxygen and fuel from that to maintain life and reproduce according to the genetic design and maintenance process. Those nutrients are formed of molecules, which are formed of atoms and subatomic particles. These very particles can be entangled with other particles and other energy in the environment of a planet or other planets forged by the same super-nova event.

Those molecules form minerals that exist in the soil. Those minerals are absorbed and utilized by plant life to make beans, seeds, fruits, vegetables, and so on. These plants are consumed by humans, cattle, fish, and birds. One way or another, the bones, muscles, and other tissues are constructed from the particles that are entangled with other particles on this world, and upon other worlds made during the same super-nova event.

So, when we say, "You are what you eat," we mean it. What's more, it means that over time we may accumulate a new set of extremely advanced and highly sensitive *sensors* in the body that pick up the energy fields generated near particles in other bodies or on other worlds. Some of these fields are not so much made by the physical body as they are by the energy body of other sentient beings. These energies are transferred into the energy of the particles and energies that are entangled, and then these particles and energies have instantaneous effects on other energies and particles throughout the universe, which may have been created simultaneously from the same super-nova event. So, when we say that everything you do will eventually affect the universe, that is exactly what is happening.

Let's think of a simple experiment you can try. If you own an acoustic guitar, you can lean it up against the wall with the strings facing the room. Then, select a radio station on your stereo system. Pick something with a broad range of sound like drums or synthesizer music. Then, turn up the volume. Without warning, somewhere in that song, one of the strings of the guitar will ring out as if someone had plucked it with a pick. In reality, some certain frequency in the music *resonated* with that guitar string. In actuality, the string absorbed that exact frequency out of the music in the room. This sympathetic energy transfer is how each of us affects the universe. It is also how all information is moved through all dimensions regardless of time.

This is a very important concept for you to understand. Life energy resonates with a human soul regardless of its source or whether it is positive or negative. The effect upon any individual soul by this Life energy depends completely upon the vibration of the soul. That vibration, or frequency, is only in the control of the soul himself. The frequency at which you will resonate is entirely your responsibility. The responsibility for the tuning belongs only to the individual. If you are tuned to a vibration that will not be affected by anger, then someone's anger toward you will not affect you. If you are tuned to a vibration that will not resonate with jealousy, then you will not feel or be affected by jealousy. If you are tuned to a vibration that is not love for yourself, then you cannot resonate with the love of anyone.

If you were to learn anything from this, we want you to learn to be more self-centered. Once you are centered more in your self, specifically in your heart, then you will reach the Janus point. This is the point at which you will see clearly the past and the future, but more importantly that although you exist in the *now,* your observation of the time arrow before you and after has a profound effect. After all, from a physics point of view, it is just as far from

LA to San Francisco as it is from San Francisco to LA. Time is nothing more than distance at a rate of change.

Figure 167 - Janus is the dual-faced god of gates. Seeing the past and future of the time arrow empowers us to use the Observation Effect to the advantage of the universe.

We want you to become sensitive to how Life energy works. If you can feel it and learn how to unravel the scripts of past mistakes and misconceptions, then perhaps you can take full responsibility for that energy. And if you can take full responsibility for that energy, perhaps you can awaken to your full potential.

Our observation of any event, past or future, has an effect. We use advanced instruments to see things we cannot see with our eyes. Just because we cannot see things with the naked eye, does not mean they aren't there. For instance, pollen affects the mucous membranes of some people. People had a hard time believing in such things, until one was photographed using an electron microscope.

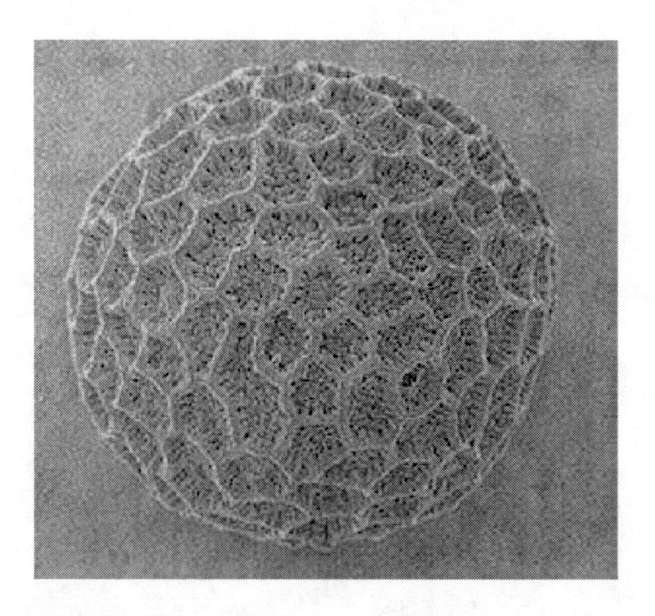

Figure 168 – Pollen at high magnification with an electron microscope

One might think this is an accurate rendition of the pollen spore. Not true. The pollen was altered by its bombardment by electrons to produce the image. When we shine a light on something to see it, because we need the light photons to strike our rods and cones in our eyes in order to see something, that subject is actually, although infinitesimally, being affected by those photons. Thus, our observation of that subject changes that subject.

When we look at a past event with open and clear understanding, the impact of that event changes for us. That does not mean you can affect anything or anyone else in your past, but you can change how it affected you.

For example, two people are taking lunch as a small table at an outside café. While they are quietly involved with each other, there suddenly occurs a traffic accident in the street right next to them.

Figure 169 – Accident reports are as varied as the witnesses

Of course, the police were called and the drivers were interviewed by an officer. He then noticed the couple sitting at the roadside table. Approaching them, he asked if they had seen the accident. He pulled out two new sheets. How many versions of the accident does he have when he finishes? You guessed it. Four. The two drivers and the two diners all gave different recollections.

About this time, the restaurant owner comes out and says that he has a video surveillance camera that has a clear view of the street. The six people then went back to the manager's office to view the tape. Within a few minutes, everyone knows exactly what happened. The four police reports are brought into a state of full corroboration.

Observing the past with a clear vision clears the distortions away and allows the full energy of truth to flow forward. The same thing happens when we review past events in our own lives.

We want to begin the process much earlier, so the human race can walk freely away from the path we have inherited in the year 2015. If the greatest teachers of Earth taught us anything, it was embodied in the two great commandments of Christ:

> "Thou shalt love the Lord thy God with all thy heart, mind, and strength, and the second is like unto it. Thou shalt love thy neighbor as thyself. Upon these hang all the laws and the prophets." Matthew 22:37–39

It is easy to see that Christ was teaching people to love themselves. Without this love, nothing is possible but despair and darkness, which are also great effects on the universe. Hopefully, these are not the effects you want to have on the universe. We are about to unlock the secret for you, so you can have the effect of light. Keep in mind that fear is far more powerful than love. A woman came to a priest friend of the authors to ask for help. She had contracted cancer and was not expected to live much longer. In her despair, she said, "My mother died of cancer. I prayed every day of my life not to get cancer, and here I have it. What went wrong?" thinking to somehow blame God for her misfortune.

To her, our priest friend replied, "Woman, how could you help but get cancer? Your fear manifested it every day of your life. I would have been shocked if you did not get it." The woman's fear had produced the cancerous result as surely as if she was falling from a ladder to the ground. Like fighting against gravity itself, she plunged toward her fear.

Add to this the ever-mounting number of spontaneous remissions from cancer, arthritis, and multiple sclerosis without any medical treatment whatsoever. To this data add the thousands of drug research volunteers who are dismissed each year by pharmaceutical researchers for positive responses to placebos. Rather than tossing out this data, we are showing you that a human being's intentions can destructively interfere with negativity n our lives. The energy of the affliction simply cannot exist in the same universe as the energy out of phase with it. It is physically impossible. And, the opposite is also true. The affliction exists, because you have made a home for it with your own environment, whether you are conscious of it or not. Your parents, teachers, food, water, sunlight, as well as other people around you are an environment from which your genes choose specific proteins that make up every cell of your body, healthy or ill. There are only around 25 thousand genes in the human genome, and more than 120 thousand proteins. Each gene may have a choice of as many as 20 thousand proteins from which it can choose, based on your total environment. Once the cell is programmed with its phospholipid liquid crystal membrane, the program will run unconsciously, without change from the conscious mind. But, prior to forming that new cell, the mind is human intention is most definitely part of the total decision-making process of the genes.

We are not the product of our genetics, but rather the product of our environment. What we need you to realize is that you can modify your complete environment by your intention on the energy within you. And, when you change that, the environment around you cannot remain the same. In fact, it has already begin to change as soon as you realize you can change it. Imagine the effects you can have if you apply the power of your focused intention.

Like the light waves in Young's experiment, the energy from one person adds to the energy of another, and then another. If the energy resonates constructively, then that fear gains tremendous creative energy. What does it create? In the year 2015, after the great cataclysms of 2012 and 2013, the results of billions of people living in fear have been felt. The great wonders made with hands and minds of more than one hundred billion souls has come to ruin through the economic and shooting wars of a few managers of negative energy.

There is a small contingency of humanity that does not live in fear. Rather, they have a pure love about them. They see the good in one another. They are charitable and merciful and seek to grow life wherever they travel. The energy of these individuals also passes into the universe instantaneously. When they gather and resonate constructively, the effect is very positive and counteracts the negative power of fear-based energy. As it turns out, our studies have shown that because of the intention and focus of these positive energies, they are like a laser beam. That is to say, the energy is polarized and focused to a fine and powerful beam that has a targeted effect. Like a small amount of explosive applied at exactly the right place inside an old building, the positive energy generated by humans who are *awake* can clear a building to rubble in a few seconds that may have taken the energy of thousands of workers months to build. This clearing makes possible the construction of something new and beautiful and functional in place of something that was old and perhaps unsafe.

Most of these people are passive in nature. They are humble and work many hours at employment, then save their money to buy a week of freedom to study or travel to places where they can share their peaceful natures with others. They are a cheek-turning people, accepting the aggression of others in a forgiving manner. They are easily taken advantage of by their employers, their neighbors, and even their governments. Throughout history, they have been forced to flee to the wilderness so they could have liberty from oppression. In the year 2015, there is no more wilderness.

Since the beginning of recorded time, these humble souls have blazed new trails across deserts, barren ice floes, oceans, mountains, and even into space. They sold everything they had for passage on a small wooden ship, or they pulled a handcart, or they indentured their lives and the lives of their children, so their grandchildren could live in freedom and liberty.

The result has been that the massive and chaotic power of fear has overcome the world. Like weeds, rapidly growing and ever consuming, never producing anything, the fear-based populace has shadowed every light and nearly wiped innocence from the Earth.

But there is hope. We discovered that fear has an allergy. We found that in the light, the dark energies of fear are cleared away. The challenge for us was to find a way to awaken and enlighten enough people in enough places around the world to flood the planet with light.

We discovered that when a person focuses their *attention* on something they want to accomplish, and then applies their *intention* toward making that manifest in the three-dimensional world, fear was replaced with love. Staying focused on the love, and not manifesting with one's fear, is the challenge of mortality. Teaching that one's attention could be consciously directed is powerful.

Teaching how to master one's intention, was perhaps the most powerful lesson anyone could be taught. When people began to work the formulas of manifestation, the Earth began to change. Those methods were discovered thousands of years ago and lost or suppressed as leaders forced people to become dependent upon them for salvation and survival. They were rediscovered in the early 1990s and applied to a few people. The effect was almost good enough to change the course of humanity. Almost.

That is why we came back to the year 2007 to give you this book. We need the effect of awareness, enlightenment and conscious intention to be larger and more powerful earlier than our present conditions display. In other words, we need you to realize that you are a creator and that you can affect the universe with your intentions. We need you to do that in your day.

We need people to focus their attention and muster their intention to manifest the most beautiful paradise in all of the cosmos, right here on Earth. That is why we have worked so hard to return to begin the Spirit Race in March of 2007. There is a huge difference between what we are asking you to do and what other leaders or prophets have asked you to do. In the past, you may have been told to relinquish your will to someone else's. Do not do that. We need you to realize that your will is the most powerful thing you have. It is the envy of the universe. Not all sentient beings have free will. We are asking you to realize that your life condition, and thus the condition of the world and the universe, are altered by the moment by your intention and Life energy. You are one hundred percent responsible for that energy.

We are asking that you take responsibility for that energy and direct your will to the creation of a peaceful and prosperous world. We know you want to be prosperous. We know you want all peoples to be prosperous. We also know that you fear this is not so, nor can it be so. Your fear is preventing it from becoming a reality. We are asking you to master your fears and apply your will with all of your strength to loving yourself and then loving your neighbor.

We are about to teach you the tools you need to control your body, and then to reach your heart. When you are there, you will soon be able to see where you want to be and where you can apply your energy. First, we will teach you these four steps to ensure you are successful in working the Law of Attraction:

1. Formulate and direct your intention into the universe.

2. Listen for the resonance of the universe.

3. Apply your sequence energy at the exact moment for constructive interference.

4. Continue for at least eight iterations to reach the Golden Mean.

Ringing bell?
I heard you today,
Do I offer thanks
To the rope,
A passing wind,
Or my wish,
At this moment
To hear your sweet tone?

Unlocking the Secret

What understanding and tools are needed for unlocking the Secret? How can the relationship between the behaviors of energies in the universe have anything to do with the state of a human being? How can the energy of one human being make a difference in the universe? What you are about to learn will empower you to change yourself. When you change yourself, everything you touch, love, or think about will change as well.

Generally speaking, there are two types of people in the universe. The first believes that he is acted upon by the universe. The second believes he acts upon the universe. Let's discuss the first type. A common misconception is that bad things or good things happen to a person based on their knack for being in the right place at the right time. The idea that luck determines if someone is successful or a failure at life is engrained in this type of person.

If a person has bad luck, they are poor and chronically in debt, moving from illness to illness and never tasting of the good things in life. They yell at their kids in the grocery store. They gossip and argue easily, refuse to forgive others, and seek remedy often in drugs or alcohol. They rarely draw the pity of others nor do they offer charity to anyone. They consider themselves to be humble, due to their circumstances, yet they harbor a pride rooted in resentment of those who have somehow won life's lottery.

If a person has good luck, they take family vacations every year. They drive new cars that are paid for. They start and succeed at businesses, sometimes selling their added value in those businesses for a profit. They are generally happy and well dressed. They love to meet people, travel, and forgive others easily. Their children all go to college, marry in storybooks, and have ne'er a weed in their perfectly manicured lawns. They go to church every Sunday, reach out and help others, cheerfully without thanks or recognition. They smile at and greet strangers, sing songs, and fuel the hobby and leisure industries with billions of dollars each year. They dream and follow those dreams, receiving great satisfaction and joy from that pursuit.

Now, let's discuss the second type of person, those who believe they act upon the universe. Many outside observers might not observe these individuals at first. These beings may be living in poverty or they may be wealthy. They may be leaders of large corporations or street artists. The key attribute is the knowledge they hold that they are affecting the universe on purpose. The idea that one is *on purpose* brings more fulfillment than all the wealth and human association imaginable. We will elaborate on this for you later.

When surveying people, the author provides a question with multiple choices. Here are the question and the choices:

If you were to choose the result from a five-sided die (an idea originated by Ken Payne), which would you say more closely describes your life in its current state:

a. My Current Life Condition is determined one hundred percent by destiny.

b. My Current Life Condition is determined seventy percent by destiny and thirty percent by choice.

c. My Current Life Condition is determined fifty percent by destiny and fifty percent by choice.

d. My Current Life Condition is determined thirty percent by destiny and seventy percent by choice.

e. My Current Life Condition is determined by my choices.

These surveys are conducted verbally. The reason they are conducted in this fashion is so the *energy* with which a person answers can be observed as well as the choice. When a person chooses "a", he invariably adds energy with his voice. When a person believes that nothing he thinks, says, or does has any effect on the current state of his life, it is reflected in the energy of his voice. That energy can contain hopelessness, as though surrendering to the inevitable course of the Earth around the sun. It may contain bitterness and resentment toward some force, spouse, parent, or even government. The truth is that this person may not have love for himself. The energy is passionate, but directed outward toward everything that has been working against him. Even in this display of energy, there is promise. The very fact that this person will add energy to the answer, belies a deep albeit sometimes flickering desire to rise out of that soul-poverty.

The person who thinks that seventy, or fifty, or even thirty percent of their life is the result of destiny still does not understand the power they have in their being. Even more than the person who chooses a full-destiny answer, there is hope that the truth will set them free.

The only other choice to consider is the one that reveals that the quality and conditions of a person's life are completely the result of personal choices. This realization is a huge jump from the destiny choices. It has been written, "Many are called, but few there be that are chosen."

This is incorrectly translated. The true statement should read, "**Many are called but few choose.**" The discovery that we are the total creators of our lives is the most important awakening of a person's life. This is the point at that "full responsibility" empowers the soul to reach its full potential. And this potential is absolutely unlimited.

Full responsibility is extremely important, so we want to make sure you understand this point. We are not talking about duty, where one goes through the motions of life because of expectations for performance. Duty is a poor and misguided substitute for responsibility. Scripted by churches, governments, and even scientists, duty is a form of indoctrination of the most diabolical nature. Extremes for duty are easy and too numerous to mention.

During the presidential years—those years before the North American presidential council was put in place to stabilize world politics—there was a religion that was utilized to indoctrinate young children to become human bombers. As toddlers these innocents were taught to be Trojan horses. The tactic was known as terror. This form of duty was so terrible and so shocking to the world that three wars were fought to free the people from these religious tyrants. The result was the most horrific crime against the soul since Satan drew a third of the host of heaven out into darkness with him.

The other sense of duty is much less morose, but just as debilitating to the development of a soul. Mostly perpetrated by religions, people are taught that they must sacrifice everything in order to be saved from eternal damnation. They are taught that giving up their own happiness and dreams for the good of someone else is the road to eternal life. They routinely use the life of Jesus as an example of this sacrifice. They focus on the mortal misery and death of this great soul, and refuse to teach the real lessons he taught with his life. His teachings all rested on two things and only two things. The first was to love God with all of your heart, might, mind and strength. The second was to love your neighbor as yourself. Upon these two points of guidance rest all the commandments and all the laws that the universe recognizes.

The fact that love is the most powerful creative power in the universe, and that in comparison everything else is just an illusion, is the one lesson we wish you to retain from this work. We are not talking about affection only, or about infatuation, or even about lust or sex. We are talking about the love one might have for his work, or for his soul mate, or even for playing or listening to music. There is a joy that accompanies this kind of love that will not allow violence to exist. It will only allow growth and peace. In response to love this powerful, energy will manifest into matter itself by its own free will and choice.

This love is the creative power to which mountains will move themselves and around which planets will orbit. When one person harbors this love for another person, both souls will feel valuable and glorious. The evil spoken of in the records of the ancients is akin to fear. Fear cannot exist in the presence of this kind of love. There are many ways by which this kind of love can exist in each of us. Notice that we are not saying that this love can be possessed by anyone. This love exists as a vibration that raises the soul to a new level. This vibration is the Life energy of the individual. When this Life energy is raised to a high enough level, full awareness occurs, and the individual now has a new attention level. Driving this Life energy higher in frequency is our intention. We want you to focus your intention on raising your frequency through intention. If you can do this, you will manifest a higher consciousness. The righteousness described by those ancient writers is nothing more than the continuous correction through internal feedback to achieve Christ consciousness.

A few people have felt this kind of consciousness in their lives and know what it feels like. They have also been able to overcome the challenges of life because they were able to send out the positive energy it took to manifest success.

Most people do not have this experience. They are generally unaware of the energies around them, feeling instead like their lives are the result of chance or even worse, that of destiny.

The reality is that they have mirrors or blockages in their individual flow of Life energy. They have had past events in their lives that create eddy fields in their Life energy that result in repeating errors and preventing success. This is the primary reason why people are not able to unlock the secret of the law of attraction.

The law of attraction exists and functions for all conscious beings. *All entities have consciousness. They are not all, however, conscious that they are conscious.* Nevertheless, they work the law all the same, some to their benefit and thus the benefit of the universe, and some to the destruction of themselves and those around them. They do not see out of their own eyes with purpose.

They are deep inside of their bodies, controlled by them, and wielded by them like wild animals. They are slaves to forces in the third dimension, such as lust of the flesh, the lust of the eye, and the pride of life.

There are those few who are conscious that they are conscious. There are more intelligences stepping into their beings every day. These intelligences are more inspired by *being* than they are by *having*. They are functioning by *doing* those activities that develop their being rather than by *doing* those activities that gain them things. There is a massive difference in the energy of these people. They are changing themselves, their relationships with one another, and they are changing the universe on purpose.

Of course, the reason we are sending this book back to you in the year 2007 is because not enough people were able to operate this law for positive. They lost hope, which a major was a setback for the planet of human beings. We are trying to prevent this setback from occurring. You are the key to accomplishing this. But you are unable to do it on your own.

We discovered, perhaps too late, that there is a very special key to unlocking the secret of the law of attraction. People need to have a clear path for their Life energy to flow. The vast majority of people cannot clear their own way through the baggage and patterns of their past life. How far past can that be?

Well, that is a powerful threshold for people to cross. The truth is that not all beings have mortal human lives past this experience on Earth. They have no history to carry forward. That does not mean they do not have experiences or lessons

Ok. This is probably a good place to talk about soul wounds. Every soul encounters challenges that cause pain. This can come in the form of the death of a loved one, the loss of a job, or merely the realization that one did not achieved a dream. It can come from harm that we have done to another soul. It can come from divorce or the heartbreak of a lost relationship. It can come from war, oppression, and slavery. The victims of ancient cities were able to manifest fire and brimstone with their cries for vengeance.

There is a dual cycle of human social groups that has never been broken. It can be broken, but it will take the conscious intention of masters of Life energy to accomplish it. The cycle looks like the graphic below:

Figure 170 - Mercy–Peace, Justice–War image imagined by Ken Payne.

The cycle begins anywhere you like, but works like this. If you begin at Mercy, then the result is Peace. When we are forgiving and watch out for the welfare of the many, then there is peace in the land. The people prosper and become wealthy together, without guile or jealousy. People live by the laws of love and look for good in all beings and help that good to grow.

Sooner or later, leadership takes a strange twist. The people raise someone up who is willing to take on responsibility as a public servant. They feel the power of using the prosperity of others to do great things. Then the lust for power set in. About the same time, the people ask for this person to take over the responsibility of protecting society from competitors. Laws are enacted. People break the laws. The public trust demands protection from the lawbreakers. Perhaps, instead of forgiving and loving people to help them grow and realize their mistakes, they begin to administer justice. At first it is a few. Then it becomes a minority. Then it becomes a majority.

Mercy gives way to Justice, and the next the next cycle begins. As soon as someone demands justice, the call for war is forthcoming. Borders are enforced, resources are hoarded and dedicated to building up the central powers that protect the people from harm. Then the central powers become their own nation, demanding their own support and never wanting to give up their job. They get good at it. That means enemies must get good at it as well. Then the factories that sell and outsmart the weapons of both sides make money and attract their own secret resources. You get the picture of where we are in the year 2015?

Souls can suffer harm from sacrifice and from fear. Very few people can clear a soul wound on their own. Most people recover from the event and build a wall around that event in their souls. Like a cyst, it sits there invisible to our defense system and never leaves. When the time comes for us to make a choice about something, or react to some stressful event, the encysted soul wound taints the Life energy again and again. It seems as though the person can never overcome this pattern. And, unless the soul wound is cleared they will never move beyond that point in this life, or perhaps in subsequent lives as well. That clearing must be done by someone who is trained in the science of discovery and soul *cystectomies.*

Full Life energy flow is the key to unlocking the secret. *Clearing* is the vital process for helping a person's Life energy to flow. Once this Life Energy can flow without the blockages from old habits, patterns, and other subconscious scripts, the failures that seem to repeat themselves will melt away.

Keep in mind that these patterns can come from many sources. They can be scripted from your parents, your teachers, your friends, and even from enemies. These are memorized by the cell membranes of your body. You react with defensive methods on a cellular level that is beyond reach of your conscious mind. In fact, the mind is normally as detached from your consciousness as your reflexive knee is to the physician's rubber mallet. What you are about to learn is how to get your conscious sentient mind reconnected to your subconscious by creating a safe and positive presence in your heart. You will learn how to get in your own heart-mind.

Through this process you can follow a future path that simply was not available to you in your negative energy state. The mathematics and physics of this process will be explained so you can understand it, not just so that it makes this book sound *scientific* and glittery with fancy terms. You will know for yourself how to open your future to the potential of all potentialities. Here we go.

Memories;
Quantum foam of intention
From that roars the Present
For one fleeting moment,
Reminisced, lamented, treasured
Notes in a symphony called Creation.

Past Life Awareness

Humans are sophisticated and cunning. They are self-preserving at all costs and nearly always react to their surroundings rather than change their surroundings to suit their desires. Human *beings* are defined as those humans who are in some stage of awareness that he or she has existed before and will exist long after this life. Many traditions teach of this, and many do teach the concept of pre-Earth lives. Yet this early life is believed to be in the form of a spirit without physical form, as if we came from some sort of *Guf* (also Gup or Guph: The Well of Souls) where all spirits await their one shot at mortality to add to the processing of their intelligence from some sort of god-thought-embryo into a full fledged god with all power and knowledge. This is nearly completely, and almost certainly, utter nonsense.

The awakened human being realizes he or she has mortal experiences well beyond the ones from this life. These are not merely deja vu, or the channeling of some other being's thoughts, or even the co-existent entanglement of your three-dimensional self with another model of your intelligence who exists in another universe, or dimension, or on this Earth. There is no god-construct around which all of us sit, like huge super-computers, imaging our many peripheral mortalities through life-force modems. The idea that life is for the entertainment of some god, or that it is some kind of punishment for tasting apples, or that we are genetic beasts of burden who became self-aware and got away from our task masters are nothing short of fairy tales. There is no all-powerful being who sends people to hell or delivers them to mansions in the sky. Most of these stories were formed by the very governing religions that used their exclusive access to truth as a sledgehammer to crush those who spoke of the intuition they were receiving from the Life energy that exists around all of us. The truth is that we judge ourselves and condemn ourselves to our own next life by the vibrations we originate. The responsibility for those vibrations, the life energy of our soul, is our responsibility and only our responsibility. Again, let us say that it does not matter how we are loved by others. It only matters how we love them. Everyone.

Each and every one of us is an individual with immense power and glory wrapped up inside. The sovereignty of that knowledge is the greatest key to freedom in the universe. But what is the source of existence? Where did you come from? Who are you? Hold onto something. You are about to hear the truth perhaps for the very first time.

Let's pick up things a picosecond after the beginning. The original Source was unaware. It was alone in the void. It was void because the void was not awake, but rather snoozing in bliss. That's simple enough. There was no up or down or left or right, because there was nothing but black everywhere. Or perhaps there was nothing but light everywhere. Either way, there was no horizon, no hill or dale or ripple anywhere.

Then an amazing thing happened. Source awakened its attention and realized it was asleep and alone and void. This *attention* is a most important concept to master. It is the first mark of sentience. The moment an intelligence can say, "I am," is the moment it realizes, "*I am* is god." Yes.

Attention is the act of a being becoming aware that it is observing something. That observation usually begins with one's self. We might look at our own feet a million times as an infant, but the first time we wonder at their shape, color and texture and movement is an amazing experience. Watch an infant the day he discovers his own feet. He'll reach for them, all out of control and flailing like some sort of robot controlled by a panel with unmarked buttons. Watching the infant punch all the buttons on the arms and legs, trying to learn how to capture that lovely five-toed object out there in plain sight is a fascinating exercise. The closer they get to associating the proximity sensors and the calcium-fired biotics that make the arms and legs move, the more excited these children become.

Until, at long last, they capture the ever-elusive foot with one reflexive grasp. Then a very strange thing happens. They nearly stop all movement. The quadriceps and calf muscles relax. The biceps and forearm muscles work together like a rod and reel to pull the foot in for a closer viewing. And then the amazing thing happens. The foot is drawn into the orifice, the mouth, in which are placed the two most amazing biological spectrometers in the universe. The tongue is a nearly perfect atomic force microscope able to discern very fine details in texture and composition. Upon it are millions of sensors able to perform molecular analysis to a few parts in one million. Salty, sweet, bitter, and sour aspects can be assessed in infinite combinations at blinding speed and to absolutely quantitative precision.

The addition of the nose brings the most powerful and unmistakable piece of analytical equipment in the universe into play. It is the single most powerful means of identity in existence. Once a molecule has been sensed with the average nose, it is permanently cataloged in the memory of that intelligence. Whatever has been associated with that smell is committed to permanent memory.

The infant is now self-aware of the foot. In a few days, he or she will be able to command that foot to its mouth for another examination, until the brain is satisfied it knows everything it wants to know about the foot, and the method for bringing it to the mouth. Depending on the boredom level reached with this new discovery, and perhaps fueled by the success event of completing the analysis of the foot, the infant will move on the next item to be examined.

Every single item picked up by this infant will be placed directly into the mouth for complete scanning.

And within a year or so, the eyes will take over as sole sensor for most objects. Energy in the form of light will take over as the rational form of negotiating one's way around the universe. The mouth and tongue are rarely used for close examination of much more than food or another human body after this point. Perhaps this comes from the hand being slapped away from the mouth by parents, or perhaps it is the result of a bad experience of something being placed into the mouth. Something too hot, cold, bitter, or just plain nasty-tasting will begin the process of using the eyes and nose for non-destructive analysis in advance of placing something into the mouth. It is a complex set of lessons that can be part of even more complex cultures and customs involving the palate and available sources of food. But now you have the idea of how amazing the beginning of self-awareness can be.

Awareness is the first defining characteristic between a human and a human being. A human may be an amazing and complex animal with speed and coordination and an undeniably robust drive to procreate and preserve its own life. But, it is an animal nonetheless. A human is brutal and violent and ever consuming of its environment. It hunts, and gathers, and mates, and will kill competitors to any of those activities. It lives on rage and lust and greed, and will watch another human starve to death without lifting a finger to teach it how to survive if it thinks for a moment that there is not enough to share. It will dig a pit for its neighbor and breathe a sigh of good riddance as the homeless are relocated to the morgue.

A human *being* is the most amazing combination of spiritual and temporal energies in the universe. A human being is the most glorious awareness and is a fascination for all other beings in the universe. The awareness of a being is often called consciousness. When humans exhibit higher consciousness, all other beings in the universe pay close attention.

A human being works in harmony with other life forms. It manages resources at all levels. A human being is not only self-aware, it is aware of all other life in its environment. At this point, we can stop calling a human being *it* and start calling a human being *he*. This is no disrespect to the female of the species. It is merely for simplicity in writing. If you are a woman receiving this book, please mentally replace the word *he* with *she*.

A human being realizes that for his life to continue, some other life form must be consumed. On the most basic level, grass or carrots or algae are consumed by simple life forms. Higher and higher the consumption continues as minerals build plants, and plants build animals, and animals build animals. A human being is aware of this entire ecology and seeks to maintain the balance between all these things. He is aware of the beauty and design of nature. He sees that bees pollinate the flowers, which give rise to fruit that may sustain his life. So, he manages the bees along with his fruit trees.

He is aware that fresh water falls from the sky and fills lakes, rivers, and streams, and is the liquid of life. So he manages the lakes and rivers and streams and oceans of the world so that they are not polluted or obstructed or lost to deserts. He may fish from them, but not take all the fish. He may irrigate his garden, but not consume all the water or pollute the river to prevent his neighbor from also watering his garden. And if there is not enough water, then he learns to collect and gather the rain and manage that resource so everyone can have some.

He is also aware that he is not the only sentient being in the universe. He can learn to freely communicate with beings from all worlds, times, and even universes. He is sensitive to the desires of others and seeks to make things better for others whenever he can. He plays with the cetaceans with the same joy he would any intelligent species in the universe. He may not even domesticate animals for consumption, because he reveres life so much that he cannot fathom one life ending so another can live. Although the feelings of a cabbage can be argued, he has no compunction for consuming copious quantities of sauerkraut. The microscopic life that feeds more complex life to sustain human life is an acceptable and comfortable component to the equation, and he is ever grateful for the bounty of that arrangement.

Let us get back now the idea of *attention*. The awakened human being realizes he has mortal experiences well beyond the present one. There is wisdom in not living in the past, but a working knowledge of these lives may clear patterns of behavior that enable the *being* to reach immortality.

We need to be very clear that the rules of observation always apply. The observation effect is an advanced process of awareness. The observation of past events will change them. The past is an infinite asymptotic tube not unlike an ice cream cone. The singularity at the end is the point of Source division. Let us explain.

The point of *I am* is the point of Source.

$$\bigcirc = \text{Void}$$

There is no attention. There is only Source or *self*. There is no up, down, inside, or outside. There is no awareness. There are only self and sleep and bliss.

$$\sqrt{SOURCE} = \Phi = \text{I am}$$

Source (Self) becomes aware. In this awakening, self shouts, "I am," and bursts into existence.

Although Self is aware, there is still not perspective. The function must be run to completion. The most difficult action in creation now has to occur. Self has to free itself from the bounds of its Source. It must somehow divide the source-circle and allow the function to happen. The square root is released into the universe.

Φ x Intention = OO

The application of intention to Phi is the creative force. There is now perspective, because in this square root function, Source becomes two. Now there is distance and there is some other intelligence with whom to share existence. This other entity is identical in every way to the other, except that one is female and one is male. One is yin and one is yang. When they swirl around each other, creation continues to happen. One without the other is just Source again, and has no perspective. This love and mating is so powerful that it is the creative force for the entire universe. Source is God, and God is you. That is to say, when the two parts are put together, aware and loving and in love, creation occurs. The variety of life in the sea, the sky, and the very energy in the universe itself are the result of the creative force of all the source intelligences in the universe agreeing to create.

When the two parts become separated by space and time, they experience mortality separately, growing and aching for one another. This is also part of the growth process. One would think that gods know everything, are omniprescient, but intimate knowledge of the third dimension is so powerful and so integral to the love that they keep coming back over and over again to either gain it for themselves, or act as a teacher and mentor to others to make sure they experience this joy at least once in their existence. They are ever seeking one another throughout the universe, being born and dying over and over again on one world and then another. When they find one another, the joy is so powerful that every sentient being in the universe and throughout all dimensions rejoices. Ascended masters from all dimensions may come to herald the event, and it is a sight to behold.

The presence of these ascended masters has been photographed. *Orbs* can be photographed with digital or film-type cameras with or without a flash. These also can be observed with the naked eye, but the vibrational level of the observer must be raised to be able to detect the energy. Like ultraviolet radiation, it is just out of the frequency band for the human cells in the eye. With proper preparation, the cells can become sensitive to this radiation and see them appear. *Orbs* come is all sizes and colors. The designs in them are not unlike the mandalas recreated by Tibetan monks in sand or with their artwork. The more high-resolution the camera, the easier it is to see the designs inside the *orb*.

Orbs are attracted to love. Numerous experiments conducted by the author have proven that *orbs* can be nowhere in sight after numerous camera shots. However, upon applying a loving intention to the area, subsequent shots reveal *orbs* appearing in large numbers.

In one such experiment, a high-resolution digital camera was set on a tripod at night in the center of a large group of observers. The reason this experiment is inserted at this point is because the feeling of remembrance and recognition is one that should be felt and should be used as a guide as we proceed with this training.

The camera was set to take a picture every ten seconds for one minute; six shots in total. The author's friend, Miceal Ledwith (author of *The Orb Project)*, stood in an Echinacea field in the dark of night with his hands down at his sides while maintaining a blank and neutral mind. The first flash occurred. He then raised his arms above his head as if beholding the stars over head and began to extend his love into the area. He was almost in an act of blessing. The second flash occurred. He continued to extend his intention for loving the people watching him in a large circle around him, as well as the space around him. The third and fourth flashes occurred. He then lowered his hands and began to return his mind to the neutral and blank state with that he began. The fifth and sixth flashes occurred.

We then went inside to a meeting hall, and the camera was connected to a computer that was connected to a projector. The images were put on the wall in sequence. In the first picture, Miceal was seen alone in the blackness around him. There were no bugs, as it was about fifty degrees Fahrenheit, and there was no breeze of any kind blowing. In the second picture, Miceal is observed with his arms above his head, and a white mist is beginning to form around him as if being conjured between his upraised arms.

In the third picture the mist is so think that it nearly obscures his face. The appearance of *orbs* is profound. There are about a dozen of them in blue, red, white, lavender, green, and even pink. In the third picture, the mist is so thick, Miceal cannot even be seen from the waist up. There are hundreds of *orbs* of nearly every color in the rainbow. In the fourth picture the mist takes on the form of a vortex or a tornado while the *orbs* are too numerous to count. Perhaps there were a thousand of them.

In the fifth and sixth pictures, the mist is dissipating and the *orbs* can be seen exiting the area, as if cooperating with the demonstration. Now, here is the remarkable thing. The camera was a ten-megapixel camera with a large lens and an external flash. The resulting detail in these shots was extremely fine. When these were shown on the wall of the meeting hall, the image was perhaps sixteen feet across. One could walk up to the *orb* displayed on the wall and observe the patterns inside the *orbs*. There were horses, men with beards sitting in lotus position, schematics, geometric patterns, and even what looked like complex machines displayed in clear detail in many of the *orbs*. No two were alike. This was a controlled and objectively observed experiment. The results were irrefutable. The *orbs* appeared as the result of loving intention, were not a flaw in the camera, nor were they the result of dust or insects in the air. One could only wonder how unaware we normally are of the presence of beings who are drawn to our love. The feelings that were recognized by the observers of this experiment were powerful and wonderful.

The reason this is a square root function is simple enough. The circumference of a circle is calculated by using π and multiplying the radius of that circle by itself. The circle gets larger as the square of its radius multiplied by π (pi). This becomes even more fantastic as one realizes that the future, emanating from this Source Point forward, is shaped like a cone and not circle.

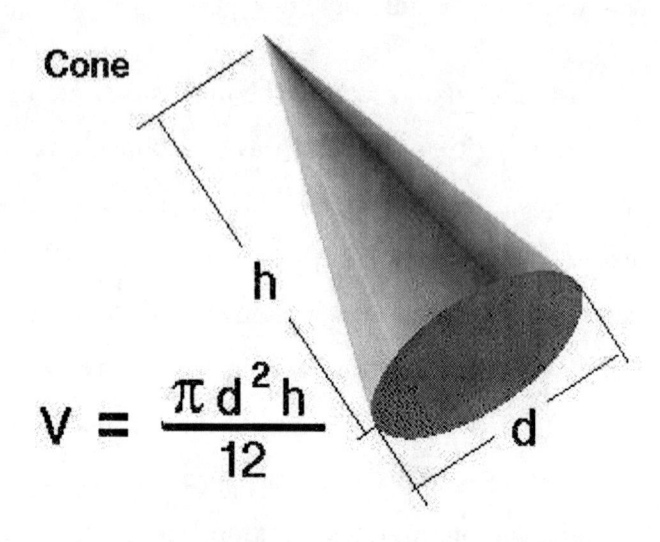

Cone

$$V = \frac{\pi d^2 h}{12}$$

Figure 171 – The square root function occurs because of expansion in all directions at once

This is the result of a two-dimensional circle moving through space with an increasing diameter. Each moment in time is a circle, but the function fits so closely together in such an immediate sequence that it forms a cone. It may not be straight, but rather shaped a little like a tornado, twisting and writhing into the future with power and glory, yet always increasing in radius. The entire structure of one's time life is always changing, and thus difficult to compute, but one can see from the parabolic cone section below that each segment is observable.

$$V = \frac{\pi d^2 h}{8}$$

Parabolic Cone

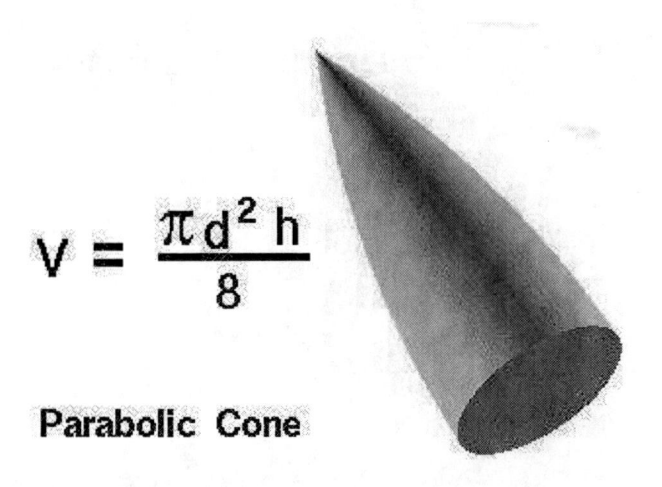

Figure 172 – The changing radius of the cone over time is a result of human intention, ever variable and unpredictable.

As the future is traced back to the present's event horizon, the past narrows to the region around the thread. As the thread is observed, the other dimensions around that thread are affected as well. There are nuances of fact and metaphysics that can be observed and therefore changed by the human being. Segments of the *tornado* or cone can be observed by themselves. Normally, review of one's past is not done from the moment of birth. We select sections of time to examine. This mathematically fits the past review process better than an entire cone formula. The thing to keep in mind is the relationship of events, and how the future possibilities expand in all directions as the square of the distance. The values in the equation are not necessary. The relationship between the different values is important. This structure is called a frustum.

Frustum

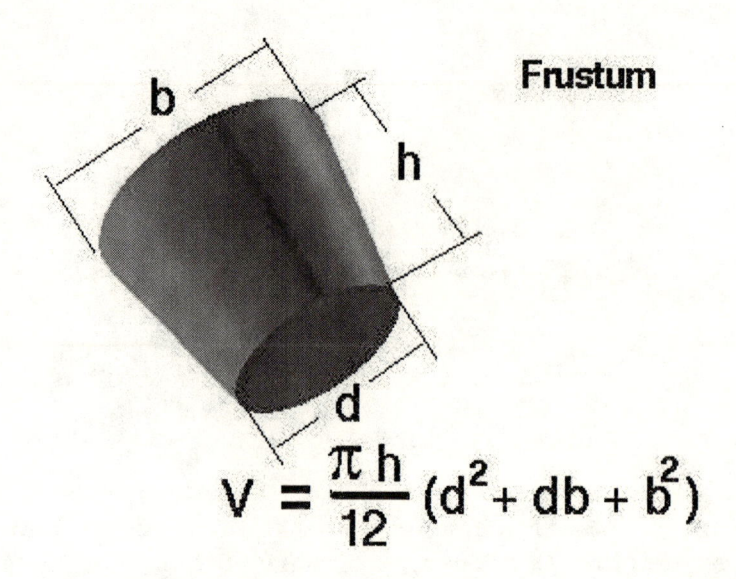

$$V = \frac{\pi h}{12}(d^2 + db + b^2)$$

Figure 173 – The frustum is a section of time examined from a starting line forward to a fixed future time.

Inside this multi-dimensional space, one can form threads or pathways of intention. Although represented by mathematical functions on strings, there are very real aspects of past threads that make up the fabric of past life, and thus of spacetime itself. The attention of a being on the past will entwine with the attention of other beings who may have been part of that experience. Even plants and microorganisms are eventually affected by the observation of a being placed upon a past thread. These past threads are real, yet each time they are observed, they are changed.

Traveling here without a guide can be done, but in order to safely and expeditiously clear an error in a past thread, it is recommended that a guide be utilized. One of the key reasons for effectively observing the past is to correct the position of the present and create a pathway to the future from here. But, let's save the future pathway process for later. For now, just learn the ability to observe the past and effect constructive changes in the now.

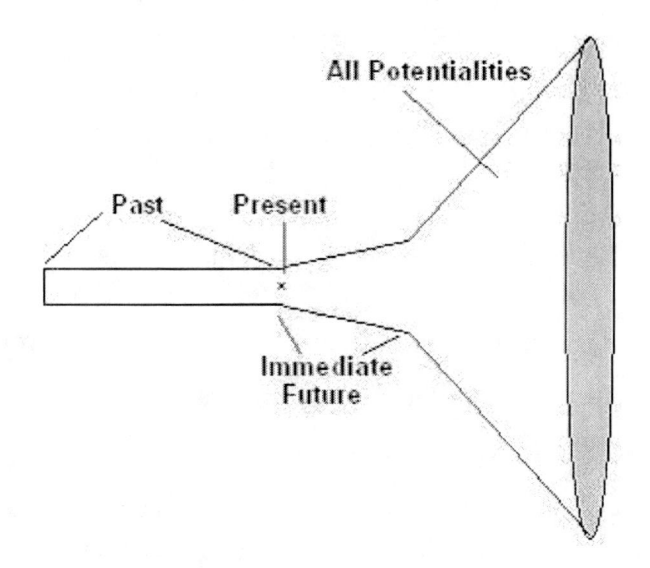

Figure 174 – The past has a narrow range of possibilities for new effects from intention

The Past-Cone is a three-dimensional cone that contains all the energy memories of all the actions, inactions, and interactions between them and everything else in the universe as it pertains to Self. This is a complex fabric of tiny threads, each with multiple dimensions. This fabric becomes more and more complex the further from Source Point Self travels. Consider a single-filament fiber under a microscope. It is sort of like a one-photon thick wire. Even though the filament is exceedingly small, there is girth to the filament. That is to say, there is a cross-section, no matter how small it may be.

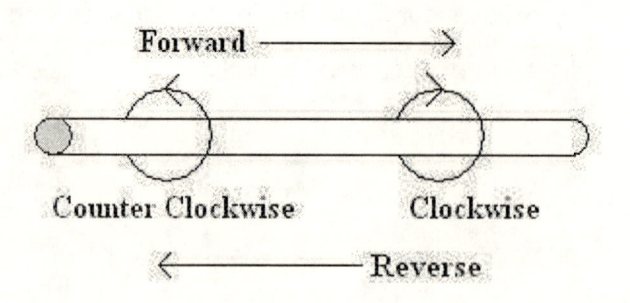

Figure 175 – Future thread with four dimensions of possibilities

Now, there are two directions of consideration around each of these filaments in the fabric and two directions for flow: forward and reverse. There is a counter-clockwise and a clockwise direction. Each of these directions will have a certain energy. Those energies are equal and opposite. When they are combined exactly out of phase, the result is zero; therefore, only one direction can be considered at once.

When the MerKaBa is rotated counterclockwise, there is a certain consideration of past events. When it is rotated clockwise there is another consideration of past events. Each human being has three complete MerKaBa fields.

The primary one is motionless. It is oriented according to the predominant sex of the being. If the female energy is the predominant energy of the being, then the upper tetrahedron, called the Sky Tetrahedron, has the flat surface facing forward. If the predominant energy of the being is male, then the flat surface faces rearward.

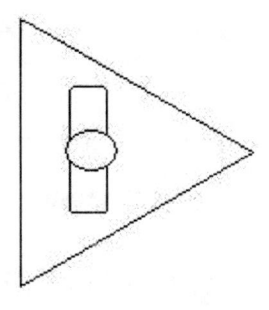

Figure 176 - The male sky tetrahedron orientation

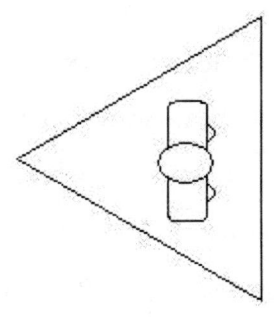

Figure 177 - The female sky tetrahedron orientation

This orientation applies no matter what the biological sex of the person might be. This energy field is normally symmetrical. It may be distorted if the being at some point in his or her life suffered emotional or physical trauma and never was cleared of that wound. Beings suffering from soul wounds may not be able to maintain a symmetrical MerKaBa field. Keep in mind that this is only the primary of three MerKaBa fields that exist around the life center of each human being.

The other two Star Tetrahedron fields are identical in size and shape, but there is a distinct difference. They rotate. Under normal circumstances, the female Star Tetrahedron field rotates counterclockwise, and the male Star Tetrahedron rotates clockwise. Remember, they cannot rotate at the same speed in opposite directions. If this were to happen, the result would be zero.

It is for this reason that they rotate in a specific ratio. Let's talk about this first.

Fibonacci was a brilliant mathematician who rediscovered the progression of growth in nature. We say rediscovered, because these growth progressions have been known for millions of years by all creators in the universe. It is very simple. The number sequence normally starts with zero, as does all creation. There are circumstances where Fibonacci relationships can arise out of other progressions, which we will explain in a moment. Here is a normal consideration for Fibonacci numbers:

0, 1, 1, 2, 3, 5, 8, 13, 21, 34, 55, 89, 144

Notice that the first two numbers are added together to get the third, and so forth along the number line. There is something even more amazing about these numbers. When the progression reaches the number 8, the following consecutive numbers form a very close proximity to the Golden Mean of 1.618 when divided into one another.

In other words, when the number 21 is divided by 13 the result is 1.616. <u>This is extremely important when considering</u>

creation. No religion or philosophy can take a single decimal point away from the mathematical truism of sequential creation. Now, does one have to go all the way back to the beginning to find these ratios? No. In fact any two numbers can be utilized in a Fibonacci method. Let's take any two numbers like 75 and 216. These two numbers are far apart. They are not factors of one another. Yet, if we add the two numbers together, and then continue in a Fibonacci pattern for 8 more iterations, the result will be the Golden Mean. Amazed? Watch.

$$75 + 216 = 291$$
$$216 + 291 = 507$$
$$291 + 507 = 798$$
$$507 + 798 = 1305$$
$$798 + 1305 = 2103$$
$$1305 + 2103 = 3408$$
$$2103 + 3408 = 5511$$
$$3408 + 5511 = 8919$$

Now observe this: $\dfrac{8919}{5511} = 1.618$ The Golden Mean!

We have shown you that if you go back to the past and add any two events on your path, no matter how distant in time, within eight additive motions the Golden Mean can be achieved. This is equally functional with future movements. This is the process of perfect creation. Rotating the MerKaBa fields in ratios of the Golden Mean, with the male rotation as the higher of the two numbers, will produce the perfect manifestation field for human beings. We'll explain this more after we discuss the other dimensions around each of the filaments.

This is vitally important for the reader to understand. Most people have dreams. If you don't have one, it is probably because you forgot the one you had when you were s child. We often make plans to accomplish the dream, but most of the time it does not manifest. The Fibonacci sequence does not need to start at zero. It can start anywhere. And, as we have now proven, once you start adding events to the sequence, within eight iterations, the process is obeying the Golden Mean, most likely in harmony with the universe.

Most people don't achieve their dreams because when a door closes in front of them, and another opens, they keep walking for about three doors. Then they quit. The universe will resonate with you intention, no matter what. But, if you quit before eight iterations, you will not succeed. Does this mean you must experience seven failures before you experience a success? Possibly, but not likely. The joy you will feel because you are walking your dream process will be so great that you will already feel successful. In fact, finishing isn't the goal of a proper dream anyway. Dreams should be all about *doing* and *being*, rather than *having*. We are always amazed at how many people dream of having things rather than being something or processing something.

Many times when we ask people about their dream, they say they want a millions dollars. Pressing further, we ask why they want the million dollars. They usually say something like they want to travel or be able to help others with their money. So, the real dream is not the money.

Figure 178 – Wealth is a misplaced dream.

We realize that dream building on *things* only gets us to a place where we are ready to die. In other words, when you get that red sports car you are dreaming about, is your life complete? Are you ready to die? Getting things or having things is a result of being and doing. Being is the awakening process we are trying to accomplish with sending this book back to you with all the knowledge of the ancients tied together with the learning of the End Times. We feel that with the access to knowledge that you have in your time and the addition of the messages left by the ancients—though some may be veiled in symbols designed to convey the truth without costing them their lives—you would have all the tools you need to manifest proper and useful dreams. Dreams of *being* will naturally lead to the action of *doing*. When we bring our dream of being into the world of work in the three-dimensional world, the doing begins. This doing is the value of a mortal life. It is the true reason why we come to this dimension to do work. And, contrary to many teachings, this Earth is one of the best places in the universe to have a mortal life. Look at who has come here to experience a mortal life. Adam, Gandhi, Moses, and even Jesus came here to experience a mortal life. Don't feel like this is such a bad place.

The truth is that when someone asks you where heaven is, you need only say, "Right here." By the same token, when someone asks you where hell is, you need only say, "Right here." What we are trying to teach you is that you and only you can make this world a heaven or a hell. It can happen within the walls of your own home, or even within the walls of your own cells. The difference between an optimist and a pessimist is that the optimist believes we live in the best of all possible worlds, and the pessimist fears that's true. Same world…different manifestations.

So, before you finish this book you should know that dreaming is about *process* and not about things. Working toward your dream is the goal, not the actual finishing of the thing. That is to say, serving as a schoolteacher is a good dream, because it is about the process of teaching. Dreaming of a red sports car is not a good dream.

Figure 179 – The things of this world are distractions from our true nature as spiritual beings.

The thing to remember is to dream. As a child you had them. As a rational grownup you have been indoctrinated to believe in three-dimensional treasures as the goals of life. Be like the child again and dream of the sand castle.

Figure 180 – Building the sand castle

Like the child building the sand castle, the process of forming the castle with one's hands is the goal, not finishing the castle. Owning a fine home or having a million dollars in the bank is not a proper dream. Being a teacher or a talk radio host is being something. These are proper dreams. The main idea to remember here is don't quit after two or three failures. Remember that the universe will flow things to you according to your intentions and your response to that flow must reach eight iterations before the Golden Mean can be realized.

Notice that there exists a pathway around the circumference of each of these photon-thin filaments. Keep in mind that a photon is considered a massless particle. We are only displaying the particle here so you can better imagine it with your three-dimensional brain. Just because it is massless, does not mean it does not exist. If you want to see if they exist for yourself, just turn on a flashlight and observe the light beam. For a simple understanding, let's assume an irreducible complexity here. This light is formed by the photons generated when electrons move from one energy state to another around a molecule. Electrical current provided by the battery excites the electrons to a higher state. When they change state a photon of a frequency exactly matching that difference radiates out from that molecule. Red, white, yellow, blue and so forth for all frequencies in the visible and non-visible range obey this principle.

So, when we say that a photon moves through time, it forms a thread through the time cone that becomes part of the fabric. As human beings, we can and do emit billions of these photons each and every moment. When these photons move through space and time, them exhibit the properties of a wave. When we stop to see their spin, they behave as particles. This Wave-Particle duality has been the bane of physics for more than a century. Each photon has a spin that is either positive or negative. For our purposes, we want you to think of it as clockwise or counterclockwise. The spin of this particle can be reversed electromagnetically. This can either be done with sophisticated instruments or with human intention.

Recall the entangled particles we discussed earlier. These particles are originated by the individual himself. They might be entangled with other human beings or even with beings who are not human. That means that when the spin is altered by you, the particle in the other being's time cone changes spin instantaneously. When the other being changes the spin on a particle placed in his time cone, the spin of the matching particle in your time cone changes as well. Without any effort of your own, your past changes. An event or an act in your past can change through the intention of another being. You can change the past of another being by your intention as well. This is conditional upon the two particles being entangled. This normally means that the two of you had some kind of relationship or shared experience.

The limits on this activity are infinite. That is to say, the past can be, and is, constantly improved and altered by the intention of the participants. In physics, giant gravitons in large numbers as dielectric gravitational waves form fuzzy cylinders that mathematically behave in exactly the same manner.

Each thread is actually a pathway formed by the passing of the particle through time. Now, we can get a picture of how complex the relationships between a human being and the universe of other sentient beings can be. Even more clearly, we can see the effect of intention upon the universe. So let us do this with purpose.

Oh butterfly,
Distant flower desired,
Supped life's nectar
Without a single
Linear stroke
Of her painted wings.

Manifestation of the Future

The intention of a sentient being is the most powerful force in the universe. It is the creative force of all things. Human beings have ego that unlike the butterfly, tries to draw a straight line between the present and the future. We bring this chapter to you because it is vital for the future of the human race for you to learn how to manifest the future. The future unfolds like a world with no horizon. The rate of movement seems to be fixed as we look at our watch or compare our performance against the timer.

But human beings have the ability to comprehend alternate time lines. We are by spiritual nature not bound to three-dimensional time. It is only our mortal bodies that are locked into the linear flow of time. This is the reason minutes turn into hours, and days or even months turn into a few minutes when we consider them. When we're on vacation, the days go by like seconds. When we're at work, the last few minutes of the day can take hours.

The only manageable segment of time is the moment. This is a snapshot of distance that can be considered by a human being. The culture of the Earth in the year 2007 was built around planning for the future of retirement and leisure. Those who could contribute to their 401-K retired on the golf course with new cars in the garage. Those who did not plan retired in poverty on Social Security. This mindset is what really destroyed the ability to manifest the future. People ended up working lives they hated for thirty or forty years so they could retire in comfort. But they usually were in such poor health and had long since lost sight of their dream by the time they retired that they could not have joy. They forced a future thread through the cone of time and passed by the bounty the universe displayed all around them every microsecond of every day.

This chapter will help you become aware of the bounty of the universe around you. It will teach you a method of preventing yourself from forcing a future thread through the cone of time. Instead, like the butterfly, you will fix your sight on the dream of the flower, and then beat your wings. The universe will not only hold you up, but will provide you rich supply all the days of your existence. The most important thing is that you will always be on your purpose, without sacrifice and without letting the sun go down without gratitude for every experience in your life. The variety and wonder of life will fill volumes of your journals. And the dream of retirement will drift away, because you will never want to stop what you are doing.

The hardest thing to do is to define one's dream. "What do I want to be when I grow up?" is the hardest question in the universe to answer. This involves a healthy exercise. We must look far into the future without much information to go on. When we are young, it is particularly difficult. Or is it? We emulate positions like astronauts or firefighters when we're little boys or actresses and flight attendants when we're little girls. What do you think it would be like to be able to stop any moment of any day and say, "I am doing what I always wanted to do"?

This is known as being *on purpose.* In the cone of time, there is always a finite number of choices we can make every microsecond. The curse perpetuated by religionists that we can never be perfect is wrong. Period. Perfection is merely a stage of completion. We can be and are perfect all the time. You are the perfect individual receiving the sum total karma of your choices from all of your existences. Nothing but this result can occur. It is perfect and you are perfect, *just as your father who is in heaven is perfect.*

So, when we look at the dream flower, the human nature is to imagine being at the flower. Then we draw a step back, and then another, and then another until we are standing at the present moment in time. Our training tells us that if we follow that path, we will have no choice but to arrive at the flower. Ta da. Retirement. Now what?

Ah ha! So the flower is not the dream after all. Have you ever gone to the beach to build a sand castle? We sit down in the sun and begin scooping wet sand into a pile, then sculpt it with our hands. The process is creative and artistic and can take an hour or more. Then, it is finished. What do you do then? Walk away. Jump on it. Wait for the tide to come in a wash it away. The point is that it is not the sand castle that is the goal. It is the building of the sand castle that is the goal. The joy comes from the building, not from the retirement. The purpose of building was the dream. When you are on purpose, there is no need to finish the sand castle. The act of building while focused on the sand castle is the true dream.

Now, what we have done holographically is to explain to you that we can move through time while focused on a target without drawing a future thread. A future thread is the "but first" list that we tend to make when we consider a task or goal. The corporate world and the *on purpose* world are compatible, believe it or not. The idea is to encapsulate or compartmentalize the worlds inside one another.

Now we have to consider resonance from the universe. Remember the example of the sympathetic resonance using the guitar leaning against the wall? What we want to share with you is the ability to present your guitar to the universe so you can resonate with the bounty that is there for you. For now, we'll teach you about this in receive mode. Then we'll teach you about the send mode.

With the understanding that there have been many thousands of books written on this subject by the year 2007, we seek not to compare this discovery to any of those. This is the discovery of the use of intention to manifest the future. It is designed to work with the purpose of your heart. Although this training may not fill your bank account with millions of dollars, as this is really not anyone's goal anyway, it will fill your life with the flow of joy that you imagined the money would bring you.

You may have thought the million dollars would give security while not having to work a full-time job, the opportunity to meet really neat people, and to travel the world. But if you could travel the world, meet all kinds of really neat people, and have security without working a full-time job without the million dollars, you have still reached your goal.

So, here we go. Step by step, this is how to manifest the future.

Step One – Getting in the heart.

The goal of the first step is to reach the heart. Being *in the heart* allows us to be aware of the universe and tunes our intention to the universe. Here is how that is done in writing. This usually takes more practice for men that it does women, but it can be achieved by everyone. The heart is a very unique organ, to be sure. But most people don't know that it actually contains some gray matter. That's right. The heart contains brain cells. This is a section of the heart that if harmed during surgery, the heart stops, and the patient dies.

The more remarkable realization is that human beings may actually have the ability to think with their hearts. The heart is the launching pad for your consciousness. There is some preparation to getting in the heart.

The MerKaBa meditation is the best method we have seen for enabling a person to reach his or her heart. With practice the person may imagine being in the heart without going through the MerKaBa meditation. The energy field generated by the MerKaBa meditation may last as long as forty-eight hours, but daily meditation is far more successful at enabling this process. Here is how it works. There are seventy conscious breaths to reach this point. Using the audio CD *MerKaBa II* recorded by Maureen St. Germain is the best way to master the timing. You can find the CD just by searching for the *MerKaBa II* recorded by Maureen St. Germain. There are some points that are critical that we will discuss in detail below.

The Breaths

The following numbered items are individual breaths in a sequence designed to prepare a physical body for conscious contact with the higher self, or source. This includes finger and hand positions called mudras. These connect energy body circuits for the body and facilitate the flow of Life Force.

1. Touch the index finger of each hand to the thumb like a ring, close your eyes and breathe in through your nose fully.

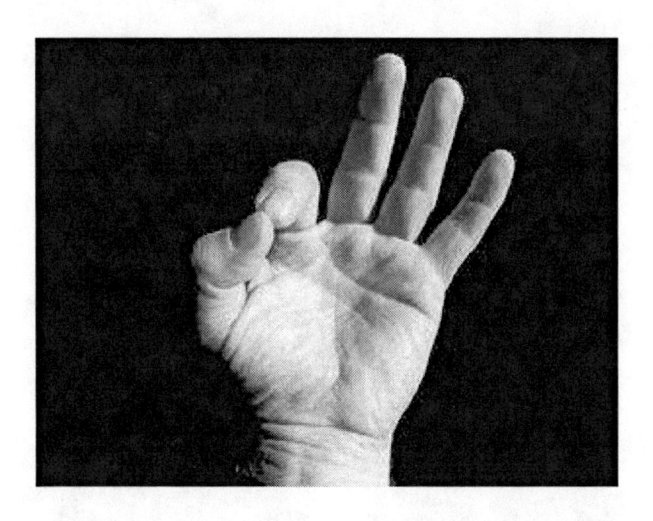

Figure 181 – Mudra with thumb and index finger.

While doing this, imagine the sky tetrahedron around your body filled with light. You're not filling it with light. It is already filled with light, marked by the solid lines at the edges of the tetrahedron as if they were strings pulled tight. Keep your throat open as though you were about to blow out a candle. It takes about three seconds to visualize the tetrahedron shape. For men, the edge of the tetrahedron faces forward parallel to the bridge of the nose. For women, the flat face of the tetrahedron faces forward parallel with the bridge of the nose. Exhale through the nose all the way until the lungs are empty. Close the throat, not allowing any air to enter the lungs. Imagine the Earth tetrahedron filled with light. Observe that there are impurities like clumps of negativity in your life floating in the light. Open the eyes, cross the eyes, and sweep them up and down, then close them again. This process is called the *Pulse*. It is designed to sweep the negativity out of the light. As soon as this is done, continue to breath 2.

2. Move the thumb of each hand to the second finger and repeat the breathing cycle.

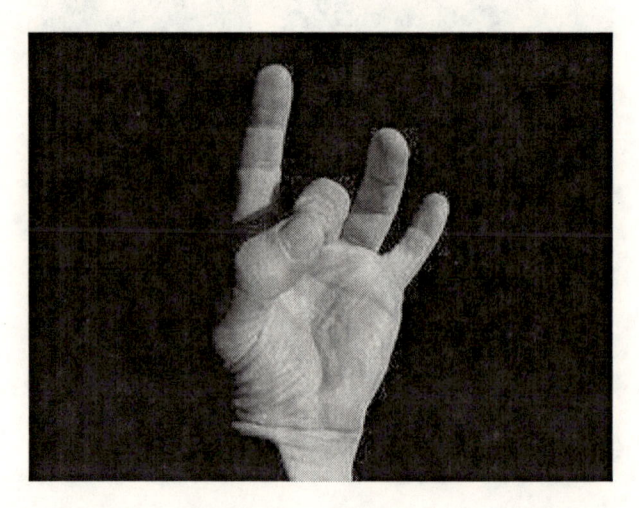

Figure 182 – Mudra with thumb and second finger.

3. Move the thumb of each hand to the ring finger and repeat the breathing cycle.

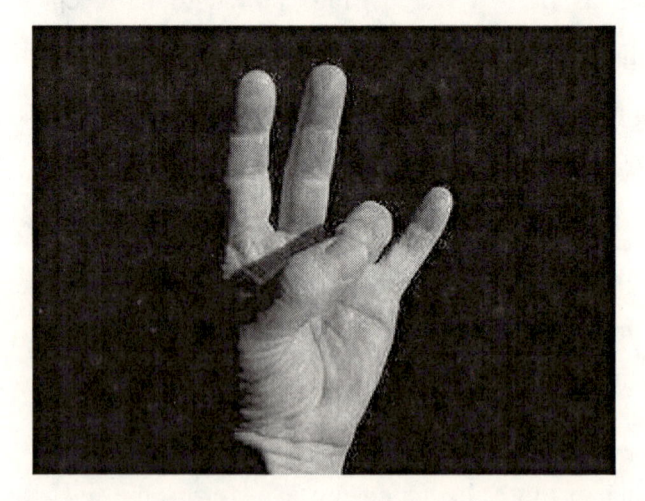

Figure 183 – Mudra with thumb and ring finger.

4. Move the thumb of each hand to the little finger and

repeat the breathing cycle.

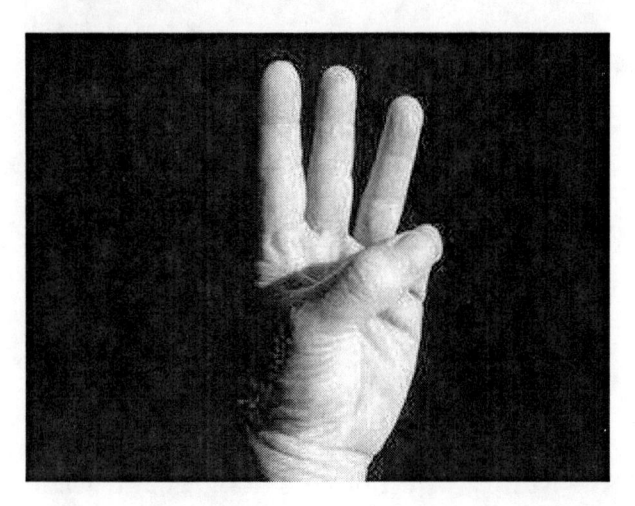

Figure 184 – Mudra with thumb and little finger.

5. Move the thumb of each hand back to the index finger and repeat the breathing cycle.

6. Move the thumb of each hand to the second finger and repeat the breathing cycle.

7. Move the thumb of each hand so that it touches the index finger and the second finger. While keeping the eyes shut, imagine a small light beam pinched between this finger union. Aim that imaginary light beam coming from the spot where the fingers and thumb meet directly at your forehead. Repeat the process of breathing.

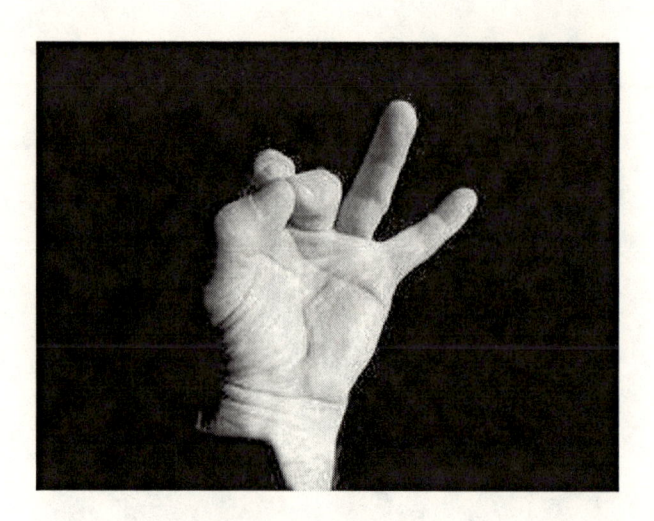

Figure 185 – Mudra with thumb and index and second fingers.

8. Keep the same finger position, except we are no longer clearing the negativity from the Earth tetrahedron. Now we want you imagine the Prana (life sustaining Force) tube that runs along the human body spine. This is open to the sky and the Earth. We want you to begin drawing energy into your body through these tubes. This energy will collect in your body just behind the belly button. With this breath, it will form a crystal the size of a baseball.

9. Keep the same finger position. Remember to breathe deeply and exhale completely and consciously. The spirit is beginning to expand away from the physical body, so concentration is required here or you will drift away and forget to breathe correctly. Keep gathering energy through the Prana tubes. The ball of light is the size of a basketball. It is gaining light and is the color of a harvest moon.

10. Keep the same finger position. When the breath is completely taken in, hold the breath slightly, building pressure. The ball of light is now the color of the sun and very bright. With great intention and power, force

the breath out like you're trying to blow out a candle five feet away. Imagine the ball of light instantly blowing up to a diameter of about six feet, with the small, round crystal light in the center. They are bright and spinning. The direction is not important at this time, only that they are not spinning at the same rate, or that the smaller crystal is barely revolving, and the larger sphere is revolving at high speed. They are not stable yet. You may have a sensation of wobbling while you are sitting.

11. Keep the same finger position. Real concentration is required here, so you don't drift away too soon. This breath is deep and conscious, in and out through the nose, using the same amount of time for both. During this breath the stability of the spheres is the goal. Try to synchronize the revolutions so the spheres do not wobble. The spheres are concentric. That is to say, they are exactly surrounding one another. All you have to imagine is the crystal spheres stabilizing. They will do this naturally, but there will be a very strong temptation to drift into sleep.

12. Keep the same finger position and use the same breathing technique. Maintain your concentration, as it does take three full breaths for this process to complete. During this breath the stability of the spheres is the goal. Try to synchronize the revolutions so the spheres do not wobble.

13. Keep the same finger position. The breath is still deep and conscious. During this breath the stability of the spheres is the goal. Try to synchronize the revolutions so the spheres do not wobble.

14. Now, imagine moving the center of the spheres from the belly to the heart. Change the hand positions so that the hands are flattened (see figure below). The male will rest the back of his left hand in the palm of his right hand, with the first knuckle in behind the first

knuckle of the other hand. Extend the thumbs and touch them, forming a triangle in front of the hands pointing away from the body. The breaths become shallow here. Stay here as long as you like, but we must keep moving along. Tell yourself that you want to be in your heart. Imagine traveling from the Pineal Gland, just above the roof of the mouth, down the trachea to a point just to the right of your heart. Consciously, move to the left, through the muscle and directly into your heart. You will notice a void there. It should feel like a point between two vortexes. Consciously, in your mind, say the words, "Let there be light."

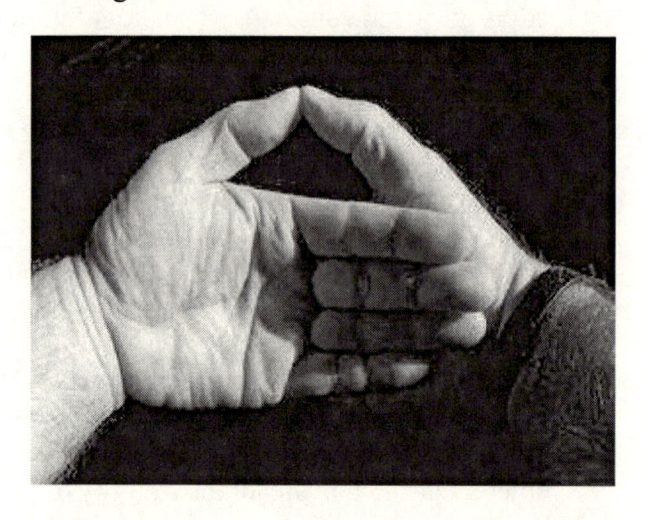

Figure 186 – Mudra with hands nested (male).

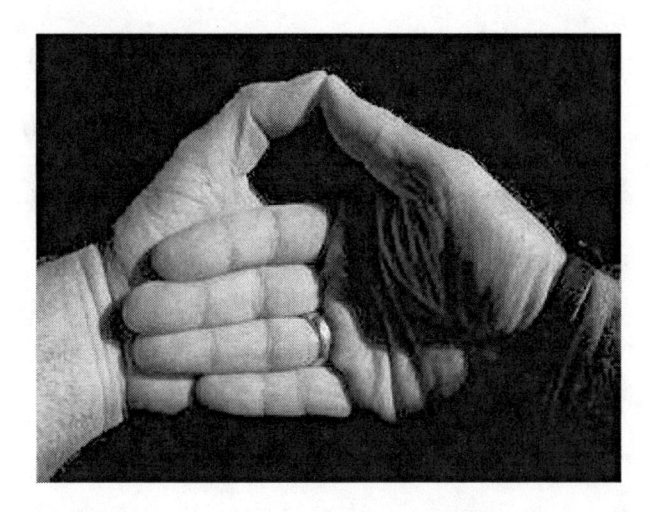

Figure 187 – Mudra with hands nested (female).

15. Keep the hands in the same mudra position. Take a deep breath in through the nose, but do not close the throat. Imagine the two star tetrahedron fields that are not fixed. One is going to start rotating to the counterclockwise or female direction, the other is going to rotate in the clockwise or male direction. Just get them spinning. These are complete star tetrahedra, and not the individual tetrahedra (sky and Earth). The sky and Earth tetrahedra are locked together as a set. Exhale with a forced breath as before.

16. Inhale completely and bring the two star tetrahedra to 9/10 the speed of light in a ratio of thirty-four to the left, and twenty-one to the right. All you have to do is say to yourself, "Thirty-four to the left and twenty-one to the right," and it will be so. This is a Fibonacci ratio that results in a Golden Mean. Exhale with a forced breath as though you are trying to blow out a candle a few feet away.

17. Inhale completely through the nose and spin the star tetrahedra at the speed of light with that ratio in mind. You don't have to over-think this. They will assume

that ratio if you command them to do so. Exhale with a forced breath as before. Your MerKaBa is now set in motion and will remain in place for forty-eight hours.

Continue to meditate as long as you need from here.

Step Two – Learning to intend with intention

Now that your MerKaBa has been activated, and you know how to get into your own heart, we can work on sending and receiving from the human being. The human being is a very capable electromagnetic transmitter and receiver. The cell membranes of your body actually function like a liquid crystal, changing state with stimuli, just like a computer, but with the power of an interdimensional transceiver. Your body is also capable of receiving energy from multiple dimensions. It is an even more prolific transmitter, whether you are aware of it or not. It can send energy across the universe instantaneously. The intention of a human being is sent out whether it is intended or not. Lest that not make sense, we want to clarify. You will send out positive of negative energy at all times, even after death. You can send out this energy reflexively, just like the knee struck with the rubber mallet, or you can change the form and frequency of that energy with your intention. You have almost all the tools. Here is the final tool you need to take conscious control of a subconscious process. Using these breaths and this process, you will be able to change the course of your life, your family, your community, and even the planet.

The Eighteenth Breath

This realm of concentration will become your most powerful

and peaceful place for manifestation and reflection. The state of body that works best is the one between sleep and wakefulness. It takes skill to master this, but one does not have to practice for forty years in a Tibetan monastery to get great results. Most of the MerKaBa meditation instructors talk about the eighteenth breath, but they do not teach it. It is an individual thing. But, there are some common attributes to this meditation, while you are in the heart, that we can impart to you. They work. They are extremely useful in helping you conquer the three-dimensional hold on your spirit. Here we go.

The eighteenth breath can be done anytime you need to concentrate, but we recommend it *after* you have completed the first seventeen breaths and activated your MerKaBa tetrahedra to 9/10 the speed of light in the 21:34 ratio.

While your hands are in the mudra assumed at the fourteenth breath, with the hands in cupping shape and the thumbs touching, change your breathing pattern. Remember, the energy body of humans for males is different that females. The body tetrahedra are oriented differently, and the mudras are different. The male cups his left hand in his right hand, and the female cups her right hand in her left hand.

This is a twelve-second cycle. Follow this procedure:

Inhale through nose

Exhale through mouth

Pineal Gland

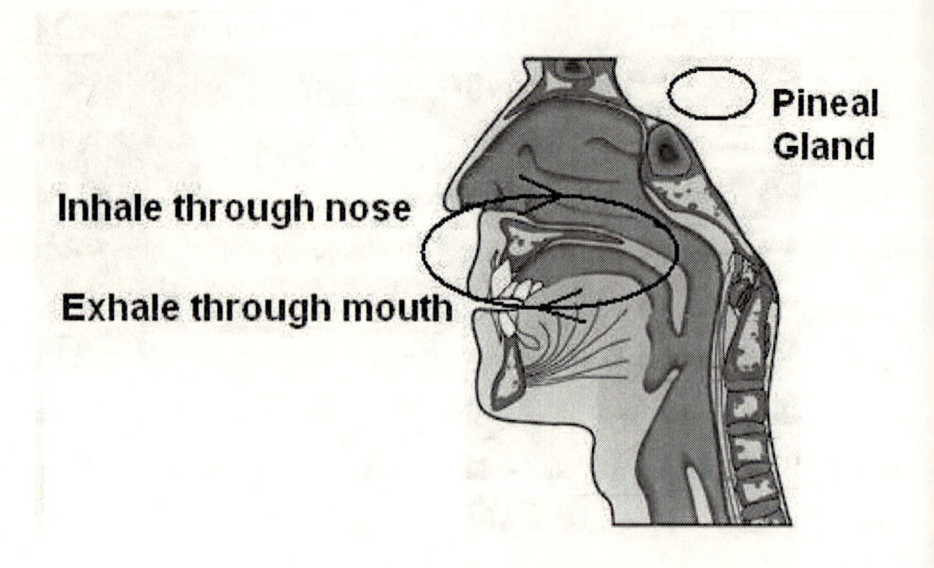

Figure 188 – Method for the eighteenth breath

1. Take a three-second breath through the nose and hold it while keeping the throat open as if you were about to blow out a candle. The depth of this breath will vary, depending on your blood-oxygen content. That is to say, some people will need to start with deep breaths to feel like they're getting enough air. Some will breathe shallowly. As you progress into the depths of this meditation, the breaths will naturally become very shallow for the three seconds.

2. Hold this breath for three seconds while keeping your throat open.

3. Exhale for three seconds through the mouth. Make the breath even all the way through. Try not to blow out quickly and then taper off the breath. Make it smooth and even all the way to the end, taking three seconds to exhale. If you keep the lips slightly parted and use the tongue against the roof of the mouth, you will form a sort of one-way valve that will accomplish two things. First, it takes no effort or thought to control that way you inhale or exhale. Second, it connects the tongue to the Chakra

directly behind the eyes. Many masters have told us that this connection is important for the energy vortex to form beneath the pineal gland properly.

4. Hold the exhalation for three seconds while keeping the throat open. Do not close the throat. It is as though you are about to take a breath, but you hold it instead. This is a very low-energy physical state and can be mastered to operate while you are nearly unconscious. This ends the twelve-second cycle. Repeat this for as long as you can.

There is an amazing physical transformation you will realize in just a few breaths. Your physical body begins to separate from your spirit body. You will feel the disconnection almost immediately, and with a little practice, you may be able to easily travel to distant places and times. It will take some discipline to control the wandering, because you have some work to do here. You do not want to drift into sleep and lose control of your conscious breathing. Your awareness will be heightened to areas of extreme sensitivity, even lucidity. Your placement in time will appear inconsequential, and thus your ability to alter the effects past events have had on your life, in the moment they actually occurred. In other words, you will actually be able to change the way you are affected in real time as though you were reliving the event again, this time with the knowledge you now possess from the future.

When a human being expresses himself with power, whether he intends it or not, the expression sends out a *karma wave*, which is very similar to the photon of light we discussed earlier, across the universe. It may sympathetically resonate with anyone or anything that is nearby or distant, present or past, that is receptive to that vibration. This means that from an energetic point of view, human beings can be like a bull in a china shop. We can display nearly unlimited power in an environment that might contain very delicate and expensive things and people. Whether we intend to or not, we may crash around destroying everything in our path. Then we may throw a tantrum that things are not going our way, having unwittingly caused the very conditions that are upsetting your world.

As we have discussed earlier, one hundred percent of your life is the result of your choices and your energy. As we have mentioned earlier, all matter and all beings are conscious. Most every being is simply not conscious that it is conscious.

Also as we have mentioned earlier, the feedback from the universe will come to you, based on your intention. You were not been given the toolbox to be able to know when it is coming, and how many steps you must take to allow your action on the universe to resonate with you. Remember, it takes eight iterations, so don't give up after the first three failures. Thousands of people we have interviewed have life books full of failure and disappointment from three-page stories. They send out their dream intention and then walk through only three or four doors before giving up.

As each karma wave yield arrives, you must be listening and ready to add your precisely measured energy to the wave so it will gain strength through constructive interference. If you are aimless, or cursing God because you have not immediately received your blessing, then you will not be capable of adding energy to the wave as it comes by. This lack of resonant energy from you almost always results in the wave dying out and never coming back.

When you reach the eighth iteration, you must be very careful to listen closely to the universe. Pay close attention to your energy output. If you are negative, cynical, or fearful, you will block the blessings coming to you from the resonance with your dream. If you force your own future threads into existence, then you block the universe from resonating with your dream much like a capo added to the neck of a guitar. All the pitches have changed, like flowers coming from rain and sunshine, and may sound nothing like the composition you imagined. The best place to do this listening is in your heart, while performing the eighteenth breath process.

When you are quiet, you can hear the universe. When the next step comes along, you will be perfectly fitted hear it, and you will be ready to step forward on it like a moving stepping stone of glass. By faith and synchronicity, you will move irreversibly toward your dream through the process of constructive interference. Even the best masters teach endurance. Every single sport is won in the last few moments. The team that walks away from the eighth inning, or the third quarter, or the penultimate play, loses. Remember this very carefully. <u>You are not playing against anyone except yourself</u>. You are trying to become what you want to be. You are trying to do what you want to do. For good or for ill, it will be so. Above all, keep in mind that it does not matter how much you are loved. It only matter how much you love others. Praying for the destruction of your enemies only lowers your own frequency. This is a self-checking system. Building darkness and fear will not resonate with light, and will result in only darkness and fear.

Praying that the hearts of your enemies will be softened and that they will receive peace and become comfortable in the light will raise you up and send vibrations that only resonate with light. If the darkness is not constructively altered by the observation of that light, then it will dissolve like a single handclap on a deserted beach.

The entire universe, and all forms of life, are inside of you. You carry the DNA of all beings inside of you. You are made of matter that is inextricably entangled with the universe, with Source itself.

Conclusion

Since the inception of this series of books in 2001, the efforts to send back Part Two from the year 2015, and nearly six years of writing our results of more than fifty years of research, we have changed. Rather we have grown. Where once we may have been indoctrinated, we have reached much further into the maelstrom of knowledge from many worlds. We have gathered our strength and testimony from direct contact with the most powerful love in the universe. We have come to know you, the reader, and met thousands of people around the country as we have toured to speak and try to raise support for our projects.

Now, at the end of *The Ark of Millions of Years* trilogy, we feel sure that these pages will leave you with the knowledge to make your lives more full of hope and excitement for your dreams and for your ability to love others. We also feel that we have left you with the tools to work the Law of Attraction to your advantage.

Sleeping souls are affecting the universe with the same empowerment that you do. Unfortunately, the effects of their intentions are nearly without exception bad for everyone. They feel that their lives are full of destiny and not under their control. Well, you feel differently now.

You know that you are not only in total control of your own life, but that your attention and intention do affect the universe in a very powerful way. You know how to dream. You know the messages left for us by the ancient races that once lived here, and we might add that they would be quite envious of your world today. That is to say if they were someone other than you.

You have worked for many thousands of years, perhaps millions of years to get to this point. You stand on the edge of the precipice along with the entire race of sentient beings on this planet. We want you to walk away from the eschatological path whereby the human race is annihilated. You have the right and the power and now have the tools to change everything. So you might as well get to it.

Peace, Love and Joy.

The authors will appear anywhere, anytime for a signing or lecturing event. Please contact us today at www.arkofmillionsofyears.com to request an appearance at your local event. Book Clubs can speak directly to authors by phone conference arrangements.

Table of Illustrations

Figure 1 - Eurasian and Indian Tectonic Plates 17

Figure 2 – Global deaths by natural disaster 23

Figure 3 – The rift in the Milky Way... 26

Figure 4 - The sky as it will appear in 2012 27

Figure 5 Our Spiral Milky Way Galaxy viewed from above with location of our sun.. 31

Figure 6 - Extra cosmic arm halo surrounding the Milky Way Galaxy 32

Figure 7 - Milky Way Galaxy "Atlas Image [or Atlas Image mosaic] courtesy of 2MASS/Umass/PAC-Caltech/NASA/NSF"... 33

Figure 8 - The Milky Way band of white light stretching across the night sky. Notice the rift or dark void across the center. 34

Figure 9 - Structure of the Milky Way Galaxy. Image credit *www.astro.keele.ac.uk/workx/milkyway/page.html* 34

Figure 10 - A (simulated) black hole of ten solar masses as seen from a distance of 600 km with the Milky Way in the background. Image taken from Wikipedia, the free encyclopedia website (Redirected from Black holes).. 36

Figure 11 - A black hole spewing out violent jets of matter and energy that can be millions of light years in length. Image credit (NASA/Reuters) .. 37

Figure 12 - Gordon Michael Scallion's *Future World Map*.............................. 45

Figure 13 – An additional *Future Map of North America* 46

Figure 14 - Serpent bar... 52

Figure 15 - Pakal's Tomb Lid. Image credit: www.Alignment2012.com 53

Figure 16 - The Mayan stylized World Tree. The Milky Way, its rift, heaven, the underworld, and the path of the sun are all depicted herein. The "+" marks the end of the aeon (age) (conjoining of sun) in the center of the cross. Earth is symbolized by the crocodile shown in the rift at base of the cross. 54

Figure 17 - Reproduction image of Panel from Temple of the Cross found in Palenque. 55
Figure 18 - Pakal with Nephilim pocketbook, a true mark of authority 59

Figure 19 - Pakal's son, Kan-B'ahlam with six fingers from 60
Pier-B. 60

Figure 20 - Pakal's infant son, Kan-B'ahlam, with six toes from Pier C 61

Figure 21 - Pakal's son Kan-B'ahlam with six toes from Pier B 62

Figure 22 - Reproduction image of panel in Temple of the Foliated Cross. Note the tremendous difference in height between the father (left) and the son (right). 66

Figure 23 - Reproduction image of Temple of the Sun panel. Note the tremendous difference in height between the father (right) and the son (left). 67
Figure 24 - 18 Rabbit in Copan holding the serpent bar in his hands. 71
Figure 25 – El Taijin's version of the Axis Mundi. Note the wormhole with many dimension fringes listed around it. On 2012 it opens…one more time. 72
Figure 26 - Ix Mayan Day Glyph 74
Figure 27 - Image redrawn from the Mayan Codex, Vindobonensis. Note the wormhole with serpent bar passing over it, denoting the End of the Age right in the center of the Milky Way. 75

Figure 28 - Close-up of serpent bar with emerging ladder 76

Figure 29 - Babylonian symbol for the sun. 76

Figure 30 - William St. Clair tomb logo for the Holy Grail. 76

Figure 31 - Stela #11 from Izapa. Note the marks of crucifixion on his wrists. 77

Figure 32 - Used with permission from John Major Jenkins, www.Alignment2012.com 78

Figure 33 - Izapa Stele 5 80

Figure 34 – Galactic cosmology in the Izapan Ball Court. Copyright John Major Jenkins, www.Alignment2012.com 83

Figure 35 - Aztec Sun Stone 85

Figure 36 - Ancient Egyptian hieroglyph for "Heaven" 89

Figure 37 - The Four Pillars supporting Heaven as crafted into the side of the Port Adelaide Masonic Centre. 89

Figure 38 – All-seeing Eye Symbol. The dot within the eye is the Precession symbol. 90

Figure 39 – Left Eye of Horus 91

Figure 40 - Egyptian Sha Star: The feminine spirit Earth symbol used in Masonic Lodges divested of its encircled dot. 93

Figure 41 - Reverse side of Great Seal of the United States............................. 95

Figure 42 - Zodiac on Temple of Hathor ceiling at Dendera, Egypt, now in Paris Louvre (picture credit: sunnyokanagan.com/joshua/Denderazodiac.html-1k) 98

Figure 43 - Egyptian Winged Disk found at Philae, Egypt...................... 98

Figure 44 - Within the sacred gateway is to be found the emblem of the Royal Arch Masonic Chapter above the door of the Port Adelaide Masonic Temple: the triple tau within a triangle, within the winged disk. ancientegypt.hypermart.net/freemasonry/index.htm........................ 99

Figure 45 - Triple Tau symbol 100

Figure 46 - Egyptian Tree of Life Picture credit: goroadachi.com/etemenanki/endgame-4-p2.htm 101

Figure 47 - Illustration from Book, *The Time Rivers*, by Goro Adachi (used with permission from Goro Adachi) 105

Figure 48 - Sagittarius Centaur 106

Figure 49 - Sagittarius pointing his arrow at the sign of the Suntelia Aeon— the End of the Age—on December 21, 2012............................ 107

Figure 50 - Celtic crosses silhouetted at sunset. This is an accurate depiction of the Milky Way World Tree with four cardinal constellations forming a Grand Cross alignment. 108

Figure 51 - Celtic sun cross. Notice the Precession *dot* in the center of the circle representing the sun conjoining the Milky Way galactic equator in 2012. 109

Figure 52 - Celtic Cross with lines continuously knitted together denoting the Union of the Polarity. 110

Figure 53 - Tibetan Stupa resembles a Tesla coil. This one in Shigatse is constructed from 4,300 pounds of gold and more than 10,000 jewels. A stunning representation of the World Tree. 111

Figure 54 - Photo of the Stargate Mandala taken by the author in 2007. 113

Figure 55 - Images of four saints in Chartres Cathedral 114

Figure 56 - Chartres Rose Window in North Transept 115

Figure 57 - The Last Judgment Rose Window Chartres Cathedral France Picture credit website: History of Gothic Architecture Cathedral, Chartres no. 27 116

Figure 58 - Typical cathedral floor plan 118

Figure 59 - The Sephiroth; a ten-dimensional diagram of human consciousness. 119

Figure 60 - Hendaye Cross Monument to the End of Time. Picture credit: *users .glory road/-bigjim/hendaye.htm* 121

Figure 61 - Base of the Hendaye Cross. The four A's probably represent the cardinal constellations forming the solar cross at the End of the Age, the cross being a representation of the path of the ecliptic and conjunction of the sun with the galactic equator in 2012. *zelator.topcities.com/hendaye.htm* 122

Figure 62 - Another side of the base of the Hendaye Cross showing the face of an angry sun at the End of the Age as represented by the cardinal constellations (stars). 123

Figure 63 - Crescent moon side of base of Hendaye Cross. The fourth side has a picture of an eight-rayed single star (not pictured) but probably represents the dual-tetrahedra that formed an eight-pointed star when they united in the Union of the Polarity (read chapter "The Tetrahedron")..123

Figure 64 - The Farr Stone in Scotland. Picture credit: www.celtarts.com/cross3.htm 125

Figure 65 - Tymphanum of St. Trophine. Picture credit: www.sangraal.com/AMET/prologue.html 127

Figure 66 - Picture above altar in San Miniato Basilica. Picture credit: www.fuka.com 128

Figure 67 - Zodiac floor. Picture credit: www.fuka.com 129

Figure 68 - Beth Alpha Synagogue sixth-century zodiac mosaic floor Picture credit: Wikipedia, the free encyclopedia, Zodiac 130

Figure 69 - St. Peter's Square, Rome. Note the eight rays represent the sides of the star tetrahedron passing through the Earth.................................131

Figure 70 - The Freemason Royal Arch 132

Figure 71 - Masonic apron..135

Figure 72 - Copyright© 1996–2000 Grand Lodge Of Pennsylvania pagrandlodge.org/tour/mtemple.html 136

Figure 73 - The entrance, or porchway, to the Port Adelaide Masonic Building. The Gateway of the Sun. The Temple of the Sun..................140

Figure 74 - Pillars of Boaz and Jachin. Note the dot in the eye represents Precession. ancientegypt.hypermart.net/freemasonry/index.htm - 28k ..140

Figure 75 - The Zodiac Floor in the Great Hall of the Library of Congress 141

Figure 76 (a&b) - Taurus and Sagittarius Rosettes in the Zodiac Floor of the Library of Congress 142

Figure 77 - Library of Congress window arches with the Babylonian Tree of Life symbol in the *keystone* position indicating the 2012 End Time date.

There are a series of windows like this on the outside of the building. Note the serpent bar arch. 143

Figure 78 - Roman god Saturn holding the Ouroborus in his left hand and surrounded by symbols of Rome and agriculture produce. 144

Figure 79 - Zodiac Clock in Main Reading Room of Library of Congress. Roman god Saturn holding the sickle of the 2012 harvest. Note the serpent bar over the top of the clock slowly measuring time till the 2012 *harvest*. 145

Figure 80 - Woman on bull in DC with sheaf of corn representing resurrection. 146

Figure 81 - Woman with sea horse in DC with zodiac water signs of Cancer, Scorpio, and Pisces represented. 147

Figure 82 - Woman on Ram with Urn in DC with zodiac fire signs of Aries, Leo, and Sagittarius represented. 148

Figure 83 - Man in DC with zodiac Earth signs Taurus, Virgo, and Capricorn represented. 149

Figure 84 - Bulfinch's Dome as depicted in this historical model. Note the Freemason symbols of Precession. 150

Figure 85 - Statue of Freedom is the keystone of 2012 atop the dome on the Capitol building. 151

Figure 86 - Sun Triangle in DC 153

Figure 87 - Cosmic Star Triangle formed by the setting sun in DC on August 15 of each year. 154

Figure 88 - Federal Triangle. Small triangle as it exists today but originally as large triangle. 154

Figure 89 - The Andrew Mellon Memorial Fountain in DC with the signs of the zodiac around the rim bowl. 156

Figure 90 - The ram of Aries and the rim bowl of the Andrew Mellon Memorial Fountain 156

Figure 91 – The authors standing at the Side Entrance to Rosslyn Chapel Scotland. Note the symbol of the Union of the Polarity in the stained glass window with the central point of the cross being the 2012 End Time date. A serpent bar arch representing Precession frames the door. 158

Figure 92 - The Casa Magna Marriott Hotel logo, representing the twelve Zodiacal Ages positioned inside a serpent bar arch. 161

Figure 93 - Lobby view at Casa Magna in Cancun, Mexico. There are twelve arches down each wall to the front main entrance representing the twelve Ages. Inside, the rays of the sun light up the arches as the sun slowly moves in its daily path, representing its movement through the zodiacal Ages. 162

Figure 94 - The Babylonian Tree of Life symbol is above each arch of the Casa Magna Hotel in Cancun, Mexico 162

Figure 95 - The Babylonian Tree of Life is located in the *keystone* position of each arch, denoting the 2012 End Time date. 163

Figure 96 - Angel in the lobby of Casa Magna Hotel holding the Zodiac Wheel of Ages measuring the time of 2012. 163

Figure 97 - Babylonian sun symbol with eight rays, a representation of Precession and polarity union, above the doorways in the Casa Magna Hotel lobby. Note the Babylonian style serpent bar. 164

Figure 98 - The Casa Magna Hotel in Cancun, Mexico. Outside, the sun slowly moves across the arches each day, carefully representing its movement through the zodiac. The large arch in center square has the serpent bar with a circle dot above in the exact center denoting 2012. Heaven's vault rests on pillars. 165

Figure 99 – Caral (picture credit *philipcoppens.com/carnal.html*-12k-cached) 177

Figure 100 - Masonic symbol. 187

Figure 101 - The Great Architect of the Universe Illumination from Bible Moralisee ca. 1250 (Picture credit: *rosslyntemplars.org.uk/Rosslyn_Symbolism.htm*) 188

Figure 102 – Five regular polyhedrons 189

Figure 103 – Four regular star polyhedrons 190
Figure 104 The Tetrahedron 190
Figure 105 Tetrahedron inside a sphere 191
Figure 106 - Spirit Earth Tetrahedron with point down 191

Figure 107 - Temporal Earth Tetrahedron with point up 192

Figure 108 - Two-dimensional Star of David 193

Figure 109 - Star tetrahedron three-dimensional Star of David
(*kalarhythms.com/theory/th.dimensions.htm*) 194

Figure 110 - Duel star tetrahedron inside a circle representing an Earth 194

Figure 111 – Star tetrahedron in two dimensions is often worn as jewelry . 197

Figure 112 – Tetrahedron crop circle 202

Figure 112 – Ground photo taken in Belgium and released to public domain of a black triangle craft that eluded F-16s with no problem. 220

Figure 113 - The Crucifixion painting. Notice the airships in the sky 223

Figure 114: Vimana carved in the ceiling support by Seti I at Abydos, Egypt 226

Figure 114 - Draco Constellation 237

Figure 115 - Draco 237

Figure 116 - Pralaya cycle represented as Shesha, the seven-headed serpent with sleeping god (Mark Pinkham, *The Return of the Serpents of Wisdom*, page 313) 239

Figure 117 – Top-of-ground igloo shelter 245

Figure 118 – Underground igloo construction (*fiberglassigloos.com*) 246

Figure 119 – Shelter design capable of housing a small family (*f5shelters.com*) 248

Figure 120 - Sample plans for an underground community shelter designed by *Earth.com* 249

Figure 121 – (left) Egyptian baptism was done by sprinkling with water long before Christian times. Thoth, son of Marduk, and Horus are administering this ordinance of cleansing of sins. (vignette from Champollion's Monuments of Egypt and Nubia, vol. 1, p. xiii) (right) The baptism of Horus carved on wall at Philae, Egypt 299

Figure 122 – Jesus with the fairy. *The Riders of the Sidhe* 304

Figure 123 - Kerubim Watchers guarding a Sumerian World Tree with three divisions. This appears to be the first representation of the pre-mortal Christ's World Tree. 306

Figure 124 - Close-up of Sumerian World Tree showing the three divisions used by the pre-mortal Christ to teach his gospel to the Sumerians. 307

Figure 125 - Buddhist Tree of Life depicted on a Laotian Buddhist Temple tile enclosed in a lotus blossom symbol of eternal life. It has three distinct divisions. Confirms Bodhi tree was the World Tree. 311

Figure 126 - Upside down World Tree 314

Figure 127 - Tau Cross World Tree symbol of Mithra 315

Figure 128 - Olmec World Tree. Note the three divisions of the cross and the serpent bar. The portal into heaven is marked by the all-seeing "eye of God" that is also a Precession symbol. 318

Figure 129 - The Crucifixion of Quetzalcoatl (From the Codex Borgianus)319

Figure 130 - The Crucifixion of Kukulcan 319

Figure 131 - Known today as the "Candelabra," "Three Crosses," or "Trident" the Nazca drawing has never been identified as to its true meaning by archeologists. It is another World Tree used by the pre-mortal Christ to teach the ancient Peruvians his gospel. Note the three divisions. Peruvians believe it marks the crucifixion of Christ and the two thieves. 321

Figure 132 - Jewish Menorah Tree of Life 323

Figure 133 – Floor plan of Solomon's Temple showing the relationship to the three degrees of glory 324

Figure 134 - Yoga Tree of Life 326

Figure 135 – Essene Tree of Life 329
Bro. Nazariah, D.D., a modern-day Essene writes: 329

Figure 136 – Yeomen of the Guard emblem. 333

Figure 137 – Byzantine Tree of Life with Christ in the branches. Note that all the true World Trees have three branches. 334

Figure 138 - Mohammad on his night flight down the Axis Mundi at the jeweled tree (Cook p. 126). 335

Figure 139 - Eighteenth-century World Tree 336

Figure 140 – The serpent guarding the World Tree..337

Figure 141 - Freemason Tree of Life 339

Figure 142 - The Rosicrucian Tree of Life 340

Figure 143 – Michael with spirit Earth in his hands (view 1. Notice the tiny cross on top of the globe...341

Figure 144 – Michael with transparent spirit Earth (view 2).........................341
Figure 145 - Alchemical Union of the Polarity 344

Figure 145 - Today's Christian Tree of Life or World Tree...........................362

Figure 146 Assyrian Cylinder 363

Figure 147 - The Assyrian Winged Disk 364

Figure 148 - A Stylized Egyptian Tree of Life. Note the three white chevrons cut into the trunk. These represent the three levels or kingdoms of glory. The very top of the tree is heaven. The palm leaves represent the serpent bar. Where they meet at the top center of the tree is a representation of the End of the Age or 2012. 364

Egyptian hieroglyphs telling the story of human DNA, Enki (Osiris) working his science, resulting in the Tree of Life. (photo at Phillae Temple, Egypt). 365

Figure 149 - Mesopotamian or Enki's Tree of Life. 366

Figure 150 - Mayan Tree of Life. The Tau Cross tree represents Christ and the fruit his gospel. Eating of the fruit leads to eternal life in heaven represented by the Bird of Paradise. The flowered branch is the representation of the serpent bar denoting the End of the Age and Day of Resurrection. Further evidence of Christianity in Mesoamerica. 367

Figure 151 - Navajo Tree of Life wall hanging. Very ancient pattern. Note the three divisions. 368

Figure 152 - Amur Russian Tree of Life motif on garment with three divisions. 368

Figure 153 - Turkish Tree of Life rug design with three divisions 369

Figure 154 - Ulebord Dutch cast-iron Tree of Life with three divisions and serpent bar denoting the End of the Age resurrection. 369

Figure 155 - This Babylonian scene is priceless. It appears a teacher is teaching the three degrees of glory by World Trees on either side of an altar, suggesting the teacher is a priest. Note the three divisions of the trees growing out of pots. Above the teacher are symbols of the sun (celestial glory), the moon (terrestrial glory), and a triangle tetrahedron (spirit Earth). The physical Earth is represented by the square cube or altar. It may be the teacher is explaining the nature of the spirit Earth departure at the End of the Age. Stars on either side of the triangle represent the telestial glory. 370

Figure 156 - Flag of Chuvashia, Russia, with stylized Tree of Life. This is an old, traditional emblem. It has three divisions and three stars representing the worlds within the kingdoms of glory. 370

Figure 157 - The Norse World Tree is a giant ash tree called Yggdrasill. It has three divisions with the serpent Lucifer guarding its trunk. 371

Figure 158 – Avalokiteshavara, the thousand-armed and eleven-headed god of compassion. The Chinese World Tree of Quan Yin. It is patterned after the Tibetan Stupa. 372

Figure 159 - Irminsul is the name of the Germanic World Tree venerated by the Saxons. 373

Figure 160 – Oriental Tree of Life as captured in a very old piece of jewelry. 374

Figure 161 - This is the Persian version of the Egyptian winged disk, now called the Faravahar or Farohar, that was adopted by the Zorastrians as their symbol. The three layers on the garment of the Wise Lord/Christ indicate he is the source of the teachings of the three kingdoms of glory or plan of salvation. 375

Figure 162 – Niels Bohr 1885–1962 391

Figure 163 – Thomas Young 1773–1829 393

Figure 164 - Thomas Young's double slit experiment..................................394

Figure 165 – A super-nova can turn entire solar systems into pure energy and give birth to higher order elements. It may be the source for entangled energy and particles. 399

Figure 166 - The star tetrahedron..................................404

Figure 167 - Janus is the dual-faced god of gates. Seeing the past and future of the time arrow empowers us to use the Observation Effect to the advantage of the universe. 408

Figure 168 – Pollen at high magnification with an electron microscope......409

Figure 169 – Accident reports are as varied as the witnesses..................................410

Figure 170 - Mercy–Peace, Justice–War image imagined by Ken Payne.....426

Figure 171 – The square root function occurs because of expansion in all directions at once..................................442

Figure 172 – The changing radius of the cone over time is a result of human intention, ever variable and unpredictable. 443

Figure 173 – The frustum is a section of time examined from a starting line forward to a fixed future time. 444

Figure 174 – The past has a narrow range of possibilities for new effects from intention 445

Figure 175 – Future thread with four dimensions of possibilities..................................446

Figure 176 - The male sky tetrahedron orientation..................................447

Figure 177 - The female sky tetrahedron orientation 447

Figure 178 – Wealth is a misplaced dream. 451

Figure 179 – The things of this world are distractions from our true nature as spiritual beings. 453

Figure 180 – Building the sand castle 454

Figure 181 – Mudra with thumb and index finger. 463

Figure 182 – Mudra with thumb and second finger..464

Figure 183 – Mudra with thumb and ring finger. 464

Figure 184 – Mudra with thumb and little finger...465

Figure 185 – Mudra with thumb and index and second fingers....................466

Figure 186 – Mudra with hands nested (male). 468

Figure 187 – Mudra with hands nested (female). 469

Figure 188 – Method for the eighteenth breath 472

Index

2012. 1, 6, 15, 25, 26, 27, 29, 30, 37, 41, 43, 44, 47, 48, 49, 51, 55, 63, 65, 68, 71, 72, 73, 74, 75, 77, 78, 79, 81, 84, 86, 87, 88, 92, 99, 102, 104, 105, 107, 109, 111, 117, 119, 122, 124, 126, 127, 131, 132, 133, 138, 141, 143, 145, 150, 151, 158, 159, 160, 163, 164, 168, 188, 193, 196, 197, 199, 201, 203, 215, 221, 228, 233, 234, 235, 240, 266, 267, 276, 277, 279, 281, 302, 309, 351, 359, 364, 376, 413
acacia bush 338
Adam. 103, 155, 185, 205, 213, 284, 285, 300, 331, 332, 356, 452
Adamic 181
AIDS 21
Akashic record 215, 351
Akkadian 104
All-seeing Eye 91
Angor Wat 73
Annuit Coeptis 96
Antarctic 29
Anubis 97
Anunnaki 103, 104
Arctic 29
Arcturus 152
Arthur Posnanski 175
Atlantis 233
attention 415, 416, 423, 432, 435, 437, 444, 475, 477
Avebury Henge 94
Avian bird flu 21
Axis Mundi. 72
Bacab 63
Beehive Cluster 135
Bernardo de Sahagun 387
Bernini 131
Beryllium Ion Modem 402
black hole 25, 27, 28, 29, 30, 35, 36, 37, 39, 41, 46, 240, 243, 401
Bodhi Tree .... *See* World Tree
Book of Revelation 96
Brahmanism 231
Byzantine Empire 334

Cacaxtla 384
caput sihil 63
Celestial Law 289
Celtic 108, 109, 110, 125, 303
centaur 107
Chaldeans 88, 89
Chandra 35
Charles Bulfinch dome 150
Chavin 183
Cherubim 89
Chichimeca 77, 180, 183
Chichimecatl 179
Cholula 320, 379, 380
Christ 15, 46, 65, 70, 75, 79, 103, 107, 117, 127, 129, 165, 167, 168, 185, 213, 216, 223, 224, 232, 235, 281, 282, 283, 285, 286, 287, 289, 290, 293, 295, 296, 297, 299, 300, 301, 302, 303, 304, 305, 306, 307, 309, 310, 311, 312, 313, 314, 315, 316, 319, 320, 321, 327, 328, 330, 332, 333, 334, 337, 346, 347, 349, 352, 354, 355, 356, 358, 359, 367, 375, 376, 382, 385, 404, 411, 424
Christos .... *See* Christ
Chupacigarro Grande 175
Clement of Alexandria 290
constructively interfere 395
cosmic sea 26
Cosmic Tree 233
CRED 22
Damkina 305
dark rift 25, 27, 37, 38, 39, 40, 41, 46, 56, 69, 72, 77, 80, 84, 99, 100, 107, 126, 136, 203, 215, 244, 302
Day of Resurrection 51, 94, 110, 119, 134, 159, 367
destructively interfere 395
Deucalion 210
Draco 234
Draconis 234
Echuac 63
El Niño 20
EM-DAT 22, 23

End of the Age 15, 27, 39, 40, 51, 56, 69, 71, 73, 75, 79, 82, 83, 88, 92, 94, 96, 99, 100, 102, 103, 107, 108, 110, 112, 114, 119, 122, 123, 126, 127, 128, 130, 131, 133, 134, 135, 137, 144, 159, 165, 166, 167, 168, 197, 203, 215, 242, 280, 302, 303, 304, 318, 320, 338, 342, 351, 359, 360, 361, 364, 367, 369, 370, 376
End of the Age. . 119, 130, 136, 137, 144, 302, 338
Enki 221, 300, 301, 304, 305
Enlil 300
Essene
    Essenes 327, 328, 329, 330
fallen sons .... *See* Nephilim
Faravahar
    Farohar 375
Farr Stone 125, 166
Feast of Belenus 303
feathered serpent ... *See* Quetzalcoatl
Ferrah Fenton 167, 345
Fibonacci 448, 449, 450, 469
Foliated Cross 55
Freemasonry 120, 149, 157, 197, 279, 337
galactic equator ... 25, 27, 51, 71, 72, 102, 105, 106, 107, 109, 117, 122, 124, 133, 159, 302
Gandhi 452
giardia lambda 256
Gita 312
Gnostic 291, 297, 327, 328, 356
Gog 283
Golden Mean 417, 448, 449, 450, 455, 469
Gordon Michael Scallion 43, 45
Grand Cross 87
gravitons 456
Great Hall 141
Great Pyramid of Giza 93, 94, 95
Guf 430
Guinsaugon 19
Hakatha 225
Heliopolis 131
Hendaye Cross 123

Hermas 294
Hermes 143
Hero Twins 68
Higgs 401
Himalayas 16
Hiram Abif 134
Holy Grail 76, 302, 303, 324
Horizon Project 160
Horus 91, 97, 299
Huaxtecs 378
Huehuetlapallan 180
Hun Nal Ye 64
Hurukan 320
Hyperdimensional 195
in the heart 461, 462, 471
intention. 8, 396, 404, 414, 415, 416, 417, 424, 426, 430, 438, 439, 440, 441, 443, 444, 445, 450, 456, 457, 460, 461, 466, 470, 474, 477
Irenaeus 291
Itzamna 63
Ixtlilxochitl 179
Izapa 78
Jachin and Boaz 331
Janus point 407
Jaredites 385
John 128
Joseph Smith 40, 137, 347, 348, 349, 383
K'ihnich Kan B'ahlam 57, 64, 67, 69
Kabbalist 119, 324
Kan-B'ahlam 57, 60, 61, 62
Kan-Xul 57
karma wave 473, 474
Katrina 15
Kerubim .... See Cherubim. See Cherubim. See Cherubim
Knights Templar 188
Krishna 313
Kukulcan 316, 319, 380, 381
Kundalini .... *See* Life Force
Law of Attraction 13, 417, 477
Lemuria 233
Life Force .. 72, 73, 81, 94, 112, 182, 200, 232, 297, 325, 345
Lord Hanab-Pakal II 51
Lords of Totonicapan 179

493

Magnificat tapestry 224
Magog 283
Mahabharata 312
mandala 113
Mani 326, 327
Manichaean 326
Marduk 101, 299, 305
Mark 128
Masonic 89, 92, 93, 95, 99, 133, 135, 138, 140, 187
Masonry 135, 136, 137, 139, 142, 187
Matthew 128
Maureen St. Germain 462
Max Planck 392
Maya .38, 50, 51, 64, 66, 73, 74, 79, 82, 86, 88, 89, 138, 180, 182, 228, 229, 233, 277, 302, 319, 377, 378, 379, 380, 386
Mayan Codex Vindobonensis 75
Mazatecs 378
meditation .. 198, 325, 350, 462, 471, 472
Mellon Memorial fountain 145
MerKaBa ... 199, 202, 404, 446, 447, 449, 462, 470, 471
Mesopotamia 104
Miceal Ledwith 440
Michlan 72
Mikvah 297
Milky Way 25, 26, 27, 31, 32, 33, 34, 35, 36, 37, 50, 51, 54, 55, 64, 65, 67, 69, 70, 73, 75, 77, 78, 80, 84, 88, 93, 99, 102, 105, 107, 108, 109, 118, 124, 126, 232, 234, 235, 244, 301, 302, 304
millennium 196, 235, 287, 288, 350, 353, 354, 355
Mithra .... *See* Christ
mitochondrial DNA 181
modulation 24
Mohammad 335
Mormon 64, 69, 70, 79, 179, 183, 236, 272, 288, 298, 307, 316, 348, 360, 377, 382, 383, 384, 385, 386
Mosaic Law 297
Mount Popo 320

Mount Wakoyama 322
mudras 462, 471
Mulekites 384
Nahuatl 180, 181
Nahui-Olin 86
Nasoreans 328
National Weather Services 20
Nazarenes 328
Nazoraeans 328
Nephilim 47, 48, 49, 57, 59, 62, 101, 103, 104, 206, 211, 212, 217, 225, 227, 228, 276, 277, 300, 301, 305, 379
Nergal ... See son of Marduk. See son of Marduk. See son of Marduk. See son of Marduk. See son of Marduk
New Jerusalem 44, 95
New World Age 78
New World Order 47
Nibiru 104
Nicea 295, 330, 332, 346, 347
Niels Bohr 391
Noah 7, 25, 38, 39, 56, 102, 103, 185, 189, 195, 198, 210, 218, 227, 242, 275, 293, 301, 315, 345, 346, 363
Nonoalca 378
Novus Ordo Seclorum 96
OFDA 22
Olmec 64, 82, 83, 317, 318, 384, 385, 487
Olmec/Jaredite 64
Olmecas 82, 180, 380
Orbs 439
Origen 286
Osiris 91, 96, 101, 298
Ouroborus 26, 46, 50, 72, 84, 96, 99, 100, 101, 107, 112, 113, 135, 144, 201, 203, 215, 238, 302, 310, 376
Pakal 56
Palenque 56
Panajachel 18
Papantla 72
Past-Cone 445
Phoenix Cycle 138
photon 390, 398, 445, 455, 473

Pictish stone 125
Pillars of Heaven 89
Pleiades 219
Pleiadian 220, 221
polydactyly 57
polyhedra 189
Pralaya 238
Precession 74, 81, 87, 88, 90, 91, 92, 93, 94, 95, 96, 99, 100, 102, 103, 108, 109, 114, 118, 129, 131, 132, 135, 136, 138, 139, 140, 150, 152, 157, 158, 159, 160, 164, 165, 166, 197, 203, 233, 279, 304, 318, 332, 342, 359, 376
process 452
Quechua Indians 62
Quetzalcoatl 63, 65, 75, 79, 168, 227, 316, 319, 320, 321, 322, 323, 378, 379, 380, 381, 382
quipu 178
Quipucamayocs 178
Ra 90, 91
rapture 136, 138, 168, 199, 215, 280, 288, 303, 351, 354, 355, 359, 361
Rapture 49
raptured . 41, 46, 136, 201, 207, 235, 281, 288, 353, 376
Regulus 152
Reptilians 222, 225
Richter scale 17
Rosslyn Chapel ... 77, 133, 158, 159, 186, 193
Sagittarius 26, 32, 104, 106, 107, 142, 147, 148
Saint Trophine 127
Sampsaeans 328
Sephiroth 119, 324, 337
SETI 219
sha 92
Shamash 221
Shesha 238
Shesha' 232
Shining Ones 103, 165, 167, 168, 300, 307, 309, 312, 313, 315, 316
Sifrala 225
six fingers .... *See* polydactyly
skull and crossbones 135

soul-poverty 421
Source 10, 63, 389, 405, 431, 432, 437, 438, 442, 445, 476
Sphinx 101, 102, 104, 105
Star of David 189, 192, 193, 194, 196
stargate 75, 105, 112, 113
Statue of Freedom 150
stela 320
stella octangula 192
Stupa 111, 112, 309, 310, 372
Sumeria 102, 103, 107, 165, 167, 168, 198, 280, 300, 301, 305, 307, 316
Sumerian 77, 97, 103, 104, 181, 220, 299, 300, 305, 306, 307, 375
Suntelia Aeon 15, 107, 112, 117, 167, 215, 302, 351
Suntelia Aeon 15, 112
Supe Valley 177
Supe-Caral 183
super-nova . 396, 398, 399, 401, 405, 406
Tahuantinsuyu 178
Tartary 179
tau 99, 100
Tehuti 91
Telestial Law 290
Teotihuacán 84, 320
Terrestrial Law 290
Tesla 111, 112, 310, 396
Tetrahedron . 99, 123, 185, 190, 191, 192, 202, 446, 447
Textus Receptus 345
Thomas Young 393
Thoth .... See Tehuti. See Tehuti. See Tehuti
Thutmose 102
Thutmose IV 101
Tiahuanaco 175
Timaeus 195
Tollan .... *See* Tula
Toltec. 64, 69, 70, 86, 179, 183, 298, 316, 377, 378, 380, 382, 384
Totonacs 322
Tree of Life ... 50, 80, 101, 118, 120, 134, 143, 162, 163, 164, 311, 313,

318, 322, 323, 324, 326, 327, 329, 332, 334, 337, 338, 339, 340, 342, 346, 347, 349, 352, 361, 362, 363, 364, 366, 367, 368, 369, 370, 374, 375, 376, 382
Trismegistus 143
Tula 74, 322, 378, 379
Tzolk'in 15, 64, 69, 84, 138, 166, 168, 240, 277, 279
U.S. Foreign Disaster Assistance *See* OFDA
UFO 223, 227, 228, 229, 230
Union of the Polarity. 26, 47, 74, 99, 108, 110, 119, 123, 126, 133, 135, 143, 152, 153, 158, 183, 192, 193, 196, 198, 203, 210, 234, 279, 280, 281, 318, 332, 338, 339, 342, 343, 344, 357, 361, 387
Uranographia 144
Vedic 226
vimana 223, 226
Viracocha .... 65. *See* Christ
Vishnu 108
Votan 56, 57, 63, 64, 315

World Tree 51, 54, 55, 64, 65, 67, 69, 70, 108, 111, 119, 124, 126, 132, 133, 139, 233, 234, 235, 301, 302, 303, 304, 305, 306, 307, 308, 309, 311, 313, 314, 315, 316, 317, 318, 320, 321, 331, 332, 334, 335, 336, 337, 347, 349, 352, 362, 371, 372, 373
World Tree obelisk 132
wormhole. See stargate. See stargate. See stargate. See stargate. See stargate. See stargate. See stargate. See stargate. See stargate
Xhixhimecatl 180
Xibalba 73
Yogi 198
Zikum 305
zodiac 88, 89, 90, 97, 102, 104, 117, 127, 129, 130, 131, 133, 139, 141, 142, 145, 146, 147, 148, 149, 150, 156, 157, 165, 332, 342, 344, 361, 375
Zohar .. 143, 206, 207, 284, 324, 344

About the Authors

E. J. is a retired medical professional. After graduating from the New Orleans Charity Hospital School of Anesthesiology for nurses, she returned home to serve her community for 38 years as Head of the Claiborne County Hospital Department of Anesthesia, Tazewell, Tennessee. In addition she provided freelance and contractual group anesthesia services to other hospitals in the area. Born with an unquenchable desire to unravel Earth's "great mysteries," she is an avid researcher of ancient texts and in the archeology of ancient civilizations for over 40 years. Not only does she have a working knowledge of ancient texts but she understands them. This rare ability enabled her to be the first to understand and write about the Union of the Polarity, to be the first to fully "crack" the Mayan calendar 2012 end time date, and to be the first to correctly decipher ancient symbolism pertaining to 2012. To date she has written more on 2012 than any other author qualifying her as an expert on the subject. Using vacation time, her career afforded her the luxury to travel worldwide to various archeological sites where she witnessed digs, explored ruins, and visited museums. Notwithstanding, she is well versed in astronomy, anthropology and ancient history. Authoring books in retirement years allows her to share her knowledge and to present ancient history in a new light for reader enjoyment. She prefers to author under her maiden name as it is the name which she is better known.

Brooks A. Agnew, PhD is the author of thousands of technical papers, booklets, and books. He has also been featured in numerous science documentaries and films. He is a patented commercial scientist and engineer with more than 30 years of experience designing and building breakthrough manufacturing technologies. During his decades of research in analytical chemistry, he generated libraries of spectrographic data on the Earth and its surrounding space. Drawing from this experience, he co-authored *The Ark of Millions of Years* series with E.J. Clark. He now commits his industrial leadership to the field of clean and renewable energy as the founder of the non-profit Phoenix Science Foundation (www.phoenixsciencefoundation.org).

He has served as college professor of mathematics and submitted papers to the Gravitaional Wave Workshop in Annecy, France, wherein he argued the mechanics of spacetime fabric oscillations detected by the LIGO project for Black Hole Research.

He currently constructs the world's most advanced biofuel facilities to convert non-food oils into high quality clean-burning diesel fuel. He is the host of one of North America's fastest growing talk radio programs, X-Squared Radio (www.x2-radio.com) and provides hundreds of hours of public service each year on the subject of world peace and ecology. His personal philosophy is, "Everything we do will eventually affect the universe. Do it on purpose."

Printed in the United States
139079LV00003B/2/P